WINDS OF DAWN

The Maran Chronicles

Winds of Dawn
Mists of Morning *

**forthcoming*

For Rebecca,
Enjoy!
Deborah Potter
3/05

WINDS OF DAWN

Book One of the
Maran Chronicles

Deborah Potter

A Mythspinner Press Book

Printed in the United States of America

Library of Congress Catalog Card Number: 96-94134

ISBN 1-888289-09-0

First Edition 1996

Prologue

The Davan Empire had been at war since its inception, responding swiftly to the plea for help from mortal worlds besieged by a savage invader. Five years later the Empire encompassed nine galaxies and the Immortals had hammered out an unstable peace. Yet the invading realm of Shandal expanded, forcing sporadic battles in what was to be a war spanning millennia.

Fifteen hundred years after the Empire's founding, Shandal's home galaxy severed ties with David, plunging its few remaining Davan worlds into ten centuries of subjugation. Within the galaxy the battles became constant, and the rebels discovered that Shandal's life of ease was not so easy to survive. With each individual regarded more important than the whole, there were no limits to which those individuals would not go. Common good was usurped by a chaos of murder and pillage to fulfill singular whims. Surviving that bloody turmoil, the rebels' descendants attempted to return to David. Their cry for help exploded into the first Universal Wars, ripping across the quadrant David considered his portion of the universe.

This war had already spanned five years of Immortal reckoning, or thirty by the scale of lesser races. The galaxy in dispute was ravaged, planets ruined beyond reclamation, entire populations annihilated or fled to territories beyond the reach of the Shanda destroyers. With Shandal willing to sacrifice half its own population to extinguish David, only the most desperate dared lone travel.

One such vessel stole away from its dying world to a planet where shelter was possible. Reaching its chosen haven, the tiny craft was engulfed in a violent vortex.

Book One

THE SETTLING

Chapter One

"The controls are frozen, Bron." The young pilot turned to his wife.

Her face was paler than usual, paler than her illness dictated, and fear tensed her entire body. He had never imagined seeing her afraid of the winds. But then, he could never have imagined this devastation of their dreams.

Bronwyn grasped his hand. "It's not our fault, Jericho."

"Our own people did this!" Jericho snapped bitterly. "Sent us astray to crash in these forsaken winds—"

The craft lurched forward into a spiraling dive.

His head ached in the blackness behind his eyes. One painful squint revealed the cabin glowing with green emergency lights, green like the leaves of his mighty trees...

Wind had coursed through those leaves, bending supple limbs, cleansing a land now gone to ruin. The powers were lost, no longer understood, and the trees withered to nothingness.

Nothingness...Jericho forced open his eyes, then covered them with one hand. Somewhere in this wreckage were the crushed remnants of his last ten seedlings, lost along with his final hopes. His one remaining task was to find some shelter for his wife.

Helping Bronwyn through the twisted hatchway, Jericho at first lost his footing in the wind's fury. Lashed by sand, he shielded Bronwyn's face with his jacket as he struggled into a battered supply pack and threw the chains of two heavy staffs over one shoulder.

An errant gentle current stilled the sand long enough to reveal a cave several paces to Jericho's left. Reaching the rough entrance, he turned to look back, but the storm obscured his ship. Sighing, he pulled a hand-lantern from his pack.

"There's a tunnel, Bronwyn. We'll go down a way to get out of the wind."

She nodded absently, pulling the jacket around her slight shoulders. "Let me carry something, Jericho."

"There's nothing to carry." Jericho put his arm around her shoulders. "Our supplies are splattered all over the cargo hold. We'll just follow the tunnel, and go back to the ship when the storm's over."

Descending in ringing darkness, the tunnel wound for almost a mile until its confining walls widened to admit a dim light.

Vast and silent, an underground cavern opened before them. Minerals veining rock walls and outcroppings shed the faint light, layering the area with shadows. Swift water bubbled in the distance beyond a desolate arena crumbling with age.

The weary couple stopped to rest on the arena's broken steps. Bronwyn shivered in a chill draft, uncomfortable in its touch. This was not her wind. "Jericho, I don't like this place."

"We'll move on soon; we can follow the river." Jericho leaned close to examine a bruise on her forehead, then straightened slowly, his scalp prickling. Squinting in the half-light, he spotted several hulking beasts creeping into the ruins. Pushing Bronwyn behind him, he reached for the handgun in his vest.

A soft wind swept past the couple, raising a small eddy of dust before the menacing creatures. Stopping abruptly, the beasts eyed the couple, then retreated with wistful howls. The wind swirled languidly behind them.

Jericho holstered his gun uneasily, wondering why the beasts feared the wind. He understood to a degree the winds that his people commanded, but this was beyond his knowledge.

"Fine damn place we picked," he muttered.

"We may as well explore it since we aren't leaving," Bronwyn said simply. "There are lots of tunnels leading back up, so it shouldn't be hard to find the ship."

"I suppose we can't get too lost." Jericho adjusted the pack and staffs, then reached for his wife's hand. "We'll be outside soon."

Outside.

There was no such place. Slouched against a rough rock wall, Jericho pulled the jacket more closely around Bronwyn as she slept in his arms. Exhausted and in excruciating pain, he could only imagine how she felt. She must realize it was too late for them, yet she could sleep.

They had followed the river for days as it gurgled over open terraces and through tunnels. Ruins lay everywhere, shadowy havens for the beasts watching the couple's progress. The wind kept the animals at bay, but Jericho found that no comfort. Something had long ago obliterated the occupants of these linked caverns and somehow the winds had been at the heart of it. The currents obeyed no natural laws, arising and subsiding on whims. Clusters of sparkles teased the periphery of his vision. It had ceased to be a curiosity and now grated on his nerves.

Their rations dwindled until they cut back to mere crumbs daily. Then the river vanished into a subterranean channel. Without water, they wandered upward at every chance but the tunnels always descended again with no higher outlets. At junctions Jericho had begun to stare blankly, eventually taking whatever direction the wind seemed to nudge him toward.

Feeling his throat flaking, he had heard distant water and veered toward it. Struggling against a stubborn gale, he half-carried Bronwyn into a narrow chasm. Within the confining walls he realized the beasts blocked the path back and that smaller creatures dwelt in the cliffs on either side. The wind pushed him backward, but he was determined to reach the unseen water. Bronwyn clung to him as he battered aside raking fangs and talons with his staff. Flurries of agitated sparkles swirled before him, frightening some of the animals back into their lairs. By the time the couple exited the chasm Jericho's back and arms were badly torn and a creeping nausea set his surroundings to spinning.

Trying to orient himself, Jericho had seen the water to his right. Cascading from a cliff top, it plummeted to a terrace so far below that the river seemed a strand of thread. The waterfall was beyond his reach, around a sheer curve of rock.

Groggily feeling a persistent breeze at his back, Jericho had absently gone on. His legs gave out after a few steps and he thought it might be better to sleep.

He had not slept, only drifted in and out amongst fevered dreams. Now he had no idea how long they had sat there, Bronwyn breathing evenly at his side.

After several moments he identified a new roaring in his ears, and dismissed it as the fever. It persisted, however, flowing steadily down the tunnel from some point far ahead.

"Bron." He gently shook her shoulder. "Bron, I hear the wind! Wake up."

Sitting up stiffly, Bronwyn listened intently. "Oh Jericho, finally." She scrambled to her feet, taking the pack from his torn hands. "We must get you to fresh water."

The thunderous roaring increased progressively, the combined forces of wind and water. The temperature dropped until Bronwyn's teeth chattered as she reached the mouth of the cave.

Jericho drew her into his arms, his last hopes blown away. Still raging after so many days, the storm raised tidal waves on whatever body of water lashed the slopes below.

A blinding light flashed past the cave, then swung back to focus on the couple before winking out. Rubbing his eyes, Jericho saw a giant moving through the swirling dust—a giant man.

"Are you hurt?" the man asked as he reached them, relighting the brilliant lamp. Pushing a face mask to the top of his curly head, he saw Jericho's flushed face and tattered tunic. "You're very sick; come with me and you'll be well."

Taking a step forward, Jericho pitched face-first into the blackness of his fever.

Awakening, Jericho found himself in a large bed covered with heavy spreads, in a dark silent room. Unable to see in the darkness, too exhausted to think, he tried to go back to sleep.

"Bron!" He sat up, feeling across the disheveled bed. When his frantic search proved futile, he threw back the covers. "Bronwyn, where are you?"

A strong hand forced him backward onto the pillows. He struggled weakly as a concerned voice said, "Your wife sleeps; she is well. Please be still."

"Where are we? Who are you?" Jericho strained to see through the darkness.

A soft golden glow dispersed the shadows. Blinking, Jericho recognized the man who had rescued them. The man was attired comfortably in a close fitting tunic of rich scarlet silk, dark hose, and supple boots of garnet tinged leather. A silver medallion hung around his neck and Jericho felt he should recognize it, but the memory eluded him as the man spoke.

"You're in my temple, safe from the winds. I am Anders Barria." He smiled warmly, his blue eyes gently stern. "Right now you must rest. I'll answer your questions when you've recovered."

"I can't rest." Pushing himself up, Jericho shook his head. "Bronwyn is ill, she needs medicine. I can't remember when she last had it."

"Ill? But she seemed well..." Anders grew worried. "What may I do?"

"If you could get my pack, I have her medicine."

Anders retrieved the battered pack from a closet, then hooked his thumbs through his jeweled belt and waited.

Jericho rummaged through the pack. "What did you mean about the winds? How long do these storms last?"

Anders smiled wryly. "They last forever—the winds are always like that. That's why I remain underground."

Jericho frowned but did not reply as he pulled a small box from the pack. He forced himself to his feet, every movement a throbbing ache.

"Where is she, please?"

"In the next room." Anders led him to the adjacent room, stepping back into the hall as Jericho entered the richly appointed chamber.

Pulling the shade from a delicate crystal lamp, Jericho smoothed Bronwyn's hair, gently waking her. "Bron? I have your medicine." He slid his arm behind her slight shoulders as she sat up, noting that a warm woolen robe had been slipped over her ragged tunic and leggings.

Sleepily taking the glass of water from the bedside table, Bronwyn swallowed two of the tablets. "I'm so glad you're better, Jericho. I feel like I've slept forever."

"You keep resting." Jericho fluffed her pillows, kissed her forehead, and smoothed the quilted satin spread. "I'll be back shortly."

Softly closing the door behind him, Jericho turned to his host. "Thank you for your help, sir." He paused, his voice becoming bitter. "We were sorely tricked, sent here as a route to murder."

"Murder?" Anders glanced down the hall, lowering his voice. "Come with me." He led Jericho down the wide passage to a comfortable room with heavy furniture and bright crystal lamps.

"I suppose we must leave," Jericho sighed, sitting on the edge of a high-backed maple chair. "I didn't know there was a claim on this world."

"Don't worry about that." Anders took a seat opposite Jericho. "Why would someone wish you dead?"

"It's hard to explain. My home was Adane, and their lifestyle is warfare and technology. I'm sure you know of it."

"How well I know of Adane," Anders said tautly, emotion briefly flooding his eyes before he locked it away behind a formidable door. "They are killing themselves."

"I fought it, as did my father. My family has always been the keeper of the trees, and versed in the sciences." Rubbing one hand absently along the chair arm, Jericho savored the warm smoothness. Wood was scarce on Adane, too scarce to waste on furniture. "When this war began I sought a new planet in the hope of saving some of our people."

"And they falsified your data," Anders said sadly. "I'm sorry your journey met such an end."

"It seemed an end to everything. What were those caverns we

passed through?" Jericho studied the big man, wondering how he came to be in this beautiful but silent haven.

"The caverns honeycomb the mountains of this world, running for vast spans underground at some points. The temple was redesigned to seal it off from the caverns in this area. How long were you down there?"

Jericho shrugged. "Days, that's all I know. If it hadn't been for the winds the beasts would surely have killed us."

Anders leaned forward, resting elbows on knees. "The beasts are deadly if provoked. But there has never been wind in those caverns."

Jericho returned the man's gaze, sorting through his disjointed memories. "There was wind, and these strange bits of glitter, unless I imagined them. But the wind held back the beasts, and pushed me in the right direction. I thought it was something of this world."

Anders shook his head. "You seem to have awakened something. But there is time ahead to investigate." He hesitated, his eyes guardedly hopeful. "Will you be staying here?"

"Well, I didn't know of the claim on this world," Jericho said again. "But I don't see how we can leave; my ship is ruined."

"My people did claim the planet, but filed no name. We finished the temple two years ago to be our new home." His words faltered. "My people were killed in an attack. I am the last man remaining of the people of Stalasia."

Jericho drew back sharply. The Stalassi had been a mystical race, and their planet was one of the first to fall to Adane's rampaging armies. The silence of the structure now made sense to him, the lonesome stillness of a home with no occupants.

Not daring to look Anders full in the face, he managed a strangled voice. "You wish us to stay, after what our people did?"

"You did what you could to stop it," Anders said simply. "I believe we are outcasts together. Please do stay. The temple is safe from the storms."

Jericho relaxed a little, leaning back in the chair. He realized now that the medallion was the seal of Stalasia's Keeper of the Temple. An almost desperate hope shone in Anders' gentle blue eyes. The Adani thought he could perhaps, in a small way, give something in exchange for what his people had so cruelly taken.

"We will stay, gladly, but not forever in the temple," he said. "The name I chose for this planet is Maradane, which means planet of the winds. I did not know their strength then. But when Bron is well we will teach you how to control the winds."

Anders considered the statement for a long moment. "I will accept your name for this world. In return, may I ask what ails Bronwyn?"

Jericho saddened again, rubbing his right palm across the gold band on his left ring finger. "It's something to do with her blood, she's been ill since she was very young. Our medics said it was hopeless and refused to help. My uncle taught me how to control the symptoms."

"I haven't the powers of many of my people, but perhaps I can help you." Anders spoke slowly, weighing his words. "But it grows late. Why don't you and Bronwyn look around while I prepare supper? I'll come for you when it's ready. I have just one small task to complete first."

"Thank you, we'd like that." Jericho returned to Bronwyn's room as Anders disappeared down another hall. Bronwyn was gazing thoughtfully at the ceiling. Approaching the bed, he asked, "Are you feeling better?"

"Yes, though my pride is achingly bruised." She reached for his hand. "They tricked us, hoped we would die."

"But we are alive and safe, with shelter and a good friend." Jericho helped her stand, hugging her close.

"Then we're to stay? I like Anders, though he has said little."

"He's Stalassi." Jericho nodded at her startled look. "And yes, we will stay. Anders said we should look around before supper."

Several doors along the hall stood open and the couple glanced into the rooms. In each they found heavy furnishings of lovingly polished wood, carpeted floors, crystal lamps, and an abundance of gems. Woven tapestries, painstaking visualizations of life on Stalasia, adorned many walls. Other walls displayed jeweled tiles intermixed with wooden panels, all gleaming in the light of recessed ceiling lamps.

Bronwyn paused in one doorway, saddened by a building meant for so many lives and housing but one. The tapestries gave mute testament that the mystics had sought to save something of their home but had not moved swiftly enough.

Coming to the central point of the structure, they sat on a stone bench. It faced a tiered fountain, and was surrounded by a large garden.

Seeing the flowering shrubs, Bronwyn turned to her husband. "Jericho, the trees?"

"They're lost." Jericho scowled at the plants, his broad shoulders slumping. "Like a fool I've told Anders we can master the winds, but I haven't got the trees."

Bronwyn looked silently around the garden, at the colorful flowers amidst golden walkways, at the smooth, shining walls. She listened to the comforting silence, unintruded upon by the sounds of furious crowds or noises of war.

"I shall greatly miss living above with the winds," she said gently, "but this will be a good place to live. Anders must be lonely here."

"I was amazed that he wants us to stay. Maybe we can find peace here." Jericho gazed at the fountain, his thoughts wandering to a not-distant future when he too would be alone, his wife claimed by her illness, and the temple would house only two men with no people.

Kneeling in a chapel, Anders bowed his curly head to listen to the stillness. He favored this chapel because it was close to the gardens, near the gentle sounds of the fountain. Muted candlelight reflected off satiny wood polished by loving hands, an act of crafting that had been, for many, the last work of their lives.

Rising to smooth the altar cloth, Anders wondered yet again if he was doing the right thing. Time spent in his quiet chapels usually yielded satisfying answers, but lately he was unsure. Resting his big hands on the pearly linen, he spotted several small tasks in need of doing. It was time-consuming to keep each chapel in perfect order, and perhaps foolish when there were no groups of worshippers.

Picking faded blossoms from the altar's bouquet, Anders returned his thoughts to his guests. All of Stalasia's powers were not dead, and things had been learned as Jericho slept off his fever. He knew the Adanes were no threat, but he was unsure of his own attitude.

Perhaps he should tell Jericho of the extra ship in the hangar and allow them to leave. This lonely place was not what they had built their dream upon, and they could get safe passage from the Paladins, the guardian units of Immortals.

But where would they go? Replacing a spent candle and preparing to fill the censer, Anders envisioned the war-torn galaxy. There were no safe worlds—Stalasia was a prime example of that. Even guarded journeys were dangerous, and young Bronwyn needed a place to rest and regain her strength.

Kneeling once more, Anders smoothed and arranged the soft pillows on the low step. Running one finger reverently over an open prayer book, he dreamt of again having people in his chapels. From a very young age he had felt drawn to serving others, and thus had he dedicated his life. But so much was now gone.

In his temple Jericho and Bronwyn would be safe, and his life would regain purpose. He had felt adrift for two long years, but suddenly a dream was forming, of life on the surface, and colonists to his home. They could build a world of peace and beauty.

Gazing into the flickering candle flames, Anders realized he was being selfish. By not mentioning the ship he was paving the road to later resentment. He could not deceive this couple into staying only to please himself. Perhaps the age of Stalasia had truly passed and the time of forgetting arrived.

Sighing heavily, Anders stood and turned toward the door. It was time for supper, and time to give Jericho and Bronwyn a choice.

Hearing the sound of quick steps Jericho turned, expecting to see Anders.

No one was in sight.

Thinking the steps too light for Anders' eight foot frame, Jericho stood up. "Bron, keep behind me. It seems that someone else is here."

Bronwyn followed closely, worry creasing her fair brow. Jericho cautiously opened a door where he thought the steps had gone.

The room was spacious, lit by many lamps and carpeted with a sparkling white material. Small tables held assorted books, and scattered throughout the room were Stalassi sculptures and paintings.

Bronwyn hesitated. "This must be Anders' room; we really shouldn't go in."

Jericho was about to agree when he caught a slight movement behind a tapestry.

"At least we won't be the first intruders. Stay by the door." Drawing his handgun from his vest, surprised to find it still there, Jericho stepped forward. "Come out of there."

A young woman slipped into view, short black hair framing a round face with pale blue eyes. "There's no need for a gun," she said calmly.

"I don't mean to hurt anyone. Who are you?" He studied her slight frame. "You can't be traveling alone. Why are you here?"

Before she could answer, a low voice issued from another doorway. "Anders was not certain he could trust you, until he spoke with you. The last visitors here caused great harm." A tall man stepped from the shadows, with another slender woman behind him. Strands of pale hair fell across his violet eyes. "Anders tries only to protect us. I am Bryce Jeremiah; this is my wife Prudence." He nodded to the blonde at his side.

"And I am Shara, Anders' wife." The first woman stepped forward, smiling. "We apologize for not greeting you at once. Raiders have come under the guise of refugees, destroying our rooms and stealing precious things. Yet I felt you were different, or Anders would have taken the gun."

Jericho holstered the weapon, motioning for Bronwyn to enter. "We intend no harm, and I understand your caution."

Entering the room, Anders stopped abruptly. "Jericho...I see you've found the rest of us." He looked sheepishly at the dark Adani. "I'm sorry for deceiving you."

Jericho waved aside the apology, offering one of his own. "I feared intruders. You've helped us; I didn't want harm to come." Reaching for Bronwyn's hand, he saw that Anders carried a large bowl of fruit.

Following his gaze, Anders smiled. "Supper's ready. I was going to tell you of the others before I took you to meet them."

"This is a good time to get acquainted," Shara said, ushering everyone into the adjoining dining room. Prudence set out the plates while Bryce brought a pitcher of ale from the kitchen.

Taking a seat, Jericho studied the richly furnished room. A crystal and sapphire chandelier provided muted light from the high ceiling, which was decorated with a pastel mural. Jericho was awed by the minute craftsmanship; art was non-existent on his home world. "It's so beautiful here..."

"We've preserved many things here," Anders said half-heartedly. "I came ahead to prepare the temple, before the attack. Shara alone survived to follow."

Jericho stared bitterly at his plate until Shara put one hand over his.

"You are not accountable for your people. We have the material things of our world and will preserve the history. If you were to go to Stalasia you would find, in the great ruined city on the plain, that the mystics remain. Stalasia is not dead." She hesitated, trying to temper the news she had envisioned as the newcomers slept. "Much more remains of our dear world than of Adane."

"They are gone, then?" Jericho turned miserably to his wife. "It's no loss to the galaxy; perhaps it's a gain."

"We have gained, thankfully." Bryce tried to lighten the mood as he passed a platter to Jericho. "We hope to preserve that which was good about all our worlds. My Stefanovia was a world of builders, and I'm very hopeful now to continue that tradition on our newly named Maradane."

Reaching for his mug, Anders said, "We're very interested in your talk of mastering the winds, Jericho. Will it really be possible to live on the surface?"

"It should be," Jericho said slowly, passing the platter to Bronwyn. "But I fear we will never have the control we would have had with the trees I was bringing. I can sacrifice our two staffs to control the winds, but the trees would have allowed so much more."

"So that is their purpose!" A sudden smile wreathed Shara's face. "Jericho, your trees aren't lost. They're safe in your ship."

Jericho frowned uncertainly. "How could you know that?"

"My Shara is one of our most gifted," Anders replied affectionately. "She envisioned the trees as she helped Bryce counteract the venom in your blood. They remain for us to retrieve."

Jericho closed his eyes briefly, then smiled at Bronwyn. "You can't yet know what this means, Anders. The trees are part of our ancient heritage and provide more control than the machines can accomplish.

"Are you familiar with Adane's earliest history? The people controlled the winds in ways we no longer understand, and styled their lives around them."

Anders nodded. "I've read of the Wind Rulers. But they abandoned Adane over three thousand years ago, didn't they?"

Bronwyn answered, allowing Jericho to eat. "They disappeared when the younger people spoke of war. The ancient True-Bloods bred the trees, but took the knowledge with them. We no longer understand why the windwood works as it does, but Jericho's family followed ancient manuals. The rest of our people retained very limited abilities, losing the rest by abusing them.

"What small powers remain allow us to control the winds through windwood staffs, and through the mechanical networks. Once in place, control towers will lower the wind velocity to allow life on the surface. We need the wood for the heart of the network."

"This is intriguing." Anders refilled his mug of ale as Shara took empty serving dishes to the kitchen. "I don't know what's on the surface, but it would be wonderful to see the sky and stars."

"We'll need to build towers and satellites, then we can plan our homes." Jericho reached for a small pastry from a tray Shara brought into the room. "We'll need materials from a supply planet."

Anders shook his head. "We stocked metals and mechanical equipment. It's at your disposal."

Jericho nodded, then sobered. "Anders, will those beasts move to the surface if the winds lessen?"

"I doubt it. They dislike light, and on the whole are shy of groups of people, unless aggravated. In any event, the Paladins will help us if need be."

"I don't care to see those caverns again soon. How did you ever find us? Did we end up near here?"

"You surfaced halfway across the world from here," Anders answered. "Shara sensed your presence and sent Bryce and me out to search.

"We should get your trees now," he continued. "We need only attach the flood lights to the ship." This would be the opportunity to explain about the extra ship, as well.

"Go ahead and let us clean up," Shara offered, glancing at the other women. "We'll meet you in the hangar."

Reaching for two empty plates Bronwyn said softly, "It's been so long since I was able to do any work in a kitchen. We lived at the scientific complex after our marriage and ate in the automated cafeteria."

"Pru and I take turns, and you may help if you wish." Shara showed Bronwyn to the kitchen. "Anders says you are ill."

Bronwyn nodded, tying her thick hair back with a ribbon from her pocket. "Jericho has tried to help, but has so little medical background."

"Bryce is a very skilled medic, and Prudence an aide. I could help them diagnose and treat your illness. I have empathic powers."

"That would mean so much to me, so very much." Bronwyn's eyes shone hopefully for a moment. "But please don't tell Jericho; his hopes have been broken so often. I've begun to give up hope myself."

"You must never do that." Shara squeezed her hand. "Come, let's join the men. It's been months since I was above ground."

Many worlds away a figure stepped cautiously into another subterranean hall, glancing furtively up and down the dark passage. It was unlikely that he would meet anyone so far beneath the palace this long before dawn, but care must be taken. His black eyes found nothing unusual, no sign of anyone on this deep level.

Leaving his sheltered alcove, he strode through the deeper shadows along the marble walls until he reached a partially open door haloed with candle light. Resting one hand lightly on the hilt of his sword, he pushed gently on the door.

It swung soundlessly inward, revealing a small, bare chamber lit only by candles on the central table. A much taller man stood in a shadowy corner, the fingers of his right hand drumming rhythmically against the brassard on his left arm.

"David?"

The man turned, candlelight playing across a face grown anxious with waiting. Seeing the figure in the doorway he relaxed and smiled, his blue eyes relieved.

"Asher—I worried lest ye be found out."

Asher crossed the tiny room and bowed, stray locks of black hair tumbling over blacker eyes. Straightening, he spoke softly. "I apologize, my lord. There was some difficulty following recent actions."

David nodded, frowning inwardly at his father-in-law's thick Shanda accent and the manner in which he spoke. Granted, the Immortal language was only a twisted remnant of its original form, but it was far better than the guttural tones of the enemy empire. He did not relish Asher's job.

As if reading his thoughts, Asher glanced with a wry grin at his grimy fur vest and leggings. "'Tis certainly not a pleasant aroma."

"An understatement." David grinned, motioning to the chairs at the table. "But Elizabeth awaits thee at home nonetheless."

"The dutiful wife—I won't make it through the door without a bath at the lake," Asher chuckled. "And how is my daughter?"

"Leah is fine, as always." David marveled anew that his delicate wife was the child of this rugged man. "She tried to visit Scott, but he wast away again."

Asher frowned at the pain in David's voice. He and Elizabeth had no more idea how to help their grandson than did their daughter or David. Until the boy helped himself nothing would change.

"I can stay only 'til sunrise." Asher changed the subject, not daring to lapse into his native speech for this short visit. "But I knew you would wonder about recent events."

"I am wondering why Adane wast razed by its own allies," David said bitterly. "And how much of my daughter's realm remains?"

"The Vale is untouched," Asher offered, knowing of no way to ease the next words. David's past was such a tangle of ties to a mortal wife and children and links to the future. "Your granddaughter died saving the Vale, and her son has assumed the rule. The rest of the world belonging to the rebels is dust."

David stared at his hands, eyes closing finally in an effort to compose himself. "Sometimes I think I shouldst ne'er have wed Mara, as if that couldst have changed what happened."

"It could not, and you know it. They were dying when you met them. Mara's life was practically over when you married." Asher looked sternly at David, his keen eyes glittering in the wavering light. "Without you there would be no Wind Rulers at all. And now you have Leah, who will not leave."

"In other words stop feeling sorry for myself," David said crisply.

"Why wast Adane razed?"

"I wish I knew." Asher expelled a frustrated sigh. "The command came from the Seer, and he reveals his reasons to no one. Orders are simply carried out. But what bothers me is that regular patrols have been instituted around the world settled by the Stalassi. Apparently one couple escaped Adane and ended up in the temple."

David smiled, satisfaction mingling with the shadows of his bearded face. "They art going home, Asher. Three couples art there, then, with three people yet to come. Doth the Seer know of their identity?"

"It seems likely, even if I do not." Asher's gazed hinted at curiosity. "This is all I have to report."

"'Tis enough." David returned the steady look, then shook his curly head. "Asher, I canst tell no one what is within my memory. It is written nowhere, and mayst not be written until the history surfaces of its own accord. That is my oath to the Wise Ones."

"I understand," Asher said with a nod. "What shall I do now?"

"Keep me informed of the spies' activities around young Anders' home." David stood and extinguished the candle with his thumb and forefinger.

Chapter Two

The men had finished connecting the floodlights when the women entered the hangar. Anders was saying, "The visibility is always the same, day or night. We have gear to protect against the blowing sand. The winds at first protected us, but Shandal's new ships survive the gale."

"Once the wind control is established we must apply for more steady monitoring by the Paladins," Jericho said as they boarded the craft. He grinned at Anders, amused by the big man's explanation of why he had not mentioned the ship sooner. Jericho had no intention of leaving this place. "The Paladins should control the raiders when the wars are over."

"I pray so." Anders seated himself at the control panel, pressing a button to open the hangar bay. "Strap yourselves in—this will be a bumpy ride."

"Bumpy isn't the word," Jericho said dryly as the winds howled into the hangar to buffet the rising ship.

"We'll be fine once we get above it." Anders guided the ship upward. After a few moments they broke free of the turbulence and settled into a straight course beneath the night sky.

"It's so nice to see the stars." Shara leaned her elbows on the rim of the nearest viewport. "Everything up here is so quiet."

"At least it seems so," Bryce said grimly. "Yet possibly half the galaxy's people are dying out there."

"Most will be small loss." Jericho glanced briefly at the roiling clouds of dust below. "Compared to many of this galaxy's worlds, Adane was a model paradise."

"Our paradise is much different than Shandal's. What is lost will be more apparent when someone wins the war." Anders glanced over his shoulder. "We're going back down now."

The ship spiraled into the ring of mountains. The floodlights created a dusty illumination as Anders began circling in search of Jericho's ruined craft.

"There it is." Bryce pointed out a port window. Glinting dully, Jericho's crumpled vehicle was visible in a shifting mound.

"Nothing stays covered here," Anders said, smiling. "The winds don't allow any accumulation." He settled the ship and strode to a storage compartment. Pulling out insulated jumpsuits, face masks, and tethers, he said, "Walking is difficult, but the wind is less here and the tethers will keep us secure."

Ten arduous steps carried the men to Jericho's ship. Crawling inside, Jericho discovered his trees in their container beneath the fallen seats of the rear compartment. Anders grabbed one handle and they returned to their ship.

Inside, Jericho stripped off the cumbersome gear and hesitantly opened the container.

"They're all right," he breathed. He sat back on his heels and gazed at the looming black mountain beyond the viewport. "The winds can't have been like this for long."

Anders looked uneasily outside, a frown creasing his freckled brow. "No, I believe something happened to unbalance the winds. Each time I come to this valley I feel that something terrible happened here. Yet the mountains are small compared to what they once were. That peak is twice the size of the others."

"Let's go home," Shara urged plaintively.

They took their seats silently, all feeling the strangeness of the area. For Bronwyn it was the strangeness of being frightened of the wind. This was not her wind, whose sound and caress had comforted and calmed her people for ages. There was something wrong there, and she did not relax until they were gathered outside the hangar.

"Can you control that?" Anders asked eagerly as they neared the gardens.

"It's possible, but we need more power than first planned." Jericho turned to his wife. "Bron, you do have the blueprints?"

"They're in the pack. We'll need to build four towers instead of two." Bronwyn brushed her windblown hair into place. "I'll work on the plans while you build the portable control."

Anders led them all through the archway into the gardens. "Shara and I will open a suite of rooms for you. Bryce and I will help as much as we can with the construction."

"It won't take long to build the portable control. That will suppress the winds in a small area so we can work," Jericho said. "Right now I have to get these trees in the ground, and then I'd like to see your supplies."

"Certainly," Anders agreed. "Bryce and I prepared a bed for the trees. Shara, why don't you and Prudence take Bronwyn down now to look at furnishings?"

Nodding, Shara turned the other women down the hallway. "I'll show you the rooms first, Bronwyn."

As the women strolled away, Jericho carried the seedlings from the container to the bed.

"This is perfect, even the ceiling height." He removed his outer vest and took the shovel Anders offered. "The trees should be about fifteen yards apart. Spread the roots over a mound in the center of the hole."

Anders took off his heavy tunic so he could move more freely. "We have an underground irrigation system, and hoses stored in compartments for easy surface watering."

"How about room for the roots?"

"The soil is about thirty feet deep." Anders picked up his own shovel. "This whole area was hollowed out, probably part of an old arena, and we just brought it up to a level with the surrounding terraces."

The holes were soon dug and the men began unwrapping the seedlings and setting them firmly in the bed.

Reaching for a second seedling, Jericho noticed a strange scar on Anders' left shoulder, near his collarbone. It resembled an elaborate letter 'Z' with an added scroll:

"Anders, may I ask how you got that scar?"

"This?" He tapped his freckled shoulder. "I don't really know. It's been there since I was a small child. Does it mean something to you?" he asked hopefully.

"I'm afraid not. But it's very curious."

"Shara says it is a mark of destiny, but does not know what it signifies. Even Leahcim Tierrah's great libraries have no mention of it. I pay little attention to it anymore." Anders packed the soil firmly around a seedling. "Jericho, how are these trees to help tame the winds?"

"Most importantly, they provide the heart of the mechanism, a focal core of wood at the center of each tower. Though most powers and knowledge were lost, the trees remain a material link to the wind. For the last thousand years my family has kept the lore out of the hands of our enemy. The Donnyas never accepted alliance with Shandal." He dusted his hands on his trousers. "As soon as these are watered we can look at your supplies."

On the next level below, the women stood in a vast chamber filled with furniture. Running one hand over a richly upholstered rocker, Bronwyn said, "This was such a loss, and for nothing."

"There is a purpose in everything, Bronwyn," Shara said softly. "My people shipped all this ahead, to be here when needed. Now there will be a new need for it."

Bronwyn looked to where Prudence sorted through a partitioned box of fine porcelain figurines. "True, we hope more people will come...Shara, is it your psychic powers which help you cope so well?"

"It helps, sometimes." Shara glanced around the room. "But Anders and I have put the hurt behind us. Foresight has had little to do with it."

Moving on to a row of deeply cushioned sofas, Bronwyn said, "I don't believe I'd like to be psychic. I've heard you can foresee your own death."

Shara laughed gently. "Few are burdened with such knowledge unless their passing is of vital importance to some event. We generally see things not so near to our hearts."

"Do you foresee many things? I suppose there must be advantages." Bronwyn made a mental note of several pieces for her rooms.

"The powers of a psychic are greatly misunderstood by most people. Only Gray, of the Immortals, remains truly prescient. That's too agonizing for mortals and the Gift was altered long ago to be what we call psychic." Shara sat on the carved arm of a heavy chair as Prudence drew closer to listen.

"I see snatches, bits and pieces of what will be at a given time, and can cause action to ensure or prevent this particular future.

"A true prescient, on the other hand, sees every consequence of every deed and action. Gray searches constantly for a true path of action, compiling data incessantly. He learned finally to close off part of his mind to store information, so he could still function normally."

Prudence looked up from the tiny statue in her hands. "Do you know any of the Immortals, Shara? What are they like?"

Shara shook her head. "I only know of them, and understand why they exist. Each Immortal is meant for a special purpose, certain ones more special than others. They exist to bear burdens that mortals cannot."

"Like Gray," Bronwyn offered. "Can he be wrong in sorting the information he gets?"

"Well, it's complicated." Shara sought the proper explanation. "Gray can't reach a wrong conclusion from data he receives, so in that sense he cannot err. But it's possible that at times he doesn't have all the information, or that somewhere an enemy psychic causes a change in what Gray sees. David has spies working to get crucial information to Gray, but lapses are possible."

From behind her Anders said cheerfully, "I see my Shara is on her favorite topic again." He enclosed her small hand in his big one.

Jericho put an arm around Bronwyn's waist. "Bron, we have more than enough material here. As soon as we revise the tower plans we can get started."

Asher rolled onto his side as the Seer paused close by. Tugging distractedly at the cape doubling as his blanket, Asher feigned restless sleep. What was the Seer doing in the midst of the sleeping infantry? Such close proximity was not comforting to a spy, who could be discovered by the psychic. Asher forced his tense body to relax as he tried to capture the man's whispered words. Daring to open his eyes to slits, he found the man's back to him.

Pulling his own oily fur cloak more closely around his slight shoulders, the Seer bent toward the corps commander.

"The destruction was too late," he rasped. "She escaped. I've ordered a search for information on her new companions. I'm not comfortable with their association."

"What am I to do, Seer?" the commander asked hesitantly.

"Maintain the patrols around her new home." The Seer pulled his hood forward, shadowing his gaunt face and lank hair. "But speak to no one of this. I am still uncertain of the implications. All may be stilled before the war is done. Many have escaped battles only to fall to raiders."

The commander nodded and turned away. Asher closed his eyes as the Seer passed in a rank swirl of gritty furs and unwashed garments. The Immortal breathed deeply when the man was gone, only partly due to the return of acrid but reasonably clean air. Safe for another day, Asher rested his head on one arm and dozed. He now knew whom it was from Adane that interested the Seer.

Bronwyn set aside the tower plans and wandered to the gardens for a break. The men were busy constructing the portable control, while Shara and Prudence were organizing the morning's food shipment from the suppliers. The Adani woman relished the quiet surroundings, still unused to not hearing the constant nerve wracking noises of her home world. This afternoon she sat near the fountain, content to listen to the water's music.

She was daydreaming about Maradane's surface when a soft breeze caressed her shoulder. Straightening, she looked to see if anyone else was near to follow the errant current.

Anders, more than anyone, was pleasantly puzzled by this occurrence that had begun with the Donnyas' arrival. The temple complex had a vast air purifying system that created drafts, but now there were random currents even when the system shut itself down. Breezes played amongst gardens and hallways, teasingly leading the curious residents along passages only to abruptly disappear.

Hoping yet again to discover the source, Bronwyn followed the breeze down the hall. It remained strong, leading her through the central passages. It led not to one of the filtering shafts from the surface, but to the elevator. Seeing that someone was on the fifth level, Bronwyn decided to take a look.

Stepping from the elevator, she realized she should have brought a lantern. The lower levels were rarely visited, so the central lighting system was shut down below the third floor. The only illumination was shed by small lamps far apart in the high ceiling.

Cool air tickled her shoulder once more and she moved uncertainly forward. There could be no source for the breeze down here. Yet it played about her knees, tugging the hem of her grey silk tunic, and tousled her thick black hair. Her searching steps led her down several dusky passages until she dead-ended in a dark corner.

Swathed in shadow, she stumbled over a protrusion in the floor and knelt to investigate. She found a small tube sticking about two inches out of the floor. Several others were imbedded closely around it, and Bronwyn began digging in the loose dirt.

"Bronwyn?" Anders called curiously, lantern in hand. "I thought it was you who passed the storeroom."

"I was following a breeze," Bronwyn explained, glancing up at him. "I found something..." She brushed more dirt aside as the floor yielded its treasure. Standing, she held the object beside Anders' light.

"It's a set of chimes," she cried softly. The chimes were so caked with dirt she could not identify the materials used, yet they had a sense of delicacy.

Anders eyed the chimes thoughtfully, then glanced at the floor. When his people had closed off this passage they had found no evidence of the chimes. "I'd love to know who used to inhabit those caverns. Somehow these chimes have worked their way to the surface after our work here. And the breezes only began after you and Jericho passed through the caverns."

Bronwyn was fascinated at every mention of that race, now long dead or gone, inhabiting her new home. The temple meandered through ancient caverns and terraces, and in some places occupied newly excavated tunnels. She felt that the new structure was now intertwined with the crumbled ruins, and found it a comforting thought.

"I'll go clean these right now. Maybe we'll learn something from them." She hurried away as Anders chuckled fondly at her eagerness.

"They're very beautiful," Prudence said as Bronwyn hung the chimes in the garden.

"I thought we could all enjoy them out here." Bronwyn stood back to admire her treasure.

An evening of meticulous scrubbing and polishing had yielded a set of delicate chimes of etched crystal and silver with a tone so clear it carried throughout the first floor. The etchings were subtle, swirling, and gave no evidence of any language. Bronwyn thought they were a representation of the wind.

"The center is very strange," Shara said, reaching toward the chimes. The tubes hung from a circular silver frame webbed with fine silver strands. Embedded in this web was a large crystal disk with faceted edges. Suspended from the center of this disc was a plaited silver thread supporting an iridescent crystal prism halfway down and a tiny black orb hung at the bottom. Touching the dark stone, she said, "This is warm."

Bronwyn nodded. "I know something of gems, but can't identify that one."

Shara cradled the stone in her palm, gazing intently at it. At last she said, "It was carved from the mountain. That is the only place I've seen stone like this."

"Is it safe, do you think?" Bronwyn shook off the memory of the looming black mountain and its uneasy feelings.

"I think so. Whatever happened in that valley is in the past of this world."

Everyone eyed the chimes for a moment, but their tones on the gentle breeze were comforting and the people soon returned to their apartments.

Jericho returned to the gardens late in the night, seeking the still-new peace to sort out his thoughts. His aimless steps led him to the chimes near the fountain.

He had watched silently as Bronwyn polished her little treasure, seeing a new joy in her gentle eyes. In the past days she had discovered the feeling of having friends, people who returned what she gave so freely. On Adane Bronwyn's compassionate heart had been an oddity, the thing that had drawn Jericho to her in an effort to deflect the cruelty of their people. Since then his life had been one continuous battle to keep her alive. Somehow this struggle had landed them on this world where hope first died and then flared to new life.

Initially feeling stranded with people he had inadvertently wronged, he found Anders' gentle soul confusing. But he would not leave this quiet place, this shelter where Bronwyn was truly safe from outside harm. With the support of his new friends he would soon see Bronwyn safe from her plaguing seizures. Hope had returned in his talks with Bryce, who assured him that when travel was safe Bronwyn could be taken to David's court physicians for treatment.

Touching the chimes, Jericho berated himself for his past ignorance. Bryce had explained that Jericho could have contacted the ruling center for help at any time. Native to an enemy world, Jericho had never imagined that possibility. His family had survived the past centuries only because they controlled the little remaining wind lore and their threats to discontinue the verbal records were taken very seriously. He would now remedy his past lack of knowledge. He owed it to those who took them in to tame the winds. But he owed more to the one who had so touched his life that he dreamed of a better way. As soon as the towers were in place he would take Bronwyn to the court physicians.

He turned back to his rooms, his thoughts intent on the portable control, the first step to completing the towers.

The compact knee-high machine began to hum and the three men peered expectantly into the swirling winds. Blowing dust scratched their goggles and worked itself into the cuffs of their bulky jackets as they knelt in tense silence, looking for some slight change. They had returned to the sheltered valley to test the new equipment.

The machine groaned ominously, then slipped back into its contented hum. A moment later the control's rippling effect was in full force, pushing the winds away from the trio in an increasing circle.

Jericho yanked off his mask with a whoop. "It works!" He patted the machine he had spent the last ten days constructing. It vibrated slightly as it worked, forcing the winds to the limits of its preset boundaries. Jericho gazed up at the mountain peaks beyond which hung the seething wall of dust. "There will have to be a few adjustments. But with this we can calm an area sufficiently to allow erecting the towers."

Pushing his heavy goggles and face mask atop his head, Anders looked around the valley. A fine powdering of grit covered everything, creating a russet glare in the bright sunlight. "It's so desolate...Well, it leaves a clean slate."

Jericho nodded, squinting as he peered around the ring of mountains. Towering above the rest, the eerie black peak cast a shadow pointing to the center of the valley. Eager to leave the area, Jericho got to his feet. "Let's move this to the airlock before shutting it down." He gripped one handle while Bryce grasped the other.

Bronwyn spread the new plans on the worktable in the study, removing the shade from the delicate crystal lamp. The solar prisms providing the light could not be turned off, so lamps were shaded with heavy fabric when not in use.

Jericho entered the room as Bronwyn made a quick notation on the blueprint. As she glanced up he announced triumphantly, "It works quite excellently—we can start the towers now. But we definitely need four instead of two."

Frowning, Bronwyn straightened. "That will take so much longer."

"About a year, with training the others to help. Actually I estimate about sixty months to build the towers and twelve more to lower the winds." Jericho sat down, reaching out to squeeze her hand. "A year is not so very long, not if it will open the surface to us."

"Did you find anything out there?"

"Very little; nothing alive. We can get everything we want from the supply planets after the war. Anders knows far more about that than I." He paused, noticing a small nick on her forearm. "What's that?"

Bronwyn glanced at the mark left by one of Bryce's needles. "Oh, I cut myself on the blueprints. It's nothing. I'd better get going—it's my night to cook."

Bryce put down his notebook, exasperated as he realized it was already early evening. He was making little progress with Bronwyn's diagnosis, despite the shining equipment throughout the room.

He and Prudence had arrived bereft of all possessions save the few taken to the medical conference that inadvertently saved their lives. Had they been home they too would have perished in the sudden violent upheavals of their planet. Abruptly alone, they sought out Bryce's friend Anders and his new world, only to learn of his tragedy.

The Stalassi helped them set up rooms that were bright and airy, filled with shipments from the suppliers. The royal court physicians at the empire's heart were making vast strides in medicine and Bryce was now able to keep pace with them. Yet none of it helped with Bronwyn. His recent tests had proved his last theory wrong.

Treating a culture, Prudence frowned at her husband's perplexed expression. She took great pride in the fact that Bryce was one of the sector's most skilled medics. "Do you suppose, Bry, it's something peculiar to Adanes?"

"Could be," Bryce sighed. "If so it wouldn't be in the general texts. I think I'll just go contact the medical libraries at Leahcim Tierrah." He grabbed his notebook and left the room.

Beginning to tidy up, Prudence offered a prayer that the librarian could help Bryce. Leahcim Tierrah was the heart of the empire, a vast city housing the collected knowledge of the realm. The Paladins would set up a relay through their communication satellites, and perhaps Bryce would have some answers at the end of the call.

Washing out a sink, Prudence remembered her only visit to the city from which David ruled. It was a blur of shining stone structures and rainbow-hued gardens, and people from every corner of the empire. Bryce had been invited to a seminar on working with empaths, and there they had met Shara and Anders. But to Prudence's great disappointment they had met no Immortals.

She laughed softly, recalling she had hoped most of all to see Michael, one of the four High Under Kings second only to David. It was said that his mother so loved the gardens of the city that she named him for it, turning the gentle name Leahcim into the hard-sounding Michael. Prudence had been fascinated by the thought of so creating a new name from an old one, but was never able to see the king. She often wondered what David's wife Leah thought of the new name, since the city was named for her and for the great tiers of gardens with which she encircled the central buildings.

Bryce returned as Prudence finished mopping the ceramic tile floor. Holding his notebook aloft, he planted a kiss on his wife's forehead.

"I gather you have good news," Prudence laughed.

"Excellent," Bryce replied with a satisfied grin. "And I never would have discovered this."

"Well?" she demanded, leaning on the mop handle.

"The librarian researched a volume on ancient Adane," Bryce began, glancing at his notes. "The symptoms seem to be a variant of an old disease of Bronwyn's people. Depending on various elements, some women of the ancient lineage were prone to a thinning of the blood leading to seizures. Bronwyn's illness is most likely caused by the compounds used to propagate the wind trees."

"And a whole shipment is arriving within the month," Prudence said wryly.

Bryce nodded. "The medic is sending a complete treatment schedule and everything we need. It will be a long bit of work, but Bronwyn will be cured."

Prudence clapped her hands joyfully, but resisted sprinting from the room.

Bryce grinned at her. "Go on, tell her. I'll finish up here and meet you in the gardens." He sat at the desk to complete his notes as Prudence dashed off to find Bronwyn. If all went as planned Bronwyn would be well when the towers were complete.

Chapter Three

One evening as Bryce sketched out plans for houses, Jericho looked up from his worktable with a frustrated sigh. "It just won't work. We need another family, or at least one more person."

"What are you mumbling about?" Bryce dropped his pen to look quizzically at Jericho.

"I'm sorry, I didn't mean to disturb you." The Adani rubbed his eyes tiredly. "We need to have someone near each tower, in case of a malfunction. With only the six of us, any unattended broken circuit could lead to failure of the tower. Then where will we be?"

"About three planets away," Bryce said wryly. "We've worked too hard over the past year to lose it for lack of one man."

Jericho nodded, his thoughts drifting to the long, tedious days spent building the towers section by section. Then there had been the construction and stationing of the six satellites that enabled the towers to do their work. Jericho had been vastly relieved when the controls were set at the final level barely a month ago.

Bryce, a happily impatient man, had found it tiresome waiting through the twelve reduction levels. When the final level was established he had been overjoyed, but less open about it than Anders.

Jericho smiled fondly at the thought of Anders, a gentle giant who marveled more than anyone at the change in the planet. The small group had recently spent the day surveying the landscapes from their small airship. Before returning home they had stopped near one tower.

All but Anders were daunted by the emptiness, by the endless stretch of bare brown soil. Standing there with hot dust blowing in his fair face, Anders had given a whoop of joy and swept his wife into his arms.

"Now we can build our homes, Shara! We'll live outside once again."

Kissing his blond curls, Shara had demanded to be put down. She pushed a strand of hair out of her eyes, looked over the barren land, and said weakly, "It will be beautiful, Anders."

"But it will be beautiful," he had cried, kneeling to smooth a small patch of ground. "It's all clean and waiting. Trees, jungles, meadows—animals and flowers—it's all waiting for us to build."

Shara had looked quickly at the group's half-hearted smiles, then at her husband's beaming face. Touching his cheek she said, "For you to build, my Anders. You'll work with the suppliers and surveyors to design our world. For you see a beauty that even I cannot."

"Well, I know there's little now," Anders admitted grudgingly, standing. "But it will be beautiful," he said earnestly, looking at each person in turn. "Truly it will."

Jericho had been the first to smile with any conviction. "It will, because you will make it so."

Turning away from the tower, Bryce had urged them home. "It's time for Bron's medicine."

Bronwyn had sighed forlornly, but returned to the ship. The treatments of the past year made her violently ill for two or three days, but were destroying the sickness that had plagued all her young life. Upon first hearing the news from Bryce, Jericho had left the medic breathless from a bear hug, then shut himself away with Bronwyn to plan for a future that was actually possible.

Pushing the memories aside, Jericho stared at his thick notebook, frustrated.

Bryce absently rolled his pen across the papers before him. "Well, I can think of no one at the moment. My people are gone, and yours are scattered or dead."

Jericho's expression brightened. "That's it! A cousin of mine left Adane several years ago, headed for a desolate planet. Maybe I can persuade him to come here."

"Can you find the planet?" Bryce pushed the papers aside, eagerness touching his violet eyes.

"Oh yes. I almost went there with Bron. It's only two days from here; you and I could go."

Bryce nodded. "Anders should stay with the women. He's an expert with that laser cannon of his."

Jericho laughed. "I'm glad the raiders are learning that. Let's go tell the others, and contact the Paladins for an escort." He dropped the notebook into his chair.

Four days later Jericho brought the small ship to a soft landing on a planet as barren as Maradane. He and Bryce stepped into the stifling morning air to find an armed group of men surrounding them.

Towering above the rest, one man with fiery red hair and beard demanded harshly, "What do you want? Strangers aren't welcome."

Jericho looked coolly at the man. "You have an ill memory, Aric Donnya. Have I changed so much since you fled Adane?"

"Jericho?" Aric stepped closer, than grasped his cousin's hand. "You have changed. I'm sorry for this reception, but the raiders plague us. Why are you so far from home?"

"Bron and I left Adane, just before it was razed." Jericho glanced doubtfully at the shabby structures and the poor attempt at a community garden. "This is Bryce Jeremiah. We came to see if you might care to move."

"Move?" Aric hesitated, not daring to give hope a foothold. "Come inside; Shonnie's just fixing breakfast."

Inside, Jericho squinted as he looked out a dusty window. The house, sparsely furnished, was situated amidst bare dusty ground with one twisted tree leaning against the east wall as if for support. Parched plains surrounded the tired cluster of ramshackle homes, and a fine powder clung to everything in the sticky air. There was no vegetation large enough to provide shade from the glaring sun.

Returning from the kitchen, Aric sat on a bench near the door. "Sometimes I wonder how terrible Adane must have been, that I left it to come here. Yet I stay because I know of nowhere else to go."

"What about the others?" Jericho asked.

"They arrived two years ago, barely able to limp here in old ships abandoned by Shandal. They are very simple and look to me for guidance. And I can't give any!" Aric pounded the plain table as he got to his feet. "We must beg the soil to grow even meager food, and chase shifting water sources. Days are hot and nights cold, and there is no wind. There's no sound unless we make it."

Watching Aric's tense pacing, Bryce asked, "How many people are here?"

"Seventy-five or so, I guess," Aric answered absently.

Bryce glanced at Jericho, who said, "Aric, come back with us. There's ample room for your people, and supply ships bring food regularly."

"What is your world like?" Aric asked tiredly, rubbing his hands over his face.

Jericho frowned at the desolate look in his cousin's blue eyes, a reflection of the surrounding land. "It's called Maradane, and shall be lush given time. We've spent a year installing wind towers to tame the surface. Right now we live in a sheltered home underground, and will build on the surface when the war ends. Join us, Aric. You'll have a tower when we settle the surface."

Aric stopped pacing and gazed thoughtfully at the floor, mumbling, "*Planet of the Winds*. Truly, I miss the wind..." He looked up. "Very well, I'll go talk to the others. They need a better chance than we have here."

As he left, his wife Shonnie entered with a platter of bread and cheese. She bent to hug Jericho. "It's so good to see you, Jericho."

"You look well, Shonnie." He kissed her cheek. "This is

Bryce Jeremiah. He and his wife Prudence have found a cure for Bron."

"Jericho, that's wonderful!" Shonnie sat down across the table from him. "She is well now?"

"Very soon. She'll be so happy to see you all again."

"It's only Aric and I now." She lowered her gaze. "Kerry took a fever and died two years ago."

Jericho closed his hand over hers.

"We've no medics here, no one to help. Everything on this world just waits to die." She turned as Aric entered the house, stomping dust from his booted feet.

Aric smiled hesitantly, afraid to hope for much. "The others are willing; indeed, they're already packing."

"Great; we can leave tomorrow if all is ready. I'll go over the route with the pilots." Jericho reached for a slice of bread before beginning a detailed description of Maradane.

"Jericho sent word that they'll arrive tomorrow," Anders said, meeting the women in the gardens. "And they're bringing almost eighty people."

Bronwyn's eager response was drowned out by a violent clanging of the chimes behind her. Spinning, she saw the chimes swinging on a breeze that stirred nowhere else in the garden. "What in the name of David?..."

As a much stronger gust burst down the entrance tunnel Anders saw a flicker of movement near the chapels. "Raiders! Get your weapons."

They scattered, Anders dashing to get his shoulder-mounted cannon. Prudence retrieved a long rifle, and Shara grabbed a small handgun. To everyone's surprise Bronwyn reappeared with her staff, but there was no time for questions.

Anders ran toward the farthest chapel with Shara close behind. A lookout just inside the door dodged forward, his knife glancing off Shara's hand as one of his companions hurled a jeweled candlestick at Anders, knocking him to the floor.

Prudence swung the butt of her rifle into the lookout's stomach and Bronwyn disarmed him with a deft movement of her staff.

Anders stumbled to his feet, shaking his head to clear the effects of the blow. One intruder ran toward him, to be swept aside by Anders' powerful blow. Shara fired at the others in the chapel.

Fleeing, the three remaining raiders careened past Anders and the women, grabbing their companions as they sprinted up the passage.

Intent on capturing them, Anders followed with his cannon. Dodging gunfire, he tripped over a discarded censer and triggered the big gun. Reverberating through the narrow corridor, the blast ripped a jagged hole in the tunnel door.

"Damn!" Anders swore as Bronwyn ran past him to dodge through the smoking door. "Bronwyn, have you lost your mind? Get back here!" He and the others ran after her, only to halt in amazement just beyond the door.

Scrambling atop a dusty knoll, Bronwyn raised her arms, her staff held aloft in her right hand. The strong wind whipped around her, twisting her long skirts tightly around her legs. Her fine hair lashing her pale face, she closed her amber eyes and cried, "*Astonal natha mare bec!*"

Rising with numbing swiftness, the winds pounced on the fleeing raiders. Staggering across the dusty expanse, the men were buffeted into one another. Reaching their ship, they dragged themselves inside and fought to secure the hatch.

"*Stonal!*" Bronwyn lowered her staff and the winds subsided, allowing the ship to soar away.

"Bronwyn, that was incredible," Anders cried jubilantly as Prudence tried to stop the flow of blood from his forehead.

"Anders, Shara, you're hurt! Get inside where Prudence can tend you." Bronwyn herded them down the passage with her staff.

Prudence bandaged Shara's hand, then examined Anders' shallow wound. Shara accompanied Bronwyn to the gardens. "They left rather easily this time, like the chapel was an afterthought. What do you think?"

As Bronwyn nodded a movement near her feet caught her eye. Her terrified scream brought Prudence and Anders running.

Snakes slithered throughout the gardens, snakes of every size and hue. In one brief instant the effect counted upon by Shandal had set in, and the fear inherent in most races had so paralyzed everyone that even screaming was impossible. Prudence could only whimper helplessly as a giant constrictor nosed around her ankles.

A low hum filled the huge chamber, rising in pitch until almost inaudible. The small black orb in the chimes trembled slightly, turning red with fire that shot up the silver thread into the crystal prism. White light seared outward from the enmeshed disc, fragmenting into myriad splinters that pierced the coiling snakes but never touched the dazed people.

Bronwyn collapsed onto a bench, staring at the wisps of smoke wafting toward the ceiling. Anders pulled Shara close as he tried to his calm his own trembling, also reaching out to Prudence. The snakes were gone, disintegrated by the light, and the chimes rattled softly, then stilled.

A distant howl pierced the structure. Grateful for Anders' support, Shara fleetingly envisioned a crumbling arena where one old beast bowed its head low, its cry echoing through the carved stone chambers.

Chilled, Bronwyn relaxed as a warm current caressed her shoulder. Feeling the breeze, the others sat down shakily.

Anders stared at the chimes, thinking of that sad yet thankful howl. "I'm grateful to our predecessors, whoever they may have been, and whatever magic they possessed."

"I think we found a safe home," Shara said softly, still clasping his hand. "Somehow it is protecting us."

"We certainly have a tale for Bryce and Jericho."

Escorted by a unit of Paladins, Jericho's seven ships landed safely only to find things in disarray. Stepping from his craft, Bryce spied the jagged hole in the tunnel door.

"Blast that confounded cannon!" he sputtered. "That's the third door we've lost." Then, worry creasing his brow, he climbed through the hole shouting, "Prudence! Anders? Anybody?"

"We're all right." Anders strode up the tunnel, his blond head bandaged. "I see you got through safely."

"No one wants to bother six Davan warships." Bryce nodded toward the man behind him. "This is Aric Donnya, Jericho's cousin."

Anders grinned in welcome as he exchanged a friendly handshake with Aric, who stood a foot taller than the Stalassi.

"What happened?" Bryce demanded. "Is anyone else hurt?"

"Shara's hand is cut, but nothing serious." Anders scowled toward the sky. "Raiders broke in last evening, but we discouraged them. I admit to a misfire that hit the door. But do you know what really got rid of them?" He turned to Jericho with wonder in his blue eyes. "Bronwyn grabbed her staff, charged out to that rise there, and shouted something. The wind actually attacked the raiders and they were hard put to get away."

"My Bron." Jericho frowned, then chuckled. "She's one of the few queens of the wind. She can summon some of the ancient powers."

"Those are very handy powers." Anders looked again to the sky, this time in the direction of his home world. "I think Stalasia would have had little to fear from the first Adanes."

Aric drew a sharp breath. "You're Stalassi?"

"I wish people would stop doing that," Anders grumbled, perturbed. "Shara and I know things that no one else knows. Many things yet lie ahead for our Stalasia.

"Let's get inside and we'll see that everyone is given rooms. Once you're all acquainted with the temple and we've fixed the door, we'll have a conference."

Leading them toward the gardens, Anders related the tale of the chimes as he went.

After installing the replacement door delivered by a supply ship, Anders attempted to gather the leaders of the new arrivals. The nearest man looked blankly at him. "But Aric is our leader."

"No, I'm not." Aric shook his head. "You must choose six men to represent your views."

"But you've always told us what to do, always known what is right."

Aric ran a callused hand over his face. "Kana, I've done my best to help you and solve your problems, but—"

"That's what a leader does," Kana interrupted emphatically.

Aric turned helplessly to Anders. "What am I to do?"

"Pick five men to join us, leader." Anders forced back a grin. "Once the meeting begins they will see that life here is a joint effort."

When the men were seated in the library, Jericho placed a large map on the table. "This is Maradane. The planet has been divided into four almost equal sectors with two small neutral areas at the sector junctions. We are in one of the neutral areas, with the other on the opposite side of the planet. The four wind control towers are situated across this large continent, one for each sector.

"Aric, you'll have responsibility for one tower, with daily checks until we move to the surface. The people will be free to settle wherever they choose."

Aric nodded thoughtfully. "I'd like the north, if no one else has claimed it. What's the climate like?"

Jericho shrugged. "The towers haven't been in control long enough to tell."

One of the settlers reached for the map. "Who is going to rule Maradane? Will there be a king for each sector?"

Dumfounded, Jericho and Bryce exchanged glances with Anders. The Stalassi looked from Aric to the newcomers.

"We haven't given thought to a kingship, there are so few of us here. After the war Leahcim Tierrah will appoint proper rulers."

"But we don't want to be ruled by a stranger," Kana protested loudly, eliciting a resigned sigh from Aric. "We must have laws. There are four of you—you can be the kings."

"Now wait," Anders cried. "We can't rule, we know next to nothing of government."

"Very true," Jericho agreed quickly. "Adane was ruled by warlords, and Bryce's world had a voting system."

Anders scowled at Aric, who had a faint smile tugging at his lips. "Stalasia was ruled by common bond and had a governor to handle records. I only assisted, as Keeper of the Temple."

Kana leapt upon that statement. "There, you do have experience. You shall guide the others and be kings together."

Aric motioned his friends toward the hall. "Kana, we must discuss this. Please just wait here."

Beyond the closed door, Anders bellowed, "Shara, come here at once!" Turning on Aric, his composure flown, he snapped, "Why didn't you warn us about those men? They're positively the most stubborn—"

"Oh, calm down," Aric laughed. "You enjoyed my being labeled their leader. But I never realized how they believed that until now. Half my time was spent guiding them, ironing out problems. They are very simple in nature, living happily at a slow pace, and they desire solid leadership. And once they get an idea in their heads your cannon won't dislodge it."

"But we can't proclaim ourselves kings. Kingship is appointed by David."

"They don't understand that," Aric said, exasperated. "They only know it is David's law that each planet have a king. They're like children and expect to be told what to do."

Anders turned to Shara as she joined them. Catching the gleam in her eyes he said, "This isn't funny."

"My love, it's neither a disaster," Shara chided gently. "Agree to act as governors until a proper appointment is made by David. Our new friends will not want to oppose the law, any more than we would."

Aric brightened immediately. "An excellent point. Kana won't want to be responsible for breaking David's law, nor be presumptuous enough to appoint a king."

"Well...we do have the right to appoint colonial governors," Anders conceded hesitantly, worried over something in Shara's expression. She was keeping something from them. "And we do have to offer guidance until someone with authority arrives. Come on, we'll try to explain it to them." Shaking his head, he opened the heavy door.

Kana reluctantly accepted the idea of governors, then waited expectantly to be governed. To keep him satisfied, Aric and Jericho spent several days initiating and training an armed guard against the raiders. The men were eager to join and the Adanes were able to schedule night and day shifts.

Gathering for dessert in Shara's kitchen one evening, the four couples shared tired sighs.

"This is terrible," Anders sighed, frustrated. "I've run out of ideas, short of having them polish everything in storage. Aric, don't they think at all for themselves?"

"Rarely," the big man grunted. "They're excellent workers once they have something to do. But they seem fearful of initiating anything."

"What planet are they from?" Bryce asked.

"Kana called it Barteg or something. I never heard of it," Aric answered.

"Bartaj?" Anders' eyes brightened. "Lord, we've got the only survivors of a suicide planet! Shandal sacrificed that world to defeat a rebel sector—it was mostly lower caste and slaves who built and manned warships. If these people were Shanda slaves it's no wonder they can't think. It's been beaten out of them."

Bronwyn reached for a mug of hot cider. "Hadn't we better begin some classes for them? We can teach the basics, until real teachers arrive."

"That's just the thing, Bron," Prudence agreed. "I can teach simple health care and home medicine. They're sadly lacking in those skills."

"And I can do letters and numbers," Bronwyn offered. "And teach people to use the staffs."

"Aric and I are going to start a crop of seedlings," Jericho said. "We'll seed the first groves just outside the temple, until we have more accurate climate records."

"It will be nice to see trees outside," Bryce said. He and Anders had spent several days in the airship surveying terrain and using the computers to map the planet. In the evenings Anders sifted through the materials, looking for possible village and farming sites.

"That reminds me," Anders said, looking around the group. "I'd like all of you to write a paragraph detailing something special about your home worlds. I want to use them in my plans."

"Won't take me long." Jericho winked at Aric. "The best thing I recall about Adane is it's gone."

"That's ridiculous," Anders chided. "Surely there was something in Adane's history you'd like to remember here. Maradane is to be a melding of all our worlds, not just a conglomeration of new ideas. I need something from each of you within the next couple months."

"Yes, sir." Jericho teasingly clicked his booted heels and saluted Anders. "I guess there were ancient things worth remembering. But we should acknowledge Stalasia most strongly—you settled here first."

"Nonsense." Anders reached for a platter of chocolate cookies. "This must be home to everyone, and special to everyone."

Prudence lost no time in starting her classes, as well as scheduling patients for her husband. Bronwyn found simple books in one storage chamber and began her classes in the garden. Every other day she taught a few of the settlers the proper use of the wind staffs.

"Wind control is very simple," Bronwyn said, standing with a small group outside the temple. "You need only a few key words, and to be certain the safety chain is hooked to your belt. The winds will never drop anyone bearing a staff, nor will they ever harm them."

Gripping their staffs, the people watched excitedly as Bronwyn summoned a wind and was lifted gently into the air, then settled back on her feet. Kneeling beside one child, she showed him how to hold the staff with one hand in the lower half.

"To begin, you say '*astonal*'—begin, or start. '*Mistra*' means lift, and '*nathor*' means land. To move in any direction you point your staff and say '*becca*'—go there. When you're all done and have landed, you say '*stonal*'—stop—to dismiss the wind." She nudged him forward. "Hold tight now, and try it."

The boy looked around shyly, gripping the staff with both hands. After a moment he said hesitantly, "Astonal?"

A gentle current swirled around him, tousling his hair. He whispered, "Mistra," and began to be lifted every so gently. Seeing the ground receding beneath his feet, he giggled and waved to his parents. Then he forgot the other words and simply hung there.

"Nathor," Bronwyn said laughingly, waving her staff toward the child. He floated lazily to the ground.

Facing the group, Bronwyn concluded. "Those are the basics necessary for control. You must practice a little every day, and as soon as we have more staffs we will see that each person has one of their own."

The propagation of the wind trees had become the focal point for the people's interest. Setting up a propagation bed in the gardens, Jericho and Aric used special growth compounds to begin the tiny seedlings. After several days the seedlings were ready to be planted outside, an event that was always accompanied by a crowd of children and adults. The children also managed to be around each time Jericho harvested a few of the mature trees' slender branches. Carefully tended and treated with mending fluid, the hybrid trees swiftly regenerated the severed limbs.

In the evenings Bronwyn stripped the bark and drilled a small hole at each end before several sandings. The wood was then sealed and buffed to a high gloss, and the staff was equipped with a carrying chain. Once given to a permanent owner, each staff could be carved, decorated, or wrapped in leather strips or ribbons, to suit the owner's fancy.

Content with their hesitant governors, the settlers never realized how eagerly the four men awaited a reply to their message of thirty days ago. Explaining their situation to the nearest commanders of the Paladins, the men had requested prompt relief of their forced command.

"Something unusual has happened, David." Asher sprawled on the shore of the lake behind his home, his legs half in the water. Throwing his head back on his arms, he relished the pure air filling his lungs and the starlit sky above.

David smiled, laying back to rest his head in his wife's lap.

"More unusual than thou knowest, I wouldst guess."

"I thought you'd understand this end of it." Asher glanced at his king. He had been given three days' leave from his unit and had wasted no time going home to clean up and relax. "The Seer nearly had apoplexy when the raiders reported an attack by the winds. Then he realized that the snakes had been nullified. The Seer's called a conclave of the psychics and locked them all up in his palace."

David nodded, more to himself than in acknowledgment. "Gray and I hadst a very long council these past days. Something e'en I know nothing of turned up, in the form of wind chimes. There is very great and very ancient magic in those chimes, but it wilt be long years before we understand it. How art thou progressing?"

"Better," Asher replied with mixed feelings. "The corps commander learned I can read and write, but my history held up to Clan scrutiny. Deciding I had the proper lineage to hold the right to read, they promoted me to archival duty."

"Just where we want thee," David said, satisfied. "At least thou wilt be in easy access to the information as it arrives. And somewhat out of the general filth."

"The archives are cleaner," Asher agreed slowly. "But only so the war records and accounts will be easily legible. Maybe I can trade those rotting furs for simply dirty fabric. And the archives are so deeply buried within the palace that the major abominations will be out of my sight."

"I have heard enough of Shandal for now," David said wearily. "Tomorrow our emissary leaves for Maradane, and the reunion wilt be complete." He reached up to bend Leah's head close to his, kissing her lovingly in the moonlight.

Jericho and Bryce tried unsuccessfully to neaten the desk in the large library where the four men worked. Shuffling through a stack of papers, Bryce sighed. "It's hopeless. We'll never get this room organized."

"It's impossible this way—what's that?" Turning toward the open door, Jericho listened to a distant thumping noise. "There's someone at the entrance."

Running toward the tunnel the two men were joined by Anders and Aric, carrying the big laser cannon and a long rifle. Behind them Bronwyn hurried the children toward their rooms, away from the class in the garden.

The pounding persisted, though less forcefully, and the men readied their weapons and unlocked the door.

Grasping the edge with a torn hand, his forehead caked with blood and matted hair, a young man leaned heavily on the door.

Chapter Four

Catching him as he toppled forward Bryce called, "Prudence, ready a room!" He motioned for Jericho to take the man's feet.

As soon as the stranger was settled on a bed, Bryce ushered the others out of the room.

Pacing the hall, Anders discovered a battered pouch fallen from the man's belt. It was sealed shut. Turning it in his hands he said, "That's David's seal."

Jericho eyed the pouch. "He's been through quite a lot to get here."

Opening the door, Bryce said, "You'd better come in. Most of the blood wasn't his own."

Entering the room, the trio found the newcomer seated on the edge of the bed, fingering the bandage around his blond head. A moment later Bronwyn and Shara brought in a tray of food, which had been the man's primary request.

Anders handed the pouch to the man. "This fell in the hall."

Checking the seal, the man said, "Thank you. A raiding party attacked after the Paladins' escort left me here."

"We've had a lot of trouble with them lately." Anders nodded toward his gun by the door. "What news have you?"

"Quite a lot. My name is Caleb Bajoc." He drained the mug of ale on the tray and bit into a thick sandwich. "Is there a room where we can all talk?"

"Our library," Anders answered slowly. "Are you well enough?"

"My head aches, but things need to be discussed." Caleb finished devouring the sandwich and reached for another.

"Come, then." Anders led the way, making introductions as they walked.

Caleb's dark blue eyes surveyed the cluttered room, then he smiled. "I see you've been very busy."

"We're trying to sort things out." Anders sat at the table. "What is the news?"

Caleb broke the seal on the pouch. "The wars are over, ended three months ago. This galaxy held out, but the Paladins and the Davan Immortals are finishing up now. David and his kings have appointed new galactic rulers and will bring the area back into uniform rule with the Empire.

"All guns and like weaponry have been banned, to become effective when the raiders are all captured. It won't be immediate—we needn't worry about it now. But it will bring us in line with the rest of the realm, and the new armor will soon make Shandal's short range explosive weapons ineffective."

Pulling a sheaf of papers from the pouch, Caleb sorted through them for one with a heavy seal and bold signature. This he passed to Anders.

"Due to one of the new laws, each planet is to have one high king. David has seen fit to appoint me to this position on Maradane."

Anders read the paper—dated, signed and sealed by David—and passed it to Bryce. "We're happy that David sent us a king so quickly. Now Kana and his people can accept our retirement as governors."

"But you've done excellently," Caleb said, searching out four more papers. He passed them to the other men. "Gray has advised David that you be appointed kings over the four sectors."

Shara spoke since no one else seemed about to do so. "Gray has seen something of our world?"

"Ah, yes, you are Shara." Caleb smiled warmly "Yes, Gray has seen something important, but did not confide in me."

Anders and Bryce thumped their papers on the table as Jericho demanded, "Are you serious? We've no background, no training, no idea of how to rule. How can we pass ourselves off as kings?"

"Of course you need training, but we are beginning very small and I can guide you." Caleb retrieved the papers with a grin. "As it is, Gray advises it and David agrees with him."

He grew more serious as he continued. "The raiders are out in force with the wars over. We need authority to make and enforce Maradane's laws. While we begin setting up the government, this sector's unit of Paladins will provide the security force."

Closing the pouch, Caleb concluded, "First I must learn about Maradane and your work. We're to follow your plans. Anders, Gray said you've already created some maps."

"Yes, they're here in the library. Once you're rested we can hold a longer meeting." Anders got wearily to his feet, at last realizing what Shara had kept from him after their first meeting with Kana.

Caleb's initial reception by Kana's people was cool and confused. Their attitude warmed, however, upon hearing that their beloved governors had been promoted to kings. Crediting Caleb with this remarkable feat, they took him to heart and eagerly awaited his bidding.

Caleb immersed himself in the records Anders had so diligently compiled, expanding ideas and plans, and relying heavily on Anders' input. After his first month there, Caleb was well into a report on Maradane's future appearance.

Anders sat back in his big leather chair, propping his feet on the desk. Pen in hand, he jotted notes as he reviewed the pages written by his friends.

Jericho had written only a brief sentence. *What I remember most about Adane's history is the windblown forests, clean and pure.*

Bronwyn's memory from her studies was of a spectacular species of butterfly, more than a hand-span across each wing, that throve in the windy meadows near Adane's small lakes.

Aric's bold handwriting recalled the frozen northern lands of Adane, vast plains of wind-sculpted snow and ice upon which roamed herds of shaggy deer with gentle tawny faces.

Anders read another page in Shonnie's precise script. *In the mountains of ancient Adane there were valleys of a fragile flower with whispering leaves, and the homes of the giant eagles that soared far inland to the grassy plains.*

"Wind," Anders noted on his tablet, smiling at how the descriptions contained the essence of that word. For Jericho it was endless expanses of trees, their leaves carrying on quiet conversations above a floor where one might walk in peaceful thought. Bronwyn saw gentle insects borne aloft in the currents off the lakes, a sparkling cloud captivating the imagination of young and old alike. Farther north, in a landscape hewn by constant gales shaping fallen snow, timid deer raced the wind. Breezes caressed the faces of Shonnie's flowers, fluttering their leaves, and carried mighty birds far afield.

Making notes for future orders, Anders had a good view of Maradane's outlying areas. There the wind would rule, protecting places both wild and serene, and anyone could lose their troubles in its gentle touch.

Bryce's page reflected the man's love of building. *Stefanovia was a planet of small villages, carefully framed around nature. Rock or wooden fences rambled over hills, and broad avenues passed homes set far apart.*

Prudence remembered lakes and ponds surrounded by parks with topiary gardens, places for picnics and family gatherings.

Collecting the pages, Anders was surprised to find another one, written in a graceful hand.

On outside walls there were murals, that visitors might understand what lay in the hearts of our people. The houses and public buildings were porticoed, and walks paved with gems wandered as they pleased through gardens between the homes. The sun shone upon open markets—and the moons smile upon silver meadows through which whisper the breezes of our memories.

"My Shara," Anders whispered with a tender smile. He tucked the page in his tablet and returned to his task of planning. With the help of researchers from Leahcim Tierrah and the abundance of supply planets, Maradane's surface would soon be lush. Then they would open the world to colonists.

Gathered near the eastern wind tower, the four ruling couples recalled their last visit there. A warm, moist wind from the sea replaced the dusty gusts of that distant day. Instead of the arid smell, they relished the scent of green grasses and scattered flowers. In the year since Caleb's arrival the dry rasping wind had given way to new leaves rustling overhead.

Anders turned jubilantly to his friends. "You see, it's just as I said. Beautiful, full of life."

"Your dreams have done it, my love." Shara hugged him tightly. "And yes, you were right. It's as beautiful as Stalasia."

"Well, not quite," Anders said with a grin. "And I didn't do it—the suppliers and David's men did."

"That's ridiculous," Aric chided. "You spent almost the entire past year doing the work. No, whatever Maradane is, it is so because of you."

The big man wanted no such praise, eluding it by saying he must return to work. "Caleb needs help organizing the new settlers' records."

With the landscaping and settlement planning out of the way, Anders had turned his attention to new colonists. A slow stream of people was applying, hearing of Maradane from David's people. Anders helped them choose and catalog sites on his maps during initial visits, and saw that the houses were completed by the time of their arrival. He had quickly chosen the pattern of Bryce's world:

small villages dotted the planet, with fields divided by stone fences and wandering avenues.

Bryce designed homes to fit the landscape, and Jericho and Aric supervised the construction. Villages were built first, completing homes and public buildings. Markets were open-air, with awnings to be dropped against stormy weather, and supporting or dividing walls decorated with murals. Outlying homes were put up next. A year and a half after Aric's arrival, the settlers moved to the surface.

The kings immediately began organizing permanent offices in the temple, to be their center of government. Anders insisted that Caleb take the largest apartment on the floor for his own, converting nearby rooms into libraries, record rooms, and council chambers.

One afternoon Bronwyn dropped a heavy box onto a polished pine table in the largest record room. "I swear, if I see another sheet of paper I'll scream." She and the other queens were transferring and cataloging records in the new filing system.

"It's not so much, really," Shonnie said, pushing her dark bangs off her forehead. She was slowly overcoming her shyness, but still spoke very seldom in groups. "Once this is all filed the following work will go smoothly."

"I suppose." Bronwyn pulled a stack of reports from the box, sorting them by subject. "I didn't think there was this much paper in the galaxy."

"You're not used to government," Shara said, smiling. "I used to help with the records when Anders was Keeper of the Temple." Her thoughts drifted to the banks of shelves and cabinets in Stalasia's sparkling temple. There were kept the recorded birthdays and wedding dates, records of feast days and names of planetary champions. People came there for the names of fine craftsmen, and to study journals sent from David's court. In a galaxy of rebels, Stalasia remained loyal to David. Shara felt secure in knowing her new home maintained that loyalty.

"It must have been like keeping Bryce's records," Prudence said. Carefully placing a series of reports on jungle animals and habitats on a shelf, she recalled her husband's offices at the hospital and at home. There was nothing quite like the sight and feel of the shining tile floors and walls and the gleaming silver equipment. Or the rolls of floor plans and landscape sketches lining one wall of Bryce's study. She had thought it all lost when her world died, but now she again had the bright, airy rooms and the plans that would house laughing children.

"After my last two homes I'd be happy to live in a filing room," Shonnie laughed. "It's clean, and quiet, and it smells good, which can't be said of either other place." She filed the papers happily, knowing she was free of violent crowds, dirty cities, and dust seeping into every crevice. Her soon-to-be-built home would be on a field of snow where the wind cleansed the air. She was already choosing grey ash furnishings and silvery tapestries for her retreat from the busy world developing around her.

"I shouldn't complain, I know." Bronwyn paused to scan a report on snow tigers and envisioned Anders' smiling face. He had generated at least two-thirds of this paperwork, creating a world that came near to the ancient beauty of Adane. Because of his tireless days and evenings, her winds whispered and roared through forests and across plains, and the fields near her tower in the west were alive with every butterfly that would thrive there. She smiled contentedly as she plunged into another stack of paper.

Running steps clattered down the corridor and a young voice shouted, "Raiders!"

Chapter Five

Rushing from the room, the women found a boy from Aric's sector running toward them. Skidding to a halt, he gasped, "They hit the north village and leveled everything!"

"Come with me." Prudence led the boy toward Bryce's surgery as the others scattered to gather what might be needed. In moments they had boarded the largest airship and were on their way.

Arriving at the village east of Aric's tower they found that casualties were light. Bryce drew Prudence aside to set up an aide station. Shara and Shonnie began gathering children to check for injuries while Bronwyn handed out heavy furs to ward off the cold.

Damage estimates were interrupted by a trio of men herding several raiders, hands bound, into the village.

"What's this?" Caleb demanded impatiently.

"We saw a ship slip toward the hills," one brawny villager explained. "They figured to do damage where they wouldn't be seen."

Shonnie looked to the hills, then clutched Aric's arm. "The

cats. Oh Aric, our cats!"

Caleb motioned the Barrias to join him in checking the area. Even before their craft landed they could see slaughtered snow tigers strewn throughout the white trees.

Anders simply stood and stared at the carnage. The beautiful wild cats he had chosen so lovingly were all dead, some already partially skinned. His fists trembling, he recalled his visit of yesterday when he had watched the bigger cats cavorting with their cubs. On his world no animal was going to fear people, and the cats had not run. Now their home was desecrated, their trust betrayed. He wanted to scream his fury but found he had no voice.

As Caleb radioed for a clean-up crew, Anders heard a mournful mewing and a series of frightened, sneezing snarls. Turning, he spotted a grey-dappled ball of ivory fluff beside one carcass.

The cub circled its mother slowly, pausing often to butt its head against her paws or flank. Sniffing her bloodied head it hiccoughed another snarl, then looked quizzically into her still face. Finally it flopped onto its haunches, mewing for attention.

Anders stole forward, step by cautious step, until he could kneel beside the frightened cub. It almost bounded away, then sniffed his outstretched hand tentatively. When it sidled closer he lifted it to the cradle of his arm.

"You'll come home with me, little one." He returned to the ship, where Caleb looked questioningly at the cub. Scratching the downy head, Anders said, "My people often tamed the cats of our plains. This will be my pet."

"The Paladins will arrive shortly," Caleb said tiredly. "Are you coming back to the village?"

"If I go I'll kill those men," Anders growled. "Shara can bring our ship for me."

Left alone in the icy stillness, Anders tried to understand why the raiders would destroy the cats. He had spent countless moments in this same confusion, always led to the same answer. Shandal killed simply for the killing, stole simply to steal. They were the complete antithesis of both Anders' people and the citizens of David's empire.

Gathered together, David's people tried to be caretakers, for the right of dominion was not the right of domination. Understanding that everything was alive, down to the rocks binding the planets, all was thus treated with love and honor. Supply planets were tended with respect, and the living things—plants, trees, animals—needed to nourish other living things were raised with love and gathered with gentleness and prayer. Even battle was entered into with the Warrior's Prayer: *Guide my hands that I may protect our right to be, to grow and learn. Let me spare life where I may.* Yet those they fought did nothing with honor. Their prayers were for domination, destruction, eradication. They had killed these cats simply to deprive Maradane of their beauty, much as they slaughtered countless species for ornamentation.

On David's supply planets fur-bearing animals were shorn of long hair, which was then processed into countless articles. Other animals that lived extremely short lives and grew at rapid pace were tended by shepherds and upon their deaths their pelts were taken for furs and leathers.

Anders shook his head, patting the cub soothingly. "I don't have the ability to understand their thinking."

Cloistered in smoky shadow, the Clan Seer peered at the commander standing stiffly opposite him. The chamber was hot, comfortably heated by the open brazier centered in the floor. The Seer cast a fond glance at the row of skulls in a window niche and heard the man swallow loudly.

"I have a task for you, not to be done by underlings this time." The Seer leaned back in his elaborately carved chair, sinking deeper into darkness.

"I understand, Seer," the man croaked.

Rolling a grape-sized ruby back and forth between his gaunt fingers, the Seer enjoyed the blood-hued reflections of candlelight playing over his hands. The teeming city was alive with the screams of slaves as their children were taken for the Festival of Battles. The young Clan warriors gathered before the High Altars, their live offerings bound in the shed skins of the Great Snakes. The Seer closed his eyes briefly, savoring the scents of blood and flame borne on the languid air.

The commander shifted nervously, ruining the Seer's concentration. Looking up angrily, the psychic barked, "I want those accursed wind lovers gone! Destroy the satellites that control their towers and the winds will do the rest."

"But Seer, the temple..." the man pointed out reticently.

"They've moved to the surface, fool!" The Seer closed his fist around the ruby. "The winds will rise so swiftly no one will reach the temple. Then we will take the treasures they are too perverted to value." He opened his hand to stare at the gem. "The wealth of a world lies in that temple...I shall add the mystics' heads to my collection." He smiled slowly.

"Yes, Seer." The commander bowed low. "I will leave at once."

Responding to a report from his sector, Jericho asked Aric to accompany him to the western tower. Stepping from the airship, the men were buffeted by a tremendous gale. A quick inspection of the control panels brought a perplexed frown to Jericho's face.

"The final level is failing."

Aric scratched his chin thoughtfully. "Is it the wiring?"

"No, it's the signal from the satellites. We'd better gather the others and check the other towers."

That evening the five kings stood at the base of the northern tower, an icy wind whipping around them.

Caleb pulled his cape more closely around his shoulders. "What will happen?"

"The levels will go, one by one, and the winds will rise." Aric scowled at the sky.

Pushing his windblown hair out of his blue eyes, Anders said, "We have to get the people back to the temple until repairs are made. Things will be damaged soon."

Caleb nodded grudgingly. "We'll begin calling them back. Jericho, you and Aric had better stock the repair ship. It'll take a while to check all the satellites."

"We'll leave tonight." Jericho and Aric set out for the hangar adjacent to the temple.

Three days passed as the people returned to the temple and the winds broke free of the three lowest control levels. The repair ship shuttled between Maradane and the satellites, gathering materials for extensive repairs. Once finished, Jericho and Aric reset the tower controls and returned to the temple.

Smudged and grimy, they trudged into the library where the others were waiting. In answer to Caleb's glance, Aric said, "The winds will be normal in a few days. But we've got a serious problem."

Jericho leaned on the table, his hands burnt by hot wires. "Each satellite was damaged in a different place, by a blasting cannon."

Caleb looked at Shara, then back at the two men. "Was there any sign of who did it?"

Jericho shook his dark head. "Whoever it was apparently thought they could kill the whole system through the satellites. We need a shield around them before someone decides to come back."

"I'll call the Paladins now." Caleb left the room.

Anders turned his gaze to Shara. "Tell them what you told Caleb."

Shara frowned as she faced Jericho and Aric. "It was Shandal. It came to me only this morning."

Aric's shoulders slumped as he leaned against the wall. "We should have known. Especially with most of this galaxy's worlds returned to David. But why us? We're barely on our feet."

Shara shrugged. "I glimpsed very little. Shandal has its own psychics, and one never knows what powers may arise on a given world."

Caleb returned, slipping into his chair. "The Paladins will be here by morning to set up the shields.

"While we're all here, there are a couple things I should mention."

"Yes?" Jericho settled into the chair beside Bronwyn.

"First, something of interest to Bryce." Caleb took out the tablet in which he kept notes of all their meetings. "Since all the people's homes are fairly well established we must begin constructing the palaces. I'd like Bryce to design them."

"Palaces?" Anders frowned deeply. "Being a king when not fit for it is trouble enough. I won't be imprisoned in a rambling pile of rock."

"I did have marble in mind, not plain boulders." Caleb made a hasty note, stifling a grin. "Simple but elegant structures to house our royal families. Bryce, would you create four similar designs, and sketch out the surrounding landscape?"

Bryce nodded eagerly, always willing to start a new project.

Rubbing his tired eyes, Jericho said, "What else?"

"Something more serious." Caleb paused to review a document in his notebook. "David has asked that we keep the temple location secret from all but our citizens and emissaries bearing his seal. One of the lower floors is to be converted into a records house. Coupled with the offices here it will safely house all our records."

"What is David keeping from us?" Aric demanded, his temper ready to flare. "Is the danger from Shandal to be constant?"

Caleb shook his head. "These are purely precautionary measures, to be carried out while the palaces are built."

"That's something to look forward to," Jericho said, more interested in the palaces than was Anders. "But right now I'm exhausted. Is there more to discuss?"

"No, go on and get some sleep." Caleb adjourned the impromptu meeting.

Ground was barely broken two months later when a fierce storm shut down work on the northern palace. The storm spread to all colder regions of Maradane, causing a second appraisal of the towers.

Jericho reported to Caleb. "The towers are all running perfectly. The weather patterns have not completely established themselves, so we have to expect fluctuations."

"Well, we can continue the other palaces while we wait." Caleb turned to the maps covering the wall behind his desk. "How are the people up there?"

"Shut in, but well supplied and warm."

"Good. We'll have quite a landscape when the storm clears."

"Aric, it's beautiful!" Shonnie turned to her husband, holding closed the collar of her fur cloak.

"It will be a fine place." Aric looked approvingly around the snowy plain. "We'll import winter plants for the gardens. Bryce, how long to finish?"

Bryce squinted in the glare of the snow, thankful his home was in the south. "Well, contending with storms, about fifty months."

"But that's almost a year!" Shonnie cried impatiently.

Caleb laughed at her perplexed expression. "All four palaces must be dedicated together, Shonnie, so the others will wait with you."

"I'll wait, but not patiently," Shonnie assured him good-naturedly.

Asher wandered through the seething market place, trying to do David's will and see this place through the eyes of its people. Shopping for food that he never ate—he relied on stores from home—he tried to understand why those in the market reveled in this gloomy place and called his people evil. The market was a miserable place to Asher, but he had to go regularly to maintain appearances. To his bewilderment, the citizens enjoyed the constant chaos.

Located in the center of Donthas, the market sprawled haphazardly over several acres, encircled by large stalls and shops where furnishings and services were sold. The market's heart was the slave complex, stalls where people chained together were inspected by prospective buyers. Radiating outward from there were booths selling everything imaginable, from cloth to stolen gems to pottery, from thick oily perfume for unwashed bodies to cloying spices masking the already rotting foods hawked by shouting merchants. The heat was intense, glistening bodies pressed into an ever-shifting throng in the midst of which sly hands lifted heavy purses. In dark alleys, throats were cut over rare gems smuggled out of merchants' stalls. The maze of paths between stalls was strewn with filth that no one wanted cleaned up, and forgotten dogs and hopeless people scavenged for grimy scraps.

Asher wrinkled his nose against the stench held down by the oppressive clouds smothering the planet. The throng swayed almost imperceptibly to the constant drumming broadcast from a series of towers. This low rhythmic thundering grated without ease on Asher's nerves, but the people could not live without it. If by some emergency the drummers ceased their work, the citizenry shrieked as if in pain, covering their ears against the deafening silence where it was said they heard taunting voices. Asher believed it was their imagination, fears instilled in toddlers by parents who knew that in the silence of idle thought was proof that Shandal was wrong. Eager to quell dangerous thoughts, the warlords filled the silence. Soldiers and spies had to be carefully trained to function on enemy worlds where silence prevailed.

Asher found no understanding here. He was used to open-air markets with roomy walks and roomier stalls, roofed by blue sky or awnings of vibrant materials. Gold tassels dripped from those awnings of crimson and sapphire, swaying on soft breezes. Leisurely shoppers talked in small groups or hummed as they strolled, filling wicker baskets with small items and ordering delivery of larger choices. Jewelry and ornamental pieces glinted in the sunlight, and colorful bottles held fine perfumes from every corner of the realm. Finished crafts as well as hobby materials lined neat shelves above racks of fabric bolts in every hue. Fresh foods were set out continuously, the grocers taking orders for meats and fish to be delivered over the following days. Tables beneath cheery canopies offered the ease to savor snacks readily available from marble counters. Children begged candy from the confectioners and cats wheedled a fish or two from the grocers.

Shaking his head, Asher turned his steps toward the quarter housing the Clan hierarchy. Reaching the fringes of the market, he felt someone tugging at his purse. Angered, he broke the thief's wrist, then threw the bag of coins at his feet. Stealing was such a vile offense, and there was no reason for it. It was unforgivable to take from someone any cherished object when a similar one was available for the asking in any market. It was available for Shandal, but they repeatedly refused David's outstretched hand. Asher left behind the market, but not his distaste.

He moved onward, one hand resting on his sword, passing the homes of the most powerful people in Donthas. High, windowless stone walls faced a street of open sewers and unwashed beggars. There were no courtyards—Shandal's people found flowers cloying and wasteful of building space, and none would grow on their dark worlds.

Asher had been within walls like these. Each house was a fortress of disheveled living quarters, the structures wedged between stinking alleys. Narrow ventilation slots were heavily grilled against thieves. Doors were barred and guarded inside and out. Deep within each house, below ground beneath the family's private altar, lay the treasure room. Barred and chained shut, with guards who dared not enter, the vault was packed with wealth: gold, silver, and jewels stolen and bought, all piled where no one could reach or see them.

The vaults were filled in many ways, and closely inventoried by their owners. To fund his present needs the overlord could sell slaves, or marry a daughter to a rival for a high price. Wives and children were often leased to admiring friends in a prospering market. Or offspring could be sold to the Seers for use in sacrifices preceding battle. Highborn young men brought an astronomical price because they were so rarely offered, but daughters also elicited a respectable sack of jewels.

Asher's disturbed thoughts were broken by a harsh young voice. Ahead of him two Clan children were dueling in the street. The older one, about twelve, cracked a whip over his brother's head. The younger boy was armed only with a singlestick and already bled from several cuts. Dodging the snaking whip, the boy rolled head over heels to crack the stick against his brother's knees. The youth doubled over, but recovered quickly enough to loop the whip around his brother's throat.

"Guess you lost again," he panted. "You're worthless, you know that? The first Davan scum to cross your path will run you through."

Silent, the younger boy pulled a dagger from his boot and

sliced through the whip and into the other boy's hand.

Asher watched from the shadows. This activity was encouraged by parents, preparing sons for future battles and feud matches, and weeding out weaklings who would be an embarrassment. This fight seemed over as the older boy sulkily wrapped his hand in a strip of cloth.

Going on his way, Asher knew he would never understand these people—he did not possess the ability to think as they did. They murdered their mates as easily as they wed them, and children were only routes to power. Wives drifted from man to man until they accumulated enough gold to murder their husbands and attract wealthier overlords. Sons slipped into the vacancies of their fathers, the new generation of warlords and overlords for the new generation of young women. The Clan leaders would always refuse David's rule for it meant loss of power and domination. They enjoyed their intrigues and tortures too much to accept a system where one could not profit from another's misery.

Finally reaching his room, Asher closed and locked his door and buried his face in a cloth soaked in clean water. It smelled better than any perfume ever could—just a clean cloth. There was probably not another one on the entire planet.

Sparkling banners were unfurled from Maradane's palaces upon completion after almost a year of anticipation. The citizenry gathered for the dedication festivals as their rulers gathered for farewells of a sort.

Caleb looked around the temple gardens, studying Jericho's trees for a long moment. The couples gathered nearby in an awkward silence, small boxes of precious trinkets in their arms. Listening to the bubbling fountain, Caleb realized how quiet his home would now be.

At least there would be the daily worship. Anders had trained Caleb to be the Keeper of the Temple, over the high king's urgent protests.

"The Keeper of the Temple is the leader of the people, of the world," Anders had insisted. "I am king of a sector, but you are king of the world. It is your due."

So Caleb gave in and undertook the training, feeling Anders was giving up too much. But prayers were in the morning, as each person came on their day of a six-day cycle. The rest of each day would be quiet, and he was already contemplating a project to fill the empty evenings.

Catching Caleb's eye for an instant, Anders squeezed Shara's hand and looked lovingly over the gardens planned such a short time ago to soothe his people. He had new people now, and this was no longer his temple. He would step aside for the rightful Keeper, to concentrate on his sector's people who would be his life from now on. Grief had turned to joy in these years, for he left behind a place built for a dying race to be a caretaker of a growing world. He would ask for nothing more than the gift of serving these people and cherishing his friends. But still, leaving was hard. Hardest perhaps for Caleb, who would remain alone.

A gentle current rustled through the leaves and Anders grinned at Caleb. The young king would not be entirely alone.

Seeing the big man's reassuring look, Caleb broke the silence. "David sent word that the last raiders are captured, and the Paladins will maintain a routine patrol around Maradane. After they retrieve our firearms David will send instructors for the new weaponry. And counting our world in the new census, there are roughly two thousand planets in ten galaxies claiming membership in the empire."

He paused, smiling at Shonnie, who was now not so impatient to move to her palace.

"I'll visit each palace shortly to give the dedication. Go on now, and enjoy the day."

Standing in the palace gardens that evening, Jericho drew Bronwyn to his side. "I never dreamt of this when we crashed four years ago. I'm still not certain about this kingship, but I'm happy to serve the people."

Bronwyn squeezed his hand. "They're such good people, especially Kana's group. And Anders has made Maradane so beautiful."

She pulled Jericho to a seat on a marble bench and looked up at the dusky sky. It seemed adventurous to try living outside the temple, but her final doubts dwindled on the warm breeze. The first moon was rising as servants lit festive lanterns amidst the trees.

The wind grew chill as a flurry of sparkling lights enveloped the lantern across the path. Staring at the golden glow Bronwyn saw, in her mind's eye, the sparkles expand into blazing flames. Her palace lay ruined, blackened by fire within this vision of flame, and the gardens were strewn with twisted bodies.

She shivered and the surreal scene was gone, the warming breeze trailing apologetically across her shoulders. Realizing Jericho had seen none of this, Bronwyn pushed the scene from her mind. It was for the future, not this moment.

End Book One

Book Two

THE HOMECOMING

Chapter Six

"Jericho, must you toy with your food? You haven't eaten a thing." Bronwyn watched as he used his fork to make canals through his mashed potatoes and then filled them with gravy.

Jericho stared absently at his plate. "I'm not hungry, Bron. Things just aren't going well." He sighed heavily.

"Really, Jericho, you are in a dismal fit." Bronwyn folded her cloth napkin. "I haven't noticed anything unusual happening."

Jericho glanced at her, frustration flooding his amber eyes. "The Paladins came today and took all our weapons. How am I to see that the people are protected when we have no weapons? Shandal won't rest just because the war is over. I don't see how this planet is ever going to work." Resting his chin on his crossed arms, he stared dolefully at the scarlet tablecloth.

Reaching out to smooth his unruly black hair, Bronwyn said, "You really are worrying over nothing, you know. New colonies can't avoid problems, but it can be worked out.

"And you know very well that David is sending armorers to

each world as quickly as possible. In the meantime we are in easy contact with the Paladins."

"If only I had your endless faith." Jericho smiled weakly, sitting up. "Things seem at such a standstill..." His words trailed away as he glanced out the window. Alarm replaced the weariness in his eyes as he cried, "Look at that ship!"

Bronwyn spun in time to see a blaze of light plummet to the ground in the northern sector.

Shoving his chair back, Jericho strode to the door. "We'd better see if anyone was hurt."

Glinting in the moonlight, the ship crashed to a halt in the lush northern gardens. As Shonnie and Aric raced across the snowy lawns a battered door was pushed open and several people stepped shakily to the ground.

A young woman rubbed a bruised arm as she wailed, "It's beyond hope! We shall never be able to repair it." The entire lower level housing the propulsion unit was torn asunder, parts strewn across broken shrubbery and paths alike.

Reaching the group, Aric asked anxiously, "Please, can we help you? Was anyone injured?"

The woman regained her composure with well-trained efficiency. Her thick black hair, braided and wrapped about the back of her head, was disheveled and wispy strands blew across her dark eyes, but she smiled shakily. The others in the group waited patiently, quietly studying their surroundings as she replied.

"We received harsh bumps, but naught serious, thank you." She looked uncertainly at a tall man who moved silently to her side, then continued as he nodded.

"We're very sorry about this damage. If our engine had not burned out we'd have gone on to the next galaxy. I am Tiea Mashun—"

Her words stopped abruptly as Bronwyn and Jericho, grasping their staffs, dropped lightly from the night sky. Tiea backed away. "Great Dacyn! Do people fly on this world?"

Shonnie laughed softly, but was quick to reassure Tiea. "Our planet is Maradane, and we frequently travel by Adane's ancient methods. It is usually faster than bothering with a ship."

"Well," Tiea said uncertainly, glancing again at her companion. "We were forced to leave Dacyn, and seek a new home."

Aric studied the group intently. There was only one reason anyone would be forced to leave that ancient world. On the other hand, they would not be free if it were David's work. He decided to let the matter slide for the moment.

"You are welcome here." He offered his hand to Tiea's silent guardian. "I'm Aric Donnya; my wife Shonnie and I rule this sector. This is my cousin Jericho Donnya and his wife Bronwyn. They rule in the west." His companions nodded as he continued.

"Come inside and have some hot drinks. We can then see that your bruises truly are not serious."

"Thank you, very much." Tiea's voice was relieved, if still shaky. As they crossed the lawns she introduced the silent man as her brother Salar, traveling with his wife Cita. The others included five young married couples, all characteristically colored with the deep bronze skin and thick black hair of Dacyn's natives. Barely out of their youth, the five men—Talos, Mikar, Tay, Gar, and Karal—were armed with shortswords and crossbows. They waited hesitantly and kept their unarmed wives safely behind them.

Aric saw that they were comfortably seated around the long table in the paneled dining hall, then murmured to Shonnie, "Let Caleb know we have guests." As she left the room Aric pulled up a chair for himself. "Please forgive me if I seem ignorant, but I was unaware that Dacyn's people still use swords."

"No apology is necessary, milord." Talos gratefully received the steaming mug a servant offered. "You would not know of my people unless you were a student of our culture.

"We hail from a small island in the far south and have served for many ages as Royal Guard to the High King. It has been our tradition to serve with armor and swords."

Pausing to sip from the mug, Talos glanced at Salar. The quiet man seemed to need no words to communicate with his friends. This fact was not overlooked by either king as Talos continued.

"Might we remain here? We do wish to travel as little further as possible, but if you aren't taking colonists we will acquire a new ship from the Paladins."

"We'd be happy to have you stay," Aric said readily. "We need colonists, and can find rooms for you in the palaces until homes are built." He paused again, wondering what clash of wills had sent them from their domed cities.

Jericho's worried expression eased considerably as he scanned the swords left in a neat row near the door. "We're fortunate to have you here. Aric and I can work a forge, but we don't make weapons, and David moves too slowly for my impatient mind. We need someone who can make and use this new weaponry."

"I can't understand what the kings thought they were doing with these new laws." Salar's voice was touched with bitterness. "It's been well over a thousand years since most planets in this galaxy used swords for any purpose at all, let alone in battle. Now the unarmed worlds are at the mercy of any unexpected attack slipping past the Paladins. Millions are fleeing, hoping for a better peace elsewhere."

"For whatever good it will do," Bronwyn said in exasperation. "Though Shandal has plagued this galaxy so heavily, they do not forget the rest of David's empire." She turned to look Salar in the eye. "May I change the subject and ask why the royal family has fled Dacyn in the guise of the royal guard?"

Salar raised one brow slightly. "You've studied Dacyn?"

"I was ill for many years and found the old library my best companion."

Sighing, Cita twisted a heavy gold ring on her finger. "Salar opposed Dacyn's Elders in the council after the wars, and again in a recent council. He proposed lifestyle changes disagreeable to the Elders, and the Mashun family has been deposed and banished from our home." She looked up as Caleb entered the room with the two other ruling couples.

Caleb's gaze flicked around the room, pausing briefly on Salar's face. "For the benefit of our unexpected guests, I am Caleb Bajoc, High King of Maradane. These couples are Bryce and Prudence Jeremiah, rulers of the southern sector, and Anders and Shara Barria, rulers of the east."

Anders smiled at each of the newcomers, then turned to his friends. "Shara feels all is well. Tell us what has happened?"

Shonnie looked quizzically at Shara before replying. "Simply, the Dacynites' ship crashed, no one was seriously hurt, and perhaps they will settle here. Shara, have you seen something particular?"

"No, it's really only a feeling." Shara blushed under the curious looks from Salar's people.

"My wife is gifted with psychic powers," Anders came to her rescue, squeezing her hand. "Perhaps we should first acquaint you with Maradane, to aid your decision."

"An excellent idea," Aric agreed after seeing no objection from Caleb. "Please, everyone come with me and we'll look at the maps." He led the way to his vast study and began spreading maps on the large table.

As he did so Salar exchanged a puzzled glance with his party. "May I ask a question?"

"Certainly." Aric straightened to face the dark man, noting for the first time that Salar matched his own nine foot height.

"You mentioned Adane earlier, and you call your world Maradane..."

"It's not easy to miss our major oddity," Aric answered, chuckling. "Yes, Jericho and I escaped Adane, and are thankful to be away. Bryce and Prudence are Stefanovians, and Anders and Shara hail from Stalasia."

"I had wondered, due to her gifts." Salar turned and found Shara smiling shyly.

A mere five feet two inches tall, Shara looked up at Salar with merry blue eyes. "We've come to enjoy the expression our companionship brings to most faces. Please be assured that in no way will Maradane follow the steps of the recent Adane. Our roots lie in the long past." She saw another question in his eyes and added, "No, my Anders has no unusual gifts, except that of great love." She closed her small hands around her husband's larger one, then invited proudly, "Come, look at our maps."

Aric traced a series of lines with a slim metal wand. "There are four sectors on Maradane, each ruled by one family. The two neutral zones are under only Caleb's rule and no one lives there, beyond the sector boundaries. We have planned several other uses for the neutral zones."

Salar looked with a seasoned ruler's interest at the detailed notes along the map's outer regions. "Have you many people yet?"

"Not yet." Caleb sat on a nearby bench. "But our colonization has barely begun."

Salar turned away from the maps. "Where would it be best to build our homes? We don't want to interfere with your plans."

"This is to be a planet of villages and towns," Caleb answered. "You may settle where you wish."

Mikar turned from gazing out at the moonlit gardens. "Is there perhaps something we may help you with, while we learn about your world?"

Jericho looked up hopefully. "We do need instruction in the new weaponry. I want my people prepared to defend themselves."

Salar looked obliquely at Caleb, who nodded almost imperceptibly. "We will be happy to help, Jericho. It will make the change of worlds not so harsh." He turned back to Caleb. "We'll sketch out some plans over the next few days. Once you approve them we can begin work."

"Excellent. I do share Jericho's concern over being unarmed. But it's getting late now. We'll settle you in the palaces, then you can get to know the planet."

Bronwyn took great delight in showing Salar, Cita and Tiea through her home, excited over her first guests.

"And this is our library, where I am often found." Bronwyn opened the double doors to the vast room. Crossing to a pair of delicately etched glass doors, she said, "This leads to the gardens. There's a little alcove just outside where I enjoy reading."

Stepping outside, Tiea gazed upward. Maradane's six moons hovered high above the horizon, patterned by tracings of silver cloud. The soft scents of night blooming flowers laced the breeze, and jeweled walks glittered beckoningly.

"It's so beautiful here! And to see the stars from outside a dome!" Tiea tore her gaze from the star-flecked sky as she sat on a marble bench. She bent to touch a tiny flower, fragily transparent on its slender stem. "It feels daringly free not to see the dome overhead."

"Didn't you ever leave the cities, to visit another planet?" Bronwyn pulled her shawl more closely around her shoulders. "'Tis quite breezy tonight."

"It's lovely. And no, I would not have been allowed to leave Dacyn until I was twenty; I am only fifteen. It's wonderful to be outside, to feel an honest wind."

Salar nodded. "After traveling to many worlds I came to despise the domes which protect us from Dacyn's dangers. Everything is recycled and man-made, not even an ocean of any account where the people rule the waters. No sight is as sad as those artificial seas."

Smiling, Cita tugged gently on the golden chain encircling Salar's neck. "It was such attitudes which caused our trouble, my husband. Perhaps you opposed the domes too much."

Joining them, Jericho overhead the comment. "Why do you oppose the domes, Salar?"

"Ah Cita, you see, you have him thinking me some faithless king," Salar chided with a loving smile, then faced Jericho. "My hatred of the domes arises from the agonies of the people during the wars. We should have abandoned the planet when Shandal first poisoned it, instead of retreating to those unnatural cities. Our very life source is too fragile, too easily destroyed."

"But with the ban on explosive weapons the domes should be safe."

Salar's green eyes grew icy. "We both know how much water that holds. Of course Shandal will abandon guns now that David's court has developed this metal called tirrschon. Bullets are of little use on impervious armor. But bombs will still destroy cities. What recourse will we have? At least David will take a more active hand in this galaxy now."

"That's considerate of him after so many centuries." Leaning against the cool stone wall, Jericho crossed his arms. "But I guess that was the price of our own folly. The galaxy forsook the empire, not the other way around, and has paid dearly for the action."

Salar nodded, the breeze tousling his thick bangs. "Who could stand against a galaxy of fools who valued technology over wisdom? Especially with Shandal at their heels? But David returned when asked, and perhaps this unification of weaponry will draw us together."

"Speaking of drawing together, what test did I and the others fail so miserably tonight? Your shared looks with Caleb weren't totally unnoticed." Jericho smiled ruefully.

Salar repressed a laugh. "You are too unwary of strangers, Jericho. You dove in asking for help before you really knew who we were, and offered us a home without any background information."

"We knew full well who you must be. An ally is an ally, and had you been criminals in David's eyes you'd have been in prison. And Shara said it was all right," Jericho countered, embarrassed. "Caleb wasn't protesting very loudly."

"Caleb and I go back quite a little way. Had I known he was here we would have made this our destination. It lessens the hurt to be among friends."

Bronwyn moved closer to her husband. "It's more difficult for you and our friends. We of Adane didn't love our world. At least now one is either Davan or Shanda; the shaky middle ground is gone. And actually so is much of the night," she finished, looking toward the risen moons.

"Yes, we'd better show you to your rooms." Jericho followed them inside, closing the door and shading the lights in the library.

Asher strode silently through the interior courtyards toward the archives of Donthas, capital city of Shandal. Passing the royal altar he averted his eyes and held his breath against the stench of standing blood. It was a sacrilege against Shandal's gods to remove remnants of any sacrifice, leaving these sticky pools all over the city. The stifling heat of the world did nothing to alleviate the odors.

Entering the musty libraries, Asher breathed at last. This was a clean smell, a conglomeration of dust, old parchment, and ink mingled with the stone and wood scents in the dark halls of knowledge. These people hoarded knowledge as tightly as their gems, doling it out to a chosen few to maintain clan lineages and records of wealth. To be a lower class and caught able to read was to become an immediate meal for one of the enormous snakes worshipped in ancient chambers.

Sitting at his table, Asher frowned as he began cataloging the latest communiqués. Already there was word of the Dacynites' arrival on Maradane. Davan movement was monitored closely, but no written record was kept of Shanda spies' identities. Only the Seers knew their names and assignments.

Asher smiled slightly, realizing David still had the upper hand in that situation. Every ambassador and visiting dignitary and worker in Leahcim Tierrah underwent routine physicals to detect the slight anatomical differences in the Shanda. Spies were either executed, if their crimes mandated it, or their memories were erased, to be retaught the ways of the empire. David loathed needless killing, and many of the younger spies were thus reborn into better lives.

The Shanda, however, had no way to detect David's men unless a Seer stumbled upon them. Physicians were almost non-existent, and their sole purpose was to minister to Clan overlords. Davan spies were always Immortal and thus able to escape through the misty teleportal zone, barring pursuit by mortals.

Sifting the records for useful information, Asher dismissed mention of the Dacynites as a routine notation. The Seer would have little interest in Salar's group—his interest lay with others on Maradane.

Salar formed a quick friendship with Jericho and chose to settle his family near the western palace. Caleb reminded Salar that he could appeal the Elders' action to David, but the displaced king had no wish to rule a world that did not want him. His attention was focused on his new home and new duties.

Settled in, the Dacynites began exploring the wonders of an open world with vast spans of natural ocean. They also planned a small-arms factory, large forge and open training pavilion for each sector. Caleb submitted supply orders along with those for a new phase of planet-wide construction designed by Anders and Bryce.

"It's going to be a splendid sight, Bryce." Anders looked from the sketches in his hands to the skeletal framework rising near the eastern palace. "I like the dolphins in the waves on the pillars." He reached down to absently scratch the ears of the massive snow tiger rubbing against his legs.

Bryce studied the structure with satisfaction. "I've tried to design each school to blend with its surroundings. With the harbor here as a backdrop, I had to make use of sea life."

"The children will love it, especially the courtyards and windows overlooking the harbor." Anders rolled up the sketches as he glanced at another half-constructed building across the harbor. "How's the hospital progressing?"

"Wonderfully," Bryce said. "My sector's school for medics was just completed, and several medics have arrived from Leahcim Tierrah to begin the classes. David's also sending teachers and books for the schools." He looked thoughtfully across the sparkling waves. "Why do you suppose he has such an interest in us?"

"Even Shara has no idea." Anders shook his curly head, then grinned. "But I'd certainly rather have his interest than someone else's."

"I'll second that," Bryce agreed. Things had been pleasantly quiet since the attack on the satellites. "But if I don't run I'll need the Paladins to save me from Salar—I'm late for my lessons. So far I find little love of swordsmanship."

"Bring Pru to supper tonight and I'll commiserate with you." Anders chuckled as Bryce hurried away, then he strolled down the beach. Nearing a group of children he saw that a brisk wind was blowing puffs of sea spray into their ruddy faces. It stopped abruptly as he reached the breathless group, leaving him to wonder anew about Maradane's winds as the children turned their attention to the gentle tiger.

Chapter Seven

Tiea wandered absently through the temple gardens. Everyone else was so busy, seeming to know exactly what to do each day. She had yet to discover a task in which she could be useful and her days were long and tedious.

Sitting on a low bench, she looked aimlessly around. The white marble fountain created gentle music as water cascaded over its basins, streaming between wispy blossoms carved of colorful gems. Delicate crystalline birds perched around the topmost and lowest bowls seemed alive in the shimmering reflections.

"May I help you?"

Tiea whirled to face Caleb, startled. "Well...not really, I guess. I just wondered...well, you rush to and from meetings so quickly, I wondered what kept you so busy." Quite shy, she tagged along with her brother to various councils, content to listen to the plans discussed.

Caleb smiled down at the girl, realizing he did exit evening meetings perhaps a little too swiftly. "I fear my archival spirit thrives on writing even when I'm supposed to be resting. I'm writing the history of Maradane. Come and I'll show you." He led her through a maze of corridors to the very back of the building.

The small room was furnished with only a long table and chair, and strewn with papers and pens. Caleb offered Tiea the chair, removing a crumpled apron from the seat.

"My people have always recorded the history of our world by hand, providing a rich heritage for the future. Of course the material is later transcribed and printed for distribution to libraries. But we maintain the tradition of the handwritten volumes. What do you think?" He handed her several pages filled with beautiful, flowing script.

"They're lovely." Tiea studied one page, admiring the elegant lettering. "I was never allowed to study very much on Dacyn. How do you go about writing the history of a planet?" She looked up hopefully.

Pleased to have such an avid listener, Caleb sat on the edge of the table. "For Maradane it's not complicated, because we know nothing of the history before our arrival. But all events since then, and those leading to the arrival of the original settlers, have been documented here. The chronicles will provide a reference source, with further information in the temple libraries. I've been working on this first volume for the three years I've lived here."

Tiea frowned. "I'm sorry. Salar said you are fifteen, but surely you cannot have been king here since you were twelve." Although twelve was the age of manhood throughout the empire, she envisioned all kings as reflections of her older brother.

Caleb laughed lightly. "No, I'm twenty in the years of my people. But I have a new home with a different year, so I'm fifteen. Do you understand the Universal Time Code?"

"I don't quite, no. The Elders were very strict in keeping off-world education from those not meant to rule." Tiea put the papers on the table. "Could you explain it to me?"

"Certainly," he said amiably, resting his elbows on his knees. "Since David's empire has accepted so many worlds he found that a universal year used in all trade and discussion is easier to follow than the varied years of individual planets. A Universal Year is precisely seventy-three months long. As a coincidence, Maradane's year is also that long, with each month containing thirty days."

Tiea nodded slowly. "I see now, it's a guideline for interaction. And the people have lived on the surface for only a year? What will be done now with this building?"

"Anders and I closed off the chapels from the other rooms, so people won't be disturbed at worship. The rest of the structure has been converted to a governing complex and space for refuge during war. The five floors will house many thousands."

Tiea's response was snuffed out by a tremendous howling reverberating through the passage.

Jumping to his feet, Caleb ordered, "Run to the gardens after I've gone. If I don't come to you, call Anders." Grabbing a rifle kept by permission of the Paladins, he ran down the hall before Tiea could sputter a protest.

Peering cautiously around the door frame, Tiea looked past Caleb. Careening toward him was a beast almost five feet tall, armed with massive claws on its forelimbs. Its yellow eyes focused on Caleb and it lunged forward.

Caleb fired the rifle over its head. The noise made the beast hesitate, then retreat into darkness with Caleb following. A door clanged shut and silence followed, but the young man did not return.

Pulling a slim dagger from her boot, Tiea ran after him.

Caleb was slumped against a thick metal door that was barred shut. Blood streamed from a gash in his forehead as he struggled for breath.

Tiea dropped to her knees beside him, warily eyeing the door. "What's in that room?" She gently pressed a kerchief against his forehead.

"The door leads to underground caverns," Caleb answered shakily. "That was a native of Maradane."

Tiea grew alarmed at his rapid loss of color and the obvious pain. "You were hurt elsewhere..."

He shook his head weakly, then slumped into unconsciousness.

Reassuring herself that the door was secure, Tiea sheathed her dagger as she stood. Slipping her arms under Caleb's broad shoulders she took a deep breath and pulled. His resisting weight made the corridors seem endless as she struggled toward the gardens.

Gasping for breath, she settled Caleb against the door of his office and ran to the panel of buttons behind his desk. There seemed no order to the confusing array, nor was Tiea certain of what she wanted. At last her frantic gaze settled on a small tag: ALARMS—EAST AND NORTH. She pressed the two buttons and returned to the hall. Placing herself between Caleb and the rear of the temple she waited with drawn weapon.

A short time later she heard heavy steps, but they came from the gardens. Tiea turned as two men skidded to a halt near her.

"Tiea, what happened?" Anders looked from Caleb's torn face to the knife in the dark girl's hand.

She dropped the dagger, tears flooding her eyes. "I don't know! Some beast attacked him...I dragged him here, but didn't know which buttons to press."

Anders drew her close as Aric knelt beside Caleb. "You did very well, Tiea. Aric?"

"He's not good; the poison has a firm grip." Aric stood up. "Shonnie will send more men if I sound the alarm again, so I'll guard the door until they arrive. Take Caleb to Bryce."

"We'll discuss a second wall later." Anders gathered Caleb into his arms and strode up the hall.

Anders and Tiea waited impatiently while Bryce examined Caleb. Prudence hurried past them with an armful of supplies and disappeared into the examining room.

When Bryce entered the hallway his face was taut. "I have nothing to counteract the poison. Tiea, would you be kind enough to stay and help Pru?"

"Yes, of course." Tiea hurried away to join Prudence.

Anders looked grimly at the medic. "Truth, Bryce."

"I can't say," Bryce sighed. "Since he is half-Immortal he may awake without treatment. As soon as we complete the blood tests I'll contact Leahcim Tierrah."

Anders nodded. "Aric and I are going to close that door permanently. We'll come back here later." He headed for the door as Bryce returned to the lab.

That evening found the three kings and the men from Dacyn unloading a supply ship outside the temple. A call through the Paladins' network had brought a shipment of rough marble blocks to complete a new wall. The blocks needed only to be squared and cut to fit.

Hefting a block onto the growing pile, Anders grumbled, "My people were foolish to put a door there."

"I don't like the thought of that animal running loose," Gar grunted, dropping a block to be squared. "But it seems to have some intelligence."

"That's one reason we hoped to study the caverns." Anders straightened, flexing his arms. "But in recent months it has seemed there is something in the temple which the beast wants. It's best to close the door totally."

Putting aside the tool with which he was edging the blocks, Mikar reached for his canteen. "How did you first encounter them? Are you certain there's no cure?"

"We're certain of nothing." Anders rubbed one hand across his tired eyes. "Our researchers were attracted to the caverns because they cut down on excavation. The beasts are usually docile unless cornered, and dislike light so they don't venture to the surface. But there are certain areas in the caverns where the animals will attack, chiefly the arenas. The rear of the first floor is built over one of those arenas. Our men who were attacked never regained consciousness."

Caleb lay in a fevered coma. Bryce fretted away the time while the researchers in the royal libraries scoured their volumes. The royal physicians were running their own tests from Bryce's data, but a day had already passed with no word. At the temple the men were completing the new wall.

It was late into the night when the men wearily shouldered tools and leftover supplies and headed home. Starting up the hall with a heavy cutter in his arms, Anders stumbled over the fragments of a block shaped for a narrow space.

Hearing him fall, Aric turned to give him a hand up. "Too tired to walk, my friend? Anders?"

The blond man did not stir. Throwing down the tools he carried, Aric shouted, "Jericho, Salar! Anders is hurt!"

Kneeling to move the cutter, the weight of which had propelled Anders backward, Aric saw no visible injury. As Jericho and Salar ran down the hall he saw a spreading crimson in Anders' blond curls. Lifting Anders' head gently, Aric's questing fingers felt a small hollow behind one ear and he saw a sharp rock fragment on the floor.

"Oh, dear God," Shara murmured as she ran into the gleaming white room and saw her husband's still form. Instinctively, she put her graceful hands on his temples and closed her eyes.

"Shara, no!" Bryce pulled her roughly away from the table.

"Bryce, let me help him!" She stared disbelievingly as he shook his head. "No medic may stand in the way of an empath!"

"Shara, his skull is cracked." Bryce steered her gently toward the door. "I'm going to repair the fracture and check for damage. Wait outside now."

"Bryce." Shara now looked tearfully at him. "Don't let him die."

"Shara, I'm doing my best." Bryce ushered her into the hall.

Bronwyn and Shonnie took the distraught woman to a bench near the garden door. Their husbands and Salar stood nearby.

"I don't understand," Shara said weakly.

Shonnie pressed a flowered handkerchief into her friend's hand. "Aric says he stumbled, hit his head. They brought him here right away."

"I know they did." Shara dried her eyes, only to begin crying again. "Why in the name of David is this happening? First Caleb, now my Anders...I felt such agonizing pain in my head, worse than when our people died. Bryce won't let me help."

"You know you'd lose consciousness, and control." Bronwyn hugged Shara, trying to calm her trembling. "We must let Bryce work."

It was nearing dawn when Bryce emerged from the surgery. Closing the door softly behind him, he turned to face the small group, an agony in his eyes.

Shara clutched Bronwyn's hand as she saw the grim set of the man's lips. With some effort she managed to ask, "How is my husband, Bryce?"

Bryce rubbed his eyes, trying to find his voice. "He's in a coma, Shara. There was a bone fragment lodged in the tissue..."

His legs refusing to support him any longer, Jericho sank onto a bench. "Oh, God, not Anders." Aric ran his hands helplessly through his fiery hair as Salar glanced morosely toward Caleb's room.

Bryce knelt before Shara, tears in his eyes. "I can't do any more now." He took her hands lovingly in his. "I'll call for help from Leahcim Tierrah. There's static now, but it will clear soon."

Shara gazed numbly at him. "Will he be alive when they get here?"

Bryce nodded slowly. "Pru is monitoring the life support. You may come sit with him."

Bronwyn watched Bryce lead Shara into the still room, then looked at the stricken people around her. Suddenly she could bear the silent hall no longer and bolted outside to the gardens.

The waning night was unusually cool and dreary, chilling the woman's bare arms. A petulant wind rustled the leaves overhead as Bronwyn wandered the maze of paved walks. The flowers had long ago folded their petals; the trees possessed neither color nor shape. All was a dark, shadowy blur as the queen tilted her head back to gaze at the sharp, cold stars.

Only a few remained bright, unwilling to surrender to the paling of the sky. Bronwyn wondered if the worlds circling those suns held such hidden horrors or felt such pain. Did their people feel this helpless? A tear escaped the tangle of her lashes to leave a moist trail across her pale cheek.

Passing a shrub Bronwyn broke off a little flower that had not closed fully for its nightly sleep. Cradling the blossom in her hands, then absently twisting the stem, she felt her heart crumbling within her.

There came a distant sound behind her, as of dry leaves in a misty wind. A soft voice touched her ears. "Thou wouldst not be happy elsewhere, milady."

Bronwyn turned toward the man who had appeared from the darkness. He was clothed head to foot in furs, as if coming from cold climes. Beneath his hood a halo of fine white hair framed his tanned face.

Bronwyn's attention was drawn to this face, youthful yet marked with all the age of time. Lamplight from an open door glanced off a lyre over his shoulder, tracing shadows across his dark green eyes. He seemed content to wait while she collected herself.

In a halting voice Bronwyn said, "You're of the Immortals, aren't you?"

"Yea, I am Richard, firstborn."

Her tears burst forth at last. "Please, can you help us? Caleb is poisoned and Anders is so terribly hurt...everything is so wrong..." She realized she was making little sense.

Richard stepped close to take her hands in his. "Do not cry, milady. Gray sent me to help your kings. Please take me to them."

Wiping her eyes with a trembling hand, Bronwyn led the man into the palace. They were met with distracted glances, then Salar snapped to attention.

"Richard!" Crossing the floor to his old friend, he gripped Richard's hand pleadingly. "Richard, you must—"

"I have come to help, Salar. All wilt be well." Richard turned as Bryce answered Bronwyn's knock at the surgery door.

Bryce saw Richard and hope flared in his weary eyes. Without a word he practically dragged the Immortal to Anders' beside.

Her head resting on Anders' shoulder, Shara did not look up until Richard moved beside her.

Reaching into a pouch over one shoulder, Richard drew forth a small cube of copper that he placed on his open palm. Intoning a brief prayer, he passed his hand in a circular motion over Anders' head and heart. Pausing, he traced one finger along the scar on the man's shoulder. "So, he hath found the first one," he whispered almost inaudibly. Then he shook his head and smiled at Shara.

Bryce appeared at his elbow. "Caleb is in the next room."

Nodding, Richard followed him to Caleb's bed, where he performed the same procedure with the copper cube. Tiea watched curiously from her bedside chair, and Salar bent to explain the actions to her. For the Immortals, healing was a combination of prayer and the use of a specific metal to focus energies. All but the most deadly injuries or illnesses could thus be cured by any Immortal, and those known as Healers had powers to eclipse Richard's small gift.

Returning to the first room, Richard found Shara holding tightly to her husband's hand. She smiled hesitantly. "They will be well?"

"They shalt be well; they wilt sleep whilst the wounds heal." Richard put away his copper.

"But how did you know to come?"

He smiled faintly. "Gray sent me, milady. He wast told something wast terribly wrong here, and that we cannot allow."

Salar looked oddly at Richard, his disheveled hair trailing across his eyes. "Are we so important, then, that our tragedy would affect any but us?"

"Thou knowest not the importance of this world, Salar. Thine people art fortunate to have landed here."

"Ah, and how much of our fortune was coincidence?"

Richard grinned broadly this time. "Salar, David promised only to send armorers to Maradane, and made no mention of method of arrival. Although if thou hadst not been in such haste to depart Dacyn, thy arrival wouldst have been less bumpy. I must leave now, leave thee to rest." Gripping his travel stone, he left the room before anyone could speak.

Looking after him, Salar thought back over his recent studies of Maradane. It had been obvious to him that someone was watching, averting potential disasters. Now he was left to wonder why Maradane was so important, until David chose to speak of it.

Bryce looked up from examining Anders' injury. "The wound

is healed. Please, everyone, go home and rest. I'll send word as soon as he wakes.

"Shara, you may use one of the guest rooms."

Tiea looked up with a smile as Anders and Jericho entered the temple library, escorting a tall man carrying a thick portfolio. After the accidents she had volunteered to help Caleb in his work until he felt well again. Two months later, she remained as his assistant, organizing his files and bringing order to the general chaos he created daily. Putting a heavy book on a shelf, Tiea said, "Excuse the clutter—it looks like our king worked into the night to keep me busy today."

"How thoughtful of him," Anders said wryly. "We're to meet Aric and Bryce here and speak with Caleb."

"He's back working on his histories; I'll get him." She left the room, waving to the two kings entering the gardens.

Caleb joined the group moments later, still in his stained work apron, and Aric began the introductions. "Caleb, this is Devon Shanot, Assistant Armorer from Leahcim Tierrah. He's come to check our progress with the new weapons."

"Welcome to Maradane." Caleb shook hands with Devon, quickly appraising the man's greying hair and bright brown eyes.

Devon handed over several envelopes. "May I offer my papers of identity? For the moment I'm to monitor your progress in learning the new weaponry. Later I'll follow my superiors' directives to help you coordinate with the rest of the empire."

"Excellent." Caleb read the papers carefully, examining David's precise signature and heavy seal. "You'll be working most closely with Salar Mashun, who is our Arms Master. Jericho, can Devon stay with you until a home is found?"

"We already have a home," Jericho answered with a satisfied smile. "A young villager recently married and offered her house for a new resident."

Caleb returned the armorer's papers. "Devon, we have a council in my office or the library each month. That should be the best time for discussing your work as a group. Have you any immediate questions?"

"No, I believe I'll get settled in my home and meet with Salar."

"Fine. Let Jericho know if you need anything." Caleb turned to Anders. "Would you like to help prepare a chapel? Kana's daughter is being married this evening."

"Gladly." Anders started down the hall, then stopped abruptly and put both hands to his head.

"Anders?" Bryce moved quickly to his friend's side. "What's wrong?"

"A headache." Anders shook his head, straightening. "It started so suddenly."

"Lean over." Bryce looked intently into Anders' blue eyes, then examined the back of his head. "Have you had any other pain?"

"No, none at all." Anders shook his head again. "It's letting up now."

Bryce bit his lip. "Well, I doubt it's related to the injury. Let me know if it happens again."

"I will." Anders turned to Caleb, feeling the sharper pain settle into a dull ache. "Let's get to work."

The two men busied themselves preparing the chapel, laying the altar cloth and arranging flowers from the gardens. Caleb lit the incense that would lightly perfume the air, and began lighting the candles to provide a soft glow.

Kneeling before the altar to position the large pillows upon which the couple would kneel, Anders saw the dimly illuminated room waver before him. The altar and its pale yellow tapers melted away, replaced by the vision of another dusky room.

Confused, Anders recognized the interior of the great library of Stalasia. The etched glass doors were dark, indicating night outside, but only a handful of candles flickered around the central desk.

From behind, Anders saw a man seated at the desk, a troubled man resting his bearded face in his hands. He was powerfully built, clothed in a sleeveless tunic that freely revealed heavily muscled arms. He ran his hands repeatedly through a mass of red-gold curls, then pushed his chair away from the desk. Turning, he looked searchingly around the vast room, his brown eyes distraught, before the scene faded into the familiar chapel.

Sitting back on his heels, Anders found Caleb eyeing him.

"Anders? Where were you? You didn't even hear me speaking."

"I'm sorry. For a moment I was seeing the library of Stalasia, and a man..." He paused wonderingly. "It's possible that something has happened there."

Caleb was immediately concerned. "I'll contact the Paladins to check the city. Thanks for your help."

"I enjoyed it." Anders grinned, then looked lovingly around the chapel. He missed the quiet days here, tending the places of worship. "I'd better head home for supper. Have a good evening, Caleb."

Closing the chapel door, Caleb hurried to contact the Paladins.

Chapter Eight

Seated in the gardens of the western palace, Bronwyn shared a puzzling conversation with Shara.

Putting down the bit of needlework in her hands, Shara asked, "Bron, what do you think of Devon?"

"He's nice enough." Bronwyn lay a handful of flowers in the basket by her side, then slipped the scissors into her apron pocket. "He says we're progressing wonderfully and has nothing but praise for Salar. But he keeps to himself most of the time."

"He struck me as very reserved, though he's very gracious and courtly."

Pulling small weeds from the bed, Bronwyn blurted, "Shara, there is something odd concerning Devon."

"Odd?" Shara looked up. "What has he done?"

"Oh, it's no fault of his own, and indeed he's deeply troubled." Bronwyn sat back, smoothing her long blue skirt. "Yesterday I had planned to instruct him with a staff. He was quite excited, and grasped the technique very quickly. But no wind would come for him."

"Seriously?" Shara rolled the idea around slowly. "No wind came?"

"Not the slightest puff. Shara, he was so disappointed, and I couldn't offer an explanation. This has never happened."

"It was not some fluke of nature, or his staff?"

Bronwyn shook her head. "I summoned winds with my staff and his. I tried to carry him with my staff, but the wind died. It's as if they refuse to carry him."

"What is the link between the staffs and the winds?"

Bronwyn blushed ruefully. "I fear I can't say. Almost all the lore vanished with the True-Bloods. When the Adanes turned to war the wind queen withdrew and took the history with her. We no longer know why the staffs work as they do."

"Perhaps it's a punishment of war," Shara said slowly. "Wind rule is a great power. Perhaps Devon isn't capable of handling it."

"Maybe." Bronwyn smiled at a sudden idea. "I think I'll begin a study of the wind law. There must be records in Leahcim Tierrah."

"I'm sure someone there can help," Shara agreed absently. Letting her gaze fall to her needlework, she looked for flaws in her fine stitches.

Bronwyn quietly watched her. "Is something wrong? You seem so troubled."

"I don't know, Bron," Shara sighed. "Anders has been very upset this past month, but won't tell me why."

Bronwyn nodded. "He was preoccupied with something when he met with Jericho yesterday. Let us know if we can help."

"I will. But now I'd better be going." Shara began gathering her things. "Why don't you and Jericho come to supper tomorrow?"

"We'd love to." Bronwyn picked up her basket of flowers and walked Shara to the hangar.

"You needed to see me, Bryce?" Anders asked softly from the doorway of his friend's study.

Bryce's smile faded at the sight of Anders' careworn face. "Anders, are you feeling well?"

"I'm fine," Anders grumbled, stepping into the room. "I don't have much time—Shara's having company for dinner."

Running one hand through his fine hair, Bryce bit back a reply. He could not force Anders to accept his help. "I need your approval for the harbor work to begin tomorrow. The initial materials arrived today." Bryce motioned to the blueprints spread across his massive oak desk.

"Whatever you've planned is fine," Anders said absently, his gaze straying to the wisteria outside one window.

"If I can tear you from wherever you're spending all your time, I need initials on these plans." Bryce thrust a pencil into Anders' hand and propelled him to the desk. "Anders, what's wrong with you? Why are you suddenly so disinterested in a world that wouldn't have been built without you?"

"Better it hadn't!" Anders snapped, scrawling his initials across the papers. "If you've finished, I have to get home for dinner."

Bryce threw himself into his chair as Anders left. Staring at the gently swaying wisteria, he tried to put a name to his friend's problem. Anders was losing interest in everything, even in his close friends. But Bryce could not find an explanation. He could only wait.

"I honestly don't know why I bother," Asher sighed, sinking into the warm water of the marble bathtub. "In three days' time I will be used to being clean, and then I shall have to become filthy again to return to Donthas."

"If thee insist on being a spy, thou canst at least not complain about it," Elizabeth laughed, sitting on the edge of the tub and scrubbing her husband's back. "Three days clean art better than none. And once out from beneath the filth, thou wilt ne'er be recognized by any spies at court."

"I wish I could learn who those spies are." Taking a deep breath, Asher disappeared beneath the water. He came up lathering his hair. "The Seer has been acting more oddly than usual lately.

He called another conclave and acts as if he can't quite pinpoint something. The name of Maradane has crossed my desk too often to suit me." He ducked once more, sluicing the soap from his thick black hair.

"Art there immediate plans?" Elizabeth asked, drying her hands on her robe.

Asher shook his head, laughing as she leaned away from flying droplets of soapy water. "I doubt it. The Seer is agitated over some feeling, and since he can't define it, Gray feels it is connected with the mystics. Stalasia is protected from the Seers, with rare exception."

"But they plan something?"

"Shandal always plans something," he snorted in disgust. "I can only wait and hope a lesser seer lets something slip."

"Well, at least thou mayst relax for a while and enjoy the wedding." Elizabeth smiled happily. "Richard's Leahcim is far more beautiful than her namesake, our city."

Stepping from the water, Asher reached for his heavy velvet robe. "I don't suppose Scott has left his mountains?"

She shook her head slowly. "Not even for Richard."

Asher's brow furrowed. "He must come out of his grief one day. Yet I fear the strength of what it will take to summon him. For that too we must wait."

"Many times talking is better than waiting, but I fear our grandson wilt ne'er understand that. For all his giant stature, Scott is still a boy within." Elizabeth reached for Asher's hand. "Come now, our daughter is coming for dinner. We shalt be cheerful these days, waiting or no."

Rushing into his study, Caleb headed distractedly for the desk in search of a just-remembered report. He had been forgetting too many things recently, caught up in his worry over Anders. The decision to wait for some natural solution seemed increasingly ill advised, but Anders fiercely avoided attempts at forcing the issue. He refused to discuss his inner turmoil with anyone and was short tempered even with the children of his sector.

Halfway to the desk Caleb stopped abruptly, realizing he was not alone. Turning, he spied the small figure.

"Tiea...I thought you long gone home for supper."

Tiea was neatly stacking folders at the worktable, leaving a large area clear for Caleb's work the next morning. She glanced up, smiling shyly.

"There was much to do today, milord—the bookshelves took nearly all day to straighten. Then I remembered I had yet to settle this room. Did you need something?"

"Yes," Caleb said absently. "A report for David—but perhaps it will wait til morning. The day has been busy enough." He found himself watching her precision and quickness and realized with sudden guilt what chaos the adjoining rooms must have been in to keep her so late.

Tiea gathered a few stray pens and pencils. "I wanted your reference materials ready for the council day after tomorrow." She dropped the writing instruments into a drawer, looking up. "I shouldn't have taken yesterday off, but Prudence has asked me so many times to visit."

Taking a step toward the table, Caleb grasped Tiea's hand. "I've taken terrible advantage of your initial offer to help. I haven't the patience required for neatness," he paused to scan the room, "although I greatly admire the overall effect. But you came to help while I recovered, and I thoughtlessly let it become permanent."

"But I enjoy the work, really," Tiea protested as he turned toward the desk, releasing her hand. Her gaze wandering over the back of his head, she studied the small curling strands at his collar.

As he turned back to her she blushed deeply and stared down at her hands that, having finished their work, seemed unable to occupy themselves in her pockets.

"I...I'm glad it's all satisfactory. I should go home now, if you don't mind."

"I do mind," he said impulsively, grabbing her hands in his. "I've been so distracted lately that I've let too many things slide. One thing is the situation here."

"But I thought..." Tiea looked up timidly, her green eyes wide. "Aren't things in order?"

"No, not at all." Caleb gazed down at her. "I've let you stay in your work because I enjoy your nearness, but we've both been bumbling around, afraid to speak. Tiea...if it would please you..." He raised his grasp to her slight shoulders and continued firmly. "If it would please you, I'd like to ask Salar's permission to court you."

Her heart suddenly in her throat, Tiea could only nod as Caleb drew her into a gentle embrace.

Cita was passing through the entry hall when the front door opened. She smiled with relief as Tiea entered.

"I'm so glad you're finally here. We were starting to worry...Why Caleb, how nice of you to bring Tiea home. Will you stay for supper?"

Closing the door behind him, Caleb ran a quick hand through his hair to settle the night wind's mischief. "Thank you, Cita, I'd like that. Is Salar home?"

"As everyone should be at this time," Salar called teasingly from the study. Crossing the tiled hall, he grasped Caleb's hand in greeting. Noting the small smile exchanged by friend and sister as Tiea left the hall, Salar continued. "My dear king, I suspect it was more than a gesture of kindness to bring my sister home." He leaned casually against the wall.

Caleb frowned uncomfortably. "Salar, don't tease me tonight. I'd like your permission to court Tiea."

"That's not a tradition of this world," Salar said with a grin.

Determined to be serious, Caleb squared his shoulders. "But it is a tradition of the royal line of Dacyn, and Tiea is a princess in her own right. I want this to be right, Salar."

Sobering, Salar studied Caleb's earnest face. "Our family is honored that you ask, Caleb, and touched that you honor our past. Permission is granted.

"Now, stay for supper."

Caleb nodded with a relieved expression. "I could use the company. Too many things are grappling for my attention."

Ushering Caleb into the kitchen, Salar said, "I know—I also

wish I could help our friend. But tonight we should concentrate on a small celebration."

"I don't understand it." Jericho stood at the base of the eastern wind tower.

Anders glowered up at the structure, recalling the series of tiny whirlwinds that had danced lightly across the palace lawns. "This is your damn contraption, Jericho. You ought to be able to fix it."

Jericho swallowed a harsh response, turning to face the big man. Almost a month had passed since he and Bronwyn had visited Anders and Shara, and Anders' behavior had only worsened. He had gradually ceased speaking to anyone unless it was utterly necessary.

Shaking his head, Jericho said, "Things like this have happened everywhere, but it's not connected with the towers. Aric and I just checked the entire system."

Anders sighed. "I suppose nothing's been hurt by it. These flukes are so unexpected, though, and I'm never certain it's natural or enemy tampering. Shandal has so many ways of hurting us, even over centuries."

"Anders, can't someone help you?" Jericho asked quickly, hoping for an opening at last.

"No." Anders shook his head, closing a door behind his eyes. "I must deal with this alone."

"Will you be at Caleb's tonight?"

"Do I have a choice? He required all of us to be there."

Jericho turned despondently toward his shuttle, leaving Anders staring gloomily at the tower.

Caleb motioned to the heavy jewel cases on the tables in the council room. "David sent these as samples for our crown jewels. There does seem an endless list—"

"Endless isn't the word," Aric broke in. Scanning the list in his hand he began reeling off, "Crowns, circlets, tiaras, belts, buckles, chains, brooches, scepters, seals, rings—"

"I think we get the idea, Aric." Caleb waved his hands for silence. "Look at them, don't read them all off."

Grinning, Aric strode to one table to examine a heavy circlet set with moonstones. "We don't have to choose everything on the list, do we?"

"Of course not." Caleb picked up a slender golden chain with engraved links. "Nor should those of each sector be the same as the others. Remember we are establishing the crown jewels for the history of Maradane. They will be used on many levels of state occasion, so you need variety. Tonight will give you a few ideas to mull over before you begin choosing."

Aric nodded as the others scanned the daunting display. Bronwyn gently lifted a delicate comb encrusted with crushed diamonds. "I could learn to like choosing such jewels."

"Couldn't we all?" Shonnie laughed, holding a flaming ruby clip near her thick brown-black hair. "Shara, aren't these lovely?"

"Very," Shara said flatly, tugging Anders along behind her. Her eyes had lost their light lately. Shonnie dropped the clip as if it stung.

Lifting a circlet of burnished gold set with rich amethysts, Shara held it toward Anders. "This would suit you well, my love. Won't you try it?"

Anders took the circlet in his freckled hands, but only stared at it. Finally he mumbled, "Let them have them."

"Let who have what?" Shara asked distractedly.

"Let Shandal have the jewels," Anders barked hoarsely. "End the killing and deceit over worthless stones. End the hurt. Maybe it will repair the past mistakes of fools." He turned and left the room, dropping the circlet to the floor.

Wiping her eyes with the back of her hand, Shara said tremulously, "I'll choose our pieces later, Caleb. I must stop him from wandering the beach all night." She scurried from the room.

Caleb turned to the medic. "Bryce, can't you talk to him?"

"I've tried, Caleb," Bryce snapped. "He only mumbles about making amends for old debts. I can't reach him."

"Maybe by the next council we will think of something. These jewels will wait for another day." Caleb shaded the lamps as the others went home.

Gnawing thoughtfully on his thumb, Bryce stepped back to inspect the newly built display cases in his council room. The jewelry patterns had been chosen and orders sent to Leahcim Tierrah several days ago. Upon arrival, the pieces would be displayed in each king's council room. He had been glad of the work on the cabinets, eager to keep his troubled mind busy.

Turning pensively, he wandered to the window overlooking the village down the hill. He smiled as he gazed at the recently opened distribution post. The past month had been monopolized by the final establishment of these open-air markets in each sector.

In working out the plans Bryce had found that linked pavilions worked best. The villages remained very rural in setting and he utilized the timber and stone incorporated in the regional fences. The central markets had been opened long ago, but the smaller village posts had waited for further settlement. Now produce, meats, and fish were brought daily to the posts, and established artisans had a place to distribute their work.

Moving to his desk, Bryce rustled aimlessly through a sheaf of papers from Caleb. A corps of workers had recently installed several plants for disposal of litter, utilizing decomposition and disintegration chambers, as well as sewage treatment facilities. The plants generated clean water and compost, and disintegrated unreclaimable residues. The growing population was assured of a clean, carefully tended world just as it had been designed.

Bryce's troubled thoughts came full circle and he threw the papers aside. Anders drew further away each day and Bryce, in his hectic schedule, was unable to enlist more than clipped conversation. Even the new work to maintain Anders' cherished planetary design was met with indifference. Bryce held little hope that the upcoming council would find a solution.

The early evening breeze tugged at the corners of the gaily patterned cloth spread on the soft grass of the bluff. Looking toward the beach below, Caleb saw shipwrights and other workers gather up their tools and head home.

Following Caleb's gaze, Jericho spied a group of children trotting in circles and laughing merrily. Squinting, he saw that as each child skipped along, a following tendril of wind erased their footprints from the sand. The children thought this was great sport, speeding up or slowing down in efforts to trick the gentle puffs teasing their heels.

"It's at it again," Jericho breathed wonderingly.

"What?" Caleb looked searchingly in the direction of Jericho's gaze, then chuckled. "And what have you discovered about these oddities since we last spoke?"

"Only that they're odd," Jericho quipped, settling back on his elbows and watching Bronwyn empty their wicker hamper. Caleb had convened the council near the eastern palace. "As embarrassing as it is for a person descended from the Wind Rulers to say this, I'm baffled. For now we'll have to accept that Maradane's winds are unique."

"If it's natural I won't be concerned about it." Caleb glanced once more at the harbor.

"It was a wonderful idea to hold council here for a change, Caleb." Bronwyn set a serving spoon next to a steaming casserole.

Behind them lay the palace, rising from a grassy hill. From there a series of one hundred marble steps, each riser carved with sea life and waves, led to the beach below, where the workers had finally departed.

Lured by Salar's presence, a large contingent of colonists had arrived from Dacyn and requested permission to establish a sea trade. Accepted readily, the idea afforded many opportunities. Aside from cutting down the number of airships necessary to move goods from continent to continent, it opened up sailing for pleasure as well as the means to study the sea life of Maradane. While the surface had been lifeless, creatures accustomed to the depths lived unrecognized below the waves.

As the arrivals collaborated with Bryce, the result was an ingenious series of quays and piers resembling nothing more than natural rock formations jutting into the harbor.

The setting sun reflected in ripples of gold off the wave-splattered piers and scattered playful shadows throughout the skeletal shipyards. The shipwrights promised to complete the first vessels within the month and Bronwyn looked forward to seeing the sails against the horizon.

"It's so beautiful here—somehow different than the waters around our home," Bronwyn continued, breathing deeply of the tangy air.

"Better than the council chambers," Caleb agreed, his glance flicking to Anders. The evening was an attempt to draw him out, but even this seemed to have no effect.

Looking toward the school and hospital, Bryce said, "Anders, how are the art museum and music school coming along? I haven't had time to check lately."

"All right, I guess," Anders replied absently. "I haven't visited them."

The group fell silent, subdued as they began eating. The museums and schools of art and music were Bryce's latest attempt to capture Anders' interest. Modeled after Stalassi architecture, the structures should normally have been the center of his day. But Anders remained the only disinterested person.

"Well," Shonnie offered softly, balancing her plate on one knee. "I think the new buildings are splendid. We needed centers of education and imagination to draw people to us."

Buttering a warm roll, Aric glanced at Caleb. "Speaking of more colonists, how are plans progressing for proper military forces? The Paladins can't be our personal guard forever."

"We're getting there," Caleb answered. "Salar and Devon left this morning for Leahcim Tierrah to meet with the Master Armorers. There aren't enough colonists yet to set up armed forces, but Devon has been instructed to begin uniform training of all the people."

Aric nodded, satisfied with the plans. "What else are we to discuss?"

"Little, actually." Refilling his mug of ale, Caleb glanced up at the first stars glimmering overhead. "It's been a quiet month. I hoped we might just enjoy the evening together."

Leaning into Jericho's arms, Bronwyn gazed sadly at Anders. He had lost weight and his tired face now seemed gaunt. If spoken to he responded vaguely, too intent upon his own tangled thoughts. She wished Caleb had not suggested this picnic, for it had falsely raised their hopes.

Laughter from the beach drifted up over the bluff, carried on the cooling harbor breeze. Bronwyn closed her eyes, relishing the caress of the wind across her arms and face. Letting go of her gloomy thoughts, she retreated into the sounds and scents of the winds as her ancestors had done for ages.

Below the bluff the waves lapped languidly against shore and quay, and wind whispered through the shipyard. Behind her the soft meadow grasses murmured to themselves, a comforting echo of the waves. The saltwater smell mingled with that of mown grass and sprawling gardens. Bronwyn felt better as she pulled her silken shawl closer around her.

A new sound intruded upon her ears, a forlorn sighing borne on the breeze. Opening her eyes, she saw a flurry of agitated sparkles high above Anders. A chill swept through her as she recalled her first sighting of those bits of glitter. But as she was about the speak, both sparkles and sighs evaporated. No one else had noticed them, so she remained silent.

Aric turned once again to Caleb. "I've seen very little of Devon since his arrival. Is he capable at his job?"

"Immersed is a better word," Caleb laughed. "He speaks with me often and spends a lot of time in the library. I suspect he has no family and is wed to his work. He's good company if you're eager for conversation."

Shonnie smiled wryly. "Tiea said much the same to me. It seems Devon is prone to inquisitiveness and floods her with questions."

"Oh yes, he hinders her work. But she agrees he's probably lonely." Caleb's gaze wandered over the group. "I'd like to invite everyone back home for cake and tea. If Devon has a propensity for talk, Tiea has one for baking. I can barely find my pantry now."

Shara smiled for the first time that evening. "I'm sure we all accept. Anders, wouldn't you like some dessert?"

Anders looked up from an intense study of his hands, his eyes bleak and haunted. "I'm sorry, Shara, did you ask something?"

"Oh Anders," Shara wailed softly. Calming herself, she repeated, "My love, wouldn't you like some cake and tea? Caleb has invited us."

Looking distractedly toward the palace, Anders shook his curly head. "I'd like to go home, please. I have work to do." Without any farewells he scrambled to his feet and wandered away.

Seeing Shara close to tears, Bryce demanded, "What work is so pressing?"

"Nothing." Shara bit her lower lip. "He sits nightly in the library, staring into the fire. I'm sorry—I'd better go too." She fled across the meadow in pursuit of her husband.

Caleb pursued a drifting thought. "It seems this began when we were preparing a wedding chapel. Anders saw a vision of the Stalassi library. I thought nothing unusual since the mystics have such deep ties to their world. The Paladins checked the library and found no damage, but Anders was little comforted."

Bryce thought back to the day of Devon's arrival. "Anders had a strange headache that day." He hesitated, then stood. "This has gone on long enough, and our patience isn't helping him. One way or another I'll learn the cause of this tonight."

"We'll wait in the gardens," Caleb called after him, then began helping to pack up the picnic.

"Bryce, I don't wish to talk about it. It's no concern of yours."

Bryce glared at his friend, the last shreds of patience tearing. Upon arriving at the library he had found Anders alone in the dark room, the crackling fire his only company. Slumped in a leather chair, long legs outstretched, Anders had been so far lost in thought it took Bryce several moments to reach him. Shara stood beyond the half-open door, listening with timid hope.

Kicking the footstool from beneath Anders' booted feet, Bryce slammed his fist down on the massive oak mantle, scattering portraits of Shara and their friends. "Anders, this is my concern! It's everyone's concern!

"Anders, talk to me. Shara deserves much more, and so do your people. You don't even care about them any more."

Without looking up, Anders said bitterly, "My people deserve a ruler who is fit, and I have found that I am not. I care too much to continue as the king I have been. I won't carry on the deception created to destroy us."

Bryce knelt by the chair, pleading, "Anders, please, talk to me. What possible reason could you have to say that?"

Anders faced Bryce at last, his eyes tortured. "Maradane does not deserve to have an enemy upon her throne. I have seen the past, and that past is of my descent from ancestors who betrayed our people, ancestors born of Shandal."

Chapter Nine

Shara rushed into the room as Bryce cried, "Anders, that's nonsense! If you are an enemy then David has no friends!"

"I know what I've seen. My lineage is one of traitors." Anders sank back in the chair, stubbornly knotting his callused hands around his wide black belt.

Kneeling on the other side of the chair, Shara lovingly smoothed his tangled curls. "Anders, my beloved fool...I have an idea now, if you will only talk to us. Tell us, if you love me at all."

"Shara." Anders gripped her hand tightly, seeing her tear-filled eyes. He should have told her from the first, but he could not bear to bring such shame on her. "There is no reason to it, I don't understand it."

Pausing, he grudgingly collected his thoughts. "It begins always with a headache. When the pain passes I see things, scenes of the distant past. I recognized William Barria, Keeper of the Library, and his son Justin who was, as I now know, a foundling. Justin was a spy, sent by the Clan of the Snake, and together he and William destroyed David's chance of thoroughly crushing Shandal.

"Shara, how can I claim a crown when I am descended from the enemy trying to destroy us?"

Shara leaned over to kiss his cheek, then asked, "Anders, tell me how you bear to share our world with Jericho, whose race destroyed our home, our people?"

"Shara!" Anders straightened at once. "How can you say such a thing? Jericho had nothing to do with that. How can we blame him?"

Bryce pounced on that. "Then how can you blame yourself for your ancestry? Anders, you are my dearest friend. If I loathe Shandal, still would I thank them for the accident that brought you to us. Jericho is not of the bent of his race, nor are you the temper of an enemy."

Unconvinced, Anders looked pleadingly at Shara. "But why do I see these things? Is something wrong with my mind?"

"Of course not." Shara squeezed his hand, the proud light returning to her eyes. "Anders, you have a power of our race after all, a very rare and precious power. Don't you see? You have the Sight Link."

Anders looked as blank as Bryce for a moment, then smiled tentatively. "Do you believe so?"

"What is this sight link?" Bryce asked at the same time.

Shara hugged her husband's arm, relief flooding her voice. "It is a gift, Bryce, that few of our people have ever known. And it is always brought into play by some injury to the head. I would have recognized it sooner if Anders had only talked to me.

"Sight Link is a key to the past, one through which a person is linked to the events of the past. He is, in a sense, present as they occur. And it always, *always*, comes to bear as a measure against crisis."

Bryce digested this, then grinned. "Then somehow Anders is to help someone through this power?"

"Most certainly. Please Bryce, go tell our friends all will be well. I can help Anders now. And I have news which will cheer him."

Bryce smiled, getting to his feet. "You have not told him...I'll see you both tomorrow." He left through the garden door.

"Told me what?" Anders asked, confused.

"That you are the father of a son," Shara said softly.

Asher stood stoically in the rear of the throng, as close to the door as he could get, and smiled despite his revulsion. It seemed a reflection of the avid smiles around him, but Asher's joy was stoked by the events of the preceding evening. This Plea for Blessings ceremony had almost been canceled because of those events.

Grabbing what little air he could from the doorway, Asher planted his feet and resolved not to smell the unwashed bodies packed into the humid chamber. Steam rose in heavy clouds from braziers at the central altar, naked slaves repeatedly dousing the coals with fetid water. The Immortal felt blanched in the stifling heat maintained as comfort to the great snake lolling across the altar.

Closing his eyes, he recalled the insane screams that had shattered last night's sleep. The entire palace had fallen over itself in a mad race to attend the Seer. Asher knew the keening shrieks meant the bone-thin psychic had lost whatever trace of insight he had been seeking since before Richard's wedding. Somehow, if Gray was right—and Gray was seldom wrong—the Stalassi on Maradane had solved their problem and the Seer would have to discover its nature through the spy network.

Wiping his sweaty forehead, Asher offered a silent prayer of gratitude for a danger passed safely by for once.

An agonized scream burst upon his unwilling ears and he steeled himself to the beginning ceremony. To reveal the slightest errant emotion would mean the end of his mission, and David desperately needed him in these libraries. Swallowing, Asher began his own mental litany to his own God as the enormous snake devoured the living child trussed before it. How he ached for his airy home and the crystalline lake beside it.

"Hear your poor servant, our Great Lord," the Seer intoned, resting the blade of his sword on the head of a bound slave woman at his feet. "As we offer our yearly Plea for Blessings, hear our words, Great Lord. Bless once more the Vision of the Clan, your Clan, that we may destroy our enemies and end the horrors inflicted upon us. Empower our Vision, that our children may inherit worlds free from the perversions of these vile aliens. Imbue us with the Sight to conquer their derangements and warm the icy blasts devouring worlds once plentiful in wealth. Empower the Seer of your Clan, our mighty god,—"

Hollow gods with no feelings, no words, Asher thought dryly. Yet the people of Shandal were awed by the size of these monsters—size meant power. Asher laughed inwardly, for the Immortals were giants among many tall mortal races, and still they felt helpless and futile at times. But they had words, words to heal and words to guide, and they saw to it that these words were spread to every nook of the empire. They were words of strength and depth, not like the shallow things issuing from the Seer's lips.

Asher's attention snapped to the Seer, the shallowness hitting him for the first time. The Seer spoke in measured beats, carefully studying his audience, gauging the impact of his words. There was laughter in his eyes, cold and vicious laughter mocking the very words he spoke. Asher closed his eyes as the Seer turned his way, knowing his attitude would be taken for the rapture stealing over the gathering. He carefully tucked away his discovery, his realization that this particular Seer held no belief in his own words, to be analyzed later. For the moment he wanted no more sight or sound of the reptile's haven, the Great Altar. It was the vilest of places, with its putrid steam and fungal growths streaming downward from ceiling and pillars.

Sinking deeper into his mental litany, Asher envisioned the chapels of his people: altars of polished wood and marble, high-ceilinged rooms lit by candles and open windows, fragranced with balmy incense and clusters of flowers. Small groups of worshippers would be gathered there for prayer, kneeling on soft cushions and sharing the comforts of their faith. Asher decided he must one day travel to Maradane and see the temple of the people who caused the Seer such wonderful turmoil. It would have a special beauty for his weary eyes.

The small chapel was silent, the comforting stillness enveloping the lone figure kneeling on an embroidered pillow. Muted tapestries on the walls swayed gently as the temple's air-purifying system activated. Candles in wall sconces and those ringing the flower-bedecked altar flickered, casting a soft glow. The gold censer centered between the silver tapers emitted the fragrant aroma of windflowers. It was, as intended, a peaceful room devoted to quiet contemplation. People were free to come and go as they pleased or needed, as well as for daily prayer, knowing the airy rooms were always ready to receive them. The air system had been adjusted to mimic the gentle winds of the surface, providing the feeling of spaciousness.

Carrying a box of new candles, Caleb entered the room humming lightly. He diligently maintained the chapels as Anders had taught him, finding the work a meditation in itself. Halfway to the altar he stopped and turned.

"Anders, excuse me. I didn't realize anyone was here."

Anders raised his head with a bright smile. "It's all right—I left the door open so I might hear the fountain." He sat back on the polished oak bench.

Caleb sat nearby. "How is everything? Is Jeremiah well?" The young king reassured himself gratefully that Anders was again robust and cheerful.

"My son is wonderful," Anders answered with a proud grin. "He is exactly twelve months old today."

"Is everything else all right?" Caleb absently counted the candles as he spoke.

"Yes, Caleb, all is fine," Anders answered chidingly. "I hoped some quiet meditation would sort out the confusion of these past months and find some acceptance of my power. I don't like this gift, and so far can see no purpose in it."

"Ah, but Shara is so proud." Caleb laughed softly. "Have you learned nothing from these visions?"

"Oh, small things." Anders sighed, rubbing the back of his neck. "I'm learning little bits which no one previously knew about William. But there seems no point. And I dislike the time taken from my work. Things are happening quickly now and need my attention."

"May I make a suggestion?" Caleb set aside the box. "I've heard that Shara sometimes shares your visions through a psychic link. Would it help for you to keep a journal? If you write down the details as they surface I'm certain a pattern will reveal itself. Are the visions still far apart?"

Anders nodded. "They come with no regularity, and much time passes between. Perhaps a journal would be helpful.

"How about you? Anything unusual in your work?"

Caleb shook his head wryly. "It's all fairly dull routine—endless paperwork because of the colonists, and my new project of documenting the library. We received a large shipment of books from Leahcim Tierrah, which Tiea and I are indexing for the time being until they are moved to the Hall of Books. Aric expects it to be finished in a few months.

"In the meantime," he continued, grinning, "Bronwyn fairly dove into the stacks in search of anything on the winds."

"Sadly, her research is proving futile." Anders bent to retie his sandal lacings, sorry that Bronwyn's enthusiasm was so harshly rewarded. "It's odd that so little was documented of so great a culture—"

"Caleb, the western forge exploded!" Tiea raced into the chapel. "Jericho and Aric are badly hurt."

Caleb ran from the room with Anders close on his heels, his flying steps carrying him up the tunnel and across the valley to the hangar. Shouting orders to the attendant, he jumped into his shuttle. Anders boarded his own little craft, fretting until the hangar bay opened.

The two men arrived together at the forge and small arms factory near the western palace. The forge was a smoldering ruin, its roof collapsed and smoke billowing toward the sky. People were carefully moving the injured away from the scene, while others attempted to search the scorched rubble lest anyone be trapped. Prudence and women from the village tended minor burns and scrapes as children gathered bits of rubble scattered across the landscape. Cries of pain and shock mingled on the steady breeze.

Bryce and several students from his medical school worked

frantically over Jericho and Aric, while another bandaged Salar's hands.

Anders joined Shara in comforting Bronwyn and Shonnie. Caleb knelt a few paces from Bryce. "How bad is it, Bryce?"

"Very bad," Bryce answered grimly, working on Aric's left hand. "They're so terribly burned...Aric's lost two fingers." He turned to locate the hospital's aircraft. "Get those burn tanks ready! We have to get them to the hospital."

Sobbing into Anders shoulder, Bronwyn choked out, "It shook the palace—Shonnie and I were walking the babies in the gardens and debris fell on us."

Anders smoothed her hair with gentle fingers, holding both women close. "Shhh...Shara and I will tend Garth and Aarek while you're at the hospital." His angry blue eyes catching a signal from Salar, he said, "Shara, take them to the hospital. I'll see that the boys are taken to our home." He then strode over to the Dacynite. "How are you?"

"My hands are a little burned. I had to move a timber off Jericho." Salar glanced at his bandages.

As Caleb joined them, Anders said, "Can you tell us that was not a bomb?"

"It had to be," Salar said hotly. "The roof blew off as I went outside with one of the armorers. But the furnace itself didn't explode."

"Damn!" Caleb slammed his fist into his hand. "What good are the Paladins if they can't keep marauders away?"

"There were so many people through here today, I can't remember them all." Salar squinted against the eye drops a medic administered. "Two rough metal shipments were delivered, as well as leathers for scabbards, and tirrschon plating for armor. There must have been forty people here today."

"Go home now and rest," Caleb urged, concerned. "I'll send word as soon as Bryce tells me anything."

"I'll be right along, Caleb." Anders turned toward the palace.

Locating the housekeeper, Anders directed her to take Garth, ten months old, and Aarek, one month younger, to the eastern palace and put them in the nursery with Jeremiah. He then made the trip to the southern hospital.

Caleb motioned him to one side. “Anders, we need to set up a radio communication system between the palaces and the temple. Bryce lost valuable time while a messenger went after him.”

“I’ll find a man to design it, one of Jericho’s students.” Anders paused as Bryce entered the hall. Knowing his friend’s moods, he was relieved even before Bryce spoke.

“They’ll be fine.” Bryce knelt before Bronwyn and Shonnie, taking each one’s hand. “Aric has lost two fingers of his left hand, but there’s no other irreparable damage. Jericho has several broken ribs, but no injuries that won’t heal.

“I’ll keep them here for a month, then they can go home for bedrest with a student medic in attendance.” Leaving the women to visit their husbands, Bryce joined the other men.

“How long will they be confined to bed?” Caleb asked.

“Four months or so. The court physicians at Leahcim Tierrah have made several advancements in burn treatments. Any chance of finding the man who set the bomb?”

Caleb shook his head. “None. He’ll be long away. Will you two be able to take over some of their duties while they recover? I’ll handle the rest.”

“Certainly,” Bryce answered. “Shall I work with Jericho, and Anders with Aric?”

“That’ll be fine.” Caleb stepped toward the door. “I’m going to talk with Salar now.”

Entering Salar’s study, Caleb found him meeting with Devon, who was preparing a report and supply order. The older man’s expression turned grim as Salar spoke. Closing his notebook, he said, “I’ll supervise the cleanup and get the new equipment in place, Salar. You rest for a couple days.”

Turning to Caleb, Salar asked, “How are they?”

“They’ll be fine,” Caleb answered thankfully. “I’ll be taking over some of the work while they recover. I’ll have to see how much of my work Tiea can handle.”

“You’ll be surprised, my friend,” Salar laughed.

Devon spoke up quietly. “May I offer a suggestion?”

Caleb leaned back in his chair, nodding.

“My cousin Arling just completed work in the libraries at Leahcim Tierrah. He’d be free to help in your offices.”

“But surely he wishes to relax before taking a new position, see his family.”

“No, Arling has no family but me. Should I invite him for an interview?”

After a moment’s consideration Caleb agreed. “If he’s capable he can split my lesser duties with Tiea.”

“Very good, I’ll write at once.” Devon gathered his materials and stood up.

“Have a pleasant evening, Devon.” Salar gazed after him, then said, “I often wonder what he does to occupy his evenings. He must be quite accustomed to being alone.”

Pulling the heavy curtains across his front windows, Devon paused to study the thick envelopes in his hand. After some indecision, he dropped two on the table for the courier who would arrive shortly.

He took the third, heaviest envelope across the room to the fireplace and knelt before the hearth. Pushing on the left andiron caused the hearth to tilt upward, revealing a narrow compartment beneath. Dropping the envelope atop a sheaf of papers, Devon closed the hiding place as the courier knocked on the door. After handing the envelopes to the man, Devon locked the door and fumbled for another key on the ring. Going to the rear of the house, he slipped into the comfortably hot room, leaving behind the biting chill of the outer chambers.

Caleb leaned back against the stone bench, relishing Tiea’s gentle touch as she kneaded his tense shoulders.

“Is that better?” she asked softly.

“Wonderful,” he sighed, closing his eyes and listening to the wind rustling the leaves overhead. After supper he had taken Tiea for a stroll through the western gardens. "I was tied in knots."

Sliding her arms around his neck, Tiea rested her head on his. "Why are they doing this to us?"

"I wish I knew. We must be more important than we think." His tone was sarcastic, but then he sobered, grasping her hands. "I don't know, Tiea. Ever since Bronwyn arrived here, even before I came, these attacks have been happening. But why would they fear her?"

Tiea was silent, then smiled. "Wind, and wind rulers."

Caleb nodded slightly. "Perhaps their psychics have seen her gaining new, or rather regaining ancient, powers. The true Wind Rulers held Shandal at bay for centuries."

"Come on, let's walk on the beach." Extricating her hands from his, she steered him toward the bay.

Arriving six days later, Arling presented his records of employment for Caleb's inspection. Caleb assigned him to begin lessening Tiea's harried schedule after settling into Devon's home.

Arling seated himself at the supper table and glared across it at his cousin on the night of his arrival. "If you'd been any slower I'd be in prison. What took so long?"

"It's difficult getting past Salar." Devon set down his goblet with an annoyed thump. "He's too sharp for risky moves. We must go slowly. I left you room to spare before the annual physicals."

"You're an idiot!" Arling flared. "The examinations were moved up; I got your orders only after I'd been checked and it took two days to elude the Paladins. In one transport gate and out another for two stinking days! Do you know what will happen if David learns I'm here?"

"He won't." Devon pointed his knife toward the newcomer. "The Immortals have little enough to do with this world; Caleb sends reports regularly, but no mention is made of new citizens or staff. If you do your job efficiently we'll have the information within the year. Once we're home an assault will be launched on the temple, and the planet will die."

"Temple, hmph." Arling scowled blackly. "All that light and stinking flowers and incense. I thought I'd choke on it."

"If you haven't learned to conceal your revulsion you'd better go home," Devon snapped. "It's critical that we have transcripts of all operations on this world, including the forming military. You are now in the position to copy materials in the temple."

"What difference does this foundling planet make against us?" Arling asked grumpily.

Devon slapped his palm on the table. "Maradane has already survived two of our attacks, as well as other accidents that should have crippled them. Anders has developed a power to see the past and is learning the secret of Justin's work. And Bronwyn is delving into her history, as a queen of the winds."

"Are you serious?" Arling leaned forward. "I thought the Wind Rulers dead, and their books locked away by our people."

"Obviously we overlooked a line of descent. And it is possible that the Adani warlords overlooked some volumes of lore. If any surface in the shipments from Leahcim Tierrah you are to take them."

Arling nodded. "What are my duties here?"

"Copy as much information as possible, keeping an eye out for surfacing wind lore. I've been ordered to cease shipping copied documents because of the Paladins' increased surveillance. I'll carry all papers with me later."

Devon paused, then continued. "One final task, not yet confirmed by the Clan Seer. Keep an eye on Caleb and Tiea. We may be able to use the girl."

Chapter Ten

Aric was propped against many pillows, his attendant seated nearby studying a medical text. Anders had drawn up a table and was spreading out several sheets of schematics.

Leaning forward to study the sheets, Aric said, "All of this in two months is fine work."

Anders nodded. "Jericho's approved them, so installation will begin tomorrow."

"Excellent." Aric settled back again. "How are things with you? Caleb says you've begun keeping a journal."

"It was his suggestion, and very helpful." Anders carefully folded the papers. "Yet so far I've learned little that seems useful. During the initial rise of Shandal one of their people was adopted by William Barria. Why this was arranged I have yet to grasp. William was merely a librarian, not able to offer guidance in resisting Shandal."

"It sounds fascinating, nonetheless. I've had precious little to occupy my mind since the explosion. Are there any books in the temple documenting the early years of Shandal?"

"David had a complete history sent for the library. I'm meeting with Caleb this afternoon and will ask to have a couple volumes sent over." Anders gathered up his records. "I have to run, promised to be home for lunch."

Entering his kitchen, Anders found Shara studying his journal at the table, Jeremiah on one arm. He bent to kiss the top of her head. "What are you up to, my love?"

"I'm trying to copy these passages in some proper order." Shara pushed the book aside and stood up. "Why don't you read it over while I fix lunch? Maybe you'll recall something to fill in the gaps."

Nodding affably, Anders drew the book closer as Shara settled Jeremiah into his walker near the garden door. Her work did give new light to the entries, and as Anders read he began to see the events as in his first visions. ***

*** William Barria stood upon the hill overlooking Shalanar, ancient home of the Stalassi. The largest of four vast cities, Shalanar now housed the dwindling remnants of the mystic race. William loved to roam the hills at night, immersed in their beauty.

The silver grasses of the plain shimmered in the light of three moons, surrounding the city of broad avenues of bright stone and buildings decorated with colorful mosaics. Small houses in neat lawns lined the outer reaches of the city. Ages-old mansions in the central circle stood amidst lush gardens.

The main avenue, lined with crystal lanterns, led the giant man's gaze to the temple, with it high turrets and graceful balconies. Layered with gems and intricate carvings, the veined stone glittered in the moonlight.

Sighing, William thrust his massive hands into the pockets of his tunic. So much was gone already, with frightening changes following close behind. Shalanar spread her majesty almost to the distant horizon, beyond which lay three dead cities whose people had long ago passed away. Once the Stalassi were millions, living peacefully with their temples, libraries, and the mysticism inherent within them. One of the most ancient races, the time of their greatness was past. An enemy had entered the realm, and William's people had approached the young Immortal race for protection. A wise man, the Immortal king, David, responded swiftly to form a network against the alien invaders.

William rubbed his neck in a tired gesture. For five years now he had worked closely with David, the king's son Scott, and their close friend Richard. As Keeper of the Library, William had been elected as most learned to help David draw together the besieged worlds and form a resistance. Correlating the information was exhausting work and the big man relished his evening walks.

His meandering thoughts were disturbed by a faint whimpering behind him. Turning, he scanned the shifting grass and discovered a cringing figure in the shadows above him.

Three long strides brought William up the slope to the figure, which was a boy of about ten. The child cowered as William knelt, covering his face with bone-thin arms.

"Here now, I won't hurt you," William said softly, gently pulling the boy's hands down. "Where are you from?"

The child stared at him with blue eyes made huge by the gauntness of his face. His swarthy skin was grimy, sparingly covered with tattered clothes.

Glancing toward the hilltop William realized the child had stumbled through the portal beyond the next plain. Others had passed through the invisible door, coming out confused and frightened. Shalanar's people made them welcome, offering care and shelter.

"I'll take you home, get some food into you." William spoke soothingly, knowing the boy did not speak his language, then lifted him into his brawny arms.

William's small home was next to the library that he so lovingly kept. He carried the boy to the study and settled him on a cushioned window seat.

"You just look at the city while I get some food. Stay right there." William motioned for the child to remain seated, then hurried to the small kitchen. Returning moments later with a tray of bread and fruit, he found the boy admiring a painting centered above the fireplace.

"Isn't she beautiful?" William set the tray on the boy's lap and gazed at the painting. His tender smile faded as he added, "Her name was Khrista; she and our daughter died of a fever."

Pausing halfway through a large apple, the boy spoke in a language William did not recognize. Yet his questioning look and pointing finger conveyed the message.

"I'm William." He tapped his chest. "William." Then he pointed to the boy.

After a moment the boy said, "Justin."

William studied Justin as the boy ate. He must have wandered for many days to have become so gaunt. So small, he weighed nothing in William's arms. He needed clothing and care.

His gaze strayed back to the painting of the woman whose passing had left such a void in his life. Ten years had passed since then; his daughter would have been Justin's age.

"You will stay with me, Justin. I'll care for you." ***

*** Anders closed the book, leaning back as Shara put their lunch on the table.

"He was very alone, my love." Anders reached for his wife's hand. "But I don't understand how I know what he was thinking and feeling."

Sitting beside him, Shara said, "Sight Link has many complexities, Anders. Most obvious is that you see William as if from nearby, all that takes place around him. But in another sense you actually are William, feeling and thinking as he did. That's the most important link, because the unseen is often the key."

"So far we have more than our share of unseen keys," Anders said dryly. "At least I now understand Justin's presence. William would have had valuable information in his offices. And who would suspect a child?"

"There obviously are no children of Shandal," Shara said bitterly. "It worries me, Anders, to know that anyone could be spying on David's plans. I wish the psychics weren't so limited, so we could pinpoint these enemies."

"Gray's People cannot foresee every detail of every day," Anders comforted her, using the collective term for all psychics. "David takes his own measures."

"I suppose. Here, your lunch is getting cold, and Caleb's expecting you." She took the journal and handed Anders a basket of hot, buttery rolls.

Caleb was deep in concentration at his overflowing desk, trying to finish two tasks at once. He looked forward to the day when Jericho and Aric could resume all their duties, leaving him a bit of free time once more.

Tiea burst through the door, accompanied by remnants of the breezes spiraling into the gardens behind her. Seeing Caleb adrift in his sea of paper, she stole up behind him to slip her hands over his eyes.

"Tiea." Prying her fingers loose, Caleb grumbled, "I haven't time for foolishness today. Anders will be here soon."

"Bookworm," Tiea pouted. "It's a glorious day and you must come outside." She brushed his ear with the end of one braid.

Swatting at the offending lock, Caleb said, "These papers have to be finished today. They're already overdue in David's offices. We'll have a picnic tomorrow."

"Not good enough," she chided. "Tomorrow it may rain, while today is beautiful. And you need some distraction." She snatched the pen from his hand.

"Tiea!" Caleb spun to retrieve his pen but she danced out of reach, deviltry in her green eyes.

"Okay, fine—I have more pens." Caleb reached into a drawer. Before he set pen to paper a dark, slender hand wrested it from his grip.

Refusing to look up for fear he would relent, Caleb set his jaw resolutely and again opened the drawer.

With a cry of triumph Tiea dove past him, grabbing every pen, and dashed toward the tunnel.

"Tiea!" Caleb roared, running after her.

Hearing the reluctant laughter in his deep voice, Tiea sprinted across the meadow to the willow grove. Seeing a flurry of sparkles amidst the leaves she thought of a new course of action.

Just as Caleb reached her, Tiea flung her arms high above her head, crying, "Take them!"

Hearing the chattering breeze, Caleb looked up and plaintively murmured, "No," but it was too late. He watched in frustration as his pens danced to and fro overhead, whirling out of reach in the twittering cloud of sparkles.

"Don't be so sad, Caleb," Tiea drawled from behind a tree. "There's still one left." She waved the pen before racing away again.

"I just wanted you to walk with me," she called over her shoulder. "But I guess running will do. If only you hadn't sat so long, you could catch me—"

Too intent on her teasing, she caught her foot on a root and sprawled in the tall grass. Before she could catch her breath Caleb had pinned her to the ground.

"I want that pen, princess. Hand it over!"

"I fear I can't," she sighed. "It broke."

As Caleb allowed her to roll to her knees she held aloft the pen's remnants. A smudge of ink stained her pale yellow gown.

"You realize," Caleb said sternly, "that I must discipline you. This is no way to treat your king, not to mention future husband."

"Oh no." She put one hand to her cheek. "What will you do?"

"Well..." He rubbed his chin thoughtfully. "Tonight you must bring me a dozen new pens and help finish the reports. But first you must make one of those awful casseroles I've been obliged to eat so often."

"Awful casseroles!" Tiea stifled a grin. "Oh, if only I had those pens, I'd spear you with them."

A renewed twitter reached their ears, followed by a shower of pens upon Caleb's unsuspecting head.

"Hey, ow! That hurts!" Batting the pens, he grinned broadly. "All right, I surrender. We'll walk for a while."

Head bowed against the stinging cold, Arling stepped from the hangar at the northern palace and began the long walk through the gardens.

"Cursed flower lovers," he snarled under his breath, stumbling over a chunk of ice fallen from a silvery tree overhanging the path. His surly gaze followed the maze of paved walkways fighting for passage through the choking collection of winter flora. Rather than following a straight, short path to Aric's palace, he was forced to wend his way past ice roses and pallid snowdrops, gagging on their stench. As if the clinging snow and cloying smell were not enough, he had to suffer the knifing gale howling around him. The abominable winds never stopped on this frigid planet. It was all he could do to stumble along and keep his teeth from chattering.

"If I could just get to those tower controls," he spat out, "I'd show these damnable wind worshippers something about wind."

Something buffeted him from behind, knocking him to his knees and scattering the books he carried. Swearing, Arling reached for the nearest volume.

A cloud of agitated bits of glitter enveloped him, and a growling filled his ears. A vision of his home city wavered before his gaze, but it was a twisted, horrid replica of his beloved Kalanth. The protective cloud cover was stripped away by ravening winds, clearing the way for the blinding sun on snow-covered ruins. The Temple of the Great Altar lay in pieces, and scattered before it were the frozen remnants of its god.

"No!" Arling shrieked, shaking his head violently and rubbing his eyes.

Aric's snowbound palace sprawled before him. Forcing composure on himself, Arling gathered up the books and fought his way to the main doors.

A sharp knock on the door drew Aric's attention from watching his son examine a set of nesting blocks.

"Come in," he called, settling Aarek between his legs so the baby would not fall off the bed.

Arling entered, several books under one arm, appearing to Aric a trifle windblown. "Good evening, Aric. Caleb asked me to bring these books for you."

"Please thank him for me." Taking the books, Aric glanced quickly over the titles. "These sound very good—oops, come back here." Reaching out, he gently pulled his son back to the middle of the bed.

Looking around the room, Arling asked off-handedly, "Are you a student of history, then?"

"Not really. I'm bored, and interested in Anders' new power." Aric put the little blocks one within another and returned them to Aarek. "History was not stressed on my previous world."

"I've studied a bit, and was quite fascinated with Adane." Arling sat on the edge of a chair. "I'm eager to learn more about your wind powers, and Adane's technology was remarkable."

"Hmph," Aric snorted. "Technology is what killed Adane, for it possessed no wisdom. Fortunately the sciences of David's realm far surpass anything Adane could claim. Perhaps now we may regain some of our powers."

"But I thought everyone here could control wind."

"Our powers are ridiculously limited. When the Adani youth first turned to war for gain the Wind Rulers departed, taking all documentation of their powers. My people are able only to use winds for transportation, and the queens may summon brief storms. I wish Bronwyn could locate the ancient books."

"She searches every shipment that comes in," Arling said. "But none seem to have turned up."

"I'm afraid they've been destroyed," Aric said resignedly. "Adane's warlords turned as much as they could find over to Shandal's Seer, and my family retained our knowledge of the towers only because it was a verbal tradition. If we had sided with Shandal as well I fear David's realm would be long lost. But perhaps if we from Adane work together Bronwyn can fit some of the pieces into place."

Shonnie entered the room and lifted Aarek into her arms. "Time for bed, my little one...Arling, will you stay for supper?"

"Thank you, but no. I have to get back to work."

"Let me walk you to the door, then." Shonnie led him down the hall.

Reaching his home in the western sector, Arling found Devon seated in a dark corner gazing into the fire. He looked up as Arling closed the door. "Where have you been?"

"Taking history books to his majesty Aric," Arling answered snidely. "He's decided to study the origins of Shandal. He also seems to believe they can gain more wind power without the old books."

"Really?" Devon studied his nails closely. "There is a great distance between an initial idea and final success. They have not told us something about these staffs, else we could operate them. Perhaps we will learn as well from their new research."

Arling sat back, relaxing. Ever since the Wind Rulers vanished Shandal had been studying the stolen books of wind lore. They had never been able to decipher the ancient language. Now they had finally gained possession of the staffs, but they would not work. Bronwyn pretended to be perplexed over the mystery.

"Perhaps they make new citizens wait before full explanation of wind control. We aren't going to be permanent citizens."

"I hadn't thought of that." Devon looked uneasily around the room. "Something odd happened today, which I can't explain."

Arling tensed. "Are we suspected?"

"I don't think so." Devon hesitated, searching for some explanation. "I had set up the altar before the flames, after darkening the room. I was deep in worship when a cold wind blew the sacrificial ash into the room. I looked around outside, and when I returned the altar was broken and everything scattered."

A ripple of horror scurried up Arling's spine. "Someone was in the house?"

"No one could have entered unseen, yet something did. We must move with care, slowly. We'll monitor Anders and Bronwyn, and perhaps pick up some clues to the wind as well."

The younger man nodded as silence settled over the room.

Settling back against his pillows, Aric opened the first volume. The room was lit by a single lamp above the bed, and the curtains swayed softly in the window. Low singing drifted from the nursery as Shonnie tried to soothe Aarek to sleep. After reading several paragraphs, he felt someone watching him, but saw no one when he looked up. He dismissed it as one of the night birds sitting on the window ledge. As he returned to the book a soft curl of wind shooed the birds from the ledge.

Aric skimmed the pages, interested in a brief overall view before he began deep study. Nestled in the soft bedding, he took little heed of the growing roar of the winds except to note the comforting sound. Several basic facts caught his interest, such as the short span of time encompassed by the history. He had always thought a great many more centuries were involved than was stated in the books.

* The time line covered by the book's spanned four thousand, eight hundred ninety-one years from the emergence of the Immortals to the present day. That made the Immortal race much younger than Aric had imagined. The episodes which Anders spoke of concerning William Barria occurred little more than twenty-five hundred years past.

Prior to the birth of the Immortals there had been magic within the universe, co-existing with other races. Five hundred years later the evils that evolved into Shandal entered through a new portal, and before another century disappeared the magic fled and the Stalassi began to fade. Many such races died with the ebb of magic; others followed their life-essence through scattered portals. At the last only the Stalassi and the Elves of Aubrey remained of those touched by magic. Not yet organized and lacking understanding, the young Immortals looked on, helpless.

As another thousand years passed the world of Shandal grew more powerful, her savage clans united under the hope of domination of other worlds. Their newly formed ranks began conquering small or weak worlds with no ready defense.

Shandal's progress ground to a halt as Mara of Adane, leader of her people, rallied the Wind Rulers to battle the enemy. She held Shandal at bay for three centuries, until the youth of her world was corrupted and sought war as a means of gain. At the first misuse of wind control, the Wind Rulers went into hiding and took the major powers with them. No more were seen the planet-scouring vortices or storms that crushed armies in one sweep.

A century and a half later, David was named king of his race and the Immortals were united. His reign was only five hundred years old when Stalasia begged his help. Since then there had been constant wars with Shandal, neither side gaining nor losing much ground. The Davan Empire encompassed all worlds seeking the aid and protection of the Immortals, evolving into its present state over twenty-five centuries. Each planet ruled by its own royalty was under the higher rule of High Immortals, Under-Kings, and finally David. The network was complex but ran with awesome efficiency. The Empire was bathed in riches and education, the people rooted in tradition and light, and Shandal hated them.

A clan-based society, the Shanda engaged in blood feuds to swell their clan's ranks while nullifying opposing families. All members of the ruling class came from the dominant Clan of the Snake. Education was for only those of high rank, and all labor was provided by slaves. Their lands were dark and their gods were the giant snakes from the marshes of the home planet called Shandal. They relished heat and dank air, smoke and heavy clouds, and many died when forced into sunlight and pure air. Living in vast, open spaces, the Immortals were a disease to Shandal, an enemy promoting heathen worship and exterminating Shandal's god-symbols. At the end Shandal's sole focus was the destruction of David, the reaping of endless wealth and slaves.*

Aric closed the book, realizing it was very late. Shonnie lay close beside him, and outside the wind continued to wail. He shaded the lamp, but did not sleep. Staring out the window, he cursed the ancestors who had deserted them because of one group's actions and consigned everyone to these endless wars. It would have been better to never know of the Wind Rulers, than to be left alone with a power that would never be enough.

Beyond the panes the wind softened to moan sadly through the trees, and something stirred the chimes in the palace alcoves.

Across the continent a young man gazed toward the western palace. The night was alive with musical chiming borne on the wind, and soft lights flickered in nearby homes. Far away the palace rose from the rolling plain, moonlight glittering on gems embedded in the structure. The scent of night-blooming flowers drifted from the sprawling gardens.

Shuddering, the youth yanked shut the heavy drapes, trying as well to block out sounds and smells. He longed for home, for the dark, comforting, light-absorbing colors and the rich, pungent aromas of warming fires. There the carefully cultivated clouds obscured the fierce sunlight and smothered the biting winds. The air would be alive with sounds of the arena and the running of slaves, and would be gently enfolding. The scents of burning sacrifices and sounds of revelry were borne softly there, not whipped into oblivion as were all sounds on this world. He ached for the looming, blood-stained altars of the gods and the festivals where young men of his world offered slave children for blessings in their coming battles. Too many times now he had missed the blessings of his lord. Perhaps that was why he had been so attacked earlier that day. He felt vulnerable and pined for the comforting presence of the mammoth snakes.

Devon was old and no longer thirsted to participate, but Arling had only to close his eyes to see the scene—the thrill of capturing and binding the offerings, ceremonial blades warm with blood.

He clenched his fists as an errant current blasted down the fireplace chimney. He hated this world with its constant winds, gales biting through his body like knives, and the blinding light of sun and moons. It knotted his stomach to have to hide in order to make his worship. Hide, when his gods were stopped by no one. Even the stripling snakes, the tiny cousins of the lords, terrorized these imbeciles into total immobility. How did these weak people persist in the face of his gods? Was it a test of Shandal's worthiness that they must overcome? Else the lords would command to be carried forth to devour David's people.

A smile teased Arling's lips. Not even the evil-spawned beings who would not die could stop themselves being devoured alive as a sacrifice. David's realm held nothing to stop these gods.

The unbidden image rose again before his eyes, of his gods desecrated, slashed, the pieces frozen by the winds.

"No!" he roared, but a voice persisted in his ears. It was the voice that the sounds of his world drowned out. It remained, he knew—everyone knew—, but unheard beneath the crackling fires and arena cheers. On his world the voice was drummed into silence, but on this barren planet it screamed to him—"Wrong. You're wrong." It echoed endlessly and he could not drown it out as his people had done for centuries. It was the voice of something he knew could devour his gods without a thought, the voice of the minions of a great power, and he began to imagine what loathsome force these people idolized.

"No!" he screamed to the empty house, covering his ears. "I will not hear. We are right. We were first."

The voice was too strong on this world. Maradane itself had to be silenced.

Chapter Eleven

Asher dashed through the busy halls, his dusty cloak snapping at his heels as he dodged startled ambassadors and court personnel. Keeping his face hidden, he turned down the corridor to his son-in-law's apartments and barked a password to the tensed guards, who relaxed their grips on their axes.

Something had told him the past forty-eight months had slipped away too quietly. The Seer's preoccupation with Maradane had seemingly waned as the enemy empires settled into an uneasy calm.

For Asher that calm had been shattered by a call from Gray and the mad race home. Banging through the door of David's rooms he recalled a distant comment to Elizabeth about their grandson. He had never dreamt of the force behind Scott's exodus from his mountains.

Leah was weeping in her mother's arms as David paced the floor. Hurling his cape into a corner, Asher demanded, "What happened?"

David turned, holding an object behind his back, his eyes black. "She wast murdered, viciously."

Asher waited impatiently, catching his breath. Richard's wife had died in David's arms five days past, moments prior to Richard's return.

David clenched his jaw, then continued. "Someone poisoned her, a poison not e'en our Healers couldst counter. Leahcim died within the day, after agonizing pain. I hadst to tell Richard. Then I went to Shalahana only to find Scott cruelly wounded."

"What have you done for Richard?" Asher asked flatly.

"I sent them both to Maradane. Scott and Richard wilt both benefit from that world."

Asher nodded. "Why was I called here? Gray could have relayed the news."

David held up the object he had been hiding, eliciting a new flood of tears from his wife.

Asher's black eyes blazed as he studied the weapon, a shaft with barbs that opened on impact, attached to a weighted wire that pinned the victim's arms. The whole of it was caked with dried blood, causing Asher's skin to crawl.

David gazed steadily at Asher as he growled, "My son hadst to hammer this out of his own body. Thou art to hunt down the man who fired it."

Retrieving his cape, Asher left the room with two parting words.

"He's dead."

Jericho and Bronwyn woke with a start as a loud pounding drifted to their room. Sitting up, Jericho pulled the shade from the light. "Who'd be out this late?"

"I can't imagine." Bronwyn slipped into her robe. "I would think one of the servants would have opened the door by now."

Nodding in exasperation, Jericho pulled his own robe across his scarred shoulders. The scars were his only reminder of the explosion almost a year ago. Tying the robe's fabric belt, he strode from the room.

One of the younger servants met them on the stairs, timidly answering Jericho's sharp question. "Milord, I feared to let them enter. One of the men is near ten feet tall and looks very mean."

"I'd look mean myself if locked out in this storm," Jericho chided gently. "Go and prepare some hot cider." He smiled as the girl flushed with embarrassment and scurried away. Then he ran to the door.

As the door opened, a silver-haired giant stepped inside, followed by Richard. "I beg forgiveness for arriving so late," the giant said. "I am Scott, and my father David wished us to come at once, if thou wilt have us." His pale blue eyes betrayed his discomfort.

Jericho nodded, confused, as Bronwyn focused on Richard's grief-stricken face and cried, "What has happened?"

"One moment, milady." Richard's voice was barely audible as he unstrapped a sturdy basket from his back and placed it in Scott's arms. Folding back the fur cover, he lifted out a baby wrapped in warm blankets.

"Please, come and sit down." Bronwyn led them to the study where a servant was starting a fire in the fireplace. "Richard, what happened?"

Holding the baby close, Richard answered haltingly. "This is my son Lachlan; he is twelve months old... my wife died only days ago..."

Bronwyn motioned to the girl entering with a tray of steaming mugs. "Jana, please show Richard to one of the guest suites. Tell the other servants not to disturb him."

Richard stood distractedly. "I thank thee, milady. I really cannot speak right now." He followed Jana to the stairs.

Scott watched his friend depart, then faced his hosts. "It wilt do Richard a great good to be here."

Something about his speech sounded wrong to Bronwyn, but this was not the time to question it. She listened patiently as he continued.

"Richard and Leahcim wert wed shortly after he healed Anders. She wast poisoned five days ago. My father felt thou couldst be of comfort to Richard."

"Couldn't anyone help her?" Bronwyn asked, distressed.

Scott stared bleakly at his hands. "E'en our Healers couldst not save her. It hath devastated Richard."

Jericho set aside his mug. "We'll do whatever we can. Will you stay for a while?"

"Actually, my father wishes us to live here. But that wilt be spoken of later. Richard needs time to adjust, I pray better than I." Scott sighed as he gazed out the window.

Exchanging worried looks with Jericho, Bronwyn stood up. "You both need time to rest, Scott. Let me show you to your rooms."

The giant did not answer, his gaze locked on some distant point. His thoughts were not on Maradane.

"Scott," Bronwyn said a bit more loudly. "Shall I show you to your rooms?"

"Yea, please." Scott followed her silently up the stairs, speaking only when they reached his suite. "I fear I am no comfort to Richard."

Bronwyn paused to gaze at Scott, whom she had liked instantly. His silver hair was shaggy, framing a scarred face. He looked savage, but there was a soft light in his eyes.

"Scott, how long have you known Richard?"

"Since I wast seven...a very long time indeed," Scott answered sadly. "I have no other friend as dear to me, yet in time of need I know not what to say to him."

Bronwyn put a hand on his brawny arm. "Scott, I feel you help him more than you realize. Words are not always necessary."

Scott showed a wisp of a smile as he entered his room. "Good night, milady."

Moving down the hall, Bronwyn hesitated before knocking on another door. "Richard?"

"Thou mayst enter, milady."

Bronwyn went in quietly, sitting on the edge of a chair. "Is there anything I can do?"

"Not now, milady. Perhaps later, if thou wouldst help with my son." He looked down at the baby as he spoke.

"Of course...He's such a beautiful child." Bronwyn leaned forward to smooth Lachlan's golden curls. "Do all Immortal children have such wonder in their faces?"

"Not all. Lachlan is an E'er Young; they art the most beautiful of our children, a great gift."

Bronwyn bit her lip as she saw a tear fall onto the baby's hand. "We're all your friends...Good night, Richard."

Back in her own room, she sank into a cushioned chair and stared out the window.

"Aren't you coming back to bed?" Jericho asked.

She shook her head, feeling useless as she rested her hands in her lap. "I don't know what to do. There's such terrible pain in Richard's eyes."

"There's little you can do, Bron, except care. You'll find the way." Jericho shaded the bedside lamp and stared into the darkness, wondering what was heralded by this new event.

Bronwyn was fixing her breakfast the next morning when Scott entered the kitchen. Attired in suede leggings and a tunic over a brown flannel shirt, he carried a heavily decorated gold and leather belt, fumbling with the buckle as he walked. "Good morning, milady."

"Good morning, Scott. Please call me Bronwyn." She added another serving of sausage to the griddle and began mixing more pancake batter.

"As ye wish." Scott took a seat at the long table, finally repairing the belt and buckling it around his thick waist. The tight sleeves of his shirt seemed unhappy at being expected to contain his massive arms and he tugged on the cuffs to reposition them. "Hath Richard come down yet?"

"Yes, he said he needed to speak with Caleb." Bronwyn set a plate and goblet before Scott. "Jericho has gone to the forge. Excuse me a moment...Jana?" she called into the hall.

The girl hurried to the door, eyeing Scott apprehensively. "Yes, milady?"

"Please bring Lachlan to me, then take Garth for his walk. I have a list of things for you to pick up at the post, then you are free for the day."

"Yes, milady." Jana scurried away.

Bronwyn set the food on the table and filled the goblets with milk, setting the stoneware pitcher beside the platter. After Jana brought Lachlan and departed, Bronwyn asked, "Scott, it is true you've seen no one since your wife died?"

"I saw David and Richard; no one else. I spent seventy-nine years in the mountains of Shalahana, and wouldst not be here on Maradane if it wert for anyone but Richard." Scott filled his plate and reached for the syrup.

"But you had to know she would die eventually, for she was mortal." Bronwyn settled Lachlan in her lap and put a bottle of juice into his chubby hands as she buttered her pancakes.

"Yea, 'eventually.' But Tanya wast only sixteen and we hadst been wed just six months when she wast murdered." Scott spoke almost mechanically, as if he had no feeling for the words. Yet his eyes were sad, and Bronwyn decided he was just unused to conversation after his years alone.

"If we hadst chosen to wed our own race, Richard and I, we wouldst not face such grief. But 'tis common practice to wed mortals. We lose more of them to murder than to natural causes—'tis Shandal's way of torturing us, since we canst not be killed. Undying, we live with memories." He trailed into bitter silence.

Tales of the Immortals reached even Shanda worlds, and Bronwyn had thought Scott's story only a fancy made up about an antisocial being. Looking into his haunted eyes she now saw the truth in the story of a man who could not bear death. Rather than lose those he loved and needed so badly, he hid where he thought death could not reach him. Yet it had, through his one friend, and he grieved deeply.

For a silent moment Bronwyn alternated deftly between eating and feeding Lachlan his hot cereal. Then she ventured, "I'm curious about your language, Scott. You speak not its true form, yet neither is it wholly our speech."

"It couldst be called a hybrid, I suppose." Scott seemed thankful for the new topic, though his tone remained flat. "Truthfully, 'tis only a bastardized remnant we art too stubborn to bury. Mortals canst not understand the majority of our ancient words, yet we must deal extensively with mortals. O'er the passing ages the two most common tongues wert melded, and the original Immortal language lost. We paid a high price for our offering of help, for only a handful of scholars know the whole of our tongue. We shouldst abandon it, but 'tis a remembrance."

"It still has a great beauty," Bronwyn said slowly. "Of tradition, strength, and of sorrow. It should not be forgotten." She set the baby's bowl on the table and wiped his chin. "Scott, you will stay here, please, and not shut yourself away again?"

"I shalt stay as long as there is a Maradane." He glanced out the big window and saw Jana walking in the gardens with a black-haired child. "How old is thy son?"

"He's sixty months old now; I can't believe almost a year has gone by already." She rocked gently, trying to quiet Lachlan's fussing. "You poor love, shuffled around with all these people."

"Let me take him to my room." Scott reached for the baby.

Bronwyn smiled as Scott left the room, cuddling Lachlan and making him laugh. Clearing the table, she wished Scott had been left with a child of his own. He would not have hidden then and somehow she felt things would have changed if he had been with his people.

Arling burst into Devon's study, eliciting a sour glance from the older man. "Aren't you supposed to be at the temple?"

"I was at the temple, which is where I ran into Richard." Arling smiled coldly, rewarded with instant attention. "Perhaps you'd care to know that Scott is at the western palace."

"Scott hasn't left Shalahana in practically eighty years," Devon scoffed. "And we've certainly been grateful to him."

Arling yanked aside the nearby curtain, pointing toward the palace gardens. "Look! He's out talking to Salar."

Going to the door, Devon focused on the small guard station at this corner of the sprawling gardens. Salar stood with his head tilted back, conversing with a silver-haired giant who dwarfed the Dacynite. There was only one man in either empire who stood that tall, or could wield a sword as massive as the one strapped at this giant's side.

Devon closed the door quietly. "I believe this confirms our mission. Continue your work carefully. He'll be looking for things to report to his father."

Arling looked once more toward Scott, realizing a short reign of luck had ended. The fear was back and the old warriors of this generation would stoke it with their tales of horror—seven old men who had survived out of the thousands who had met Scott in individual combat.

That evening Jericho and Scott settled comfortably in the library, a fire warming the room and reflecting softly off the polished wood of shelves and furniture.

"Thou hast a fine home here, Jericho. And a fine world, from what I have seen." Sitting in the largest chair in the room, Scott stretched his feet toward the fire. "I am unused to being among people."

"Your arrival's been the talk of the planet, according to Caleb." Jericho passed a plate of cookies to Scott and reached for a mug of hot cocoa. "How is Richard today?"

"Awake. Sometimes 'tis all to be said for my race," Scott answered slowly. "He is coping by taking on extra work. I suspect that is why my father sent him here."

"And why are you here?"

"I wonder." Scott smiled grimly. "I have caused many people sadness, not on purpose but nonetheless sad. I do not cope well with death." He studied one scarred hand intently. "I am here first to help Richard. After that I believe my father seeks to keep me busy until I canst accept returning to an inhabited world."

"I somehow envision this encompassing the rest of us, too." Jericho brushed crumbs off his embroidered doublet. He instinctively liked this moody man, which somehow made Scott's pain more bitter. Scott was a gentle man who loved others and was as easily loved in return. Yet he had grown into being a key figure in the warring history of the empire, surrounded by the death he sought to escape.

Scott caught Jericho's eye, and seemingly his thoughts as well.

"I wast seven at my father's coronation. Since then I have tried avoiding losses I do not wish to accept. 'Tis time I worked as I am able. Tell me what is happening on thy world."

"We've begun building again." Jericho was quite pleased with the newest work. "During the last year we've completed schools, museums, and our Hall of Books to be the central planetary library, as well as other libraries across the planet. Now we're building observatories and scientific academies."

"I took a cursory look around the planet this afternoon. What is the purpose of the sea platform in this harbor?" Swirling the cocoa in his mug, Scott reached for another cookie.

"That's our first oceanographic laboratory. We're beginning to study samples from various depths, and to monitor the deeper dwelling creatures. We need to study what is here to determine if we need to import more species later."

"I noticed the platform is manned largely by Dacynites. Thou hast quite a combination here—wind and water rulers."

"Salar's people have been experimenting with the first real seas most of them have encountered. But tidal waves and whirlpools aren't much in demand here."

"But the talent mayst be maintained, for elsewhere," Scott said causally.

"War is never distant, is that what you mean?" Jericho added a log to the fire. "Well, we haven't really forgotten that. Salar's establishing a royal guard. And the planetary colors were initiated when the crown jewels were installed a few months ago. We'll have all the proper war standards, never fear."

Scott nodded, having browsed through the council rooms in the western palace and the temple. Each room displayed on one wall the flag of Maradane, a variegated sunburst of colors around a golden center, as well as the sector flags in their respective colors: blue for west, yellow for north, green for south, and purple for east. These smaller flags depicted two crossed staffs with the Adani symbol of the winds, and the names of the sector, king, and planet. In each corner of the room stood one of the planetary standards, with the heraldry of the ruling family. Scott found the crests interesting, for they all depicted animals as the central figure. The

Donnyas' imprint was the winged ice tiger of Adane, gone with the True-Bloods. Bryce's crest was a wolf under a silver moon, and Anders' the unicorn of Stalasia. The planetary crest incorporated all three animals with the sunburst pattern, Caleb's crest.

"Caleb says thy people undergo routine defensive training."

Jericho nodded. "No one will be forced to serve with the military, but we do insist that everyone become proficient with one chosen weapon as well as hand-to-hand defense. The children enjoy the initial training, making a game of it. And we have the peace of mind that our people can protect themselves."

"What of military units?" Scott asked. "Hast thou decided upon any certain form yet?"

Jericho studied Scott, sensing his intent to be more than casual. It was becoming apparent just how David intended to keep this Prince of the Realm busy.

"Devon is now reporting our decisions to your father's Master Armorers." Jericho paused, hearing the breeze rattle the ancient chimes in Bronwyn's alcove. "Our four forces will include the guard, an army, navy, and air corps. In times of battle the navy will merge with the army for ground combat. Their main purpose will be downing attack vessels over the oceans.

"Bryce is now training field medics, and Prudence has begun classes in general first aid."

Scott's attention drifted to the music of the chimes. "I heard a temple librarian mention thy wife's search for wind lore. What is planned?"

"We're trying to collect our rather feeble knowledge of the wind law," Jericho said wryly. "But we four of Adane know pitifully little. Bron has decided to write down her commands and see if she can vary them for greater control." He paused, waiting for the giant's reaction.

"'Tis late, and everyone else abed," Scott said quietly, wishing to speak with David before pursuing this matter. "I wish to see the forge tomorrow, and thy process of making armor."

"We can go right after breakfast," Jericho offered, letting the other subject drop. He began shading the lamps as Scott went to his suite.

Jana eyed Scott nervously as she served breakfast, shrinking back each time she passed his huge form. Scott seemed the only one to notice her behavior, and his uneasy gaze followed her movement. This served only to further upset her and she scurried from the room.

Taking note of the abrupt departure, Richard asked, "Bronwyn, is something wrong with the girl?"

Jericho choked back a laugh, eliciting a scolding glance from his wife.

"She's a very sweet girl, Richard," Bronwyn said quickly, "but very timid, and I'm afraid a little clumsy. I've let in more servants than we need so no one has a very heavy load. Jana's been here the longest." She bent to retrieve the spoon Garth had dropped.

Richard turned to Jericho. "I shalt be retrieving my things from Leahcim Tierrah today, before meeting with Caleb. Couldst thou suggest home sites near this palace for Scott and me?"

"Actually, there are a couple nice spots at the western and eastern corners of the gardens," Jericho said as he finished his breakfast. "They're secluded, and not as far away as the village."

"As ye wish, then," Richard said, then excused himself. As he left, Bronwyn turned to Scott.

"Scott, what is the big horn Richard carries strapped to his belt?"

"'Tis the Horn of the Rijo. As firstborn of our race Richard hath the right to bear it." Scott pushed his chair away from the table. "'Tis a gift from a higher race and is used as a signal. It makes a noise which wilt encircle a world."

"It sounds wonderful," Bronwyn said, awed.

"'Tis used in emergency. Let us hope thou hast no occasion to hear its call." Scott reached for his cloak.

Jericho grabbed up his own cape. "We'll stop to see Salar's recruits for the guard before we go to the forge." He turned to blow a kiss to his wife before leaving.

"Well." Bronwyn glanced at her son, laughing. "It looks like we've been abandoned for the day."

"Can't we go see Drahcir?" Garth asked hopefully. He and Prudence's son were becoming close friends even at their young age.

"I think we can manage that," Bronwyn said. "We must be sure Drahcir meets Richard, his namesake."

"What's a namesake, Mama?"

"A person or place after which someone is named," Bronwyn explained. "Prudence wanted to honor Richard for saving Anders and Caleb. But no one is ever given the names of the Immortals closest to David, another matter of honor. So she turned it around to be Drahcir."

Bronwyn bundled Lachlan into her son's outgrown basket and set out with the boys for the southern palace, stopping briefly to return a book to the temple library.

Tiea sat in her favorite spot near the central fountain in the temple gardens, waiting patiently for Caleb. Bronwyn had chatted briefly that morning, but was preoccupied with Richard's son and the slow progress of her search for wind lore.

She sighed, idly watching the water cascade from basin to basin.

"Sorry I'm late." Caleb bent to kiss her. "I had to finish some notes."

Tiea stood, laughing as she slipped her arm through his. "Caleb, you're always late because you always have to finish some notes. Yet your notes never, ever seem to be finished."

"I'm an archivist at heart, my love," Caleb admitted as they left the temple. "I can't help getting lost in the papers and pens."

Hugging his arm, Tiea said, "It seems something else is lost, or held up..."

Caleb stopped halfway across the meadow, tilting her face up in the moonlight. "You're troubled, and I haven't noticed. What's wrong?"

"Wrong isn't the right word, really." Tiea tried to pinpoint her feelings.

"Come on, let's walk." Caleb turned toward the gentle slopes beyond the hangar. "Talk to me."

"Everything seems to have stopped," Tiea said quietly, enjoying their nearness. "It's as if we're suspended and waiting to fall. Bronwyn had such hopes for her wind lore, and she's found nothing. Anders is still puzzling over his visions." She paused to look up at him. "And you've been troubled since Richard spoke to you."

"Is it that obvious?" Caleb was annoyed with himself. "I can't speak of it now, not until council. But I fear you won't feel suspended much longer."

Tiea accepted the comment quietly. He would tell her when he could, as he always did.

"We'd better hurry to supper," she said, tugging his hand. "Cita will be waiting. Then we can walk on the beach."

From the shadows of the grove nearest the hangar an angry figure followed their progress. Seeing their small airship depart, he forced a pleasant smile onto his swarthy face and strode to his own ship. It would soon be time to act.

Chapter Twelve

Caleb convened a council of the ruling families six nights after the Immortals' arrival. Wishing he were elsewhere, he looked distractedly around the table.

"Before we begin the central discussion, has anyone got any work reports?"

Bryce handed Caleb a sheaf of papers. "We're putting up the guard buildings now, including the main barracks and four posts at the corners of the palace grounds."

"Fine." Caleb slipped the reports into his notebook with only a cursory glance, a gesture that surprised his friends. "Salar, how is the guard progressing?"

"Excellently." Salar checked his own small notebook. "To date we have about eighty men in each sector. Ultimately there will be three hundred sixty-five for each, allowing quarter-day shifts and extra men at the tower."

Caleb nodded, making hasty jottings, his thoughts far from the work.

Richard shifted slightly in his seat, drawing Caleb's glance.

The Immortal was tired, strands of his snowy hair falling across his green eyes. In the brief discussion prior to the council his voice had been hoarse with grief.

Shaking his head, Caleb turned to David's son. "Scott, you may as well begin."

"I suppose I must," Scott sighed, noting a slight nod from Shara. "My father hath knowledge of another war on the western reaches of the realm—"

"Scott, that can't be!" Bronwyn cried. "This galaxy won't survive another war."

"Unless David's warriors halt these first stages, this war wilt sweep the realm. We must prepare," Scott said firmly. "At the moment 'tis a battle of the psychics, as Gray's people seek out the plans before Shandal's seers learn of our preparation. In the meantime, our spies report that attacks on Maradane art ordered, before she rises to power."

"Power?" Aric eyed Scott. "Maradane is barely populated, too insignificant to threaten anyone. Why this deadly interest in our world?"

"Aric," Shara said evenly, "you cannot dispute Gray."

"I'm not disputing him." Aric thumped his hand on the table, rattling the water glasses. "I want to understand. How could our world be so important that Shandal fears us? If we are at the center of a war I demand to know why."

Scott cleared his throat loudly. "Thy request is fair, Aric, and those not gifted of vision require answers." He smiled at Shara, quelling her next words. "'Tis a matter of the distant past which makes the future so important."

Everyone focused impatient attention on Scott, who though sitting towered over the volatile Aric. Scott waited another moment before continuing.

"Shara wilt verify that the psychics do not shape the events they see—they report only what is already set in motion. Often we canst use their foresight to alter situations to avoid certain things or turn them to our use."

Shara nodded silently as Scott paused to consider how best to explain.

"Gray long ago saw a future time when Maradane and the people of another, smaller world mayst be the driving powers in this galaxy. In the distant future thy world and another couldst very likely be the sole deciding factors as to whether Shandal fells our empire or they themselves fall. And Shandal knows this. So before that happens they intend to destroy this world. 'Tis either that, or destroy the other world far into the future, which wilt be more complicated than they wish to handle. We seek to protect thee all."

Aric was mollified, but persisted, "What has brought this dubious honor upon us?"

Scott smiled vaguely. "I am certain few mortals know that my father David first wed a mortal woman called Mara. Their three sons and daughter wert half-Immortals who began lines which go unbroken through the ages. When small I hadst a vision of these siblings of mine, all dead before I wast born. I saw their descendants far into the future, and we now understand they art thine descendants also. And they mayst very well decide the fate of our realm."

"What is our link to David?" Bryce asked dubiously.

Scott glanced around the table. "The four children of David founded four lines of descent: one of white-haired half-Immortals and one of a line of mystics of Stalasia, the builders of Stefanovia and the wind rulers of Adane, all to come together to form this world."

Bronwyn's astonished gaze wandered from Scott to Richard, her dark amber eyes wide. "The first queen of the winds was named Mara..."

"'Twas David's daughter," Richard answered softly. "A girl of dark complexion who married into a race with amber eyes who hadst settled the world of her people. Canst thou not trace thy lineage from Mara?"

"I can; I'm the third queen of the winds." Bronwyn glanced at her friends. "When first very ill I had little to do, so I undertook our family tree. Jericho and I have a common ancestor twenty generations back, the same person from whom Aric and Shonnie are descended."

Speaking gently, Scott tried to calm the chaotic thoughts of those around him. "There is time enough to accept this; 'tis indeed not a horrendous thing to be my kin." There was a hint of a chuckle in his hoarse voice, but he sobered as he caught Anders' gaze.

"Anders, thou art gravely troubled by a new gift, and still in doubt of thyself. Perhaps I canst tell thee a thing to enable acceptance and a deeper understanding." He recalled a recent talk with Gray. "If these future children of thine art truly to crush Shandal, it mayst come to be only because Shandal, in their greed for power, long ago planted the seed that is to destroy them. Remember this as thee try to sort out the confusion of thy visions."

Anders was visibly relieved by these words, his spirits lifted from the last depressions over an ancestry he cursed in his heart. "Thank you, Scott. If it's as you say, and my children may help overthrow our enemy, it is worth this accursed mark on our family." He glanced proudly at his wife. "And through Shara we have a noble descent."

"Through thee also, Anders. Marissa, whom Justin wed, wast descended also from my brother Alaric. But we must return to the more immediate topic." Scott looked to Richard.

"What thou must understand at this moment," the blond man began, "is that Gray hath foreseen two choices. We fight now, if it comes to that, and ensure some measure of peace for this world if we win. Or we delay retaliation until a time which wilt lead to decades of constant wars in which Maradane wilt be the focal point."

Aric leaned back in his chair with a frustrated sigh. "We've little choice, then. But I confess a lack of confidence in this new weaponry."

"Thy confusion is understandable," Richard said. "Thou must now understand two things. One: David ne'er doth anything rashly. Two: Shandal swiftly abandons any situation in which they cannot hold the upper hand."

"And what is significant about those two things?" Aric asked, drumming his fingers on the table.

Richard smiled briefly. "Tirrschon, new to thy galaxy, hath actually been in use for seven centuries throughout the realm. 'Tis impervious to any weapon in Shandal's arsenal, though we know the secret of its cutting and shaping. Trust me for the moment that Shandal wilt ne'er have the ability to manufacture tirrschon."

"Never?" Jericho asked skeptically.

"In David's realm art certain secrets, some of which thou wilt later learn, which enable us to keep safe such knowledge." Richard awaited the next question.

Aric studied both Immortals warily. "It seems like we are going backward rather than forward with this weaponry."

"A step back to look at something, a pause to consider appropriate change, is not in itself a step backward," Richard replied. "We know from experience this action wilt work. Death wilt not be a convenient matter inflicted from miles away—the enemy wilt suffer as do we."

"But do they suffer at all?" Aric demanded. "They seem all too adept at avoiding retribution."

"It is on their horizon," Scott said ominously. "Shandal is very methodical in their actions, and they depend upon our people living by a standard which they themselves find laughable. They inflict upon us every conceivable injury, then hide behind hostages and slaves, knowing that in our decency we wilt not hurt those innocents. They wish to slaughter at will, then accuse us of ill treating them if we retaliate. But before they fall Shandal wilt learn that I wilt get around those slaves and I wilt fell the people behind them. It mayst take a thousand more years, but they wilt see how well I have learned from their tactics."

Richard sighed. "We art not moving backward, as ye think. By converting the arms and armor we art providing a balance, a necessary balance to keep ourselves from destruction. Our best defense is nullifying the bulk of their explosive weapons, and our best offense is becoming lethal with weapons they art too lazy to master."

"My father seeks to save lives," Scott said, "in our empire, but also in Shandal as well, though I see no point in it." His bitter tone brought his late wife's name vividly to Bronwyn's mind. "And being the creeping slime they be, Shandal gave up explosive weapons when tirrschon kept David's armies safe but left Shandal vulnerable to slaughter. Rampant use of firearms hath existed only in this galaxy for six centuries, and wilt now vanish with the appearance of tirrschon."

"And why does David want to offer any ease to Shandal?" Aric demanded. "Slaughter would save us pain."

Scott rubbed his thumb over his left ring finger, which had not born ornament for so long a time now. Finally he said softly, "Slaughter ne'er comes easily or leaves tidily, Aric. There art helpless slaves, in our enemy's strongholds, who wilt fall at any such action from us. There mayst be citizens who cry for salvation. And those who slaughter find holes gnawed in their souls."

Richard looked grievingly at Scott for a moment, then turned to Aric. "I fear, newly made king, that my people must once again ask thy race to trust us on slim hopes. But be aware that our weapons masters have devised countless ways to defend our realm, all excruciatingly thorough. Bullets ne'er saw the day to inflict such damage as we canst loose from our hands."

"I think I know enough for now," Aric said tiredly. "What do we do first?"

Caleb looked at the mess of jumbled words on his once neat tablet. "Is there more to discuss tonight, Richard?"

The blond man shook his head. "There is time enough to let this sink in. 'Twouldst be best for all to return home now."

Sighing, Caleb said, "After conferring with Richard and Scott I'll send out work schedules to each of you. That's all for tonight, then. We meet again in one month."

The Immortals nodded agreement and departed as Caleb gathered his papers. Tucking the book under one arm, the young man sprinted down the hall.

"Richard, may I speak with you?"

"Certainly." The Immortal halted his stride.

Brushing a strand of hair out of his eyes, Caleb said hesitantly, "I realize this is not proper timing, but if things are as Scott says this will not wait." He paused uncomfortably, wishing he did not have to ask. "Tiea and I have planned to be wed for some time now, but things keep coming up. We'd be happy with a simple ceremony."

"Ceremony is important to the people, Caleb," Richard said

slowly. "Wouldst six months be soon enough for a traditional ceremony?"

"Certainly," Caleb said quickly. "Thank you, Richard." He hurried away to find Tiea as Richard left the temple, lost in sad thought.

Watching the exchange from a few paces away, Anders shook his head as his slow steps wandered toward the hangar. Such a question should never have been necessary, nor the pain it had brought to Richard's dark eyes. Weddings were times of joy, mingled with many other joys large and small that the people of David's realm wove throughout their lives. Yet always Shandal loomed forth to mar the picture, to throw grief into the midst of the people's efforts to live.

Looking up at the rising moons, Anders wished his world could just be left alone to exist, as the moons existed without hindrance. The Davan people were striving to be, to follow the will of God as it appeared in their daily lives. The empire's peoples were vast and varied, but they all followed God and strove to be. They would, at any moment, accept a treaty with Shandal and allow them to be as they wished, but Shandal did not want David's people to be at all. That was the heart of the fight. David's people would battle forever to uphold the right to be, to roll back the tide of unbeing which was Shandal.

Slipping into the pilot's seat, Anders smiled at Shara and headed the craft home. The war would come or not, but in the waiting his people would continue to strive.

"Are you sure this is all right?" Tiea asked hesitantly. She was not eager to postpone her wedding even longer, but the timing seemed bad indeed. "Maybe we should wait until things are more settled."

Caleb shook his head firmly. "No. We will be moving slowly at first. But I refuse for us to be lost in the shuffle. Richard said six months, and that is when it will be."

"I'm happy, then, if you're certain." Tiea tucked away the folder of notes she had been organizing while Caleb held council.

"Let's go tell Cita and Salar. They'll be pleased."

Caleb reached for her hand as they set out.

The next morning Bronwyn knocked softly on Scott's door. "Scott?"

"Enter, milady."

"I wondered if you need anything for your rooms..." Her voice trailed away as she entered.

The chamber, formerly empty of all but a bedroom suite, overflowed with varying objects that coalesced into all that was Scott. A lyre and flute lay on a table near the bed, while ceremonial and battle armor and swords hung on the wall above. One wall was hidden by sundry weapons and wistful paintings of quiet lands. A half-finished battle scene lay propped on a stack of poetry books; a nearby easel held a portrait of a young girl.

Objects of war, peace, art and music contrasted madly throughout the chamber. Statues adorned shelves and tables, while small crystals refracted light from the open window.

"Why Scott, when did you bring all this?"

"A few nights ago, milady. Please sit down—something troubles thee." Scott waved his hand in the direction of a large chair.

Sitting on the edge of the seat, Bronwyn frowned as she smoothed her skirt. "I'm upset over the council, that's all. I'd so hoped this world could be one of peace."

"Maradane is too peaceful." Scott sat up straighter, his legs outstretched on the long bed. "If thou wert faced with a sudden attack most of thy people wouldst perish. They must be prepared, slowly, to defend their home. My people wilt supply all possible help, but the people must learn to fight."

Bronwyn was not comforted. "I'm so confused by all this. It seems it ought to be a great thing to be descended from David, yet I feel no different and it obviously does naught to intimidate our enemies."

"Ah, that wilt put my father in his place," Scott laughed, then sobered. "Lineage, my queen, is what thou art by blood, not what thee feel. We hold it significant that all these descendants of David shouldst come together at this time, in this place. And Shandal is all too well intimidated, else they wouldst not put such focus on thee."

Bronwyn clasped her hands nervously. "Will there never be peace, Scott? Shara says you have some bit of foresight."

Scott was touched by the grasping hope in her voice. She needed something to hold onto.

"I have seen peace, Bronwyn. If these wars art won, Maradane shalt see many ages of peace. I have seen descendants of Anders who shalt be quite special."

"It's difficult to comprehend such a distant future," Bronwyn sighed. "But it's easy to believe your words about Anders."

"Thou shouldst heed him well."

Bronwyn brightened. "Oh, we do, and love him dearly. Anders is such a dear man, his strength is forever there. Yet he's so quiet you'd barely notice him. When we all doubted, faced only with dust and dry wind, he saw paradise. And he formed it."

The big man nodded, saying softly, "The pillars of the world...Yea, Anders is such a man as is seldom found on any world."

Bronwyn was greatly comforted by Scott's understanding of the shy Stalassi and his presence in their lives. Looking once more across the walls, she asked, "Did you paint all these pictures?"

"Most of them." Picking up his lyre, Scott began to play softly. "Milady, what dost thou do to pass the time?"

"Oh, I like to make jewelry and tapestries. And I do love to work in the observatories...Are there words to that piece, Scott? It's very lovely."

"Yea, but my voice is too coarse for song... I have some errands, now that we have talked. I shalt return for supper." Scott stretched to his full height and left the room.

Bronwyn remained alone for a while in the quite chamber, pondering the clutter of news and hope.

Asher bent over his cluttered desk, trying to appear oblivious to the voices in front of him. Every so often he dared a fleeting glance up, knowing the men faced away from him.

"He should not have bragged so, Seer," a young man said, stroking the head of the mangy wolf at his side. Lanky and skulking, the beast bore no resemblance to its silver cousins living on so many of David's worlds.

The Seer of Donthas tossed his ruby into the air and caught it with a rhythmic gesture, watching the wolf's baleful eyes follow the tumbling red orb.

"Yes, well. I suppose you're right," the Seer reflected with a hiss of breath.

The two men were contemplating the recent death of one of their assassins, the man who had so grievously wounded Scott. Asher had easily tracked the man by his excessive bragging about the incident.

"For his words to reach Donthas so swiftly all the way from Seryl's domes his tales must have been great indeed. But still, to have him murdered like that, impaled on the very weapon he used on that vile spawn of David and then lain across the altar... Are you certain no one saw the man who did it?"

"No one, Seer," the youth affirmed. "The Immortal scum slink through the night and shadows, using that accursed travel plane of theirs. Perhaps the next men will be more subtle in attacking David's family."

"We can ill afford that sport now," the Seer said, snapping his fist shut around the gem. "It will take all our energies to force this war—years of preparation. Our forces are numerically superior, but my spies still talk of the Adanes searching for more wind control. If that wind-scoured abomination isn't extinguished now we will have to weave our way to the very heart of power on another world in years to come, and I like not the hardships entailed by that route." He gazed at the gaunt wolf through narrowed eyes. "Don't you ever feed that thing?"

"He's being trained for information retrieval, and he's rather stupid." The youth cuffed the animal's ears to emphasize his words. "Until he learns to sniff out our men from a drop point in the mountains he gets only two kits a day."

The Seer nodded and began strolling toward the door. "A fine idea, if it works. The information will move faster. Keep me informed."

Nodding, the youth grabbed the wolf's chain and dragged him to his feet. "Come along, my pet. If you don't do better tonight I'll send the whole supply of cats along with you to the lords' food stock."

As they disappeared through the door, Asher ground his teeth, thinking of his own fine, limber cat at home, a beautiful creature with eyes veiling the depths of history. Raven roamed the fields and courts with him by day, and rumbled contentedly upon his pillow by night, a medley of green eyes, ebony fur, and whiskers curving perfectly to touch below his chin. He was Asher's sea of calm on his too infrequent visits home, climbing onto his shoulder even before the man could strip off his foul clothing.

Something in the eyes of a feline disturbed the people of Shandal, and the feeling was mutual. No cat could be let loose on any Shanda world without immediately attacking the nearest citizen. As a result they were bred in cramped cages and their offspring used for sundry purposes, including training of the wolves.

Closing his notebooks, Asher slipped into the bleak shadows huddling at the outskirts of the room and reached for his travel stone. The Paladins must be warned of this new development. All incoming ships would have to be searched, especially those landing on Maradane. No coded papers had ever come from that world, but Asher did not take that to mean there were no spies there.

Leaving the library behind, he melted into the teleportal zone, realizing now there were still several years of quiet ahead for most of the realm. But for the Davan forces the time for action had come, the time to begin harassing enemy outposts to slow their progress.

With the news that the war would be slow in coming, Maradane's rulers settled into long-range defense plans and plans for their first royal wedding. Five months passed swiftly, and one afternoon found the queens gathered at the eastern palace.

Spreading out several bolts of cloth, Shara said, "Prudence, how are the medical classes coming? I wish I was free to attend more of them."

"Nearly all the women are attending now." Prudence tied a multi-colored scarf around her fluffy golden hair. "Drahcir is becoming a problem, though, for he wants to forsake his proper lessons and attend all my classes. Or else he wishes to run off and plague Richard, fascinated by his namesake."

Bronwyn laughed softly. "If only Garth would content himself with medicine. He spends every free moment at the barracks to watch the guards...Tiea, turn a bit." She pulled a tape measure from her apron pocket. "I hate all the noise, the clashing of swords and marching. The first sound I hear each morning is the horn calling the change of the guard."

"Jeremiah thrives on it," Shara said as she smoothed a crease out of some fine silk. "Ah...here it is." She picked up a bolt of satiny iridescent fabric that shimmered in the sunlight. "Tiea, this is perfect for your complexion. Do you like it?"

"It's lovely!" Tiea ran a hand over the cool, smooth material. "What is it?"

"This is spun opals, though you get a similar hue from pearls. Shall I set it aside for your gown?"

Tiea nodded as Shonnie cried, "That's impossible! Cloth can't be made from stone."

"Not impossible, but extremely complicated." Shara put the cloth on a table beside her chair. "It's similar to breaking gems down for printing purposes, using a longer series of additives to alter the composition for spinning thread. We end up retaining the colors, but with a more pliable texture. Perhaps I'd better find the texts and train some students. This is a purely Stalassi art. People used to travel across the realm for our cloth."

"I don't know how to thank you all." Tiea smiled at each of her friends. "I'm so glad we stayed here."

"No more so than we," Prudence assured her. "It's too bad the weather's so miserable lately; we could work in the gardens. Sunny one moment and raining the next...Tiea, what about the wedding tour?"

"Caleb says we'll use a shuttle to tour where the weather is bad. Arling will pilot it for us."

"He seems to be working out well."

"Oh, he's a tremendous help." Tiea sat down as Bronwyn finished her measurements. "He maintains all the records, often staying in the evening to finish up. And he's been helping me with errands while I'm redoing our apartments."

Shara looked up from a small book in her lap. "I must say, Tiea, what a vast improvement you've made in Caleb's living quarters. I feared he'd get lost in that mess and never surface." She laughed lightly as she gave the book to Tiea. "These are some of the patterns of my world. Perhaps there's one you will like."

"Thank you so much. I'll try to choose a gown this evening." Slipping the book into her little carryall, Tiea glanced out at the setting sun. "I fear I must go. Arling is to meet me at the sector post here to pick up an order, then I must hurry home. Cita isn't feeling well."

Shonnie prepared to follow her out the door. "I should go too. I'll get a scolding if Aric's supper is late."

Prudence could not help laughing as she and Bronwyn helped Shara tidy up. "I'd like to see the day Aric raises his voice to her; he adores her."

"Oh, if only he adored everyone else so," Shara laughed, recalling many of Aric's extremely loud outbursts. "At least someone on Maradane knows a quiet side of our storm king."

Bronwyn was just setting the big table in the kitchen when the clear notes of four rams' horns filled the evening air. Jericho burst through the kitchen door.

"David has arrived, and the four High Under Kings are with him!"

A knot tightened in Bronwyn's throat. "They are coming here, now? Will they want to eat with us? Maybe I should change my dress." She looked sheepishly at her plain blue gown and travel-dusty slippers.

"Milady, there is naught to worry about." Scott entered the kitchen with Richard and removed his billowing cape. "Call Jana to finish preparing the meal and have another girl set additional places at the table. Father wishes to be treated simply. They have come to see this world."

"Well...if you're sure." She looked nervously around the cluttered kitchen, then followed the men to the council room.

The five kings left their ship a mile from the palace and proceeded the rest of the way on foot, the custom for leisure visits. They were escorted by a guard of twenty men in ceremonial garb who stationed themselves at the palace doors as the kings entered.

Jana fumbled open the council room doors and tried desperately to recall the proper introduction. Richard smiled reassuringly at her. "Thou mayst leave."

All present bowed low before their king, who bade them rise as Richard began the formal introductions.

Bronwyn's gaze traveled from person to person as she carefully noted the features and mannerisms of each. David was precise in every way, from his close-cropped hair to his resonant voice. Nicholas was tall and lanky, with almost gaunt features. His hair was short in front, brushed back from his forehead, and long and curly in back. His dark eyes were sober and he seemed a man of few words.

Michael grinned as Bronwyn's curious glance reached him, a mischievous light in his eyes. She found him very pleasant, with an amiable rounded face and short, thick hair. He was obviously amused to find her more than a little awestruck.

Robert had a vague, dreamy look about him, yet he seemed to miss nothing taking place around him. His trim mustache crinkled as he exchanged a smile with his wife Rachel.

Bronwyn spoke briefly to each, welcoming them to her home and admiring the Immortal woman's waist-long red hair. Yet her greatest attention was drawn to the fourth High Under King.

Short for his race, Gray was only two inches taller than Richard, yet he compelled intense interest. Shoulder-length black hair with a blue caste framed a face that was a far cry from handsome but still pleasant.

His most striking feature was his eyes—a deep, rich golden hue that scintillated with an inner light. Looking at him, Bronwyn saw those eyes drinking in every minute detail and could imagine his mind constantly devouring each new bit of information. Part of his being was incessantly preoccupied, and he seemed distant.

Returning her full attention to David, Bronwyn found him looking at Scott with a father's concerned eyes. "Thee look well, my son. Art thou happy here?"

"Yea, 'tis a lovely world."

"I am sure." Putting one hand on Scott's shoulder, David looked wonderingly at him. He did not understand something new he saw reflected in his son's eyes. "When is the royal wedding to be held?"

"On the last day of this month," Scott answered as Jana sidled into the room to announce the meal.

As they took their seats around the kitchen table David turned to Richard. "How fares Lachlan, my friend?"

"Very well, sire. Milady Bronwyn is helping in his care."

"I thought as much." David turned an amused face to the queen. "Thou seemest most capable, milady, though nervous."

"David, do not tease her," Rachel said firmly. "It is unnerving to be descended upon by so many people unannounced." She squeezed Bronwyn's hand.

"I'm happy to have you here. It's just..." Bronwyn was nervous, for the Immortals were held in awe by almost everyone. Though they supplied so much aid to her world, she knew only Richard and Scott.

"We art only people, my queen, and thou needst not worry about thy every manner." David smiled gently from the head of the table. "Indeed, thou art all very precious to me. Please accept us and be at ease."

Bronwyn nodded slowly as the men turned the conversation to the progress of defense plans. Rachel turned again to her.

"Thee see, men art men where'er they be. Do tell me about the wedding plans."

Bronwyn was about to comply when Salar entered and made his way to her chair, pausing only briefly to greet David.

"Bron, did you see Tiea this afternoon?"

"Yes, of course." Bronwyn laid her fork beside her plate as she looked up at him. "She left Shara's quite a while ago to meet Arling. She was supposed to pick up something at the eastern post."

Salar gazed perplexedly out the window. "I don't understand this. Cita isn't feeling well and counted on Tiea fixing supper."

"She did mention that, Salar, and left in quite a hurry. It was just sunset at Shara's then, mid-afternoon here." Bronwyn grew worried. "What about Arling?"

Salar thumped one hand repeatedly upon his sword hilt. "Caleb says he is gone also. It's not like Tiea to stay away after dark without Caleb; she's still not comfortable in such open spaces at night."

"Excuse me," David interrupted. "Who is this Arling?"

"Caleb's assistant, Father," Scott answered. "He came to help after the explosion at the forge. He hath been keeping the temple records."

David pursed his lips, exchanging a glance with Gray. "'Twas about that time that a youth called Arling Haller evaded my men."

"And landed on Maradane." Salar's hand tightened on his sword.

Chapter Thirteen

David and his men joined the massive search that began that night. Bronwyn brought Cita to stay at the palace until Tiea was found, and Prudence came to tend her. The other kings began searching their own sectors while Caleb tried retracing Tiea's steps. All he learned was that Arling had stopped at a post in the eastern sector to pick up a fur cape and a supply of smoked meat.

Devon was in Leahcim Tierrah reporting to David's Master Armorers, and David sent orders for his immediate arrest and return to Maradane.

Jericho and Caleb tore Devon's house apart inside and out searching for some clue to Tiea's whereabouts, but they found no sign. Giving up, disgusted by the dark, steamy rooms hidden behind drawn blinds, they were standing in the living room when a puff of wind showered ashes on the andiron before the fireplace.

"Look at that." Jericho watched wonderingly as the gust continued swirling down the chimney and around the metal. "There's no wind outside."

"I'm in no mood for more of these idiotic wind flukes!" Caleb kicked the andiron, losing his balance as it gave way.

Steadying his friend, Jericho took no notice as the wind retreated up the chimney. The hearth had titled upward, revealing a hoard of journals, envelopes, and papers copied from the temple offices, all sitting atop a cache of explosives.

Dropping to his knees, Caleb grabbed a handful of papers. "Spies!" he spit out furiously. "Under my own stupid nose, Shanda spies! And the man who bombed the forge."

Jericho stared at the papers, then said, "This must mean they've sent no information to their base. The Paladins have been monitoring everything so tightly they must not have dared send them out."

"I pray so." Caleb gathered the evidence and stormed out of the house. He sought David out and presented the bundle by throwing it across the room. "I'm too gullible to be a king!" he growled, wildly pacing the tiled floor.

David grabbed him by the arm, saying calmly, "Spies art a matter of life, Caleb, and they live on any world we count important. We simply didst not yet know who wast spying here.

"My own spies recently reported a plan to train wolves for information retrieval. That is why all ships art searched. Prior to that, the routine search of couriers hast kept the information beyond Shandal's reach. I am sure we have lost nothing of value as far as the papers art concerned. And Devon wilt be returned 'ere he canst flee with what he stores in his memory."

Caleb returned to the search little comforted by David's words. The only thing that seemed to help was the satisfaction he received from ordering Devon's home burnt to the ground and the debris disintegrated.

An entire day passed before Salar allowed himself a brief break to visit his wife. She was sleeping, and Prudence took him aside outside her room.

"She's worried, Salar, but otherwise fine. Bryce was here a while ago."

Rubbing his weary eyes, Salar shook his head. "It's hard enough not knowing where Tiea is, but I can't stop worrying about Cita. We've lost two babies before..."

Prudence silenced him with a gentle gesture. "Bryce is taking care of her, and I won't leave her. Find your sister, Salar, and leave your wife to me."

Jericho collapsed onto a chair, resting his arms on the edge of the kitchen table. Bronwyn gently rubbed his shoulders after pouring him a mug of ale.

"I just don't know, Bron." He rested his head on his arms. "We have so few men in proportion to the area to search, assuming the fur cloak indicates a cold region."

"How is Caleb?"

"Frantic. Can you blame him, after six days?" Jericho stared blankly at the mug. "Salar is little better off. Is everything all right here?"

"Yes, I suppose so," Bronwyn sighed. "Jericho, I'm worried about Jana. I don't understand her behavior."

Jericho let out a sour chuckle. "No one understands Jana's behavior."

"Be serious, Jericho. The girl's a nervous wreck and I can see no reason. She broke our set of crystal yesterday. Scott came back to eat, after being gone three days, and when he asked her for a sandwich she screamed, dropped the tray, and cut herself badly. She refused to let Scott help her, insisting that Pru do it."

"That girl's not entirely with us, Bron." Jericho sat up and drained his mug in one gulp. "I'd best return to the search. Robert and Nicholas are trying to wring information from Devon, but I fear only footwork will help us."

Watching him go, Bronwyn found her thoughts wandering worried paths. If they found Tiea would she be well? And what of Caleb if she was found hurt, dead, or not at all? He was overcome with guilt for trusting Tiea's safety to Arling and letting him see guarded plans. He would soon be in no condition to rule, and then where would Maradane be? She realized with a chill that this was just what Arling wanted, just what his superiors had planned.

Bronwyn was jarred out of a fitful doze by the echoing reverberations of a horn. It began as a low, barely audible call but with each subsequent sounding it rose in intensity until its rich tones were ear-shattering as they vaulted to the sky.

Shara was visiting Cita. As the call echoed again, causing the chandelier to tremble on its chain, she ran to the hall. "It's the Horn of the Rijo! Richard and Anders have found Tiea!" She waved a hasty farewell to Cita and Prudence as she stepped toward the stairs.

Bronwyn threw a cape to Shara and grabbed her staff. "I know where Richard was searching."

Anders dropped to his knees beside Tiea as Richard fastened the massive ram's horn to its strap on his belt. Knowing his copper cube would not cure Tiea's multiple injuries, Richard would wait for Scott and meanwhile began looking for Arling. The cave was dark, a single sputtering torch giving off a feeble light above the girl.

"Tiea?" Anders gently slid his arm behind her shoulders, looking at her bruised face. "How badly are you hurt?"

"I don't know," she answered weakly, tears flooding her dark eyes. "He beat me. He said he wanted to hurt us all." Her words turned to a cry of pain as Anders ran a gentle hand over her leg. "He's insane, Anders. He keeps screaming about some voice he hears on the wind."

"Sshhh." He smoothed the hair away from her grimy face as he leaned back on his heels. "Caleb will be here soon, and Scott will heal you."

At the rear of the cave Richard was on one knee, examining tracks in a narrow tunnel, when something crashed down on his head. He pitched forward into the dirt.

Arling spun around, preparing to use the club similarly on the Stalassi. He was dazed by a blow from a heavy fist, followed by searing pain as his arm was twisted violently behind him.

"Be still or I will surely break you in half," Anders hissed in the man's ear. "If David didn't need you I'd finish this now."

Arling gasped with pain, but managed to spit out, "You have little more time to finish anything!"

Richard stumbled to his feet, shaking his head, as Anders demanded, "How much information has been sent to your base?"

Arling refused to answer and Anders repeated the question. When the short man still did not reply Anders hooked one arm beneath his chin and with the other applied agonizing pressure to the already twisted limb. "Answer or I'll rip this arm from its socket! It will hurt you more than if I break your neck!"

"Nothing, we sent nothing!" Arling screamed as several men ran into the cave. "Only a few military tables that Devon could take..."

Scott, Caleb, and Salar all dropped to their knees beside Tiea, the giant Immortal reaching for a flat oval of silver in his belt. Jericho and Aric bound Arling's hands, ignoring his cry of pain as the rope aggravated the hurt inflicted by Anders.

Richard and Anders joined the men gathered around the girl's battered form. Scott held the silver tightly in one hand, intoned a silent prayer, then put the other hand on Tiea's forehead. There was a surge of energy between the two, from Scott to the girl. He then put away the silver. "She wilt be well."

Caleb gathered her into his arms and held her tightly as Bronwyn and Shara knelt beside her, offering their comforting touch. Salar grasped Tiea's hand, then turned to face Arling with drawn sword.

Before anyone could speak, David propelled Devon into the cave and halted before Arling.

Eyes narrowed, Devon spit contemptuously into his cousin's face. "You idiot! All our work, all these days on this stinking planet, gasping in this thin air—you've ruined it all! You've set us back years!"

"Be silent!" David shouted, and a guard thrust a gag into Devon's mouth. David turned to Arling, fingering a palm-sized circle of black metal.

Arling's eyes widened in terror at the sight. "No, no, I beg you!"

"Thou art in a position to beg nothing. Where is thy base?"

David demanded.

"The second moon of Seryl." Arling's gaze never left the circle of metal. "Please, spare me!"

"I fully intend to. What information hath been sent to thy superiors?"

Terrified, the youth moaned, "Military tables, hangar locations, news of Bronwyn and Anders—nothing else. We were to take the rest by hand, or give it to the wolves."

"How many people hast thou murdered to gain thy position?" David held the disc before Arling's frightened eyes.

"None!" Arling stared at David, desperate to be believed. "I was raised for my job, to infiltrate the library systems. I've killed no one!"

Putting one hand beneath the trembling man's chin, David forced his head up. With his other hand he positioned the cold metal above the man's eyes.

"Arling Haller exists no more. Thou hast no past, no memories, no other life. Thee know nothing of Shandal. Thou art training for service in my libraries after a severe illness which took thy memory. Thou wilt know nothing until thee reach Leahcim Tierrah and thou wilt recall nothing of this day."

Pocketing the metal, David turned to Devon and motioned to the guard to remove the gag. "Thou wilt go to a prison planet for execution for the murders inflicted on thy route to this position. The Wise Ones wilt confirm whether or not thee murdered the real Devon to take his place."

"Kill me, it will do you no good, you bastard!" Devon swore. "The Clan will see that you are put to an end for the evil you inflict, robbing men of their minds!"

"I spare life where I am able." David grabbed the man by the collar and glared down at him. "I do not put snakes in the beds of babes, nor do I beat women or burn children alive. I do punish killers, and try to save those who have not yet killed by their own hand. Thou art residing in my realm and by my laws thou wilt live or die as thee so choose.

"Take him away." David threw Devon into the arms of his guard.

Aric sank thankfully into the deep cushions of the chair facing the crackling fire. He wanted only to rest in the dimly lit room and forget for a moment the past hectic days. Yet he could not prevent his thoughts from wandering to events occurring elsewhere on the continent.

Tiea was resting at home and Scott had assured everyone that her recovery would be swift. While the rest of the searchers retired to their homes with prayers of thanks, the four kings awaited word from Caleb, to come the next day.

In the temple, Caleb was meeting with David, Richard and Scott. They would spend the waning night studying the papers found at Devon's and deciding what must be changed on the planet to insure safety. Aric hoped they would discover that little damage was in fact done. Members of David's own guard were stationed at the eastern and western palaces until they were certain no other spies resided on Maradane. The Paladins had sent a special division to monitor the area surrounding Maradane until the armed forces were completely stabilized.

Yawning, Aric reached for a heavy volume on his desk, curious about the ruling system established by David. Content with the soft snapping of the fire, he settled back in his chair and skimmed the pages.

* The Immortals lived by a system of group and class, according to basic skills or personality. One person could belong to only one of the four groups, but could have membership in more than one of the eight classes. The four groups were headed by the four High Under Kings—Robert, Nicholas, Michael and Gray—and were so named the Rijo, Nibru, Mikon and Graco.

Universal government fell to the first two classes, under the guidance of David and the High Under Kings, and was supplemented by the remaining six classes.

Each inhabited solar system was assigned one Under King, who worked in conjunction with the High Immortals who ruled at five hundred per inhabited galaxy. Laws were enforced by the Paladins, a military unit composed of the class of Wanderers—Immortals who also held membership in one of the seven other classes. There were sixty Wanderers from each other class for each planetary quadrant, with others available at need.

High Travelers traversed the entire realm offering counsel as their skills were needed. Under Travelers were assigned to specific quadrants as an aide in upholding currently effective Space Codes.

Healers, such as Scott, traveled at will or call, dispensing their healing gifts at need. Their work was often guided by members of the Graco, the group to which all with psychic abilities belonged.

The remaining classes were the half-Immortals, a race of kings scattered throughout the realm, and the Immortal E'er Young, known for their haunting beauty and the ability to communicate with animals. *

Aric closed the book, too tired to really sort out the facts. His mind wandered back to David's words to Devon and he needed no book to recall the history of which the king had spoken.

Throughout the realm all but the Elves of Aubrey and the Immortals had a paralyzing fear of snakes. Shortly after Stalasia called for help from David in the year 2307, the Clan of the Snake devised a new horror to unleash on their rallying enemies.

The planet Shandal was a world of swamps and marshes rampant with poisonous reptiles. The snakes of one species grew to monstrous proportions and were worshipped by the people, while other small breeds were kept as pets. The Clan leaders began a breeding program, filling artificial ponds with the snakes necessary for their new plan of assault. When ready, in the course of four months they unobtrusively shipped these creatures to worlds inhabited by their enemy. Aside from simply leaving the uncountable swarms across each planet's surface, the smugglers took pleasure in creeping into homes in the night and placing their pets in cradles with sleeping babies. Mothers awoke to find their children either poisoned or crushed.

The situation was so unexpected and so severe that people

would leave their homes only to find themselves ankle deep in the swarming snakes. Millions died, weakening the defenses of the newly awakening empire, and instilling such petrifying horror that to this day citizens of David's realm froze upon sight of a snake.

For over a century all inhabited worlds were patrolled day and night by Immortal and Elf, ferreting out the snakes as they bred and guarding against new shipments. On several worlds where the population was decimated the Immortals simply flooded the planet with gasses to exterminate the reptiles. But this could not be done on populated worlds, and the terror persisted for long years.

In retaliation the Immortals ravaged the breeding grounds on Shandal and razed the places of worship on other worlds, but David would not order the gassing of enemy strongholds. Shandal finally suspended the tactic, fearful that this destruction of their snakes would incur the wrath of their gods. From then on worlds to be colonized by David's people were first purged of all snakes. Unintentionally, this served to further anger the people of Shandal and deepen their hatred of David.

Aric frowned, stifling the repulsive memories, and realized it was very late. Shading the light on his desk, he left the study and walked the silent halls to his bedroom. On the way he peered into the nursery, comforted by the sight of Aarek curled beneath his blanket and the sound of the guards' footsteps outside.

Healed by Scott, Tiea recovered within two days and the wedding preparations were taken up once again. David decided that major harm had been prevented by Devon's capture and only the underground warship hangar locations were changed as a preventive measure. A new physical was ordered for all court workers in Leahcim Tierrah. Caleb made arrangements to clear all newcomers to Maradane through David's offices as well as through physicals by Bryce. David assured the rulers that no further damage was done, and with the royal guard established and the military growing, Maradane was safe for the moment.

The day of the ceremony arrived with preparations barely complete. Anders and Richard hurried through the last-minute tasks in the temple before the Stalassi took his place in the front of the chapel set aside for ceremonies of state.

A trio of musicians began a quiet melody as Caleb took his place before Anders. As the music changed he glanced nervously at his reflection in one of his silver brassards, adjusting the moonstone headband encircling his long white hair.

Tiea was escorted down the long aisle by Salar, rainbow hues shimmering beneath the lace of her gown. Her only ornament was a crown of fragile gold lace holding her veil, from which hung strings of tiny diamonds entwined in her raven hair.

Salar took his seat as Tiea and Caleb knelt on two satin pillows in front of Anders. Caleb grasped Tiea's hand as his friend began.

"We are blessed this day to celebrate the marriage of our king, the first ceremony of our new world to take place in this chamber. Caleb Bajoc takes this day into his house Tiea Mashun, daughter of the rulers of the seas.

"Caleb, do you promise for your life to care for Tiea, protecting and honoring her, and sharing the realm of your heart?"

"I do so promise." Caleb tightened his hand around hers.

"Tiea, do you promise for your life to care for Caleb, protecting and honoring him, and sharing the realm of your heart?"

"I do so promise." Tiea smiled shyly at Caleb, then turned back to Anders.

Anders closed his small prayer book as the couple exchanged rings of gold. "With these symbols of the circles of our lives, Caleb and Tiea begin their journey anew through this life and unto the next. Love is bound, as it was before and will be again, and though the symbols be removed the bond and the love remain eternal."

Anders closed his eyes for a moment, finding pure joy in this renewal of his first love, that of caring for his people, and savoring what would probably be his last action in this capacity. Then he concluded with a hand resting upon each of their heads.

"In the name of our God, I bless this union. May this joining of two into one be blessed for all time with joy and love."

As Caleb drew his bride into his arms, Bronwyn glanced across the room to Salar. Smiling as he gazed at his sister, he had one arm around Cita while the other cradled his tiny newborn son. Bronwyn turned back to the altar to see the couple bow to Anders and rise to their feet.

The newlyweds proceeded to the eastern palace where they were honored with a festival before touring the populated areas of each sector. Prudence and Bryce held a late supper for their friends after Caleb and Tiea were on their way.

Much later that night, as Bronwyn and Jericho sat in their study, Jericho closed his book and said, "And to what are you giving such deep thought, my Bron?"

"How good it was to have something to celebrate. It banished a lot of the tension."

Jericho nodded thoughtfully. "I had much the same thought. We should get everyone together to discuss other ideas, maybe an annual festival."

Entering the room and settling Lachlan on his lap, Richard offered, "'Tis a very good idea, Jericho. The people need things to look forward to.

"Milady," Richard paused to disengage the baby's fist from the golden chain around his neck. "Scott and I shalt be moving to our new homes tomorrow. Dost thou know two girls who wouldst keep our houses in order?"

"I'll send two of my girls. It won't be that much extra work for them."

Lachlan grumbled as his father stood up. "Thank thee, milady. I must get this little one to bed."

Jericho also rose and began shading the lamps in the room. "We'd also better turn in, Bron. I have a lot of work tomorrow."

"I suppose everyone does." Bronwyn carefully folded her needlework, putting it on a table.

Bronwyn was mending a gown late the next morning when Scott passed the window with an armful of belongings for his new home. "Oh, that reminds me...Clare, come here, please," she called into the hall.

A girl of twelve hurried in from the kitchen. "Yes, mistress?"

Bronwyn set aside her mending. "Clare, would you be willing to do extra work beginning today?"

"Surely, milady." Clare dried her hands on her apron. "What needs to be done?"

"I need someone to take care of Richard's home, and to cook when he does not eat here. Also, you'll have to help with the baby."

"I'd like that, milady. Lachlan is such a sweet baby." Clare smiled, well pleased with the new task. Lachlan was walking now and she enjoyed keeping him out of mischief.

"Very good, then. Go see if Richard needs help now, and please send Jana to me."

Clare bowed and left the room.

Bronwyn called to Scott as he passed the garden door. "Scott, I'm sending Jana to keep house for you. Is that agreeable?"

Scott hesitated. "I shouldst like that, milady, but the girl doth not like me. I want her not to come unless 'tis her wish."

"Why shouldn't she like you, Scott? Surely you're mistaken."

"She fears me, Bronwyn. Send her if she hath no objections, but force her not." Scott turned abruptly away.

Closing the door with a frown, Bronwyn smoothed her wind-blown hair as Jana entered the room.

"Jana, beginning today I'd like you to care for Scott's house for him, in between your tasks here. You need only cook when he doesn't dine here, and keep his things tidy. It should be easy; Scott is very orderly."

Jana's face fell and she took a step backward. "If you wish so, mistress...Milady, have I somehow displeased you?"

Bronwyn looked down at the girl with a renewed expression of worry. "Jana, your work is excellent, most of the time. I thought it would be a kindness of you to do this, as you have so much free time.

"Really, Jana, I'm concerned about you lately. If you feel so terribly about this I'll find someone else."

"No, milady, I shall do it." Jana bowed her head as she left the room, ashamed of her reaction and for worrying Bronwyn. Climbing the wide stairs she swallowed the lump in her throat and knocked timidly on Scott's door.

His harsh voice rumbled through the door. "Come in."

Slipping into the room, Jana mumbled, "Milady Bronwyn said I am to help you move, my lord, and keep your house...Shall I take this box to your house?" She reached for a large wooden case, but he stopped her.

"'Tis much too heavy for thee to carry, little one. Perhaps thou shouldst carry these books and I wilt take the chest." Scott piled some of his paintings atop the chest and lifted them all into his arms.

Following the giant down the stairs and out the door, Jana gazed timidly at his broad back. In the cottage's front room Scott set his burden on a polished table near several piles of books.

"Wouldst thou please shelve these books? I have only a few things more to bring."

"Yes, my lord." Jana set to work putting the books alphabetically on the shelves. Marveling that many were poetry collections, she stopped occasionally to flip through the pages. She was reading a sonnet when Scott returned.

"Dost thou like poetry?"

Jana nearly dropped the book. "Y...yes, milord, very much...I didn't mean to stop working." She hastily placed the book on a shelf.

Scott's scarred brow furrowed. "Little one, I wilt not reprimand thee for working in a way which pleaseth thee. Thou mayst read any of my books."

"Thank you, my lord." Jana gazed up at Scott. "What is to be done when I finish here?"

Scott glanced around the room. "Perhaps thou shouldst fix the kitchen to thy liking. Then thou mayst go about thine own affairs." He disappeared into the bedroom.

The house still looked empty when Jana returned to the palace, carrying one of the poetry books.

Bronwyn stopped her in the hall, concern in her eyes. "Jana, how did you do?"

"I put away some things, but milord seems to have few possessions."

"Scott still has many things in Leahcim Tierrah. He's getting them tonight." Bronwyn glanced at the richly bound book in Jana's hand, not recognizing the binding. "Is that one of ours?"

"No, milady. My lord said I could read his books if I liked. May I go to my room now?"

"Certainly, dear. I'll be out with Garth." Bronwyn pulled her cape around her shoulders.

Settling back in her alcove, Bronwyn relaxed in the warm sunlight and steady breeze, her book momentarily forgotten on her lap. Closing her eyes, she listened to the chimes echoing from doorways all around the palace.

A sense of calm had settled again across Maradane and there was nothing so wonderful as the surrounding peace. The trees of the vast gardens sighed softly in the wind, and a toddler's giggles drifted from Richard's house as the man lay beneath a willow, playing with his son. Farther away other children laughed, chasing one another toward the forest, while close by one of the gardeners hummed off-key as he worked.

Hearing quick footsteps Bronwyn looked up and saw Jana scurrying toward Scott's house. The girl worked dutifully at Scott's, though still fearful.

Seeing her startled out of her wits by his mere presence, Scott attempted to turn his steps away from of her small form whenever possible. He kept to himself, knowing his towering size contributed to the disquiet of the girl who stood only five feet nine inches tall.

Bronwyn shook her head, once again contemplating sending Jana home. True, she would rather discover the problem and help correct it, but she also had vowed to keep Scott from feeling unwelcome. Already she saw him spending more and more time alone, and she refused to allow anyone or anything to hurt the fragile progress he had made in rejoining a world of mortal friends.

Perhaps she could get Jana interested in one of the many committees now forming to organize new athletic competitions.

When she had suggested, at the last council, some form of festive event for the people, those present had decided upon competitions to be held twelve times yearly in each sector. The winners would then go to the Planetary Championships thrice yearly, and hopefully one day a few could go to the Royal Davan Competitions, held for three months once every twenty years.

"Yes, that's what I'll do," Bronwyn said to herself, getting up and heading for Scott's home. "Since I'm designing the medals, perhaps Jana would like to help me." She was quite pleased with herself as she entered the small dwelling and found Jana dusting the bookshelves, a preoccupied look in her eyes. Studying the timid girl, Bronwyn hoped that by their working together she could discover Jana's problem.

Chapter Fourteen

The hill above the slave quarter was quiet, as quiet as it ever became on Shandal's worlds. Asher stretched out on the parched yellow grass and gazed absently at the low clouds above him.

He had left Donthas on the pretext of illness, at the moment unable to stomach another of the bloody ceremonies. Feigning ill health was always a ready excuse—in Shandal one went away and either recovered alone or died quietly without disrupting those nearby. Asher felt it was not a lie to say his insides were bothering him in order to escape his work for a day or so. Just until the festival was over.

The dense clouds and sluggish air effectively muffled the cheers and screams, squelching the constant drums to a sound somewhat like distant thunder.

Below him he heard small sounds escaping the slaves' squat dwellings—an occasional cry of a toddler, the low voice of a man—sounds betraying nothing of the lives of these people. Here was the single place on Shandal where one could find the gentler emotions. In these dark hovels souls loved and grieved, hoped and despaired. In the dim alleys caring words were exchanged, and life's scavenged necessities were shared as needed. Illness was at least attended to, if it could not be greatly helped. And here was moderate cleanliness. In this sprawling conglomeration of shacks was the essence of life that had been ground into oblivion in Shandal.

Asher scowled as his glance traversed the lines of torchlight surrounding the buildings. At first David had attempted to free the slaves, to move them off the planets so the enemy could be dealt with in their stronghold. But Shandal's course of defense had been to begin slaughtering the slaves at the first sign of Immortal or airship. Ships could not reach the planets undetected, and slaves could not be taken through the teleportal zone.

David had finally halted his efforts, perplexed. If he did nothing the slaves faced endless hardship and torture followed by sure death. If he acted, they faced a more swift death, after which other worlds would be ravaged to replace them. Either way the salves did not benefit, but through the second course others were drawn into the suffering.

Asher closed his eyes, stopping the thoughts coursing in circles through his mind. There was simply no safe way to move the slaves except through total defeat of their captors. However, it had occurred to him that during the course of the coming war, when the main armies were drawn far from their worlds, the slaves might be enabled to help themselves. David and he were already working out the first tentative details.

The Immortal returned his gaze to the clouds, envisioning the sky beyond their gloomy mass, and contemplated his plan. He had time to lay the foundation.

☆

The summer was passing quietly over the four palaces scattered across the large continent, and for once the rulers of Maradane felt events could be considered peaceful. Colonists were arriving regularly, after being cleared through their own home worlds, Leahcim Tierrah, and Bryce's physicals. They settled comfortably into life on the spacious world and Caleb established a date when the planet would be officially closed to colonists.

The first athletic competitions were met with rousing approval and began a tradition of colorful opening festivals and new schools of training. Bronwyn had enjoyed the time spent designing the medals and overseeing their manufacture with Jana's help. The girl had, over the passing months, finally settled into an outward calmness around Scott, but kept to herself and seemed unhappy. Bronwyn decided patience was the best route and no longer considered sending the girl home.

The young queen felt better after realizing that Scott was once more spending time with others, avoiding only Jana once in a while. The silver-haired giant was developing a deep friendship with Anders, who seemed to understand Scott's moods without any effort. At the moment everyone was pursuing some avenue of interest in the warm, lazy days, and at least some were progressing toward their goal.

Bronwyn had begun to abandon hope of finding any lost Adani volumes, for her long days of sorting through dusty books rewarded her with nothing. Then one day David gave her a gift while visiting his son.

"Milady, I only lately learned of thy search. Alas, I hold in trust all the volumes of Adane which survived the search by Shandal, and am bound to release them not until a day long into the future. But I have for thee a gift, written out of my youth." He placed a slender volume into her hands.

Opening the leather-bound cover Bronwyn read the first parchment leaf. "Why, you wrote this yourself! Surely you don't want to part with it." She offered it back to him.

David smiled tenderly and shook his head. "No, dear one, 'tis all in my heart. I believe there is something there to help thee. At any rate, 'tis a history of Adane few now know. Keep it for thine children."

"I shall treasure it." Bronwyn took the book to her garden alcove and began reading the filmy pages.

* As a young man, long before the founding of Leahcim

Tierrah, David traveled over many worlds. In his five hundredth year he discovered a planet then called Maara, later to be known as Adane. Its inhabitants were a gentle race, slender and pale, with a thirst for knowledge and a deeply rooted love of the wind.

Long ages past they were a mighty people, glorying in wild storms and shaping the surface of their world. Over the passing centuries their lives became ever more centered on the winds and they learned their every aspect. But by so tying themselves to the winds they began a slow evolution, until their very existence depended on the winds. Thus did David meet them, a fragile but long-lived race undergoing a final metamorphosis.

Queen among her people was Mara, versed in ages-old wind lore, pale and beautiful as sea foam. David loved her instantly and remained with the Maarai for long years, learning their history. At seven hundred he married Mara, who was many centuries older. Three hundred years passed, during which time they moved to the planet of Nahcym Tarah, the place of David's origin. Also during that time David began to see what was happening to the Maarai, but it was too late to prevent it. By the time Mara bore her fourth child, a daughter named after her, her people had faded almost to nothing. She herself grew steadily more frail, relying upon the winds for her life, and David realized she was slipping away from him. In her last days they journeyed home to Maara, where she and her people faded into the winds to be seen no more.

David could not bear to remain there, and so returned to his birthplace, but soon thereafter his daughter Mara felt compelled to return to Maara. It was now called Adane by the amber-eyed race that had settled there, and there Mara wed one of their people. Drawing upon the techniques of her mother, Mara led her new people to become the Wind Rulers, and over three hundred years later led a series of battles against Shandal's advancing armies.

Of David's other children, Vincent founded a line of kings in a sheltered valley of Mars; Stephen used his deep love of building to set up marble cities on a world he named Stefanovia; and Alaric married into the mystics of Stalasia. *

Bronwyn studied the last several pages of the journal, filled with entries of wind commands which David had heard Mara use. She was so engrossed in the exciting discovery that she did not hear the steps approaching her.

"That must be a wondrous story, you're so rapt," a deep voice boomed cheerfully.

"Huh?" Bronwyn looked up, startled. Then she jumped up. "Oh Anders, this is the most precious thing! David gave it to me, a history of Adane I never dreamt of, and it contains commands so much stronger than any I know. It will be such a help in the war." She hugged him tightly, sharing her joy. "And what can I do for you?"

"I'd say you've already made my day," Anders chuckled and kissed the top of her head. "I've come to collect my son."

"He's in the playroom with Garth." Bronwyn tucked the book under her arm and led Anders inside. Snowfire padded along beside him, a gentle beast who roamed the lands around the eastern palace and traveled many places with Anders. His figure was known by every citizen and he was loved by every child. Bronwyn paused to scratch his ears and was rewarded by a pleasured squint of his slanted eyes.

They were crossing the vast entrance hall when Anders spied a miserable form sitting in a shadowy corner. Kneeling down he brushed a tear from her cheek. "Little one, why do you cry so?"

"Oh, don't call me that!" Jana jumped up, but hurried to apologize. "Forgive me, milord. I'm just sad today." With that she fled out to the front lawns.

Anders turned to Bronwyn with a bewildered gesture, dismayed that he had added to her distress.

"It's not your fault, Anders," Bronwyn sighed. "I really should send her home, but I keep hoping to help her. No one seems to know what's wrong, and Bryce assures me she's not ill.

"Well, come get Jeremiah. I do love that name."

"It's the name of my friend, and who better could my son take after?" Anders followed her up the stairs, casting a parting glance at the forlorn figure beyond the open doors.

"Anders, what's wrong?" Bronwyn asked anxiously, alarmed at

how pale he had become. They were seated in the playroom with the small boys.

Jeremiah looked at his father's drawn face and said quickly, "Papa's seeing Stalasia."

"Oh," Bronwyn said weakly, relieved that it was not some illness. "He frightened me."

"He'll be okay." Jeremiah clambered onto his father's knee and held Anders' hand in his small ones. A moment later Anders shook his head violently, then smiled down at his son.

"Jeremiah, hurry and help Garth pick up the toys. Mama's waiting for us."

As the child slipped to the floor Anders turned to Bronwyn. "I'm sorry; this rarely happens away from home."

"There's nothing to apologize for, Anders. Have you learned anything important yet?"

"I'm not certain. Things have been coming out of order more, lately, and it's confusing. But just now I saw a book that must be important."

"A book?"

"Yes," Anders said thoughtfully. "William was hiding a very old book, far back in the library; I couldn't quite tell where. He was hiding it from Justin."

"It surely must have value, then. What more do you know of Justin?"

"Little that seems of use to us." Anders sighed, recalling the disjointed visions. "He was the son of a major Clan warlord and starved himself before going to Stalasia. William at first believed the boy had strayed through the portal on our world. It was only after Justin was married and had a child that William learned the truth. And then, it seems, he hid this book. Yes, there must be some importance to that book. I'll ask Scott if he knows anything of it."

"He's away with David right now, but I'll tell him to see you when he returns."

"Thank you. Well, we do have to go." Anders bent and swung Jeremiah up to a seat on his broad shoulders. "We'll see you at council, Bron."

Nodding, Bronwyn watched him leave the room, then went to look out the window. A brief scan of the lawns revealed Jana's small figure seated dejectedly beneath a tree, an open book ignored in her lap.

Several days later, Jana paused on her way out of the palace, hearing the clank of swords and a burst of deep laughter from the gardens to her left. Turning, she discovered Scott and Anders fencing on the broad paths, and enjoying some joke.

Warding off an overhead arc of Scott's huge blade, Anders chuckled, "You're safe with me, Scott, but I fear for you if you decapitate any more of Bronwyn's shrubs."

"I am saving the gardener a little work," Scott grunted, guarding against a thrust toward his upper sword arm. "I shouldst not do so if thee stopped hiding behind the roses."

Anders only laughed and dodged behind a dogwood tree. "This is an exercise in terrain and close foliage, you know."

"It is? I thought thou wert out for a dance with the windflowers." Scott jumped over a bed of the delicate blossoms and brought his sword deftly down on Anders' own weapon.

Jana backed into a shadowy alcove, fascinated. Anders was an equal match for Scott and they enjoyed these exercises. On this hot day they wore only shorts, leaving their skin free to breathe in the soft breezes. Anders' hair was held back by a leather band, but Scott's silver locks fell wildly over his forehead and shoulders.

As he moved the sun cast a sheen over his moist skin and Jana found her eyes following the lines of his body. His powerful legs bore few of the scars so prominent on his torso. His broad back was laced with faint lines from repeated sword thrusts, and his upper arms were badly marked.

It was these arms that held the girl's awed attention, for they were thicker than her own slender legs, and their power frightened her. She shrank back at the thought of the force behind his sword. Yet something in his hoarse laugh drew her eyes finally to his battered face as the men stopped to rest. In the warm light it seemed not so scarred, with perhaps a gentleness to his mouth and harshly set jaw.

During the lull Anders' own gaze traveled over the giant's torso, which dwarfed his own powerful body. "Scott, how have you ended up with such scars?"

"We heal swiftly, but repeated opening wilt leave marks. I have been struck thousands of times in those places." Scott pointed to his right side, where Anders and Jana both saw a jagged scar. "This is the only mark born of a single stroke. I wast on Shalahana and beset in the mountains by Shanda marauders. They used a weapon which opened barbs once inside the wound whilst a weighted wire encircled my body. My right arm wast pinned to my side and I hadst left my Star Holder at home, so I hadst to reach my house before I couldst find wire cutters and push the weapon out my back. It wast in there about four days."

Jana closed her eyes and turned away, her stomach churning at the thought of the agony he had suffered. He shouldn't have to suffer such pain... She hurried away, frightened anew by the strength that withstood such torment.

"Wait until you see this system working, Bron," Jericho said enthusiastically, reaching for the fried chicken Clare had just placed on the table. "The kids are really excited over it."

"More so than you?" Bronwyn laughed. "At least you were up to some good today while Scott was decimating our garden again."

"I expect the gardener to skewer him one of these days. Where is he, anyway?" Jericho's glanced flicked to Scott's empty chair.

"He said he wanted to think," Bronwyn replied, filling her cup with tea. "He's had something on his mind lately. Tell me about your new toy."

"It's a system of viewing screens." Jericho launched into a narrative of the work done since the newest school of technology opened shortly after Caleb's marriage. It had filled immediately with young people eager to study the tower structure and principles, as well as the working of delicate machinery. "The kids at first planned to design just a few large screens across the planet to broadcast performances of plays. But they've compacted the size so people can have them in their homes and view recorded programs as well, by satellite signal from the libraries."

"It sounds nice."

"Nice?" Jericho stared at her. "Nice! Bron, we can do endless things with this system. Aside from allowing more people to see plays and events, we can set up classes for people in isolated areas, like those living where it freezes so badly every year. And we'll have an instant way to communicate with the whole planet in an emergency."

Bronwyn smiled, amused. "I'm sure it will be wonderful, Jericho. You can tell Aric all about it tonight."

"Sheesh, I forgot." Jericho gulped down the last of his supper. "All right, I'm ready. All this fuss over an ice garden."

"But it's permanent, which makes it unique." Bronwyn ushered Jericho toward the door, eager to see the collection of ice sculptures Aric had ordered for an area north of his palace. "I'm taking Jana there tomorrow; she didn't feel well tonight. Maybe I can talk Scott into going too."

Scott gazed over the dark waters, seated on the beach not far from the western palace. It was very cool and breezy, the crashing waves sounding much like the winds that rampaged through the mountains of Shalahana. Blinking through strands of silver tousled by the wind, Scott realized he need not have hidden himself away for almost eighty years to be alone. He was alone wherever he went.

Oh, there were friends, yes, but they returned to their families at day's end while he returned to solitude. Even that was broken only by one who feared him beyond his gentle understanding. He did not hurt people, or ill treat them, yet they so often ran.

No, it was only she who ran. His house was empty so much of the time, without her quiet hum as she worked or her scurrying soft steps.

He tilted his head to the sky, as if he could see Shalahana from here. There was an empty house there also, and its lonely grave. For a time there had been song there, contented joy as young hands shaped gems into jewelry. For one hundred eighty days there had been light steps and the arms of one who closed out the rest of his life, and there was no loneliness.

His left hand touched the scar beneath his tunic. For four days he had staggered and crawled to his house, his entire body on fire with the wound as it fought to heal around the poisoned intrusion. All he had wanted to do was reach his home and the touch of gentle hands, his mind grasping in the agony for the short happiness that had ended so abruptly. He had cared for nothing but reaching the one who could chase away his inner pain.

Finally he had reached the empty house, dark and cold with the wind blowing through open windows, and he stumbled over Tanya's grave marker. His head reeling, he had fumbled to cut the wire that bit so deeply into his arm and midsection. His right hand trembling violently, he had used his left to slam a hammer against the weapon's shaft, ripping open his back with a terrible scream. Finally free of the tormenting metal, he had crawled into a black corner and tried to die.

Hearing a sharp pop, Scott realized he had crushed a large shell in one hand. He dropped the pieces and began picking slivers out of his bloody palm. Mortals did not realize that those many years had passed like a day for him, an agonizing day beginning and ending with death. For his father had come to him as he lay in that corner and taken him to Richard, to see his friend broken by the loss of his own wife. So had he come to Maradane.

The wind carried a soft sob to his ears. Turning, he saw a small figure huddled a short distance from him. The moonlight reflected softly on her auburn hair as she sat with her knees drawn up, face buried in her skirts. She was a silent picture except when the undecided wind shifted in his direction and he could hear her crying.

Getting to his feet, Scott cursed his life and everything about it. Hesitating, he wanted to comfort her, stop the tears, for she should have only joy. She was small and vulnerable, unaware how someone ached to protect her, so unlike Tanya had been. This little one should have fear of nothing, yet to guard her from fear he must guard her from himself. He must put distance between them, lest he frighten her more. Wanting to stop her tears, he knew she would shrink from the touch of his big hand.

For a time he had forgotten his need to be needed, to protect and support, for there had been no one to need him. He was a good protector, because of the strength of his hands and his heart. But it now seemed his very strength secluded him. For a long time he looked at Jana, then sadly turned away.

He forced his steps away from her, down the beach in the direction of his silent home.

One early winter afternoon found Jana pulling a light cape over her head against the rain as she hurried to Scott's house. Dodging through the door, she said breathlessly, "I'm sorry I'm late, my lord. Garth was ill this morning."

"Yea, I know." Scott closed the book he had been reading, looking sadly at the girl. "I prefer to eat here this evening, little one. If thou hast not time to cook I wish to know now."

"I have time, my lord." Jana busied herself dusting the crowded bookshelves, her favorite spot, not looking at Scott. "Milady Bronwyn says I am to do whatever is needed."

Scott put aside the book as he stood, a sharp edge touching his voice. "Didst Bronwyn send thee e'en though thee wished not to work here?"

"Oh no, my lord, she only asked me to do so. I don't mind the extra work." Jana clutched the dust rag with both hands, staring up at Scott with wide violet eyes. A lock of auburn hair trailed across one cheek as she asked in a small voice, "Milord, may I borrow another book?"

"Of course, any ye wish. Thy work wilt be light o'er the next days. Tonight I return to my father's court for some time." Scott turned to reach for his cape, then noticed a questioning look on the girl's face. "Dost thou wish something?"

Hesitating, Jana glanced at a portrait done in pastel shades. "I only wondered who the girl is. You have so many pictures of her, and she is so lovely."

Scott's expression darkened and there was pain in his voice, startling Jana. "She wast my wife Tanya. She died many years ago...I loved her very much." He threw the cape over one shoulder and left the house.

Still grasping the dust rag, Jana stared after him, shocked that he had ever loved someone. She looked around the room at the paintings and books still in startling conflict with his armor and weapons. Then she looked out the window and saw Scott standing beside a fountain, staring miserably at the sky.

"Oh, no." Stuffing the cloth into her apron pocket she ran back to the palace and her room.

As Jana served supper that evening Bronwyn asked where Scott was.

"My lord ate at home, milady. He wished to leave early." Jana put a platter of meat on the table, her eyes downcast.

"Leave?" Bronwyn's face was blank. "Where did he go?"

"He said only that he'd be at his father's court for several days, milady." Jana retreated to the kitchen.

"Why didn't he say anything? Richard, do you know about this?"

Richard shook his blond head, confused. "Scott said nothing to me. David ne'er holds court this time of year—in fact he arrived here only this morning to confer with Caleb, and Scott knew that."

Glancing from Bronwyn to the Immortal, Jericho said, "Scott's been bothered by something of late, upset quite deeply. I've noticed it particularly as we work at the forge. He hammers the armor as if he wants to kill it."

"I must go to Leahcim Tierrah." Richard pushed his chair away from the table. "Please excuse me."

Bronwyn finished her meal in silence. When Jericho went to work in his study she wandered out to the gardens. The soft fragrance of the flowers buoyed her spirits, but the worry was renewed when she found Jana seated in a secluded corner.

Bronwyn sat next to the girl, who leaned against a bench with her chin on her knees. "Jana, dear, please tell me what's troubling you. I'd like to help, and not send you home."

"It would be better if I went home so I won't hurt anyone," Jana mumbled into her clasped hands. "I am a thoughtless fool."

The young queen studied the girl, her confusion growing. "Between you and Scott I'll be a nervous wreck. If he withdraws again because of some hurt...and I do so hate to see you troubled. Jana, I'm sure you've hurt no one..."

"I saw it in his eyes," Jana insisted bitterly. "I have been unfeeling and stupid, just because he is big and scarred; he's so terribly big! And his voice is quite harsh, though I've heard it gentle as the wind. I was afraid of him because I didn't think, and he was so hurt when I asked who the girl in the painting was..."

Jana's words trailed away, not directed at Bronwyn. She got up to run toward the palace, crying, "I must go home."

Bronwyn returned to the palace at a slower pace, entering the quiet library and staring into the empty fireplace. "How little I guessed."

Returning late the next afternoon, Richard found Bronwyn seated in the study, staring into the distance. He joined her, saying quietly, "I know now what troubles Scott."

Bronwyn continued gazing out the window, watching Jana trudge down the path to Scott's home one last time before returning to her parents. "It's amazing how one forgets things once they are past. I couldn't see past my joy in Jericho to discover why Jana behaved so strangely. I understand why she loves him, but I wish she had come to me."

Richard took this in quietly, sorting it out. "She is afraid of Scott, is she not?"

"She was, but I think no longer." Bronwyn finally turned to face him. "She feared his size, for she is smaller than most. And he is very scarred."

"Scott is not ugly, for all his scars, my lady."

"Don't take offense, Richard." Bronwyn smiled at his quick defense. "He is very handsome in his way. No, it's only that he can look so menacing. Jana wishes to return home as soon as I assign another girl to her duties."

Richard again took this in silence, but his face brightened. "I must go speak with Scott; he returned with me. We shalt see thee for supper."

Bronwyn watched him go, then realized irritably that he had not told her what troubled Scott.

Jana was replacing a book on a high shelf when the stepladder wobbled and she lost her balance. Grabbing a shelf to steady herself, she sent a delicate mosaic portrait of Tanya crashing to the floor.

Hearing the crash, Scott appeared in the doorway of his bedroom. Seeing the tiny tiles scattered across the floor he turned his gaze to the girl.

"I'm sorry!" Jana stared at the ruin, one hand over her mouth. Dropping her hand to her side, she said, "I slipped. I didn't mean to break it."

Scott started to speak, but Jana darted through the door, disappearing into the shadows of the forest.

Chapter Fifteen

"Jana! Little one, come back." Scott started after her, but ran into Richard just beyond the door.

Richard grabbed his arm. "What is happening?"

"She broke my mosaic—'twas an accident." Scott looked anxiously toward the forest. "Please go after her, she wilt only run from me."

"No, Scott, thou must go. Quickly, 'ere she gets lost." Richard gave his towering friend a commanding shove.

Scott's easy lope covered the ground quickly and soon he was far into the forest. "Jana, answer me!" He ran on, then stumbled to a halt beside the girl, who had fallen over a log.

"I hurt my leg," she said tearfully. "Please, my lord, I didn't mean to break your picture. I'm going home soon, and won't hurt you any more." She turned her gaze to her leg.

Scott knelt, but hesitated at her words. "Home?"

Jana nodded slowly. "I should go where I may learn to be less selfish, and to see beyond my own feelings."

"Do not cry, little one." He gently checked to see that no bones were broken as she looked timidly at his unshaven face. "'Tis only a sprain, made well with rest."

Scott then sat back on the ground, rubbing the back of his neck. "I wish thou hadst not run."

"Please forgive me, my lord. I just didn't understand, not at all." Jana forced herself to face him as she rubbed her aching leg.

"What am I to do with thee?" Scott studied her for a long moment, then reached out to wipe the tears from her face. "I am not thy lord, little one. My name is Scott. And I canst forgive any small hurt if thou wilt promise one thing."

Jana gazed timidly at him. "What may I do?"

"Thou mayst become my wife."

She ceased rubbing her leg, staring at him, and murmured, "Your wife?"

Scott's gaze fell to the ground as he shifted to his knees. "I didst not think thee wished it so—I wilt take thee home, little one." He bent to lift her into his arms.

She stopped him with a small hand on his shoulder. "Please, wait. You...just surprised me." Hardly daring, she smiled hesitantly. "I was so frightened I couldn't speak, yet I've loved you long. I could never be happier than to be your wife, my lord Scott."

A slow smile spread over his rugged face, almost of disbelief, as he smoothed a strand of hair back from her tearstained face. "Thou canst not know how I love thee, little one. My father shalt say the joining words." He kissed her gently as he cradled her in his arms.

A gentle breeze ruffled the brilliant blossoms of the gardens as guests gathered at the western palace.

Rushing Garth back to his room, Bronwyn scolded him furiously for covering his new tunic with mud from a flower bed.

In the palace library, Scott nervously adjusted the collar of his own tunic, loosening it a little as he turned to Jericho. "Do I look well?"

"You look very handsome, Scott. Hurry now, all is ready." Jericho handed Scott his jeweled scabbard.

The couple soon stood before David, Jana's auburn hair curling about her face and resting lightly against the gold of her gown. Scott took her hand in his as David spoke the simple words of an Immortal wedding, binding the two into one.

Jericho and Bronwyn had ordered a lavish feast and the garden was dotted with food-laden tables. As the ruling families gathered for conversation their children began a game of chase through the tables and chairs.

Anders bent laughingly to scoop up his son, who had sprawled headlong at his feet. "Jeremiah, have you forgotten how to walk?"

"No, Papa. I tripped over your big foot." The child angrily brushed a persistent lock of honey-brown hair out of his grey eyes. "Papa, when may I use a sword like yours? May I learn soon?"

Anders smiled fondly. "Your mother has you for one more year, my son. Then I shall instruct you in weaponry."

"I don't want to wait, Papa. Mama makes me learn court manners and things I don't like. I want to learn to fight like you. You fight better than anyone else ever." He looked adoringly at his father.

Anders tousled Jeremiah's thick hair. "Jeremiah, what your mother teaches you is terribly important, and you must learn it well to be a good king. You'll find fighting is not what you think. Too soon you will have to fight. Go on now and play while you may." Kissing the boy's head he set him on his feet. Jeremiah scampered back to his friends.

"He will be a fine man, Anders, if he grows like you," Bronwyn said softly. "He admires you so."

"He's my joy, pure and simple. I wish he could grow without going through war." He sighed resignedly. So powerful a man at eight feet, an excellent warrior in combat, Anders lived only for peace. Working now to build the machines of war, he prayed they need never be used.

"You mustn't be sad, Anders." Bronwyn tried to comfort him. "You will see peace. I believe Scott when he says most of our lives will be lived in peace."

"I pray so. I don't care so much for myself, but worry for my family. Shara has lost too much already to war." Anders thought of his daughter, a laughing child with golden curls whose life ended with Stalasia's. "I don't wish her to suffer thus again."

"She will be fine, as will we all," Aric said firmly. "Anders, that belief is all we have to cling to. I can't be like you, putting so much heart into my work, for I pray it will be needless."

"I fear no such miracle will come, Aric, so I must help assure the future Gray has seen. Though I cannot bear killing, I must see those I love safe."

Aric stared at his feet, vowing to pour more effort into his work as Bronwyn ordered an end to talk of war.

The day passed all too quickly and people began heading home. Anders hoisted his son up to his shoulders and put his arm around Shara. "It was a lovely day, Bronwyn, one of too few. Jericho, I'll see you tomorrow...Jeremiah, stop pulling my hair." He reached up a big, callused hand to grab his son's fist. "Keep that up and I'll be Maradane's first bald king."

"Nonsense," Bryce said, approaching with Drahcir on one arm. "You have more than your share of hair anyway." He pushed his own damp hair off his forehead. "It's getting humid."

"It will storm before long," Bronwyn agreed, turning to say good-bye to Shonnie.

Scott and Jana thanked Jericho and Bronwyn for the feast, then retired to their small home. Bronwyn seated herself on a marble bench to watch the purple sunset encircling the horizon.

"Anders, would you like some hot cocoa?" Shara peered around the half open door of the library. "Whatever are you doing in here?"

"Trying to organize this damnable journal," Anders said in frustration. "And yes, I'd love that cocoa. Bring it and we'll go over this together."

Shara returned soon with a tray of cocoa and confections. "I thought this would be a nice way to end the day," she said, settling next to her husband on the large pillows before the fireplace.

"It was a very pleasant day," Anders agreed. "I'm happy to see Scott and Jana together. It's a shame he didn't speak up sooner, instead of working himself into such a depression."

"Well, you certainly are the authority on keeping everything in the open." Shara smiled over the rim of her cocoa mug.

"Point taken, my love." Anders laughed ruefully. "That will never happen again. Here, let us try to put these entries into order." He pulled Shara close and opened the book across their laps. ***

*** Many years passed before William discovered the treachery of his adopted son. Justin was a wonderful son, quiet and loving, and eager to learn the ways of his new world. William taught Justin to work in the library and soon set him to work as his assistant. When Justin was fifteen he married Marissa, and soon after that their son Andrew was born.

From then on Justin began to disappear for short periods, telling his wife and adopted father that he liked to explore the three ruined cities beyond Shalanar. He was twenty before William stumbled upon a notebook of information copied from William's desk, notes concerning David's plans against Shandal.

It was at this time that William came across the ancient book in a storage room of the library. He hid it in a far recess of the libraries, telling no one what it contained. And he tried to tear Justin away from his treacherous mission. ***

*** Anders shook his head, disappointed. "Shara, I don't see where this is leading. It seems of no value to know this history."

"But there is a value to it. And I'm certain it is centered on that book." Shara kissed his cheek. "Be patient, Anders. In time it will become clear, in time for it to help us."

"I pray so. But now it's late. Tomorrow will be busy." Shading the light beside them, Anders drew Shara into his arms.

That evening in the northern sector Aric experienced another oddity of the winds peculiar to Maradane. The night was so beautiful that Shonnie had allowed Aarek to stay up late and play in the moonlit gardens. Seated at his desk in the library Aric watched the fur-bundled youngster romp across benches and leap into deep snowdrifts. He smiled, for the boy had inherited his love of the cold.

Aarek was gazing intently at the sparkling surface of one drift when a fine powdering of snow puffed upward across his face. Startled, he spun around, looking for the one who had thrown the snow. Several more tiny clouds of snow pelted him from different directions, then retreated. Aarek stared after them, wide eyed, then laughed and chased after the intermittent puffs.

As Aric watched in amazement the small boy was led a merry chase around the nearby area, ever pursuing the clouds of sparkling crystals. Then Shonnie called her son in for bed and the gusts of wind died abruptly, the snow falling in a disappointed shower to the frozen ground.

"I'll be," Aric breathed softly, sorry to see the spell broken. Shaking his head wonderingly, Aric filed the incident mentally to relay to Jericho. There was something going on with the winds beyond their understanding and they accepted it as natural to their world. But no one had ever expected the winds to actually play with their children.

Pausing to add another log to the blazing fire, Aric returned to his study of his history books. He found himself reading less often now for he spent more time with the war preparations and less at leisure. Propping the book on the desk, he leaned back in the chair.

* Shandal was the name of a small planet inhabited by a dark and angry people. During the first centuries of the Immortals a series of phenomena took place, creating the portals to other parts of the universe and to other places and times. By some fluke the planet Shandal became encircled by numerous portals.

Whether fleeing punishment in their own realms or simply seeking new places to wreak havoc, a stream of evils poured onto the planet. Coalescing into a driving force, the newcomers gathered the swarthy Shanda into an army for pillage and plunder. Up until then Shandal's populous was divided into warring clans attacking one another for gain, but their efforts had left little to gain anywhere on the planet. Had the convergence of stronger powers not happened, Shandal would have died away quietly with no harm to anyone else.

The most powerful newcomer became an overlord who drew several clans into one to create the Clan of the Snake, worshipping the giant reptiles of his new home world. At first seeking total world conquest, the Clan Overlord became aware of another voyager from beyond the portals who carried the knowledge of space travel. By uniting the two clans they first overpowered the rest of the world, then settled down to plan raids on any nearby worlds offering suitable spoils.

Attacking beneath a herald of smoky banners, Shandal's armies captured slaves and returned home, using the slaves to swell a suicide rank for total conquest of the raided worlds. Soon four planets nestled under the black flag of Shandal and the Clan of the Snake increased in power.

At the end of eight centuries, Shandal held sway over seven planets, slowly spreading as it sought increasing slaves and wealth. The clan Overlord presided over feuds for gain and arena sport for entertainment. Unruly slaves were turned into gladiators to be pitted against clan warriors and the great snakes. Vast domed cities, choked in smoky darkness and adorned with symbols of fire and torture, housed a well-ordered caste system. To be non-clan was little better than slavery. Slaves provided all labor and the majority of the entertainment. The driving force behind all life was the push for expansion and the gain of power.

In 1350 the Clan Overlord launched an attack on Adane that led to three hundred years of vicious warfare against the Wind Rulers. Mara's people would not carry the attack away from Adane, for they sought only to defend their world. But Shandal's leaders grew livid at this impregnable defense and forsook all other battles in their effort to destroy Adane. In 1650 Mara so effectively beat back the heaviest attack that Shandal gave up and spent the next seven centuries licking its wounds and regaining its strength with only minor sorties for slaves and plunder. They were unaware that, also in 1650, Mara's people withdrew from the mainstream and so deprived Adane of its wind defense.

By 2307 Shandal was once more on the rise, bursting forth to capture two more planets and wreak havoc throughout the galaxy. In desperation Stalasia called on David for help and a new force entered the fray. With the founding of the Davan Empire in 2312 the Overlord was faced with an enviable threat. David sought not to battle but to lure the people of Shandal to better lives, a tactic so underhanded in Shandal's view that the Overlord was at first stunned out of defense.

The Clan Overlord succeeded in diverting his people from heeding David, but was still faced with the problem of annihilating the Immortals—they would not die. Then, in 2313, the Clan began its attacks with the snakes. The Immortals might not die, but they could be hurt. They loved the mortals they protected, and these people Shandal could indeed kill. The Clan reveled in the century of destruction that followed. But the two sides had by then begun down the road to a stalemate. Each empire hurt the other, but total conquest seemed unattainable.

In 3800 Shandal began turning the remainder of its home galaxy against David. Adane was already rebelling in favor of war, and many other planets swayed easily. For a time David backed off, until the wars prior to Maradane's settlement. By then the majority of the stolen worlds were ready to return to him. This time Shandal backed away, but only long enough to prepare a new attack. *

Aric yawned sleepily. It occurred to him that an outside observer would see both sides as equally convinced of their way as right. Of course he knew Shandal was evil. But the people of Shandal believed that David's realm was the evil. Each side loathed the lifestyle of the other and sought its end. Perhaps the deciding factor was that David would readily accept Shandal into the Empire if it would conform to his laws, the laws of any decent race, while Shandal would rest only when the Davan Empire was dust. The true right must therefore lie with the side offering mercy, and that side was David's.

Hearing Shonnie call softly to him, Aric left the darkened room for the night.

Chrys wandered the passages of the palace at Donthas, gazing intently at his feet as he moved. He saw only the spidery lines of cracked tiles vanishing beneath his stride, and in truth had little need to see much more. Everyone seeing him made wide berth, cringing out of the path of the mightiest Seer in the realm. Anyone failing to do so would receive a painful flailing.

The fingers of his right hand toyed with his ruby as he passed wraith-like through the empty corridors. The silence did not unsettle him because he understood it, but something was awry or there would be no silence. If the Beaters of the Drum had fallen drunk during the last Feast of Offerings he would add their skulls to his collection.

Entering the antechamber of the Great Altar he paused, still not looking up, to take stock of the area. The Beaters were indeed drunk, splayed sloppily across the mossy benches on either side of the room. Their contented snoring matched that of the rest of Donthas' citizenry, their flasks of bloodfire toppled at their sides, empty. The smell of the burning liquid that drove the celebrants to frenzy filled the chamber like a cloying mist. Where had they acquired such a quantity?

Chrys shrugged his slight shoulders; he would have them dealt with later. Since the entire city was knocked out by the bloodfire the momentary silence did not matter.

Entering the Great Altar Chrys did look up at last, realizing where the Beaters had gotten their drink. An annoyed smile tugged at his lips as his dark eyes took in the severed pieces of the lesser snakes scattered across the stained floor. The altar itself was strewn with the bloody pieces, and the ceremonial axe lay across the marble surface, its blade cracked in half.

"Ah, you're a clever one, Immortal," Chrys rasped. "Have your fun. One of these days I'll learn who you are, and we shall see how well you bear torture."

Continuing through the humid room, Chrys pushed aside a

hidden door behind the altar and slipped into the adjoining room. Kneeling in the darkness, Chrys bowed his head in concentration for several moments before slipping his ruby into its niche in the wall beside him.

The window before him awoke to murky life, the flickering torchlight beyond the pane playing across a cowled figure staring toward the window. From the darkness of the hood a voice demanded, "What is your report, Chrys?"

"Something is off balance, my great lord," Chrys answered softly. "Our attempts on Maradane always fall short. Since our spies were discovered I cannot get another past the guards David established. Something interferes with my Sight of the planet."

The cowled figure nodded. "Your Sight is being blocked. Rely on the reports from David's court for the moment. What of my recent emissaries?"

Chrys smiled to himself. "The damage done by Devon's capture will soon be mended. I sent the emissaries directly to two of David's own subjects, two who are susceptible to your enticements. No physical will reveal them, and when these men go to Maradane, the wind witch will die."

"Excellent." The voice paused tentatively, then demanded harshly, "Why do I sense silence?"

"The Beaters are drunk, my lord," Chrys replied. "But so is everyone else. I'll have the drums going before they wake."

"See that you do, or burn again." The voice chuckled ominously. "There's so little left of you to burn, Chrys, you who were once as large as David himself. See that my enemies do not make their whisperings heard beneath the silence. They have a particular interest in your universe, which is my only reason for creating your worthless world."

"Yes, lord." Chrys bowed his head as the image faded. Retrieving his jewel he hurried to summon his private guard to the antechamber.

"Clean up the Great Altar before some imbecile wanders in and raises a cry, and replace those stinking snakes with new ones. Get two new Beaters in here at once. And speak to no one of this."

"Yes, Seer." The men bowed and hurried to their work.

Chrys went on his way, his attention riveted once more to his feet. He ignored the obeisance commanded by the sacrificial pools lining the entryway path, ignored the stern rule of offering some living blood in each passage. By the time he reached his rooms the drums were once more filling the air with their quiet pulsing.

Slipping into his tropical room, Chrys huddled into his fireside chair and drank deeply of hot tea laced with bloodfire leaves. He had long ago passed the stage of being susceptible to intoxication. He used the bloodfire mixture to warm him from within, chasing away the cold instilled by his master.

Staring into the flames, he envisioned a wall of pure white fire engulfing his body. His lord was right. Three times had he failed in a mission and three times the freezing flames had devoured part of his being. Once more and he was a walking skeleton.

He listened to the drums with a self-satisfied smile. His lord's enemies would not whisper this night. Centuries ago the drums had started their noise and it continued without break, broadcast to every portion of each world. The insidious voices of beings who traversed space in the blink of an eye were drowned out on the worlds of Shandal, leaving these blind fools to be led in the cause of the lords from beyond the dark portal.

Chrys settled back in his chair, caressing his ruby and cherishing the realization that the Immortal king knew nothing of the existence of his great lord. Shandal would leave Maradane to its short peace. Let them enjoy what time remained. Soon Chrys would move to a different realm entirely, a realm beyond his master's door, leaving this one blackened in his wake.

Chapter Sixteen

In the eighth year of Maradane's new culture, Jana gave birth to a son whom she and Scott named Joachim. When he was three months old the Donnyas held a christening feast in their gardens.

"Anders, have you learned anything more of late?" Jericho asked. The four families were seated around a table sheltered from the setting sun by a spreading tree.

"No," Anders said in a discouraged tone. "The visions get ever farther apart and seem to offer nothing new. At least nothing my dense mind can comprehend."

"Anders, you know the Sight Link is a very unruly gift," Shara scolded tenderly. "Members of our race often went years between visions, but in the end it all comes together."

"I suppose so." Anders' expression brightened. "At least perhaps if the visions remain vague it means the war is yet distant...if it is the war I am to help with."

Reaching for a tray of tiny cakes to pass around, Bronwyn said, "Can we please just let the war be for today? This is a celebration of life."

"Indeed it is." Bryce refilled his mug of ale. "And look at Scott."

The giant approached them, one hand on Jana's shoulder and the other arm cradling the tiny baby. Taking a seat on a bench beside the table, Scott gazed down at his son with a wondering joy.

Leaning into his embrace, Jana laughed softly. "Scott, will you always stare at him so?"

"But he is so tiny!" Scott said.

"David says you were once this small, impossible as it seems now. Joachim will one day be a big oaf like his father."

"Little one, thee hurt me deeply." Scott laughingly bent to kiss his wife's forehead, then stroked Joachim's fine auburn hair. "Small or not, he is a fine Immortal."

Hearing a faint hint of relief in Scott's husky voice, Aric asked, "How could he not be?"

"We art ne'er sure, in a mixed marriage, until the child is born," Scott replied. "Often the children art mortal, or half-Immortal. Our life span doth not always carry through."

"And how do you tell, then?" Aric's interest grew.

"'Tis a thing we feel. I canst not explain it, for 'tis not a visible thing. But we hold the babe and we know from the first touch." He settled the baby on his lap, wrapping a light blanket around Joachim's chubby legs.

"You know, Scott, I've been studying the history books your father sent and have learned quite a lot. But nowhere does it speak of the origins of the Immortals. Surely there must be something to tell." Aric reached for another of the small spicy cakes.

"Not a great deal, really," Scott answered obligingly. "'Twas obviously decided long ago that my race wast needed, so we art here."

"Decided? Who decided?"

"All creation is from God, thou knowest that, Aric." Scott paused thoughtfully, looking down at his son. "Perhaps I canst give more insight for thee.

"There exists a form of life beyond our seeing, a race of beings known to my race as the Gabrellans, or the Wise Ones. They live as more than Immortals yet less than angels, and they traverse not just our realm but the entire universe, e'en beyond the boundaries enclosing us. 'Tis upon them that we call for guidance when our own resources fail. And 'tis from them that we derive our being." Scott pushed his windblown hair back from his pale eyes, glancing toward the sky.

"Our years art measured from the first day of life of the firstborn, the day that one Gabrellan took form as Richard. Soon after, others of our race came to form, and then more wert born to us. Yet each of us is a Gabrellan soul, and to the Gabrellan form we wilt return when time as we know it hath ended. Until that time we bear the burdens necessary to guide our realm, burdens no mortal couldst manage for they span centuries at a pace. We wert given life to serve."

"I never realized any of this," Aric said, wishing he had a tablet to take notes. He would have to write down what he could remember later. "And these Gabrellans, do they decide who has certain powers, like you or Gray?"

"Yea, when a necessity is known to be arising, an Immortal to handle it is born. There art many Healers and many psychics. Yet there is only one Gray, for he alone is needed to do the work given into his hands. And then there is Chuck—"

"Chuck?" Jericho broke in. "What an odd name. Who is he?"

"'Tis rather a funny name," Scott agreed, laughing. "Actually his name is Uriel and he hates it. As a child he returned from a portal to some future time demanding to be called Chuck, a name he hadst heard there.

"But to explain," he continued, "thee all know of the existence of the portals. Portal travel is dangerous at best and best left alone, but there art also certain energy flows surrounding them that need periodic siphoning. The portals wert created out of the same energies which support the Immortal travel zone, because of some imbalance we have not been able to pinpoint. We believe it hath to do with Shandal's entry into our realm." He bounced his sandaled feet lightly, seeing Joachim smile at the motion.

"O'er periods of decades the portals build an unequal pressure on one side of the door, and this must be siphoned away before it causes the door to collapse. It is easily done for the build-up is slow and the portals art few enough to allow a person to maintain them with no danger. This job falls to Chuck—he alone traverses the portals with impunity. He alone wilt e'er have this task, and he is an example of an Immortal born to a certain need."

"That's fascinating," Prudence said. "Can the Gabrellans foresee the future?"

"Not precisely. They see, rather, possibilities, and prepare for them. They studied the portals and so understood the need for Chuck's power. They perhaps foresee brief instances as doth Shara and offer help to smooth the way. But things shift so constantly they canst not with surety tell of events years hence, and rely on guidance from e'en higher powers in those instances. They passed the gift of prescience to Gray."

"Oh." Prudence was disappointed. "Do they ever take forms other than Immortals?"

"Yea, they have been known to do so. In instances of grave danger needing immediate support the Gabrellans mayst step in. Perhaps 'tis a world of people of small stature, or located in another part of the universe. Unless it be through a portal we of David's realm canst not pass beyond the natural barriers around our universe."

Bronwyn asked simply, "Why don't they take care of everything themselves, then, if they're so powerful? Wouldn't it be easier than going through your people, easier to just come and make the enemy obey them?"

Scott laughed affectionately, shaking his shaggy head. "Bronwyn, the Gabrellans provide assistance where it is requested, and cannot force mortals to do things against their will. And I believe they already care for everything, by creating and maintaining my race. Gabrellans become Immortals in order to assist the mortals who cry for help."

Bronwyn considered the explanation, then smiled. "What of your own people? Do you ever go to worlds to study, aside from David's spies?"

"Yea, we have done so on worlds considering joining us. 'Tis to gather information, to learn about the people."

"Someone really should record all this," Aric said hopefully. "It is, after all, part of the history of the realm."

"Thou art right," Scott agreed with a thoughtful nod. "I must speak with David about it. I suppose 'twas ne'er recorded because all my people know it. Our concern lies more with preserving histories of mortal worlds and events since the founding of the Empire."

Jana leaned over to take the baby. "Bronwyn, thank you so much for the gathering. It was a lovely day. But now it's time for Joachim's supper and then bed."

"I enjoyed putting it together," Bronwyn assured her happily. "I'm going to the peninsula on the Gulf of Stalasia tomorrow to practice those commands some more. Would you like to bring Joachim and join me?"

"I'd love to. I'll see you then." Jana turned away toward her home.

"Hath the book been of help, Bronwyn?" Scott asked.

"Oh yes, very much." Bronwyn motioned to one of the servants to begin gathering the dishes from the tables. "It's taken me quite a while to understand certain words or phrases, the language is so old. And then I try to go to untrodden places since I'm apt to call up sudden storms. But it's very exciting and I believe the commands will help greatly in battle."

"Excellent. I shalt tell David when next I see him."

"I'm sorry he and Leah couldn't come today. But we'll have them over to dinner next time they're here."

David and his wife had become frequent visitors to the western palace, to see their son, but at the moment were involved in an emergency council with Gray.

Scott frowned deeply. "They sent their regrets. From what I wast told Gray hath foreseen dire consequences for Aubrey shouldst that world take part in the war. David insists that the Elves remain on their world to guard their treasured places, yet Othniel and Thais want to send their best archers to the war."

Anders sighed. "Thais is even more stubborn than her husband. But we can do battle without them, whereas Aubrey cannot be replaced."

"That is precisely what my mother is trying to drill into Thais' head. That is why she asked Richard to be there, hoping his closeness to the Elves wouldst force Thais to listen." Scott glanced down at a wooden rattle in his hand. "Well, it doth grow late. I thank thee again, Bronwyn, for the dinner. I shouldst return this home—'tis Joachim's favorite toy."

"Have a good evening, Scott." Bronwyn turned to see her other guests on their way, then settled in her alcove with her small book.

Jericho was returning from the forge much later that evening, having gone to check on an incoming metal shipment, when he heard the terrified scream of a child. Looking around in the growing twilight, he finally spotted the source of the cry.

During the change of the guard a child barely older than Garth had used his staff to perch himself atop the wind tower. Somehow he had lost both his staff and his balance and was now clinging with one hand to the upper guard rail.

Jericho ran toward the tower, where the guards were already going up by both wind and access ladder. Before any were near enough, the boy lost his grip and plunged downward.

Staffs were for transportation, not quick maneuvering. Though the guards tried, they could not move swiftly enough to catch the child as he fell.

Trying desperately to position himself beneath the child, calling to one guard to grab the other end of his cape to form a net, Jericho suddenly heard the scream turn to laughter.

Looking up, he saw the boy wafting to the ground as if he were a feather on the wind, surrounded by a flurry of what Bronwyn had come to call wind sparkles. Before the men's astonished eyes the boy was plopped into the cape with a soft motion and his hair caressed lightly by the parting breeze.

Wavering between unspeakable relief and total rage, Jericho finally sputtered, "Where is your safety chain?"

The boy hung his head sheepishly, knowing full well he should not have loosened the chain that secured all children's staffs to their waists during use. "I wanted to fly without it, milord."

Finally feeling his racing heart slowing, Jericho softened his expression. "Perhaps now you see why that is not allowed. Turn in your staff for six months."

The boy nodded tearfully, handing over the slender staff which one of the guards had retrieved. Grounding was the penalty for all misuse of wind control, the worst punishment possible for the carefree children.

"Go home to bed now, young man. This will be kept safely for you." Jericho took the staff and tousled the boy's hair before motioning a guard to escort him home. He then returned to the palace, more than ready to relax.

"You'd better sit near that overhang, Jana." Bronwyn pointed to a jutting cliff a short distance up the hillside. "I'm never certain what will happen, but the winds won't harm anyone carrying a staff. If a storm comes up you can get under the cliff for shelter until I stop it."

Nodding, Jana carried Joachim and her carryall up the gentle slope as Bronwyn walked several paces away from their landing spot. Spreading a quilt just beyond the entrance to a small grotto, Jana settled Joachim into her lap and her wind staff at her side.

Since receiving the book, Bronwyn had devoted her time to understanding the ancient language of Mara's people. It was one step away from the language of the Wind Rulers, and, while many words were familiar, Bronwyn had to practice extensively to command proper pronunciation of the more remote phrases.

Once that was accomplished she began a very cautious period of testing each phrase and recording whatever resulted. This was a long, sometimes tedious process as she committed each phrase and result to memory. After that she began excursions to seldom visited areas of Maradane to use the commands one by one until she should eventually control them all. She discovered that the main effect could be varied by placing different emphasis upon different words, thus creating countless results from the main body of twenty phrases.

None compared to the force of those used by Mara's daughter against Shandal, but they were strong enough to confuse and momentarily scatter an enemy battalion. One or two would perhaps prove forceful enough to destroy a base camp if Bronwyn could find the proper focus.

Seeing Jana settled beneath the cliff, Bronwyn raised her arms, outspread, grasping the polished staff in her right hand. Closing her eyes, she intoned softly:

"*Astonal marat norbec cai.*"

There was a deep rumbling far overhead followed by a swirl of wind through the waving grasses. After a twittering sound strangely like laughter, the wind rose in force and a torrent of rain poured down on the surrounding area.

"Well, pooh!" Bronwyn's shoulders sagged beneath her drenched cape as she noted the effect of the obviously wrong emphasis. "This would be great if I wanted to muddy up a field."

The cold winds whipped around her as she raised her arms once more and repeated the command with the emphasis on the first syllables. She was rewarded with a clap of thunder, a bolt of lightning, and an increased downfall of rain.

Two more attempts did little to slow the torrent and brought her no closer to her goal of a water vortex to flood an enemy stronghold. To make matters worse there was a persistent bellowing guffaw riding the gale, another of the unfathomable effects of Maradane's winds.

"Oh, forget it," Bronwyn finally cried in exasperation. "Get it out of your system. I shall have to ask Salar for help with this—water is his domain, after all." She began sloshing her way through the sodden grass.

The moment she gave up the storm died abruptly, with one final twitter on the breeze, and the sun broke through the dissipating clouds. Sighing, Bronwyn wrote the episode off as a loss and headed for the grotto.

As the first raindrops spattered the ground Jana gathered her things and hurried into the grotto with Joachim. It was not deep, only a shallow depression in the cliff side, but it provided adequate shelter. The mossy floor was clean and the walls dry, with a tiny stream originating in one corner and flowing down the hill. Jana spread the quilt once more and sat down to watch the rainfall. She could not help laughing at Bronwyn's perplexed stance and drowned appearance.

Bronwyn was beginning the second phrase when Joachim let out a delighted gurgle and craned his head past his mother's elbow. Jana was often surprised at his accomplishments for, he was progressing more rapidly than a mortal child of his age. Turning to see what so amused him, Jana stared in amazement.

The rocky walls of the grotto glowed dimly, glittering with flecks of minerals, and hovering just in front of the rear wall was a wavering scene. It was this picture that held Joachim's attention.

More curious than afraid, Jana scrambled to her feet and approached the illusion. As she neared it, it took on a more solid form and she could see the details clearly.

Before her stretched a golden meadow damp with recent rain, its grasses sparkling in the sunset. To one side was situated an ancient stone table and circular bench. Seated on the bench was a white-haired youth whose eyes were fixed on a nearby mist.

Jana recognized the mist of the travel zone and also recognized, with some awe, the big Immortal who entered the meadow and strode toward the youth. Rich auburn hair shone in the sunlight and he was clad in the uniform of the Paladins.

The scene faded abruptly, leaving Jana disappointed. But something else was happening.

She now had a clear view of the wall at the rear of the grotto, a wall mottled with niches of varying size. One of these niches emitted a beckoning light and Jana drew closer.

Joachim crowed in delight and reached out with a chubby fist. Timidly, Jana put a tentative hand into the niche. Her searching fingers brushed a hard object and she withdrew a small, dusty book. Joachim watched as Jana flipped through the ancient pages. It was a book of names.

"Well, my love, I will save this for you. I'm sure it must be meant for you, as sure as I am that it was you I saw." Jana carefully tucked the book into her apron pocket. "We shall tell Papa about this place and see if he understands."

She turned abruptly at the call of her name, but saw only a wavering wall before her. Holding Joachim close she sidled to the left until she could see Bronwyn standing in the doorway, her face a mixture of curiosity and concern.

"Jana?" Bronwyn paused at the grotto's entrance, shaking the water out of one sandal. The quilt, bag, and staff lay undisturbed on the moss-cushioned floor, but the young woman was nowhere in sight. In the soft glow of the walls she saw a wavering scene before her and suddenly feared it was a portal.

"Oh dear, I hope Jana hasn't gone through." Bronwyn approached cautiously, then realized the scene was more like a living picture and not a portal.

Her gaze was drawn to the figure of a youth with shaggy red hair, garbed in the colors of the western sector. He knelt wretchedly within a ring of dazed onlookers, his tears falling on the face of a young woman who lay dead before him. Troubled, Bronwyn reached out with one fair hand and the scene vanished.

The glow faded as sunlight flooded the grotto and Bronwyn saw Jana standing to one side.

"Bronwyn, did you see a meadow?"

"No." The queen shook her head. "I saw a man, in our colors, kneeling beside a dead girl in some sort of village. He wept bitterly."

"Oh my." Jana's voice was troubled as she hugged her son closer. "I saw a meadow, and Joachim as a man. Then it went away and there was a light in the wall, where I found a book.

"Bron, let's go home and get Scott. I'm scared now."

"Yes, let's." Bronwyn hurriedly gathered Jana's things and they ran to their waiting ship.

"What do you think?" Caleb looked questioningly at Scott, who knelt examining the grotto walls. The five kings and two Immortals had gone to the grotto immediately after hearing the accounts of the women.

"I think 'twas created by magic." Scott rose, dusting off his knees, and ran one hand over the rear wall. "The niches apparently appear only after a scene hath been completed. I feel nothing here now."

Caleb nodded, contemplating the stories of Bronwyn and Jana. "They came in separately, whereas we all entered as a group.

"Scott, let us all go out and see if perhaps you see something. You're most likely to understand what you're seeing."

"Yea, it mayst work." Scott followed the others as far as the entrance, then turned and waited expectantly.

Within moments the soft glow suffused the grotto and a scene took form. Approaching cautiously, Scott studied every detail.

The scene was clearly the western gardens, for Bronwyn was kneeling beside a flower bed, gathering a bouquet. It was twilight, the last sun reflected brightly from the glass doors of the library. Someone was approaching Bronwyn from behind, cloaked and head bent to hide his face.

Scott cursed as the scene dissipated, but his attention was soon drawn to the rear wall. The niches were clear now, and one shallow crevice glowed with welcome. Reaching inside, Scott withdrew a delicate bracelet set with a milky white stone. The glow receded as he called the others back.

"'Tis very clearly a magic creation." He held out the bracelet. "I saw Bronwyn in the garden and wast then guided to this. The niches open up after the scene is complete."

"I see," Caleb said slowly. "Jana was led to a book which will probably be of value to your son. Bronwyn disturbed the scene and thus lost whatever she would have found."

"Yea, and that troubles me." Scott turned to Jericho. "Please, get Bronwyn and bring her here. I wish to try something."

"Right away." Jericho dashed out of the grotto. The others went out to stand beneath the overhang to await his return.

When Bronwyn arrived Scott sent her alone into the grotto, but nothing happened.

"'Tis as I feared," Scott sighed. "Each person is apparently allowed one scene, and e'en though not completed there wilt be no other. Bron, didst thou recognize anyone thee saw?"

She shook her head. "No, no one was familiar. It had a feeling of distance, sort of. Have I done something terrible by ruining it, Scott?"

"I canst not say. But I believe thy scene, as Jana's, wast far into the future. It is likely that Gray wilt see it 'ere it takes place if it is of any import." Scott hugged her with one arm. "Meanwhile, my scene wast in thy lifetime. Please, wear this bracelet, that it mayst serve whate'er is its purpose."

Bronwyn slipped the bracelet onto her slim wrist.

Aric glanced around the surrounding landscape. "What should we do about this place? And why is it here?"

"Well, to answer thy second question first, I believe 'tis here to help people." Scott looked once more into the grotto. "There art few such places left in our realm. When the portals opened and Shandal entered, the magic fled. Yet bits and pieces remain, upon Aubrey, Stalasia, and a handful of other worlds. Some person from ages past created this grotto and bound it into permanence. My people know little of how magic works, for none amongst us hath been gifted with those insights. So I am unable to really explain the existence of this grotto.

"As for what to do about it, I wouldst suggest creating a park here. There cannot exist an object for everyone, but 'tis likely anyone coming here wilt see something of value."

Caleb nodded. "Bryce, would you like to rough out some sketches for the park?"

"Certainly," Bryce answered. "We can look them over when we gather at Anders' tomorrow."

Asher straightened slowly in his chair, rubbing his head where the blow had struck.

"Good evening, Immortal," a voice to his left hissed. Asher knew without looking that the Seer stood at his elbow. Chrys' private guard stood around him, spear points prodding Asher's throat.

The Seer tossed an object up and down, deftly catching it each time as he moved to stand in front of Asher. "Have you nothing to say, Immortal?"

Asher's gaze focused on the small stone Chrys toyed with, and a knot formed in his stomach. He did not have to search the hidden pocket in his belt to know that the Seer had found his travel stone.

"I have naught to say to thee, nor do I expect to in the future." Asher stared evenly at the man.

Chrys shrugged. "Actually I don't need any questions answered. I know approximately what information has passed to David, from the length of your work here. I realize also there are other spies. No, I have not captured you to stop the flow of information. My questions will be answered without any words from you."

Asher took a deep breath to calm his racing thoughts, but his gaze never wavered from the Seer.

Chrys examined the stone in his hand, a focus material allowing access to the travel zone of David's people. Then he casually tossed it aside, knowing that to attempt its use was to die.

"You may be interested to know it was the wolves that betrayed you," he said quietly. "I just realized we had spoken of them here one night. That explains how the plan was nullified before it even began."

The Immortal said nothing, waiting for what was to come. It was only a day before he was scheduled to report. But what a long day it would be.

Hugging his fur cloak around his shoulders, Chrys studied Asher with keen interest. "Do you not care about what is to come?"

Asher did not respond, but the Seer remained unruffled.

"My master seeks to have a study done of your person, a study in pain." Chrys retrieved his ruby from some inner pocket and rolled it between his fingers. "He has tried beheading your kind, much to his disappointment. But there remains the question of how much pain your minds can withstand. To accomplish his goals my master needs to know this. And he has sent someone here to conduct this testing, all on your behalf."

Asher complied as the guards prodded him to his feet, his mind seeking to sort out Chrys' words. The Seer had not meant his

Warlord when he spoke of his master. That was clear from the amused tone of his voice. Who was higher than a Warlord in the realm of Shandal? Asher searched his memory and rooted out the idea that Chrys' master was from far beyond Shandal. It was the memory of an episode from the early days of his people, an episode that later caused enemies to abandon attempts at beheading.

The Immortals were a tall race. Granted, Scott was a giant among them, but the mortal races rarely surpassed eight feet tall, while many Immortals were more than that in height. Up until the episodes with the snake deluge David's people had walked where they pleased and cleared a path before themselves. Wounds healed swiftly, and severed limbs were regenerated in less than a day. Thus was Shandal discomfited in its attempts to halt the Immortals.

It was as the Immortals patrolled the planets to purge them of snakes that the event Asher now recalled had occurred. Its details had been kept from the people of the realm, for even the Immortals did not understand its source. But the result was spread to all enemies by an unknown force.

The Immortals patrolling a planet that had been almost desolated by the snakes had one day encountered a group of men who would have towered over even Scott. With blades that no Immortal could have lifted, these men attacked and beheaded the patrol before anyone knew what was happening. To their anger, the alien men learned what David's people already knew.

Because the Gabrellan race could generate bodies at will for work in emergency situations, so could their Immortal form regenerate as long as any substance of their body remained. In the case of beheading, the regeneration was instantaneous, the Gabrellan soul creating a new body even before the murdered one was fully fallen. In every way it was the same Immortal as before. Thus the attackers were faced with the same foes they had just 'killed,' and the attackers vanished within the blink of an eye.

Asher nodded to himself as they entered the room behind the Great Altar. It made sense now—someone was feeling them out. He would have information for David and Gray when help came, information he could not have gotten without this action from the Seer. Within another day he would be home, for help came at once at any missed report, and then he would go on to another world to continue his work.

"I shall leave you here, to our guest's ministrations." Chrys nodded toward a cowled figure in one corner of the shadowy room. He then left, posting the guards outside the locked door.

Asher studied the figure, then the chamber. No objects were present, no tools of torture. This boded no good. Only he and the figure stood facing one another, in a pale light cast by a green orb above the Seer's guest.

The figure raised one hand and a beam of cold green light bored into Asher's chest, sending him writhing to the floor with a scream of agony.

"God be with me," he begged as the beam withdrew only to be replaced with a blaze of fire engulfing his legs. Even as he screamed again he gauged the pain, realizing how much worse it would have to get before the Sleep came, his people's instinctive safeguard against madness from pain. Before that threshold was reached they would sink into a blackness beyond all feeling and awaken only when healed. As guardians, they could not open themselves to anything that might bring them to harm their charges.

Outside the room Chrys leaned casually against the altar, kicking aside the sluggish snakes sliding across his feet. How incredibly foolish these people of Shandal were, slitting their own families' throats to please a cluster of mindless reptiles. As a psychic he had always toyed with the thought that his people's ways were somehow idiotic and useless. Perhaps that had been why the Master had chosen him.

The Master. Chrys shuddered inside his heavy cape. Years ago the cowled figure had approached him, confirming his own insights and offering the promise of power for deeds well done. With each failure and each burning Chrys had become only more determined to succeed, and more frightening to those he ruled. His power had already begun, with the knowledge of the Zha-Dhak from beyond the portal.

His lip curled into a derisive sneer as he thought of the Overlords. They thought they ruled a growing empire, an empire destined to destroy what they had been taught was evil. But they were too stupid to see the precipice before them. That they were the evil, spawned of portal travelers with one purpose in mind—to create a disposable army to crush an enemy and clear a universe for takeover.

"Such fools," Chrys murmured, studying the snakes through narrowed lids. "Give you something foul to worship and permission to revel in obscenity and you tie yourselves down more effectively than any tyrant or Master."

He shook his head. They had never understood that in order to profit from the suffering they inflicted a plan must be followed. But the plan had been plain to him, even before the Master arrived those many years past.

"Evil is as evil does, my wretched morons, and evil you have not yet seen. You look across the stars instead of into your own home. Rid this universe of what is good, and I will teach you how to profit from inflicting pain, not wantonly but with carefully calculated purpose. See how you will burn when the fires are from my hands."

Concentrating on his ruby he smiled thoughtfully as Asher's screams echoed throughout the chamber.

Curling into a ball, Asher felt his chest healing as an icy blaze flamed down his back, forcing him to straighten. Fragments of green fire pinned his ankles and wrists to the floor, holding him on his back as the figure hurled inquisitive daggers of blue flame at his midsection. Each color inflicted varying degrees of pain, the cool blue tongues sharper than the green chill eating into his hands and feet.

Trying to concentrate on a prayer between assaults, Asher closed his black eyes against the trident of fire bearing down on him and screamed as the prongs peeled the skin off his chest.

"*Elizabeth*!"

Chapter Seventeen

*** Marissa was gone. At William's urging, she had taken Andrew and returned to her parents when Justin's absences had become so long she realized something was wrong.

Seated at his desk in the library, William ran his hands through his curly hair and glanced miserably around the huge chamber. He awaited his son's return in bitter silence.

Justin had been gone without word for ten days this time. Then one evening William had discovered the notebook, hidden in a dusty records room, filled with the secret plans of David for the defense against Shandal.

In the same room with the notebook, while numbly scanning the titles of the age-worn volumes on one far shelf, William found a book whose age he could not guess. Leafing through the pages he took some heart upon discovering a series of tactics written down by some ancient visionary, tactics that could very well save David's foundling empire. Only its continued presence in the room assured William that Justin knew nothing of the book's existence.

Without thinking, William hurried to hide the book in a tiny room at the end of a maze of passages. Justin must not find it before William could contact David and Gray.

That was two nights past. William had sent an urgent call for David, but he could not come for several days. So William awaited his son's return, and the confrontation that must take place.

It was well into the night when Justin entered through the etched glass doors and found William seated in a tiny circle of light amidst many candles.

"Father?" He stepped slowly to the desk. "Father, why aren't you home? Where is Marissa, and Andrew?"

For a long time William simply stared at the dark man, then without a word he threw the notebook at Justin's booted feet.

"Ah." Justin looked down at the book. "Well, so you found out. Things needn't change. Now, where is my wife?"

"I sent her away!" William snapped, jumping to his feet. "How could you do this? How did they get to you?"

"I did it easily, for love of my people, my home," Justin said calmly. "My people are high in the Clan leadership. It was an honor to be chosen."

"Chosen!" Circling the desk, William grabbed Justin by the collar. "Justin, you can't do this. All we stand for, everything we love will be trampled. You've lived here too long not to see that."

"I've lived here long enough to see how right my people are." Justin pried loose William's fingers. "I'm sick of this putrid air and the nauseating stench of those worthless gardens. I'm sick of your temple and your libraries, and twisted values. I can't comprehend life without money, work for the love of it. No one loves work! How did you ever get so warped?"

"Warped?" William stared at him. Then he blurted, "When I found you, you were starving."

"I ate nothing for days prior to my departure," Justin said proudly. "Our spies knew of your work, and your loss. They were certain you would take in a child."

"You call us twisted, we who love beauty and build for the sake of creating? You, whose people would starve a child so he could pass as one lost?" William could not accept what he was hearing. "It's not too late, Justin. If you'll only tell David what information has been sent, you needn't return to those people."

Justin spat in his face. "Tell your king what I've done, my beloved father, and I'll be dead by sunrise. No, don't talk to me of changing sides. All that I hold true is in danger of extinction from this upstart king. I'll continue my work, and you'll keep silent if you care for me at all." He narrowed his eyes. "If I die by David's hand, it will be you who have killed me. Consider that, then come home." He spun on his heel and left the library.

William stood numbly, realizing that for five years vital plans had been sent to the enemy, and he was to blame. Had he not taken in the child...

The book. William ran dazedly through the halls to the small room, slamming the door shut behind him. He had to guard this book and be sure it was given into David's hands. If Justin found it the tactics could be used against the Empire.

But what of Justin? David would surely have him killed as a spy. Could he hand his son over to death so easily?

Staring at the book on a high shelf, William traced his work of the past years. Valuable information had been betrayed, but plans could be reformulated. At this point the scales were evenly tipped. The book would be the deciding factor, for whichever side possessed it.

When war erupted, Justin would return to his own people. If the tactics were used, those people would be obliterated. Unless he could somehow win Justin to the right side. He would plead with David for help in making Justin see the wrong of what he was doing. And no one must find the book.

Fumbling for a lighter for the old oil lamp on one shelf, William reached for the book. Once the flame was strong he touched it to an open page.

A thunderous roar split the air as blinding white light seared through the room. Shelves and bricks tumbled to the floor, half burying the ashen body by the door.

Down the avenue Justin ran out of his home, seeing a portion of the library tremble ominously before settling into stillness. Without waiting for any explanation he gathered his few belongings and returned to his home world. ***

*** Anders rubbed his face tiredly. He was seated in a corner of the gardens beneath gaily colored lanterns. A cool breeze fanned his flushed face.

"Anders, beloved, are you all right?" Shara knelt before him as their guests gathered behind her.

"Yes, yes, I'm fine." Anders hesitated, and sighed miserably. "The book was destroyed, and William with it."

He related the vision, then found his friends perplexed.

"But I don't understand what happened," Aric said.

"It was the spell on the library," Anders answered, forgetting the others knew nothing of it.

"More spells?" Jericho asked in confusion.

"I'm sorry, forgive me." Anders took a deep breath to calm his thoughts. "You see, my people protected their books above all else. Books contain all the knowledge of the ages and must be preserved at all costs. So my people bound the library with protective spells. Though magic fled, as Scott explained, we as a mystic race retained the power for that one spell. Each Keeper wove his own spell into the existing fabric, to destroy anyone or anything seeking to harm the books. Nothing that ever exists will destroy the Library at Shalanar."

Shara said softly, "This explains the locked room."

Her husband nodded, glancing around the group. "None of my race knew what transpired there, but they considered it to have been protection against harm. The room was sealed and no one ever set foot inside."

He looked sadly at Shara. "The book is gone, so it must be something else I am to see. But the visions are so far apart now."

"I know, my love." Shara squeezed his hand. "But it will all come to light. It could be something to do with Justin, or his wife and son. Time will tell."

Taking a seat on a low bench, Aric asked, "Anders, how much does Scott know of this? Perhaps he could shed some light on where this is taking you."

"Sadly, no," Anders answered. "I've spoken at length with

Scott and David, and in fact they learned much from me.

"David never knew what happened to William or Justin and only guessed about the latter as we settled this world. David did go to Shalanar in reply to William's call, but the man had vanished. Since no one had seen or heard the episode I just saw they could only speculate. Marissa still believed Justin had gotten into trouble in the ruins, perhaps discovering some ancient magic, and she gave him up for dead. At least now I can tell David what really happened to William."

Aric was as disappointed as his friend. "Are you certain the book is gone?"

"The spell works to protect the volumes in the library, but William was holding the book."

Bronwyn shuddered, though the breeze was warm. "How have we regressed so far in what is truly so little time?"

"I don't understand." Anders studied her.

"Well, this is the year 4849 of Immortal Reckoning, right?"

Anders nodded, and the young woman continued. "Now look at the facts. Shandal entered this galaxy and within fifty years the magic was fleeing and the Stalassi were dying. In another thousand years the Wind Rulers vanished. In less than five thousand years we have lost powers that would never have allowed Shandal to progress as far as it has. But Shandal in itself is nowhere near strong enough to frighten away such powers. I've learned only trifling wind commands, yet they will be enough to help distract and disorient the enemy. How then could such an enemy drive away powers it could never hope to compete with?"

"I never truly thought of that," Anders said.

"Yet it bears thinking about," Aric said, recalling his historical studies. "Shandal is vile, truly, but it could never stand against the True-Bloods, nor could it survive against the small power of Stalasia. So it could never have survived whatever magic was here. Yet the magic sought escape. Why?"

"Why indeed?" Shara wondered aloud. "And why were the Immortals created such a short time prior to Shandal's arrival? Only their unifying force has held the enemy at bay. But the Empire was undreamed of when the powers deserted us."

After a quiet moment Bronwyn ventured another question. "Who, then, is the true enemy? What force lies behind Shandal, in truth?"

"Oh my," Shara mumbled. "We really must go to Scott and Richard. This is leading far beyond our understanding."

"We can meet in my library," Jericho offered, scrambling to his feet from the soft grass where he sat.

The two Immortals frowned deeply, perplexed by the questions brought before them.

Leaning his chin in his big hand, Scott mused, "Where doth lie the true enemy?

"Bron, what doth Shandal seek in their war against us?"

"Why, to destroy us," Bronwyn answered. "They believe in all that we despise, and they despise our beliefs. So they seek to destroy us. And you must admit they have everything to gain and we only everything to lose. For Shandal to conquer us would make the Clan wealthy beyond all comprehension."

"Yea, we fight to save ourselves. But, in the end, what shalt Shandal truly gain? Shalt they retain possession of their spoils if they win?"

"I like not where this leads us, Scott," Richard said grimly. "We have truly o'erlooked something that mayst well lead to destruction. We have seen only the obvious and fought it, ne'er looking into the surrounding factors.

"I believe 'tis time to call a council, with Chuck present. He alone knows what lies beyond the portals."

"Yea, thou art right. Wait here, and I shalt gather the others." Scott headed for the nearest door, reaching for his travel stone as he went.

While he was gone Bronwyn and Shara went to the kitchen to prepare a tray of desserts and drinks. The men readied the council room and called Salar to join them. Then the group went to the gardens to await Scott's return.

Little time passed before a misty haze formed near the central fountain and six figures emerged—Scott, his father, and the four

High Under Kings.

Bronwyn looked curiously for Chuck, assuming he would be with Scott, eager to see this unique Immortal. Yet the mist dissipated with no further arrivals.

On the other side of the massive fountain a sudden wind swirled the air and a cascade of glittering particles spun to the ground to settle around a pair of booted feet before fading.

Amazed, Bronwyn watched as the short, black-clad man came toward the group. His hands were gloved in soft black material, and his black trousers were tucked into his high boots. A high black collar was partially hidden by shoulder length blond hair. Nearing, he surveyed the people with pale blue eyes.

Scott put one hand on the man's shoulder, turning to Maradane's rulers. "I shouldst like ye all to meet Chuck. He canst not speak, but he wilt try to help us with this matter."

"I've prepared the council room," Jericho said, leading the way.

"I find this most perplexing," David said as they took their seats. "To think we have o'erlooked vital facts. Yet this wouldst explain many things."

Glancing around the table, the Immortal king finally ventured, "From what my son relates, I have concluded that Shandal is only the frontal force for an attack by far superior control. And it mayst well be that my race is an unforeseen balancing weight, created when the Gabrellans learned of this plot."

Gray took up the discussion. "Scott hath explained to thee the duties performed by Chuck. In fulfilling these duties, Chuck hath traveled to most places existing beyond our rule. David wilt ask certain questions, and I wilt respond if words art needed."

David paused, then turned to the portal tender. "Chuck, is it true that many portals once surrounded the planet Shandal, and most art now gone?"

Chuck nodded, his gloved hands clasped on the table before him.

"Of the portals remaining, how many lead to a realm wherein magic is rampant?"

Chuck closed his eyes, and a moment later Gray answered for him.

"There art six portals still around the planet, David. Of these only one gives access to a universe of magic. Chuck hath ventured little into it, for the powers art black."

David frowned as he nodded. "And how many portals mayst be safely closed?"

After another brief moment Gray said tautly, "All but the one we art concerned with. 'Tis a key portal and to close it e'en from both sides wouldst result in the beginning of the warp effect."

David turned to explain this to the group. "There art certain major portals where the energy generated is so forceful that to close off e'en both sides wouldst create a rupture of the field. This energy wouldst then cause other portals to collapse into themselves, causing more ruptures which wouldst eventually sunder our entire universe. Small portals mayst safely be imploded and their energies absorbed into the surrounding field."

He turned back to Chuck. "Canst thou find the realms to which our magic fled?"

Chuck shook his head and thumped one hand, causing a flurry of frustrated sparkles. Gray said softly, "He hath searched, David, but the magic hath hidden itself. It remains inactive, as if waiting, and so canst ne'er be found until it reawakens."

"Wonderful," David muttered, glancing at the ceiling. Then he said, "One last question, Chuck—hath the realm beyond the portal a centralized base, and canst its leaders traverse to our realm?"

Chuck nodded, his eyes narrowed. Gray translated his thoughts.

"In his brief exploration Chuck discovered a fortress of sorcery located near the portal. 'Tis on a blackened, smoky world. And Chuck hath found evidence that they long ago traveled to our universe, before and after Shandal began taking form. He thought little of it since people art always stumbling through the portals, sometimes in groups."

"Yea, things become clearer now. Chuck, thou hast helped greatly. Return now to thy work and monitor that portal. But under no circumstance do further exploration. I shalt order a permanent guard mounted near the portal, though I doubt they art ready yet to enter here in force."

Nodding, Chuck stood and raised his arms above his head, clapped his hands, and disappeared in a glittering cascade.

"How does he do that?" Bronwyn blurted.

David smiled, amused. "Chuck hath the power to transport himself by opening a temporary portal where'er he mayst be. He spins wind, wind he generates himself from the energies of the portal zone."

"How intriguing," Bronwyn said. Then she sobered. "Now, how do his answers relate to our questions? Did we stumble onto something, do you think?"

"Most certainly, for one being the source of Shandal's power. I believe forces from several portals connected on Shandal, and as the people became more petty and hungry for power the sorcerers sent an emissary to begin a plot to control this universe. It mayst be that they have destroyed everything in their own realm and need this territory."

Aric nodded, grasping the thread. "They likely planned to overthrow the planets here, since there was no unified leadership. They apparently didn't know about your people."

"That is almost a certainty. The Gabrellans must have learned of the plans, leading to the creation of the Immortals. We wert yet young and untutored when the magic fled, and few in numbers. Perhaps hadst the powers of magic known of us they wouldst still remain."

Anders had been taking this all in attentively and finally offered a supposition. "It does begin to come clear. The emissaries were first sent to Shandal to check the plan's feasibility. Once established there, perhaps one of the sorcerers entered secretly to frighten away the magic powers, and to somehow begin the decline of my people."

David agreed soberly. "It hath possibility. Once those things occurred Shandal hadst free reign, until my daughter came into power. Meeting resistance, the sorcerers likely undermined the Adani youth, turning them toward the path of war. That effectively removed Mara. Hadst she known the extent of the threat her course wouldst have differed greatly."

"That leaves only us to face the threat," Aric sighed dismally.

"Not necessarily," Robert said. He and his companion High Under Kings were content to listen for the most part, sorting things for later consultation with David. "I think perhaps we alone—David's empire alone—must control the threat from Shandal."

Nicholas pursed his lips, venturing a rare comment. "Yet I feel we wilt be sent aid when the leaders of the plan seek entry here. As Chuck and Gray pointed out, the magic is not dead, nor doth it flourish openly. It lies waiting. Therefore it mayst return one day."

David considered this. "Yea, things mayst be as ye say. Also, the threats against this external force have not been truly nullified. The Wind Rulers live through Bronwyn and her family. And I preserve the Adani Wind Law where none mayst touch it until I am told to release it.

"Stalasia lives also. And it mayst be that without Anders we wouldst ne'er have learned of these possibilities."

"How so?" Anders asked, surprised.

"Didst not thy vision lead to these ideas? Without the knowledge of William and Justin perhaps none wouldst have considered these things. I believe thy gift hath served its purpose, Anders, and served it well."

"I never thought of that," Anders said, bemused, sitting back in his chair.

At the end of the table Caleb looked up from his notebook, shaking a cramp out of his writing hand. "And what plan are we to follow now?"

David turned to Gray, who said, "As things stand the major threat remains Shandal. If they win then the sorcerers wilt enter right away to wrest power. If Shandal wanes, though, 'tis my belief the sorcerers wilt wait for some time before attacking, to formulate new plans."

"I agree." David returned his attention to Caleb. "We shalt continue as planned. So done, we wilt have time to seek the guidance of the years. As soon as I return to Leahcim Tierrah I wilt seek the Gabrellans' wisdom to see if these ideas art truly born. Unless I send word otherwise thou wilt know we have guessed rightly.

"I wilt send Alex, my Master Armorer, to confer with Salar on this world's armaments progress. The rest of thee continue as planned."

Caleb closed his notebook and pushed back his chair.

David stood also. "Alex wilt arrive in a few days. He is not Immortal and must travel by ship."

"I shalt keep thee informed, Father." Scott followed him to the door.

Intent on some inner thought as he approached his apartments, Chrys did not notice that his guards were missing from their stations outside his rooms. But he did wonder if something was wrong, for he had heard no screams echoing from the secret chamber for several moments.

A slender but strong arm snaked around his throat as the cloying odor of wildflowers accosted his nose. Stumbling to a halt as a razor sharp dagger slipped under his chin, Chrys finally noticed the absence of his men.

Two hulking warriors stood before him, their silver armor emblazoned with the likeness of David. He knew a third man stood behind his captor.

Out of the corner of his eyes he saw a mass of honey gold curls falling over the arm around his neck. A soft voice breathed in his ear.

"Thou wilt take me to my husband or I wilt carve thee from the feet up."

Chrys felt a chill creep over him at the woman's quiet words, a chill worse than the thought of his master's icy fire. He recalled Asher's tormented cries and realized he could easily be made to mimic them. His carefully cultivated expressions and gestures would do nothing to strike fear into this Immortal witch. Alone, he could never overpower her guard.

He nodded finally, realizing that once they reached the hidden chamber his master's emissary would make short work of these interlopers. Sidling around, careful not to put pressure on the blade at his throat, he led the woman toward the great altar.

They had reached the altar when they were deafened by a

shriek of enraged frustration from the small room. An explosion collapsed the door, throwing aside the guards stationed there, revealing a fading blaze of green light and a broken figure on the floor.

Chrys made a desperate lunge for freedom, realizing the emissary had gone, but the blade sliced cleanly across his throat.

Elizabeth dropped the dagger and ran to Asher, falling to her knees beside his unconscious form. One hand covering her mouth, she reached the other to tremulously touch his burned face. He had mercifully fallen into the Sleep, but that only emphasized the excruciating pain he had suffered until then.

"Clay, Toby, carry him to our grandson," she said firmly, taking her dagger from Thomas, the third guard. The men gathered Asher into their arms and set out, vanishing quickly into the misty teleportal zone. She followed close behind.

Elizabeth left the teleportal zone behind in time to hear a terrified scream from her grandson's house. Guards raced from all directions and Jericho and Bronwyn collided with Richard on one of the paths.

"What's going on?" Jericho shouted, skidding to a halt at Scott's door, sword in hand. Seeing the man on the floor before Scott's kneeling figure, Jericho sheathed the sword and turned Bronwyn away. "Don't look, Bron."

David arrived then, having been turned back to Maradane only a short time after leaving. He took one look through the door, closed his eyes with a shudder, and then turned to face Elizabeth.

Forcing down the bile in his throat, he demanded, "What happened?"

"I do not know," Elizabeth said, tears streaming down her cheeks. "He didst not report, so I took the map of the palace he had given me and went to get him. I found him like this... Who couldst have done this?"

"We art only beginning to learn," David said flatly, putting one arm around her. "Apparently this wast another test....Scott, canst thou help?"

"I have healed the worst of it," Scott said, replacing his silver in his belt and pulling Jana into his arms. She had answered the door and been terrified by the sight. Smoothing her auburn hair, Scott continued. "Facial scarring wilt be minimal. The rest wilt heal in due course. I see we wert not so far wrong tonight."

"No, not so far wrong at all." David stared numbly at Asher. "What I wouldst not give if we wert all wrong. I wilt take him home, Scott. Get Jana calmed down and to bed."

Scott nodded, getting to his feet as his father and the guards lifted Asher, and the rest of the group dispersed. Soon the gardens were silent once more, disturbed not at all by the soothing murmurs from Scott's home.

Chapter Eighteen

Alex arrived eight days later and carried out an extensive inspection of Maradane's military forces before joining Caleb in the temple to review the strategies and projected work for the coming years. He returned nightly to the western palace as Jericho and Bronwyn's guest, but spent a great deal of time in his suite amidst charts and tables.

On the tenth day Bronwyn settled down in her alcove with a book, hoping for a quiet afternoon of reading. Soon she glimpsed Scott returning from Leahcim Tierrah and called him to join her.

"Have you learned anything new, Scott."

Sitting beside her, he shook his silver head. "Nothing that seems to help. Chuck reported that a group entered and returned through the portal several years ago, but 'tis extremely difficult to trace individual passages. A permanent base is now positioned there and anyone seeking entry wilt hopefully be captured."

Noticing the worry in his eyes Bronwyn grasped his thoughts. "But you fear what might happen even if one is captured." Asher had awakened after four days and was now relating everything to

David and Gray. It was not comforting news to any of them.

"An Immortal fears little for his own person, but yea, this we do truly fear," Scott said gravely. "We know nothing of magic, neither to use it nor to protect against it. And though we mayst not die, we have seen only a small portion of the tortures which couldst be inflicted."

"Oh, don't talk about it." Bronwyn shivered and put her hand on his arm. "I pray Gray is right and they will not try to enter soon if Shandal is defeated. And it certainly must be defeated."

Scott smiled at the determination in her soft voice. "And how is Alex progressing? He and his brother Hammond have been my father's Armorers for decades."

"He's a wonderful man. He has taken such care over the plans with Caleb and Salar, and spends so much time working that I rarely see him. But when he is here he's very interested in what I can do with the winds. He says it may be a vital part of the battle."

"As well it might." Alex approached from around the corner, his eyes merry as he bounced a village child on his broad shoulders. "Scott, how are you?"

"Quite fine, Alex. And thee?"

"Very well, very well indeed. Hammond's daughter is getting married in three months, a happy event."

"Wonderful, my friend." Scott got to his feet. "If thou wilt excuse me, I must go home now and let Jana know I am back."

"Please come to supper, Scott, all three of you." Bronwyn reached out for the child's hand.

Nodding, Scott took note of a pulse of light from the stone in Bronwyn's bracelet as he turned to leave. As he walked away he heard Alex saying, "Bronwyn, perhaps after supper you will show me how to use one of your staffs?"

"Certainly. I'm so happy I can help—I feel as if I'm doing something, rather than just waiting."

That evening Bronwyn took her staff and a new one to the garden outside the library where Alex and Jericho planned to meet to discuss that sector's fleet of warships.

The sun reflected a rosy glow off the glass doors as the queen knelt to pick some flowers while she waited. Humming softly to herself, she was planning the demonstration for Alex and did not hear the whispered steps behind her.

Boots gliding over the broad stones of the path, the hooded figure stole up behind the woman, head bent to hide his features. With one lightning movement he locked an arm around Bronwyn's throat and dragged her, screaming, to her feet.

A sharp point prodded painfully into the man's back as Scott snarled, "Let go!"

Moving carefully, he released Bronwyn as Jericho stepped from the library to draw his wife close.

Scott slid his broadsword beneath the assassin's chin, his pale blue eyes burning with painful rage. Putting no pressure on the blade, the captive choked out, "How did you know?"

"Milady's bracelet, a gift of priceless value. It pulsed as thee neared her this afternoon and I knew then of thy betrayal."

Metal whispering against metal, another sword point slid beneath the man's quavering chin as David spat out, "How couldst thee? How couldst thee do this to thine own people?"

"You cannot imagine the power, David." Alex faced him in the waning light. "They travel with magic, they offered us magic, spells and power. Spells that we never imagined."

"I have seen the results of those spells," David hissed, "blackened remnants of chance experiments in my own palace. Where didst murder slip so easily into thy life?"

"Those people counted for nothing, not when there is so much to gain," Alex said absently.

David tried to control the tremble in his voice. "I canst accept Shandal's deeds for they art not of our people. But thee! I canst not accept this, nor forgive it. Thou not only spied for an enemy, thou betrayed thine own blood, and murdered children!"

Jericho pulled Bronwyn into the library. "Go inside, out of sight of the guard yard. Keep Garth with you."

Bronwyn went tearfully, hugging her son close. She flinched as an agonized scream cut the air, then sobbed in the silence that followed.

She was standing in a darkened room when Scott came to her. She leaned into his arms, crying bitterly.

"How could he have done it, Scott? He was so good and kind."

"Shhh." Scott smoothed her hair, kneeling before her. "They ruined his mind, somehow lured him with false promises. Yet he knew full well what he wast doing. My father hath been searching for months for the men wreaking havoc in the night, leaving twisted bodies in dark hallways. And that is what we canst not comprehend, how these people such as Justin and Alex canst feign love so easily and do such evils with hands that wert moments ago gentle."

Bronwyn dried her eyes with her handkerchief. "What will happen now?"

"Jericho wilt go to help try the families of these men. Hammond must die, but we wilt not exile their wives and children if they art able to use the staff."

"I've never been able to understand that, why Devon couldn't use the staff," Bronwyn said.

"'Tis part of the Wind Law. And from today forward it shalt be part of the annual testing in Leahcim Tierrah. My father wilt release that much of the wind lore to protect our people." Scott paused, his expression hurt. "We ne'er thought our own people couldst betray us."

"There are always bad people, Scott, else the prisons would be empty. But it hurts all the same. How did you know what would happen tonight?"

"Thy bracelet from the grotto." Scott related the vision he had seen that day. "As thee reached up to the child I saw the gem flash and took it to be a warning of danger. So I summoned David, warned Jericho, and later waited in the shadows for the scene to take place."

Bronwyn gazed out the window at the darkening gardens. "Do you think things will go well now?"

"We shalt have time enough to prepare." Scott stepped toward the door. "Maradane is protected in ways e'en Gray doth not understand, milady. Rest now."

"I will, Scott. Thank you." She watched him leave, then went slowly to her room.

Two evenings later Bronwyn was sorting jewels in her small workroom, preparing to make a belt for Jericho's birthday, when she heard a soft voice outside. Going to the etched glass door, she slid into the shadows and watched silently.

David stood beside a marble fountain, the music of its flowing water almost masking his words. His back to the palace, he was gazing wistfully into a hovering cloud of sparkles and chuckling softly. A tendril of wind played through his hair as Bronwyn strained to hear his words.

The sparkles faded as the man hung his head and whispered, "Farewell, then, if it must be so."

He stood so long without moving, his rich black cloak hanging motionless, that Bronwyn finally stole forward, moving to touch his arm and see a moistness on his cheek.

"David?" she whispered hesitantly. "David, do you know what the sparkles are? Please tell me."

He smiled a little, but shook his close-cropped head. "I am sworn to silence, my queen. In truth I didst not guess until Jericho told me of the little boy's rescue at the tower. I hadst to come and see for myself."

"But why can't you tell me? They're my winds," she said possessively.

"That they art." David squeezed her hand. "But many know more than I, and by them am I sworn. I am sorry, but the future must hold one mystery in trust for thine children. When one we now await comes and I am told to release the wind lore, then wilt others know what guards the winds of my children."

"I shall have to accept that, then," she said, disappointed. "But who is this person you await?" She felt from his words it was someone only newly known of.

"That much I mayst tell thee," he said with a warmer smile. "The Wise Ones, those we call the Gabrellans, have answered my questions about the sorcerers. They also promise that in the future one of my race wilt come who wilt deal with the magic. At his coming our magic shalt return to us."

"Well," Bronwyn said more happily, "that at least is a thing to look forward to. Come in and have some cake and tea, as long as you're here. It's rather lonely with Jericho gone."

"He shouldst arrive in another day or so. The Paladins art bringing him home." David followed her into the palace.

Before his execution Hammond admitted that Alex had been ordered to kill Bronwyn because she proved too much of a threat with her new control of the winds. The families of the two men were proven innocent of the betrayal and remained on Nahcym Tarah under David's protection. After the incident was resolved, the years passed in relative quiet. Several attempted raids on Maradane were thwarted by the Paladin units ringing the planet, and no more spies were able to reach the world. Under Salar's exhaustive supervision the armed forces grew and trained as the population grew.

Tiea found herself often alone as Caleb travelled to Leahcim Tierrah and other worlds to confer with other kings. Evolving an organized strategy including forces from several planets was no easy task, nor was deciding where each battalion would be best placed for defense.

The four princes married within two years of one another, Garth marrying Aric's fifteen year old daughter Nahla. The couples remained living at the palaces, the princes close to their fathers for the continuous work. One task of the princes was to organize an orderly move of the children of Maradane to the lower floors of the temple and oversee construction of underground shelters for the women.

Scott enlarged his home to house three more sons and two daughters, at peace at last with his family. Each child was Immortal and Scott found no complaint with his life as he worked with his father and Maradane's kings.

Richard remained living quietly in his small home, his son grown tall over the years.

In the year 22 of Maradane, when Scott's youngest child was

not yet two, one wintry afternoon found the giant Immortal dueling with eighteen year old Jeremiah. The other princes watched from vantages around the guard yard.

Trained both by Anders and Scott, Jeremiah excelled in swordsmanship while maintaining his father's dislike for battle. He enjoyed duels, however, and Scott was hard pressed to overcome the youth.

"You make enough noise!" Garth yelled over the din of clashing swords.

"But you don't get anywhere!" red-headed Aarek taunted. "We'll never defeat anyone that way."

At that moment Jeremiah parried with a deft twist that sent Scott's huge blade flying to clatter down at Garth's booted feet. Jeremiah stepped back as the dark youth struggled clownishly to lift the sword.

Retrieving the weapon Scott turned to frown at Jeremiah. "Ne'er be fair with an enemy. They wilt not be fair with thee. Disarmed is the same as dead."

Jeremiah chuckled and feinted forward, then slipped under Scott's guard and nestled the point of his own sword atop the giant's leather belt.

"Shall I skewer you here and now, then, and let Drahcir practice for his medical fleet?"

"I think not." Scott tousled the boy's hair. "But be wary of trickery."

Jeremiah suddenly found himself flat on his back, Scott's foot still pressed against his ankle and the sword at his throat.

"I get your meaning." Jeremiah laughed as he scrambled to his feet. "But one can be fair and still not be tricked. Fairness is the basis of the Warrior's Prayer."

Scott shook his head vehemently. "Wisdom is the basis of our Warrior's Prayer, young prince. 'Tis not always wise to be fair. In the midst of rolling battle, to spare life means to leave a sword in thine own back. I have felt that sword, and I have learned. But I hear Anders' words from thy lips."

"Papa's drilled me harder than you do," Jeremiah said, affection in his voice. Anders remained the quiet ruler, ever present in the background. "Scott, do you think I will make him proud? Sometimes I think I could work harder, or do better."

Scott smiled gently at the doubt in the youth's eyes. "Thou art working well beyond what canst be asked. Thee make Anders proud each day."

Jeremiah leaned on his sword, still looking up at Scott. "I worry that I won't be able to do properly in battle. I don't like killing, and long for another way out. That makes me afraid I'll run."

"Art thou fearful for thy life?" Scott asked simply.

"My life is to be laid down for our people," Jeremiah answered with total conviction. "It is the taking of life I fear, not the losing of it."

"Then thou wilt do well, Jeremiah, for if thou dost not kill the enemy before thee he mayst live to reach thy people, thy mother, thy wife. But do not lose the fear of taking life. If it fails to frighten thee one day, thou art lost." Scott clasped the boy's shoulder. "Come on, I wilt take the lot of thee loafing boys to Jana for some hot chocolate. 'Tis too cold for further drill."

As the five men set off toward Scott's house they did not see the figure racing home from a distant meadow.

Lachlan skidded to a halt at the door of his house, gasping, "Father, the war comes! David sent word...less than one month...I must tell Caleb."

Leaving his son to catch his breath, Richard dashed to the palace council room. He pressed the council summons switch, then returned to his son. "Come, then, and we shalt give the news."

In a matter of moments the soft bell sounding in each palace and the temple had summoned everyone concerned to the main council chamber. Caleb looked expectantly at Richard. "What?"

Lachlan spoke up. "I wast in my meadow when a message wast carried by the Gabrellans—the war wilt reach Maradane in less than a month. Final tasks must be completed now."

Caleb nodded, a little envious of Lachlan's powers to pick up messages relayed on the winds. Such methods were employed occasionally to insure that no enemy would intercept the news. This guaranteed that Shandal would not know how prepared David was for the coming battle.

"Tiea, please send at once for an accurate enlistment count from each sector's base. And announce that no soldier under fifteen is to leave the planet; we need the added protection here."

His wife nodded, making notes as her husband continued.

"Bryce, call in your medic units for the final inspection. Order supplies, organize them, and see that all staff members are no younger than thirteen.

"Anders, you must see that the hospital ships are outfitted swiftly and that all equipment checks out properly." Caleb turned back to Richard's son. "Lachlan, is there anything else?"

"I am to make a sword, for Jeremiah."

"But you've had so little practice," Aric began.

"All I ask is to work in the forge. I wilt be told what to do."

"See that Lachlan has the materials he needs," Caleb told Aric. "I have faith that he will be guided as he says."

"Certainly. I'll see to it today."

"Fine. We can go back to work." Caleb closed his everpresent notebook. "Anders, please stay a while. I can use your help."

Early the next morning Richard's son began sorting the items gathered at the forge. Jericho and Aric eyed the pile curiously, but were forced to retreat when Lachlan fired the forge until it glowed a searing white.

The second day Richard and Jericho stood just outside the forge, discussing the work.

"Richard, I'm not certain this is going to work." Jericho scratched the side of his nose. "Lachlan keeps remelting the raw metals, each time adding something new. I fear he'll end up with only a glob of mush, instead of a metal which may be shaped. Why isn't he using tirrschon?"

Richard stifled a smile. "He is going about it rather strangely. But he is certainly being guided by the Gabrellans. We know nothing of weapons manufacture beyond the range of our universe. And if 'tis to be a special sword perhaps it must be made differently."

"I'm willing to wait, if curiosity doesn't overcome me." Jericho laughed as he listened to the sounds from the forge. Then he turned back toward the palace.

Richard strolled toward the forge. Catching sight of his father, Lachlan stopped his work.

"Father, wilt thou make a scabbard? I have written down the proper measurements, but have not thy hand with leathers. It must be special."

"Certainly." Richard took the small piece of paper. "When wilt thee be finished?"

"Mayhap in three days—I must be careful to make no mistake." Lachlan wiped his forehead with his arm, looking a little uncertain. After a reassuring smile from his father he returned to his task. Richard headed for his house, pondering the unusual methods and pace. But the Gabrellans had never been wrong. Given three days more, Richard would barely complete the scabbard.

Late in the afternoon of the third day Richard and Lachlan hurried from the forge to the palace, where Caleb and the other kings were working in the observatory data center next to the council room. The men put aside their work as the pair entered the room.

"Have you finished?" Caleb asked eagerly.

"I have. Thou mayst see." Lachlan took the scabbard from the velvet in which it was wrapped and handed it to Caleb.

The man ran one finger along the length of the polished leather, the edges of which were bound with silver inlaid with precious stones. Stamped in gold in the center of the sheath, between two large diamonds, were the emblem of Maradane and the Barria crest. The golden hilt was intricately carved, set with rubies, emeralds, and one giant black garnet.

Caleb grasped the hilt and unsheathed the sword. To his amazement the cold blade was as clear as glass.

Aric reached out to test the blade and quickly drew back a cut finger. "That's a fine edge. But I've never before seen a clear blade."

Lachlan retrieved the sword. "'Tis meant to be invisible in the sun's light or dark of night."

"Jeremiah's watching the guard drill. We'll take it to him." Caleb led the way outside.

Jeremiah looked down at the sword which Lachlan gave him, balancing it on one palm. "But it's so light!"

"It is very heavy!" Caleb protested. "It's heavier than any sword I've lifted."

Lachlan tilted his head as if listening to a distant voice. "For Jeremiah it weighs little. Yet it wilt guard him in battle, that he mayst lead our warriors. Jeremiah, the Gabrellans give thee this gift of Bane Slayer. Mayst it lead thee to victory."

The prince hesitated, uncertain. In David's realm swords were generally not named, with the exception of the Immortals' swords known collectively as the Golden Death. He was rather taken aback by a weapon that seemed to have a life of its own. "Thank you, very much. I hope I prove worthy of this."

"There is no question of that," Lachlan said firmly as David approached the group.

The Immortal king examined Jeremiah's sword. "'Tis an excellent blade, Lachlan. And a great gift for Jeremiah." Handing the sword back, he said, "I am needed in Leahcim Tierrah henceforth, but I came to bring thee one last bit of help. I ordered my court physicians to prepare a healing aid for our warriors." He held out a small silver box containing yellow tablets.

"When taken promptly, in conjunction with proper treatment in the more serious instances, these tablets wilt prevent most wounds from being fatal. They wilt speed recovery far beyond the natural process. But if taken after too much time elapses their effect wilt be decreased."

Bryce took the pills, looking closely at them. "This is more than I could have hoped for. We will save countless men this way." He appreciated the reasoning behind David's idea. The forces of Shandal's over crowded worlds far exceeded those of David's population-minded realm. With these tablets at least the loss of warriors would be lessened, and the armies therefore strengthened.

"My men art now distributing these to the soldiers." David paused, letting his gaze rest on each person. "Maradane is most precious to me, far beyond e'en the obvious reasons. Take great care, and keep those pills with thee at all times."

David departed swiftly, but left seeds of a new hope and the reminder that he cherished them all, beyond the fate of his empire.

During the ensuing days the queens oversaw a project moving Maradane's artistic and literary treasures to the lowest level of the temple, where all would be safely preserved. Once this was completed they began laying stores for the children to be sheltered in the remaining levels.

When the battles neared Maradane Caleb ordered all children brought to the temple. Bronwyn contributed to the sanctuary by returning her ancient chimes to the center of the gardens. This gave the added assurance of protection against any attacks with snakes.

Ten days after David's visit the raids began, randomly destroying outlying villages. The raiders were out for plunder and partook in few battles; they were only a foretaste of the ruthless men to follow.

Tiea supervised the care of the children while the other queens concentrated on settling the women in various shelters. A handful of the Guard remained at the palaces to protect the queens.

There was little left now to do but to wait until the battles reached their world. Maradane's armies were to remain on the planet to head off the first onslaught. Leaving darkened homes, the people settled into their shelters and listened anxiously for the first horns of warning.

Anders paced restlessly, ignoring the wind's harsh buffeting. He could not place what was wrong, he only knew that something was tugging at his mind.

It was the nineteenth day of the first month of the year, not long after the raids had begun. Anders sighed in frustration—perhaps it was only the tension of waiting, of not knowing when the first real blow would fall.

He sat wearily on a marble bench and looked around. It was a strange night—the winds were acting up again. The garden surrounding him was encircled by sharp, cutting winds, the plants bowed low before the gale. A terrible moaning echoed through the boughs overhead, adding to the harsh clanging of the chimes in the palace alcoves.

Anders rubbed his arms as a chill crawled slowly along his spine. Someone watched him from some hidden spot. He turned slowly, windblown curls falling over his tired eyes, and saw a sparkling of lights near one fountain.

Going quickly to investigate, Anders was caught up in a crying wind that tugged pleadingly at his sleeves. The lights spiralled eerily around the fountain and glowed beneath the water, and he thought he heard a whispered voice call his name.

A sudden shooting pain behind his eyes dropped him to his knees. The garden vanished, blotted out by the intense image of an ancient book amidst ashen ruin. But the scene was as quickly gone.

Anders shook his head violently, then glanced around the calm gardens. A moment later he was running toward the hangar.

"Scott!" Anders pounded repeatedly on the door.

It soon opened to reveal Scott, sword in hand. "Anders, what is wrong? Hath there been an attack?"

"No, no," Anders panted. "The Stalassi book, it's still there....I saw it, in the ashes...I'm going after it."

"No, wait..." Scott began, but Anders was already racing away. Scott slammed the door and ran to contact the Paladins to guard Anders' journey.

Setting the small ship softly down atop a hill four days later, Anders slowly emerged from the hatch to stand at the edge of the plain. The silver grasses shimmered mutely in the light of Stalasia's three moons. The whispering rustle of the endless plain comforted Anders' troubled mind as he looked ahead.

Beginning at the foot of the hill, stretching as far as he could see, lay ancient Shalanar. Its streets were broad and smooth, their stone bright. Mosaics undulled by the years remained on some of the buildings.

Anders' steps led him into his home city, his eyes drinking in the sights. Small houses and rambling mansions stood amidst faded gardens. The open market places were damaged, some roofs gone, but their pillars remained upright against the sky.

So intent was he upon the scene before him that he did not hear the soft footfalls behind. Heedless of any danger he turned his steps toward the temple where he had passed so many years.

A main avenue through the heart of the city led to the center of their lives, the enormous temple with its spired turrets and graceful balconies. Within its walls the people had prayed in small chapels and meditated in quiet halls. It had been lit only by flickering candles, thousands upon thousands of them, and the light of sun and moon. Stained glass spilled colorful patterns across marble floors and over the cushions that cradled eager knees. The great temple had been the cradle of their love, a place of comfort beyond mortal terms.

As he entered the first porticoed courtyard Anders' steps faltered, then tears coursed down his cheeks as he knelt in anguished silence.

The vaulted ceilings were crushed, the rubble strewn beneath starlit chasms. Shattered crystal glinted dully amidst crumbled pillars. The giant fountain was gone, its transparent basin and hidden lights pulverized by a rain of bombs. He and Shara had said their vows before that fountain, its gentle cascade their only music.

There was no way to enter the battered walls of the temple. Mountains of stone lay heaped everywhere, hiding forever any bit of hall or chapel remaining intact.

Before Anders was a narrow hole, the maintenance channel for the fountain's lights and water. It lay beneath the thick marble floor, and the cover lay half across it. There Shara had hidden when the attack began, wedged alone into the farthest dark corner, without her child who lay crushed beneath the central altar.

Anders buried his face in his hands, for the first time truly wishing to see the men of Shandal fall beneath his sword. They had torn one home away from him—he would not let them destroy his new one.

Behind him a swarthy man in heavy furs crept up slowly, sword raised. Yet before he could plunge the blade into Anders' bowed back he was frozen in mid-stride, imprisoned in a stasis controlled by many minds.

"Papa?" A faint voice reached Anders' ears, and a whispered caress crossed his fingers. Looking up, he saw a very small girl gazing intently at him, her dreamy blue eyes framed beneath a mass of silken gold. She reached out in anxious concern, a question on her face.

"Shayne?" Anders breathed, staring through tear-filled eyes. "My Shayne?"

"My Papa," she giggled softly, once more brushing her tiny fingers across his.

Anders looked around to find the courtyard ringed with shadowy figures, and only then did he finally see the king of Seryl held motionless behind him. A tall man stepped toward him, the stars twinkling faintly through his dark blue robes.

"Father?" Anders scrambled to his feet, reaching out desperately for his daughter's hand.

"Anders, you know we cannot," the man said sadly, pulling Shayne toward him. "My beloved son, it is only the pain of your first visit that clouds your thoughts. You cannot stay, no more than we can go. Now hurry, for time is so short. We will release him only after you are on your way."

To Anders' dismay his father and daughter faded into the night, leaving him to remember why he had come.

Skirting the imprisoned man, Anders hurried across the avenue to the great library. Unlike all the other buildings it remained whole, not one pane of glass or one square of marble cracked by the explosions. Knowing there was in truth little time, Anders ran through the dark halls, passages he had not forgotten over the long years, and halted at the sealed door.

Using his sword he cracked the heavy binding fabric and pulled the door open. A faint glow suffused the area, created by the people still guarding their home, and Anders saw the havoc wrought by William.

Across the entrance lay the blackened ash that was once William Barria, and at its head, partially hidden beneath a fallen shelf, was the book.

Kneeling, Anders reached gingerly for the volume, tenderly brushing the ashes from it. Resting it on one knee he scanned the pages and his heart sank.

The entries were in a script so ancient that even David would not remember it. It far outdated the Immortals; their librarians would need months to decipher it.

Yet it could be of use, late or not. Anders left the building, the book under his arm, and went home.

It was very late when Anders handed the volume to Scott. The Immortal examined the pages with disappointment.

"Yea, it wilt take precious time to decipher this. Yet perhaps what it reveals wilt be worth the delay." Scott closed the book and looked searchingly into Anders' eyes. "What is wrong, my friend?"

"I saw my daughter," Anders said quietly.

"Ah," Scott sighed, clasping Anders' shoulder.

"It's not so much that," Anders said after a moment, "as the realization that I cannot go to her. We are bound now to Maradane."

"I fear I cannot offer comfort, Anders. But in thy heart thou hast this meeting and the knowledge that she remains where thy heart truly lies."

"No, Scott," Anders said sadly. "That's the point. I have learned that my heart is with Maradane, and so it is that we are separated. I will not leave Maradane as I left Stalasia and let it fall. If I do nothing else in my life I will see to it that Maradane does not fall."

"We stand together, Anders. Now thou shouldst return to Shara. I wilt take this immediately to my father."

Scott watched Anders walk away, then turned to Jana and scooped their toddler Laryssa into his arms, holding the small child tightly and resting his head on hers.

Settled into his small craft, Anders stared at his hand and imagined once more the touch that would never again caress his fingers.

Chapter Nineteen

Warning horns shattered the early morning air as invading ships landed in each sector. Slipping into his armor, Anders warned Shara to hurry to the shelter. Kissing her tenderly, he ran to the guard barracks.

Across the continent, Bronwyn rushed Jana and her youngest children into the shelter beneath the palace. Since his offspring shared his immortality, Scott had chosen to keep them home with their mother rather than in the temple. Once everyone was in the shelter, Salar sent in a handful of armed men, then the heavy door was barred from within. Salar and Scott then raced to the aid of Jericho, who held a doorway against several men.

Peeking out a vacant archer's slot, Bronwyn tried to see through the darkness to discern what was happening. The guard barracks were already afire, throwing wavering light and shadows across the combatants. An enemy soldier brushed past her viewport and she gagged on the stench of ill-cured furs and unwashed body that assaulted her nose.

As he moved away, she saw a terrified toddler, somehow

separated from her mother, cringing against one of the fountains. Children under one year old had been kept with their mothers, too young to be sent alone to the temple. Bronwyn crept from the door and grabbed up the girl, pushing her into the crowded shelter.

At the same time she saw her son and several servants, guarding a group of wounded men, set upon by a handful of burly warriors. Before she could call a guard from the shelter she saw Garth struck down. Pulling a dagger from her sandal straps, she dashed to his side.

"Garth?" She reached for one of the healing tablets in her belt.

"Mother, go back!" Garth gasped, painfully swallowing the tablet before his head fell back. Blood ran thickly through his black hair. Bronwyn's dark eyes sought out her son's attacker and she started toward him.

"My lady! Get thee back inside!" Richard snatched her off her feet.

"Let me go!" Bronwyn flailed wildly until she broke free to race toward the dark figure. Dodging beneath his raised sword she drove her knife through a gap in his armor. She stabbed again as he sank toward the trampled grass.

"Bronwyn!" Richard's voice was panic-stricken as he locked his arms around her slim waist. "Garth wilt heal. Salar wilt stay with thee both in the palace. Thou art to wait for Gray to tell thee when to begin the winds." Dragging her back to the palace, he shoved her through a doorway before he vanished into the battle.

Bronwyn sank to the floor beside her son. "Garth, how do you feel?"

"Sore—but the pills do work." Garth pushed the bloodied hair back from his face, leaning back against the wall.

Salar stood silently by the door, his sword resting across one arm. Bronwyn listened fearfully to the clamor outside. This was not just a raid.

The Shanda leaders centered their attack on Maradane, thus bringing the Davan forces to that world and adding to the destruction spread that first day. Shandal's forces leveled as much as possible in their wake, setting afire every building they passed and using any lull in their area to gather up jewels and precious metals.

They strode across battlefields killing any wounded foe they encountered, prohibiting Bryce's medics from pulling the injured to safety. Snakes were loosed everywhere, and small bands began igniting the forests across the planet.

Late in the evening David appeared in the midst of the battle, accompanied by the four High Under Kings. More Immortals followed to spread across the planet, their golden-hued blades flashing through the air. Many of these formed groups to slaughter the snakes that were spreading their paralyzing fear throughout Maradane's armies.

With a clear view above most heads, David saw that Bryce was in immediate danger, but too far away to help. Unable to fight his way through the press of men, David shouted to the one man who could get through.

Heeding his father, Scott saw three men closing on Bryce, too far for David to reach. Laying open a wide swath with his massive blade, the giant knew he could not reach the flaxen-haired king in time either. Inhaling deeply, Scott sent his harsh voice ringing above the din of swords on armor. "Bryce, turn around!" His two-handed broadsword cut down the men before him as he ran madly at Bryce's attackers.

Bryce could only glance thankfully at Scott as they downed the three men and fought on. Bryce returned to his medical unit, battling the hulking warriors to get the wounded off the field. David quickly ordered more of his people to merge with the field medics and form a guard for the injured.

Gray left the area of his arrival to deliver a jacket of tirrschon mail to Bronwyn.

As she fastened the straps, Bronwyn asked, "How badly is it going, Gray?"

"Badly enough. Maradane hath been marked for destruction," Gray answered. "Yet there art tales arising to mystify the leaders of Shandal, of warriors who die not from mortal wounds, and of the boy who brings death with a look."

Bronwyn paused, buckle in hand, and looked up quizzically.

Gray smiled faintly. "'Tis almost impossible to see Jeremiah's sword, therefore he appears to bring death with a wave of his hand.

"Bron, 'tis time to call upon the winds. Our warriors need time to rest and heal, to regroup. They wert instructed to carry their staffs?"

"At all times," Bronwyn said. "If they are disarmed the staff also provides a weapon, so the men are never without them."

"Excellent. Take this, and be cautious." Gray put a slender golden sword into her hand. "I must go to the other queens. Call down rain to quench the fires as well."

Dashing across the front lawns, Bronwyn dodged amongst the men until she reached the wind tower. Climbing to the highest walkway she held her staff, raised her arms above her head, and repeated a command from David's book.

"Astonal marat dubor trahs."

The winds rose to biting fury and fell mercilessly upon anyone not bearing a staff. The dark warriors fell dazedly to the ground as their weapons were plucked from their hands and their forces blown in upon themselves. They stared in disbelief as the Maran forces advanced, untouched by the swirling gusts. Then the rains began, stinging downpours that doused the fires and dispersed the smoke that had hung over the fighting. Maradane's people breathed deeply of the clean air, while Shandal's forces cursed the biting chill and sharp air burning their lungs.

Bronwyn crept down from the tower and traveled to the other sectors until the Shanda forces were so scattered that they retreated to their ships to re-deploy. Hearing the news, the enemy leaders did not need to consult their psychics to know that an ancient foe was again on the rise. As it was, their psychic forces had still not totally recovered from the vicious murder of Chrys, their renowned leader, many years ago.

Altan settled back in the big chair in Chrys' old quarters, booted feet outstretched toward the roaring fire. A chill still permeated his robust body, the remnants of his new Master's punishment. At least now he understood what had eaten away Chrys' tormented frame.

Peering at the grape-sized piece of amber in his hand, Altan closed his eyes in satisfaction. As a child he had marveled at Chrys, the Seer of Seers, the one who held true sway over Shandal's activities. Still a child when Chrys was murdered, Altan was only beginning to catch a glimpse of the true shape of things. Since then he had fought doggedly to rise to Chrys' position, leaving a trail of bodies in his wake. He had not understood, in the days of that haphazard mayhem, but the Master had been watching him nonetheless.

It was amazing, the things Chrys had known and yet kept so effectively to himself. He had prattled endlessly in the laughable services before the giant snakes, all the while knowing that the people were being honed for one final battle, after which they would feel the fires of the Zha-Dhak.

The thought renewed the chill in the pit of his stomach. He had spent the last four years beyond the window, in hideously grueling training, and had seen why his Master's people needed the realm of David.

The entire universe of the Zha-Dhak was black: lifeless cinders floating in space, worlds drained of the energies supporting life. When the cold fires came all was devoured, funneling the energies into the beings of the sorcerers. There was nothing left in that universe, absolutely nothing. And the Zha-Dhak were nearing the threshold of death. That was why they needed David's realm. If they could not carry out their careful plan to successful completion, the next centuries would see the beginning of their deaths.

Altan remembered his worst lesson all too well. Failing a ridiculously simple test, his body seemed consumed by the freezing fire, and his Master grew stronger before his eyes. Now he would not forget the lesson of icy calculation. Twisting people to one's own ends must be done methodically, with care to see that there was something left to use. And all the while it must appear as something else to watching eyes. Once these wars were won the people of Shandal would learn how it was done.

"Seer?" came a timid voice from the doorway.

Altan motioned for the old man to enter. "What is the news, Becca?"

"The battles aren't going well, lord." Becca bowed, trembling.

"The wind queen has risen to new power. Our men cannot fight when she summons the winds."

"She will be taken care of." Altan rubbed his chin slowly. "My other plan is in action?"

"Yes, lord, all has been set in motion."

"Good." Altan nodded. "We will see how they stagger beneath this blow."

On the third night the western palace was set afire once again. Before Bronwyn knew what was happening her home was surrounded by a closing wall of flame, trapping her inside.

"Richard! Salar, where are you?" Everyone had disappeared. "Salar! Garth!" She ran through the empty rooms, hearing only her own voice in response to her calls. Spinning in futile circles, she tried to think of an escape route.

Jericho was crossing the far lawns, so exhausted that he was almost upon the blaze before he noticed it. Bursting through a blackened door, he shouted, "Bronwyn, are you here?"

"Jericho?...Jericho, I'm in the study!" Her frightened voice rose above the roar of the fire.

The king kicked in the door, the flames exploding behind him. Bronwyn ran to him, clinging to his arm. Tears streaked her face as he hurried her down the smoky hall and out a glass door to the ruined gardens. "Jericho, I can't find anyone!"

"Most of the men have gone with the Immortals to drive back the Shanda. This is only a lull, the enemy will return if they think they can withstand the winds." Jericho stopped walking only when he was certain no airborne debris could reach them.

Bronwyn wiped her face with a grimy hand. "Jericho, my powers are so limited. I haven't strength enough to make the winds constant."

"My Bron, the strength of your powers will buy us time when we need it. You can't win the war alone, but you are helping." He held her close for a moment.

Finally she said, "There's death everywhere now, only death to be seen where once stood our dreams."

Jericho sighed, gazing across the body-strewn landscape. "Come, I'll take you to stay with Shara. Anders went to join Richard, but you'll be safe with Shara."

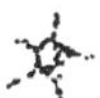

All was silent as they entered the eastern palace. No person was in sight but for a tall shadowy figure fleeing across the far lawns, cradling his arm to his chest as if injured. The Donnyas' steps echoed in the deserted halls as they neared the council chamber.

A scream shattered the stillness, followed by anguished sobs as Jericho and Bronwyn ran into the vaulted room.

The throne at the head of the room was splattered with blood, a stained sword driven into its supporting platform. Anders lay across the single step, his head cradled in Shara's loving hands. Blood pooled beneath his back, and his left arm dangled uselessly to the floor.

"Anders!" Jericho fell to his knees beside the man. When he had last seen Anders the big man was on his way to join the Immortals' fleet. "He is not dead?"

"No, but he has lost so much blood." Shara looked up at Jericho, then to her left, where lay the inert form of Snowfire, his throat severed. "We were in the shelter, and he fought so hard to get out, to come here...but not soon enough." She choked back a sob.

"But the pills...they should begin working by now." Jericho tore his gaze from Anders' pallid face.

"He gave them away, to boys who had lost theirs." Shara ran her hand over Anders' curly hair in a futile gesture. "I can't move him."

Jericho took out his own pills, still untouched, and gently forced two into Anders' mouth. It required all the man's concentration to get the small tablets down, then he let his head fall back into his wife's hands.

Jericho turned to his wife. "Bron, find Bryce—he was at Aric's when we parted. Shara, get some blankets. I'll put him on the table." He lifted Anders gently and laid him on the council table as the women ran from the room. It was then that he saw that Anders had shed his armor in what he thought was a safe moment, trying to loosen the muscles stiffened by the torso-encasing metal and long days of fighting. "Anders, my friend, what have you done?" He smoothed the man's hair away from his tortured face.

Looking miserably at the lifeless cat, Jericho imagined what had happened—Snowfire fighting free of the shelter, sensing the danger to his master, finally reaching this room too late, caught by the enemy's sword.

Shara returned with several blankets. Jericho's weary gaze rested on the plaque bearing Maradane's oath above the throne as he tried to stanch a flow of blood with his hands.

"...Maradane shalt e'er endure..." he read aloud. "David has given us the wrong oath. We aren't enduring at all. It's all been one long struggle toward annihilation."

"We mustn't despair. I don't doubt that we shall win this war, and go on as before." Shara spread a blanket over Anders, caressing his face. "Jericho, the medicine isn't helping much; he's hurt too badly."

"Bryce will be here soon."

"He's slipping away from me, Jericho...You must hold me up so I may use my empathy."

Anders shook his head feebly as Jericho ran one hand through his dusty hair. "Shara, it may be too much for you."

"With or without your help, Jericho, I will do this," Shara said tautly, tears flooding her eyes. "All I ask is that you hold me lest I fall."

"Very well," Jericho sighed, stepping next to her as Anders struggled to protest. Shara placed her hands on Anders' forehead and closed her eyes. Her face twisting with pain, she sought the internal damage, but after only a few brief moments she fell into Jericho's arms with a scream of agony.

Bronwyn ran into the room, followed by Bryce and Jeremiah. "What happened?"

"She tried to heal him," Jericho said miserably as he eased the woman to the floor.

Bryce stopped to check her. "She'll be all right. Bron, keep her quiet." He moved to the table where Anders was struggling to sit up. "Anders, be still now."

"Shara?" Anders asked weakly, falling back.

"She's fine. Be still and let me work." Bryce removed the blanket, then closed his eyes against the sight.

Shara got unsteadily to her feet, leaning on the table. "Anders?"

"No Shara, not again. You've helped enough." Anders' voice was stronger now. "I'm torn apart inside; it will kill you."

Shara held his hand tightly, pleading, "Anders, I'm much stronger than you credit. It won't hurt me..."

Anders coughed on a faint laugh. "My Shara, I love you too well to be fooled. I won't have you die that I should live."

Shara smoothed his hair and put her hands on his forehead, but he pushed her away. "I am your husband and I forbid it! I won't take your life for mine."

Shara protested, but Bronwyn and Jeremiah gently pulled her back from the table.

"You helped, Shara," Bryce said. "You gave him added strength and the pills have worked a little. We've gained some time." He and Jericho carefully rolled Anders onto his side so Bryce could examine his back. The medic scowled at the deep gash in Anders' side.

"It's no use, Bryce," Anders breathed, trying to wave his friend away.

"Be still. If I can't help you, Scott can." Bryce's voice shook as he saw the extent of the injuries.

"The Immortals are gone," Anders reminded him quietly.

Not wanting him to waste any more of his strength, Bryce held Anders firmly by the shoulder and injected him with a sedative. In a moment the man slept quietly.

Bryce turned to Shara, a small hope creeping into his eyes. "Shara, can't the mystics of Stalasia concentrate their empathic powers on a specific area?"

"Yes, I can do that. But..."

"I didn't want him to struggle." Bryce put the needle away. "He has lost too much blood, and our reserves have been used up during this battle. More are coming, but... Do what you can there, while I stitch the wounds."

Working swiftly, Bryce wondered if they were helping or only prolonging Anders' pain. With Shara's help he could keep Anders alive indefinitely, but the man would force her away when he woke.

Anders woke slowly, somewhat stronger, and irritated at being tricked. He pushed Shara roughly away. "I said no!"

"Anders, be still. You'll undo all our work." Bryce finished the final bandage, satisfied that the internal bleeding was momentarily controlled. "How do you feel?"

"You've masked the pain, that is all." Anders let his head fall back on the pillow. "I can't see well, and my legs have no feeling.

"Jeremiah, are you here?"

"Yes, Father." Jeremiah stepped closer, away from Bronwyn's comforting arms, and grasped his father's hand. "Who did this, so I may find him?"

"I don't know. I came to tell Shara I was leaving and a man jumped from behind the throne and stabbed me in the back. I never saw him." He hesitated, then said miserably, "He killed my pet. My Snowfire was old and slow, too old to fight for me..."

"I will find the man," Jeremiah vowed. "Now you must rest."

Bryce gave Anders another pain reliever before taking Shara aside. "Are you certain the Immortals have all gone?"

"Yes. Can we not wait for their return?" Shara dreaded the answer.

"If the hospitals still stood, yes, I would not even need them. I told Shonnie to call one of the hospital ships back, but that takes precious time. And I have not the instruments here to repair the damaged nerves and arteries." Bryce continued, hating every word. "He's right, the man tore him apart and I'm not sure we aren't only dragging out the pain...If only Scott were here, or someone had had sense enough to set up a surgery in the temple. But with the children there..."

A tear traced a path along Shara's cheek as Bryce fell silent.

Anders gathered strength to speak, holding tightly to his son's hand. "Jeremiah..." He paused, as if searching for a vanishing idea. "Before all else, even your life, take care of our people. Our world must live, Jeremiah. Remember that, and that I love you."

Anders looked at his son, pride filling his blue eyes as a burning pain spread through his body.

Jeremiah's throat constricted. "Father, I've no wish to be king yet—"

Shonnie raced through the door. "The hospital ship is landing!"

Anders fought off a surge of pain as Bryce and Jericho lifted him to carry him to the shipboard surgery. In a strained voice he murmured, "Take care of the people, Jeremiah. You shall be a good caretaker..."

A sob choked the youth's voice. "But you must get well, Papa..." He raised his eyes to his mother as the men lowered Anders back to the table.

Shara took Anders' other hand, smoothing the curls from his still brow. Her eyes stung with tears as she whispered, "You were the greatest of all caretakers, my darling..." With a strangled moan she buried her face in the folds of his cape. Jeremiah enfolded her in his arms, his tears falling on her hair.

Bryce hung his head, forcing himself to swallow the burning lump in his throat. "It is best to take him to temple burial chambers. I must get some things from the ship..." Stumbling over the words, he ran from the room.

Jericho stared blankly at Anders' still form, his gaze finally seeking the scar on the man's freckled shoulder. Tracing the mysterious shape with a trembling finger, Jericho whispered, "My friend, I never could find out for you what this meant. I'm sorry."

"We can't leave him in these clothes. Jeremiah, gather your father's ceremonial clothing." Trembling, Shara turned away from the table.

Leaving Jericho and Shonnie looking bleakly at the sword in the throne, Bronwyn led Shara outside. "Shara, can I do anything for you?"

"Tell me if we were right, Bronwyn. Were we right to prolong his life as we did, or did we only torture him more?" Shara sank down onto the remnant of a bench, covering her face with trembling hands. "If only he hadn't come—I would have known he went with the armies. But he thought of me, and he's dead."

"Oh, Shara." Bronwyn hugged her close, but found no words of comfort within herself. Shara had known so much grief, and knew too well how to keep it at bay until her strength was no longer needed.

"What will I do when this numbness wears off?" Shara asked plaintively, glancing around the gardens. The lovingly tended foliage was trampled, littered with fragments of statuary and fountains. Members of a medic unit were busily removing bodies from the area.

Bronwyn straightened, realizing the people around them had no idea what had happened. At the moment she could not find her voice to tell them.

Shara dried her eyes with a pale hand, turning her gaze to the palace. One section was blown away; the entire structure would have to be rebuilt.

"It will be so empty after it's rebuilt, so empty and quiet...I suppose they're ready now. I've never understood this new embalming process." Shara stood and walked slowly to the council chamber, locking the agony deep within herself. Her son needed her strength, not her torment.

The three men were just putting Anders' body on a stretcher. A heavy silence fell upon the group as they journeyed to the temple, broken only by an occasional sob.

Tiea was giving lessons in the gardens but ran to the group as they entered the tunnel. "What happened? Is he hurt badly?"

"Anders is dead." Jericho's voice broke as he gazed past Tiea to the children, tears mingling with the grime on his face. "We've come to bury him."

"I...children, move out of the way." Tiea motioned the children away from the central walk and led the way through the many passages. She stopped at the head of a long hall with sliding vaults in its walls.

Their loss pounding in her head, Tiea forced herself to speak. "I...I think you should use this vault, please." She pointed numbly to the vault nearest the door, then reached for a prayer book from a small drawer.

Shara straightened Anders' cape and folded down the collar,

fixed a pale curl over his headband, and bent to kiss his forehead. Tiea read a passage from the slim book, her tears staining the creamy page, then knelt to engrave the man's name on the gold plate of the vault. It was a cruelly brief farewell to their beloved friend and Tiea's heart ached for the ceremonies he should have had, but could not because of the war.

Pushing the vault into the wall Bryce pressed the lock, sealing away his friend. Gripping the handle so tightly that it snapped off in his hand, he rested his forehead against the cool wall, his shoulders shaking violently. Angrily forcing his voice under control, he growled, "Where is Caleb?"

"He went with the army, toward Dacyn." Tiea looked at the man, absently wiping her eyes with the back of one hand.

"Contact him, and recall as many men as possible. We'll meet him at the eastern palace."

"Tiea," Jericho explained, "Anders was murdered by a warlord of Seryl. The sword was left in the throne to declare a private war. Bronwyn and I saw the man fleeing the palace, taller than average for his race, and apparently clawed by Snowfire on his left arm."

Tiea nodded soberly, trying to grasp the full situation as they retraced their steps to the gardens. Bronwyn and Shara were discussing ways to gather whatever men remained on the planet. Their conversation trailed away as they reached the center of the temple.

The older children had gathered all the candles from the chapels and set them throughout the gardens so the children were encircled by the flickering lights. Kneeling on the floor amidst the flowers, they raised their voices in prayer and the soft sound filled the vast chamber.

Shara clung to her son, recalling Anders telling of his journey to Stalasia. He had been saved there only to be followed and killed by a man who had hidden behind the throne throughout the long battles. Seryl would pay for this murder.

Chapter Twenty

Bronwyn and Shara traveled by air across each sector, safely armed with their staffs and mail jackets supplementing Bronwyn's wind control. They sought out scattered warriors in open fields, men who had remained behind to help the wounded, or wounded men whose tablets had healed minor injuries after the fleets departed. Rage replaced weariness upon news of the gentle king's murder and each man hastened to the unit forming at the eastern palace, where Jericho and Bryce impatiently awaited Caleb's return.

Taking a moment's rest in the charred remains of the southern gardens, the women were set upon by five Shanda. Raising her staff too late, Bronwyn shivered as a sword slid beneath her chin.

"Head up, pretty witch," the man hissed. "Now what sport shall we make of you?"

Eyes narrowed, Bronwyn spat out, "*Astonal!*"

A frenzy of wind sparkles beset the men, distracting them enough for the women to slip back to back and wield their staffs. As Bronwyn summoned a stronger wind, a lone figure appeared behind the enemy, a tattered form so soiled with grime and blood that he was barely recognizable as Richard.

His voice hoarse from smoke, he warned, "Thou shalt suffer greatly if ye harm them."

Spinning on his heel, the enemy leader sneered and lunged toward the short man. "Farewell, little hero."

"I wish thee the same." As Richard's blade slashed through his dingy mail armor, the man's sneer melted into dismay. Richard impatiently tapped the blade against his knee, pushing gritty hair away from his eyes with his free hand. "Who next shalt feel the Golden Death of the Immortals?"

The group hesitated, then fled as Scott exited the silvery mist behind his companion.

Wiping his sword on his ruined trousers, Richard glared at Bronwyn. "My lady, thou shouldst be in the shelter! Why art thou here?"

"We're gathering men to go to Seryl. Didn't you return with Caleb?"

"No, we came alone." Glancing from Bronwyn's tearstained face to Shara's, he flinched inwardly at the grief in her eyes. "Gray sent us. What happened?"

Faltering, Bronwyn explained, adding that Bryce and Jericho planned to hunt down the murderer while the battles were still far from Maradane.

"Anders is dead?" Richard fought the idea, then rage flooded his green eyes. "There art no armies on Seryl! Their shields art up, preventing all landings there." Pausing, he mentally sought some way for a force to bypass the shields protecting Seryl's domed cities.

Metal clinked ominously in that brief silence, and the trio spun to identify the source.

Methodically drawing pieces of a weapon from his Star Holder, Scott fit them together in stony silence. The depth of pain and hatred shadowing his scarred face chilled Bronwyn as she watched his work.

Gripping a leather-bound shaft of heavy iridescent metal, Scott slipped an axe blade onto the top and locked the bolt. Fastening an enormous scythe opposite the axe, he finally pressed a hidden button, releasing a retractable spear.

Richard's eyes widened as Scott assembled the weapon of the giant's own design, an instrument of destruction combining spear, halberd, battle-axe, and scythe into one piece that only Scott could wield. It could be used in any one of its forms, the axe and scythe discardable to form a throwing spear, or the axe used alone with the scythe for close battle. Forged in an Elven smithy out of grief over their slaughter in retaliation for the Elves' patrols of snake-ridden planets, the weapon had not seen the light of day for many centuries. Scott assembled and used it only out of fathomless rage and pain. Had Richard not cut them down upon location, Scott would have used the axe on Tanya's killers.

Still staring at the axe, Richard breathed, "If Seryl knew what they hadst wrought..."

"No man of Seryl wilt cross my path and live." Scott swung the weapon onto one brawny shoulder, his eyes agonized as he recalled his last talk with Anders. "Truly didst he vow that night. For in this single act Shandal hath spawned its own end."

"I don't understand," Shara stammered, fresh tears touching her cheeks.

Scott gently brushed the tears away. "When Anders gave me the book, he vowed that if he didst nothing else in his life he wouldst see that Maradane doth not fall. The hatred kindled this night wilt live beyond time, and though it be not now, it wilt crush Shandal through Anders' own children. I am not Gray, but that much I have now seen."

Pressing her face to his huge hand, Shara whispered, "Thank you, for your small vision."

Scott hugged her close. "We cannot remain here. Richard and I wert sent to warn thee that the battle turns back this way."

"We're gathering at the eastern palace," Bronwyn said flatly, grateful for Richard's arm around her waist. She summoned a wind and they set out.

Upon hearing Richard's news Jericho hurled his sword to the ground. "It's like Seryl to deal in murder and then hide!"

"They canst not hide from Gray," Scott growled. "The murderer wilt face us. But now more urgent things art at hand." He pointed to the night sky.

Battle fleets raced before the dark clouds. Hurtling through the air, projectiles ripped jagged holes in hulls, plunging hundreds of men to their deaths.

Drawing his sword, Richard muttered, "I wish we hadst kept such great speeds to ourselves. Mortals shouldst not traverse a galaxy in half a day simply to maim and kill."

Scott motioned for Bronwyn and Shara to follow him. "I wilt take thee to the palace shelter. Remain there until one of my people comes for thee."

Too heartsick to argue, the women followed wordlessly. Only at the entrance did Bronwyn look up at Scott's weary face.

"Why do you allow this? Why not blow up all of Shandal and be done with it? David should save us from this agony."

"Save thee for what, though?" Scott looked gently into her dark eyes. "Bron, Shandal's worlds art no longer home to only their race. Do the slaves deserve death because of their captor's deeds, when they suffer more than thou canst imagine?" He smoothed her windblown hair, then shook his shaggy head. "We art their only hope of life, of freedom, and thou wouldst drop bombs on them. We must remember those who wait, e'en though we art torn apart inside."

Bronwyn reached up with trembling hands to wipe the tears from his face, then hugged him tightly before he turned away to join Richard. She then sank to the cold stone floor beside Shara, who stared blankly at the small archer's slot opposite them. "I seem to do everything wrong now," she mumbled to herself.

Shara grasped her hand. "Turning to vengeance alone would destroy us. We must fight because we love our people, not because we hate our enemy, and right now I hate them more than I have hated or loved anyone or anything. They've torn my life from me."

Bronwyn watched helplessly as Shara buried her face in both hands. Until today she had always known what to do to help, to comfort, but this night had crushed whatever hope was in her soul. Hugging Shara once more, she sat in empty silence.

Aric stood atop the rubble that had been his home, smoke obscuring the ruin and thankfully the bloody landscape as well. The work of his life was gone, obliterated in five brief days. He seemed unable to remember that life, to know anything beyond the burning pain in his arms, worn out from wielding his broadsword, and the depthless agony in his heart. So he stood, unable to decide where to turn, how to save what remained of his world.

"Aric?" David scrambled up the devastation of boulders to grip his shoulders. "Thou canst not stand here."

"I can't do anything else," the red-head mumbled hollowly. "I can't save my people, the enemy is too many. They'll raze the shelters, our stores, our children. I can't stop them."

"We shalt stop them at least here," David said bitterly, hugging Aric close in the acrid wind. "They shalt fight on our own chosen ground, or I shalt destroy every palace, every treasure house, every records library, until they abandon our shelters and storehouses. Come, Aric, back to our council. I wilt not leave thee here to die in ambush."

Aric followed numbly, to the cluster of rulers and Immortals gathered in one room somehow still sheltered by a wall on one side.

"'Tis the only way," Scott was agreeing with Richard and Gray. "We must not allow ground combat on our worlds, for they seek only to slaughter, not to fight our warriors."

Caleb nodded. "The air corps will remain here, instructed to take out Shandal's ships as they fly, and to douse grounded warriors with water. Bron has been instructing several warriors in summoning a freezing wind to attack those who are doused."

"Excellent." David nodded. "We wilt send a handful of those men to other worlds in this quadrant, to use the same tactic. 'Tis imperative that the shelters be kept safe, and the storehouses. Gray, help Bronwyn and Shara prepare to travel. The rest of thee gather what forces wilt not remain here. I am going to Nicholas to see that their fleets concentrate on the treasure houses of Shandal. They *wilt* fight on our chosen ground."

Shandal refused the ultimatum for three long months, bent on keeping the battles on David's most precious worlds. But their troops were being decimated, frozen in mid-battle by the howling winds that Bronwyn helped spread from world to world, and their fleets lost countless ships to air corps attacks. This alone would never sway the Seers and Overlords, but each day more treasure centers fell to Immortal ships, enormous airborne battering rams of reinforced tirrschon designed specifically to demolish buildings by repeated impacts. David refused to further imperil his people by re-introducing explosive weapons, but Shandal's governing and monetary centers fell nonetheless fully.

"It's working, slowly," Shara said wearily, sinking onto a cot beside Bronwyn's in Gray's tent. "Gray feels they will soon abandon the attacks on our worlds, and follow our fleets to barren planets."

"I pray so." Bronwyn sighed, a hairbrush held loosely in one idle hand. "I've trained the last group of Icers—in the name of David, what a ghastly phrase."

Shara rubbed Bronwyn's shoulder sympathetically. "All too apt, though."

"All too," Bronwyn agreed, shaking her head. "I was so eager to practice all those years. Somehow I never connected it with actual killing. Five men backed out of this last group. They could not bring themselves to watch others frozen to death before their eyes, by their own hand. Do you realize that almost all the Icers are women?"

"Not women, but mothers." Shara hesitated, rubbing her eyes. "Mothers who will protect their children at all cost, by any possible means. It's too detached for the men, who can justify the honesty of sword upon sword, face to face. But drawing death from the very air, it grates against their honor."

"And all it grates upon for me is my heart."

Shara hugged her. "Be glad it does, Bron. Were I in your place, I would rain death on every one of their worlds, and have no heart to rail against what I had done."

Bronwyn held her for a long moment, then kissed her cheek. "If I could, I would, but those powers are not mine. It would be easier that way, not to watch death unfold before me, not this horrible, cold way."

"It will not be cold much longer," Shara said distantly. "Shandal loves heat, and many of their worlds are desert. There will be no water in their deserts."

Nodding, Bronwyn grasped her hand. "Are you sleeping, Shara? You work so hard with Gray, you need your sleep."

"He drives me during the day so there will be no time to think," Shara said softly. "And at night he touches my forehead so there will be no room for memory. I sleep a very deep, very empty sleep, always."

Bronwyn did not know how to comfort her. Perhaps it was best left to Gray, who did push her harder every day, using her psychic powers to seek weak areas in enemy defenses, to test tactics for their own forces, to probe ahead for what was to come, and on what worlds it would happen. Yet he watched her with gentle eyes, and did leave quiet spaces in the day for her thoughts to roam. If he gave her such deep sleep each night, it was only to allow a healing of the grief that stole over her during those quiet moments. He guarded her, protected her, and in his wordless way would guide her back to wholeness.

Within the month all Shanda forces landed on barren, hot planets scattered throughout their realm. Bronwyn was stripped of her power with water and ice, as Shara had known would happen, and the Icers were left to defend David's worlds against scattered forays that still persisted.

Wind was almost non-existent, the current sluggish and laden with the smoke and clouds cultivated to shelter the Shanda from the full touch of the sun. Glorying in heat, they despised bright light. Bronwyn's efforts were temporarily turned to clearing some of the smoke and clouds, bringing clean air to David's forces and blinding the enemy so that they adopted gauze shades around their sensitive eyes. She found this a great relief, for it helped her people without injuring others. Yet it was not enough, a point brought home in the next council gathering.

Jericho massaged a healing lotion over his very red arms as he spoke. "It seems we only gain another hurt for each one we relieve. We're either choking on their acrid air, or frying in this desert sun."

Scott nodded slowly, his own skin nearly black from its reaction to avoid burning in the prolonged exposure. "Perhaps, Bron, thou hadst better concentrate on moving wind through the camp, particularly around the hospital tents. The air purifiers wilt keep our air breathable. But we need a stronger tactic for use in battle."

Bronwyn nodded, grasping the small book David had given her. "There's so little to work with here, the wind barely moves. Perhaps if I concentrate on magnifying the heat in their camps, or moving all this sand somehow."

"Any distraction will help, Bron," Aric agreed. "If I just don't melt into the ground first. I can't bear this heat."

"You spent too much time in the snow," Jericho said with a small laugh. "Scott, how are we faring so far?'

"We art holding our own, but not moving forward." Scott glanced around the group. "In this area, Jeremiah is doing the best of any unit."

"It's only because of Bane Slayer," the youth said tiredly, hugging his mother close with one arm. "At least it gets me close to their camps, to free the prisoners. What's planned next?"

Richard shrugged. "Ground combat is all too repetitive. David's scholars art studying the book, and Asher is laying the foundation for an attack on several of Shandal's weaker planets. But for us, it remains only day to day battle, with little hope of rest any time soon."

"Then we'd better get back to it." Bryce stood, stretching stiffly.

Asher strolled toward the guards at the near end of the slave camp, feigning irritation as a light was flashed into his face.

"What is your business here after dark?" the man demanded harshly.

Raising his hand to display the heavy signet on his thumb, the mark of the highest rank of librarian, Asher said simply, "I have come seeking a new pleasure girl for my home. The previous one seems to be all used up."

"Worn out, eh?" The man grinned wickedly. "There's not

much of beauty in this camp, though. Go on, just remember to return this way to leave."

"Certainly." Asher brushed past him, stepping onto the narrow lane bisecting the camp's array of clay hovels. Little beauty, indeed. His irritation was no longer feigned as he strolled the lane, looking at each slave as he passed. Any beauty existing in Shandal was to be found in these camps, any bit of tenderness and compassion. And much hatred, all of it at the moment directed at his passing form.

Few eyes dared meet his. Children vanished into the nearest doorway at his approach, and women hurried either to hide their babies or hide themselves behind their men. Someone, or several someones, always vanished when a Shanda of his stature roamed their camps. Even the men backed away, for the most part, leaving him an empty lane to trod.

He scanned each doorway, each cracked shutter, and mentally noted each instance of what he sought—defiant eyes that met his own and did not falter. Traversing the entire lane, and studying the maze of alleys branching from it, he turned to retrace his steps. But this time he pointed to men as he passed, pounding on doors if he had to, and ordered them to follow him. They did so grudgingly, knowing one shout from him would bring mayhem from the guards.

Pausing in the center of the camp, Asher intently studied the seven men in the dim light from nearby windows. They held their heads up, meeting his gaze with belligerence. Scarred and battered, they were by no means broken, neither the youngest of perhaps fifteen nor the oldest with thick white hair.

"This alley." Asher pointed to his left. "It is a dead end at a wall, with no other way in or out?"

"One door, halfway down," the old man answered warily. "Why?"

"I seek to demonstrate something. You will be my witness." Asher began pointing. "Two of you remain here, facing the alley. Two of you go to the doorway, and two of you all the way to the wall at the end."

They complied slowly, suspiciously, and the old man asked, "What do I do?"

"You will walk beside me, slowly, all the way to the wall." Asher set out.

Watching from the alley entrance, the youth looked at his companion. "What is he up to?"

"Murder, most likely. Separate us, then kill us."

"Hardly," Asher laughed from behind them.

They spun, gaping, as the old man skidded to a halt behind them, gasping, "Immortal!" under his breath.

"Silence!" Asher snapped. "Get your friends back here, with no sound."

The old man complied, quickly.

"Excellent." Asher nodded. "Take me to your secret room, the one even the Shanda know nothing of."

They eyed him again, then slowly guided him a few paces to the left, into another alley, and another, then through three small rooms. Steps led to a food cellar, where a rock wall pivoted into a narrow passage, leading to a cramped room with rock walls.

"This is very good." Asher pulled a lantern from the wall and lit it, holding it aloft. "Who is thy leader?"

To his surprise, the youth stepped forward. As Asher arched one brow, the boy turned and pulled up his shirt, revealing a back flayed to the bone more than once. "They never broke my father, and they will never break me," he said evenly, once again facing Asher. "My name is Tarmynan."

"My name is Asher," He studied the boy. "Tell me, Tarmynan, why my people have not saved thine from this camp."

"Even you cannot do that," he answered soberly. "You are strong, but you are not God. We would all be slaughtered if they saw you, or saw one of your ships. And we cannot leave without ships."

"Not yet," Asher agreed, still holding his gaze. "I believe they have chosen their leader wisely. Now let me tell thee how thou mayst indeed leave this world."

They gathered closer, intent on his words.

"This war is stripping all warriors from many worlds," Asher began. "By the time we art ready to move, the worlds wilt be open for thee to take, and then to leave. For then our ships wilt be able to land, and take thee to safety. But this entire plan is now upon thine shoulders."

"We understand," Tarmynan assured him. "What is to be done?"

"I wilt leave a message periodically in thy home, which thou art to show me 'ere I leave. That wilt tell thee when to meet me here." Asher looked once more around the room. "One night and one day wilt see thee liberated, for my people wilt move into this chamber enough weapons to arm every person in camp. Thou art now entrusted with the care of thine people, and their freedom." He caught and held Tarmynan's gaze. "One murmur of this and the Shanda wilt slaughter this entire camp."

"The man who speaks will die by my hand before I die," Tarmynan swore.

Asher squeezed his shoulder. "Upon the chosen night my people wilt bring in the weapons, which wilt be quietly distributed by thy chosen men, with no sound or light to alert the outside guards. In the morning thou wilt find those guards replaced with my people in Shanda uniform, to escort thee as usual into the city. Once at thine appointed duties, thou wilt begin to take the city. More of my people wilt come then to finish the task, and thou wilt go at once to the fleet, with no stops. By day's end thou wilt be in safety, tended and healed, and ready to settle a new world of thy choosing. But this wilt not happen for many months, so the secret must be kept."

"It will be kept, and we will wait, and there will be no trouble made before then, to endanger none of our people." Tarmynan's gaze swept the others, who nodded quickly.

"Yea, chosen very wisely." Asher smiled slowly. "Show me thy home, Tarmynan. Then I must hasten to other camps and other worlds."

The youth led him back to the lane, where he pointed to a small room facing the street.

Asher went on his way, pausing at the guard station. "That was a waste."

"No beauty here," the guard repeated.

"None at all." Asher strode away, allowing a smile in the dark night.

The camp remained quiet, the men returning home with a story of fixing a broken cart. In his one tiny room, Tarmynan caressed the cheek of his sleeping wife and gathered up his infant daughter, kissing her forehead. *You shall know freedom, heart of my life.*

"The children are there." The Shanda scout consulted the small map in his hand, a map created long ago by Devon in his months on Maradane. "They conceal the entrance, but it is there. And all the Maran children are locked inside with their treasures."

The corps commander nodded, turning to his men. "I am told there is a wide tunnel leading into a garden area, and the living quarters branching from there. You are to enter as quietly as possible, the assigned four first, and loot the chapels. The rest will begin loosing the snakes, and locate the paths to the lower treasure floors. Kill everyone you encounter."

Moving silently, they sought and found the temple entrance, then slipped soundlessly down the tunnel, sacks of snakes over their shoulders, swords drawn.

Entering the gardens, they split as appointed, some searching for chapels and elevators while their companions began freeing the mass of reptiles.

A small girl slipped from her hidden alcove and raced toward the council chamber, shouting, "Raiders! Joachim! Kimmel, raiders!" Doors slammed and bolts flew home as she ran.

Scott's eldest sons hurtled past her, swords drawn, followed closely by his youngest two and Lachlan. By the time they neared the garden the child had sounded the main alarms, and heavy grills crashed to the floor behind them and over all entrances to the chapels and elevators, as well as the tunnel itself.

Skidding to a halt, Joachim stumbled over an arm-thick serpent on the brick walkway. With a disgusted snarl, he hacked at it with his sword even as he counted the twenty confused men trapped in the gardens. Pointing to the commander, he shouted to his brothers. "Leave him alive to report home!"

The Shanda raised their swords, intent on the five youths and paying little heed to the increasing clatter of the chimes in the center of the chamber.

"There are only supposed to be children here," one man growled toward the commander.

"I am a child," Joachim informed him with a slight grin. "Eldest child of Scott, and his most apt pupil. He wouldst not leave our Maradane unguarded." He caught the man's blade on his, prepared for a struggle.

With a frenzied chiming mingled with an ear piercing hum, fire shot upward from the small black orb to the crystal embedded in its silver net. From there the fire fragmented into countless shards, each one finding its home on a writhing serpent that then smoldered into nothingness where it lay.

The Shanda dove forward with agonized cries, hacking at the Immortal youths, who herded them back toward the tunnel. Maran warriors raced toward them, and Joachim pounded a hidden switch in the wall to admit them. "Leave the commander alive!" he ordered.

The remaining Shanda seemed also interested in living, for they threw down their swords and clustered at the wall as the Marans surrounded them.

Grabbing the commander by the collar, Joachim growled, "This temple is ours, and we protect it, and those who lived here before us protect it. Do not send more men, or they wilt die, for we need only one report to reach thy Seer's ear." Turning, he found the Maran commander. "Put this one on his ship. Send the rest to the prison ship."

"At once, my lord."

As the prisoners were escorted outside, Joachim sat on a stone bench to survey the quiet gardens. The chimes were still now, and no trace remained of the snakes. A handful of warriors scouted the chapels and checked the elevators, but none had been reached by the raiders.

"I am glad Bronwyn left her chimes here," Joachim said at last. "And glad we didst not need to kill here, where the children play."

His brothers nodded, sheathing their swords. Lachlan went to tell Tiea all was well, and Joshua lowered the tunnel grate once more. "'Tis better to leave it in place now."

"Yea, much better." Joachim glanced down the hall, where Jana held Laryssa in her arms. "'Tis safe, Mama."

"I know." She came over to kiss his cheek. "Your papa would be so proud of you, all of you."

Joachim took his baby sister into his arms, hugging her close. "I hope Papa is well. It hath been so long now since he came home."

"They need him near our armies," Jana said softly. "But he will come soon, he promised."

Chapter Twenty-One

Rubbing his side where it had been pierced by a lance, Scott peered through the smoke rolling across the field. The Shanda had imported more shiploads of green wood to set afire that morning, creating choking cover for the massive assault on the Maran base camp. Leading the first counter-attack, Scott had later fallen back to protect Bryce's medic unit as they worked. At the moment, however, he could not see past the length of his arm.

"Damn." Turning slowly, he listened intently, seeking voices from the medics. The smoke billowed forth too thickly for Bronwyn's sluggish winds to clear, making direction nonexistent in the suffocating blanket.

"Curse it!"

Bronwyn's infuriated cry reached Scott, much too near. He had strayed back toward Gray's tent, away from Bryce's vulnerable unit. Following the sound, Scott found the queen framed in the tent's doorway.

Her staff stabbed into a mound of sand at her feet, Bronwyn flipped angrily through the pages of her small book, wincing at every dull cry reaching her ears.

"Bron?" Scott paused beside her.

"Sixteen months!" she snapped, barely glancing up. "Sixteen months of choking on their foul smoke. It's going to stop!"

He studied her, wary. "Hast thou found a new command?"

"No." Bronwyn hurled the book into the tent. "I've made one."

Striding forward, she planted her feet, raised her staff high in both hands, and shouted, *"Astonal! Mare nalath, natha nacht mithrac, nothrac trahs!"*

In the ensuing instant of deadened sound, Scott recognized only two of her words—*vortex* and *enemy*. The lull broke, the entire area reverberating with a low hum. Smoke and sand curling in all directions, the hum crescendoed to a roar as the winds coalesced into a vortex above the camp. In that moment Scott, like every other Maran, dove to the ground, arms crossed over his head.

Seething, black with smoke, the vortex hung for a moment, gaining momentum. The roar was shattering as the winds spun ever wider, drawing in the smoke and spiraling thick tentacles outward. With a decisive howl, it moved, bearing down on the Shanda forces.

Daring to look up then, Scott saw the vortex fragment, the main body seeking the Shanda camp while myriad smaller tornadoes danced over every part of the battle, plucking enemy warriors from the very midst of the Maran force. Empty now of smoke, the air filled with agonized cries and the sickening crunch of shattered bones.

In its wake the Maran warriors began to stand, a wave rising behind the storm. Yet as they saw what lay around them they simply turned back toward their camp.

Sunlight flooded the area, only making that part shadowed by the vortex that much more black. The blackness careened onward, at last enveloping the Shanda camp in an hysteria of terror and agony. Men struggled to flee, but were drawn upward and cast aside with crumpling indifference. Tents, arms, supplies, ships—all collapsed as if stepped upon, debris hurled wide by the howling wind. Yet the vortex grew smaller, the smoke dissipating, and as the winds themselves dispersed, a small group of men staggered from amidst the destruction.

Jeremiah's unit ran at once to help the freed prisoners back to their own camp.

Standing slowly, Scott looked first toward the tent to check on Bronwyn.

Staff lowered, Bronwyn stood numbly, staring over the sand toward the remnants of the vortex. That sand was strewn with broken bodies, a sight that drained all color from the queen's face.

Striding to the nearest body, Scott discovered why they all looked odd, why they lay as if ground beneath rolling boulders. Returning to Bronwyn, he gently touched her cheek.

"I didn't mean it this way," she said flatly. "I meant to crush as to stop, not...this."

"The language of the True-Bloods is one of picture fragments, Bron," Scott reminded her. "There is no subtlety of words to the winds. Crush is crush."

Jericho ran up, overhearing Scott's last words. Seeing his wife's pale face, he hugged her tightly. "You've helped us, Bron, and that is most important." He kissed her cheek. "They'll need days to get a new force here. By then we'll have taken better ground and have our men back on their feet."

She nodded slowly. "We had better organize units to help get the wounded into camp. But what about the Shanda?"

"My people wilt deal with it, Bron," Scott said, scanning the scene. "Any who art not dead wilt go to the prison ships. I see some movement still—" He paused, squinting in the bright light, then he focused on the distant medic unit.

Two Shanda warriors had staggered to their feet, wounded already and thus overlooked by the winds. Grasping their swords, they turned on the medics working around them.

"Jericho, with me!" Scott grabbed up his axe and loped across the sand.

Taken unawares, two medics fell before their companions drew their swords to meet the attack.

With half the distance yet to cover, Scott saw one youth abruptly run through with a broadsword. "Adric, no!" Running madly, the Immortal caught the Shanda on his pike and hurled him aside, turning to catch the youth as he crumpled to the ground.

Grasping futilely at the sword lodged in his stomach, Adric looked up at Scott and gasped, "Tell Miri good-bye, my lord."

"No!" Scott yanked his silver from his belt even as the youth fell back limply on his arm. Adric had been Jana's servant since he was eight, and had assured his young wife he would be safe in the medic unit, safe to return home to her and their infant daughter. Loosing the sword, Scott hurled it aside and gathered Adric's body into his arms, kissing his forehead. "Adric, no."

Jericho threw down his own sword, scowling, then knelt beside his friend. "Shall I take him to the burial ship, Scott?"

Scott shook his head vehemently. "I shalt carry him home. I let him die, I must tell Miri."

"But you can't save everyone, Scott," Jericho began gently.

"Adric wast my family!" Scott growled, standing with the youth's body in his arms. "I wast supposed to be with this unit! Not lost like a child in the smoke. I wilt take him home, and return before the battles begin anew." Grasping his travel stone, he strode bitterly into the mist forming ahead of him.

The temple gardens were quiet when he arrived, only a handful of older children scattered about at various tasks. One tall youth glanced up, then his shoulders fell. "Oh Papa, no."

"Find Miri, please, Kimmel," Scott whispered, turning toward the nearest chapel.

By the time Adric had been laid on the altar's stair, hesitant steps whispered on the tiled aisle floor. Miri approached slowly, then knelt beside her husband's still form.

Scott smoothed her thick black hair. "I am sorry, Miri. I shouldst have been nearer him."

"You cannot save everyone, my lord," she whispered absently, stroking Adric's forehead with trembling fingers. "I will stay with him now."

Scott turned helplessly away, following the corridors to Jana's rooms and stepping inside. Closing the door as she met his gaze, he sank to his knees and sobbed.

"Sshhh." Jana ran to hug him close.

Holding her tightly, face pressed to her shoulder, Scott cried,

"If I hadst been faster, or been where I belonged, he wouldst not have died in my arms."

"You ask far too much of yourself," Jana chided, kissing his hair. "No matter where you are, someone elsewhere will die because you aren't in that place. You do your best, always. Don't ask so much more of yourself."

He looked up, then gently wiped the tears from her face. "I love thee, my little one."

"I love you, my very big one." She settled into his arms, grasping his hand in both of hers. "Stay with me for a little while, please. Tell me of our friends, if they are well, and how the battles go. Hold me close for these moments."

"These, and all moments." Scott kissed her tenderly. "Our friends art well, my love. Bronwyn doth much with her winds, more each day."

Pausing in her reading, Bronwyn tried to remember the last time all the families had been together. It had been at the last council, now twenty days gone, where the latest rout had been planned. Precious silence once again surrounded the camp, as they awaited yet another Shanda battalion to replace the last, the fourth in ten months since the devastation with the vortex. She had been unable to summon another one so strong, but lesser ones proved just as effective. In this brief silence she made an idle mental tally of people and positions.

Shara remained with Gray, of course, throwing herself into the demanding mental work of the psychics. The small woman allowed herself rest only to seek out reports of her son. Jeremiah remained well, invulnerable with Bane Slayer in his grasp. In each battle he led his band of unrelenting warriors at the forefront of the Maran armies. As the fighting waned, he and his men haunted the fringes of the Shanda camp to free Marans taken prisoner.

Absently flipping a page, Bronwyn glanced toward the hospital tents. Prudence was in charge there, assisted by Shonnie in tending the wounded brought in by Bryce's people. The field units were still hard put to retrieve the injured warriors, and Bryce risked his life more times daily than Prudence cared to consider. Shonnie never dared think of Aric's position, for he led the central assault units and was away from camp for days on end.

Relieved that Jericho and Garth were usually close at hand, leading the protective units around the camp, Bronwyn wished the other wives could have that same peace. It was worst for Tiea, left on Maradane to guard the children and command the forces there. For long periods she was out of touch with everyone, although Immortal couriers met regularly with her. She had little to do but wait and wonder, while Caleb shuttled between his forces and David's command center in an endless cycle.

Returning to her book, Bronwyn began again toying with different phrasings. Then one word caught her eyes, and she drummed her fingers thoughtfully on the page.

Carrying the book with her, she went to glance outside her tent. "Richard? Are you here?"

"Always, my lady." Richard strode from the left, golden sword resting across one arm. "David wishes me near to thee and Shara. What dost thou need?"

"I have an idea, I think." She glanced down at the book, then smiled at him. "Richard, each of these four times we have moved slightly north, and it is still barren, but no longer all desert. The Shanda always try to push us back into the heat, where they fare so well. What I need to know is whether there are polar caps on this world."

"Really?" Richard tilted his head to one side, green eyes intent, then he smiled. "That is easily enough checked. Remain here, my lady, and I shalt be right back."

Bronwyn watched as he disappeared into the silvery mist, then waited patiently through the several moments of his absence.

Returning with a smile upon his face, Richard tossed a snowball toward the queen. As she caught it, he said, "The caps art not large, but deep in snow. Wilt that do?"

"Very well, if only once. It will disconcert them once they arrive. Thank you, Richard." Bronwyn kissed his cheek.

"Thou art most welcome, my lady." Richard laughed as he returned to his post and she to her tent. As he turned, he found

Jericho walking toward him.

"Is she well, Richard?" Jericho paused to grab a rag and wipe the grime from his face.

"Thy lady is fine, my friend," Richard said softly. "And planning some snowy mischief for our next guests."

"Snow? Well, they'll surely love that." Jericho smiled, then grasped Richard's shoulder. "It means everything to me that you are protecting her, Richard. It makes my days that much easier. That, and knowing that you'll always do so, if I do not return home."

"Thou wilt go home, Jericho, for I couldst ne'er heal her of that grief. But in thine days apart, I am the lion by her side."

"And I'm very grateful." Jericho nodded toward the Immortals' tent. "Go rest. I shall be with her for a while, until we must prepare for the next fleet from Shandal."

"Then I mayst very well seek a nap." Sheathing his sword, Richard strode away.

Entering the tent, Jericho stole softly to his wife's chair and bent to kiss her neck.

"Jericho." She laughed softly, turning to hug him. "I do seem to recall having a husband who looked like you."

"He remains." Jericho drew up a chair, then grasped her hands. "I hear you're up to mischief in here."

"I hope so, and one that won't maim this time." Bronwyn hesitated.

Jericho squeezed her hands. "My love, anything you do to distract them is a help. It is our warriors' task to kill."

"But I can save so many of them, when I have the strength."

"But it is tiring, we know that." Jericho brushed her dark bangs back from her face. "It does me nothing to win a war and lose my wife. Do not wear yourself out."

"I won't," she promised, pressing her cheek to his hand. "Besides, my bodyguard will not let me. He hovers over me at every turn."

"As well he should," Jericho said emphatically. "You do as Richard says, for you are first in his eyes."

Bronwyn sought his gaze. "Does that trouble you, Jericho?"

"It troubles me only that my friend is alone," he answered softly. "To know that you are always protected, to know that protection goes even beyond my death and can never be broken by his death, that gives me great peace of mind. Bron, I shall have to be dragged from you by powers stronger even than Scott, but if that day comes, you will go to Richard, and I will know peace."

Tears in her dark eyes, she nodded. "I would go, because he would honor my grief, as you honor his heart. I love you, Jericho."

"And I you." Jericho hugged her close. "Now, tell me of this mischief you plan."

Aric paused, surrounded at last by only his own men, and scrubbed the sweat from his face. "Five days only, and I could melt into the ground again."

"They seem to bring more heat with them, my lord," his commander said wearily. "How can they thrive so on this heat? They draw energy from it even as ours seeps away."

"I understand nothing about these people." Aric shook his head. "Except that they are as stubborn as we."

The commander nodded, seeing the battle turning toward them once more. "I'm beginning to fear they may be more stubborn. At least on this world."

"Hold on, Titus, just hold on." Aric sighed, rolling his shoulders within his armor, feeling as if he were a roast in a sealed pan. Flexing his arms, he took several limbering sweeps with his broadsword.

"My lord?" Titus pointed to the north. "Is another storm planned, my lord?"

"No one told me." Aric peered toward the horizon, seeing a huge bank of something white and dense boiling toward them. It did not look like a vortex, but more like something collected and borne before the wind. "Well, whatever it is, just stand fast with your staffs."

"Stand fast!" Titus shouted to the men behind him, and the command rippled outward through the ranks.

The Shanda paused as well, those in combat and those laying

the green fires to choke their enemy. The Overlord nearest Aric's unit rubbed his arms briskly. "Cursed witch, she's cooling the air somehow. Stoke those fires, now!"

Smoke began rolling forth, but was swiftly blown southward on a wind gone frigid. The Shanda gaped at the white wall bearing down on them and wondered at this new terror even as they slapped their arms to keep warm.

Aric gaped as well, breathing deeply of the clean, cold air and at last recognizing the billowing whiteness. Throwing his arms wide as the first soft flakes caressed his cooling face, he laughed, "Snow! Heaven bless you, Bron, you brought snow!"

"Snow?" Titus hesitated, then rubbed the cold moisture into his skin. "Ah, my lord, I can breathe again!"

The reaction spread on the cold wind, the Maran warriors stretching and straightening, breathing deeply and soaking in the touch of the snow.

The Shanda fires sputtered and died, the bits of smoke faded on the gale, and the warriors shivered in their heavy fur boots and capes.

Seeing the swarthy enemy's movements, Aric laughed and turned to Titus. "Form the ranks. We shall fight now in our own element."

"At once, my lord."

Aric watched as his warriors fell into formation, shaking off the fatigue of the heat and relishing the soothing coldness surrounding them. Glancing at the wavering enemy, Aric laughed again and ordered his unit forward.

In the camp, the four queens gathered to look over the field, already deep in snow.

"Oh Bron, look at them!" Shonnie cried thankfully, watching the Maran forces course forward with sudden energy. "This is the best you could ever have done, to let them feel home again."

"Indeed," Gray said as he joined them. "Look behind thee."

Turning, they saw the entire camp turn out, even those from the hospital tents. Men and women alike fell to their knees and gathered handfuls of snow, scrubbing it over faces and arms. Then they simply knelt in a growing silence.

Shara hugged Bronwyn tightly. "Bronwyn, you've brought life back to them. Only an instant, but it will stay with them."

"I can do it once more, from the southern cap," Bronwyn said happily. "If we move to other worlds, or with time here, I can do it again. I'm so happy it worked."

"It worked beautifully." Prudence watched their warriors beat back the Shanda, all the way to the enemy camp. "A small step on a long road, but this day is ours."

"I shall see how to make more days ours, and shorten the road." Bronwyn glanced at the book in her hand, then returned to her tent.

Altan accepted the steaming mug from Becca's gnarled hands, exhausted from the lengthy conclave. With dozens of worlds as battlefields and hundreds more open for plunder, all he was able to focus on was one small desert world and one cursed witch. If her powers were not nullified, the entire empire would fall in years to come, even if the present war were won.

"Lord, are you better now?" Becca asked nervously, wringing his hands.

"I will never be better," Altan said dryly, glancing at his withered leg. It froze through to the bone, a coldness that no heat could burn away. "But I am learning. As my Master learned from his mistakes, so will I. When toying with the beloved of the Gabrellans each step must be carefully taken. I realized too late how the love of Anders would drive his people onward." He paused, then frowned wearily. "I created the very force I sought to destroy. And I have paid for that slowness of wit."

"What shall you do now, Seer?"

"I, nothing. For the moment." Altan sipped his tea. "No, my Master has a plan now, and we will see how he fares. David prepares tricks with his secret little book, but the Zha-Dhak also prepare. Progress has been made since their experiment with the spy Asher. The Immortals will pay a high price for their stubbornness. But before that, the witch will fall and our armies shall conquer."

The ensuing months saw the fighting deteriorate into an all too predictable pattern of stalemate and retreat. Setting up their camps and attacking for as long as they were winning, Shandal abandoned the fortifications and fled in search of better terrain as the tide turned. In many instances this tactic worked, but where Maradane's armies were concerned it proved futile. A shifting wave of battle and flight established itself around those forces, and tactics of wind attacks and harrying forays settled into tedious regularity.

For the Maran forces it was a constant struggle to pull the battles northward, away from the searing desert heat of the world that Shandal refused to abandon. For Bronwyn it was a daily struggle to derive new commands from old, a constant experiment seeking ways to deter the enemy without inflicting the casual mayhem she was becoming unable to bear.

A secondary battle raged beyond locked doors, far beneath the city of Leahcim Tierrah, as David's researchers arduously tried to decipher the text of the ancient Stalassi book. The better part of a year had gone with no clue to the script. Its language was far older than David, and his days became burdened with frustration.

Pushing aside stacks of field reports, David rested his forehead on his crossed arms.

Shaking his head, Gray drew the shade from a second lamp. "Thou canst not sit forever in the dark, my king."

Leaning back in his chair, David rubbed both hands over his face. "I have led us to ruin, Gray."

"Thou hast not!" Gray countered, sitting opposite him. "There wast no other way, not if we wert to save the future."

"There is no future now," David sighed. Lifting several reports, he tossed them across the table. "Half our worlds are devastated, and wilt ne'er rebuild with most of their people dying in our armies. My children of Maradane bear up the best of any, yet they shalt fall any time now."

"They shalt not." Gray caught his gaze. "David, leave thy charts and tactics and reports of despair, and go to the Maran base. See the heart of thine children, and let them see thee. Here, thee only brood. There, thou wilt learn to fight once more."

"I feel as if all I do is fight."

"But the fight is with thyself, and gets thee nowhere. Please, David, come to the camp. It wilt give thee a new perspective, if nothing else. And it wilt give thy scholars the ease of not having thee breathing down their necks."

Gray paused at a slight knock at the door.

"Enter." David straightened in his chair.

"Pardon, sire." The young man slipped into the room with a deep bow. "My lord Peter asks that I tell thee there is an initial break in the script. 'Tis only small, and many months remain ahead, but it is a break."

"Thank God," David breathed, then smiled. "Thank Peter for me, please. I shalt be leaving him in peace for a time whilst I visit the armies."

Chapter Twenty-Two

The general stood stiffly before the heavy chair, hands clasped behind his back, and tried not to meet the Overlord's gaze.

Huddled in heavy robes, the gaunt man scanned several dog-eared papers in his hand. He had arrived only that morning, sent to see why one small enemy force had not been put down in the course of sixty months.

Tossing the papers onto a small table, the Overlord looked up. "Our Seer is intent on destroying these Maran forces. Not simply defeating them, but destroying them. What is their significance that four of our battalions have already been wasted on this effort?"

"I do not know their significance, Overlord, but I've seen their power. It grows daily, and we'll need many more battalions here to crush it."

"I will admit to being out of touch with that world. I've been posted most of my life on our far borders, holding territories against the Immortals."

"Maradane is their bastion in this quadrant, Overlord," the general said reluctantly. "I am told its rulers, though mortal, are descended from David himself. And I do believe it, for the Immortal hierarchy itself protects them, especially the wind witch."

Nodding, the Overlord glanced toward the papers on the table. "Tell me what you have seen here, of the enemy's strengths and powers. From this I will derive our strategy."

The general considered carefully. Overlords rarely asked for such candid appraisals and he did not wish to overstep his bounds. "I've been here only a brief time, Overlord, but I believe these Marans have four strengths which must each be crushed if they are to fall."

"Yes, well, tell me of them!" the Overlord snapped. "Come on, get on with it. I'm not some worthless sot from Donthas, I've fought all my life in the borderlands. I expect my generals to express themselves."

"Yes, Overlord." The man paused, then nodded toward the tent flap. "I would suggest you look outside, sir, while I explain."

The Overlord complied, throwing the flap wide. "Your name, general?"

"Barac, sir." He pointed to a skirmish at the far side of the camp. "Our first enemy, Overlord, is the youth with the sword called Bane Slayer."

"A named sword?" The Overlord arched one white brow, following Barac's gesture.

Shanda warriors swarmed to the prison quarter, seeking to stave off the latest raid to free the captured Marans.

The raiding party appeared ordinary except for their boldness, bearing down on the Shanda camp in bright mid-day. The warriors rallied around their honey-haired commander, who at first glance looked unarmed as he strode forward.

The sun caught something then, cascading off a blade as clear as any glass, a blade that was now seen slashing through armor as it might through water, leaving a trail of mayhem in its wake. Shanda blades were turned aside, Shanda arrows thinned the ranks but fell always short of the youth, who strode onward. Faced with his determination and the lethal touch of his sword, the Shanda fell slowly backward, until the prisoners were running to freedom.

Scowling, the Overlord eyed Barac coldly. "Who is that boy,

and where did he get that blade?"

"They call him Jeremiah, sir, only son of their king Anders. The sword was forged by an Immortal, but created by their invisible guides through his hands. I have seem him simply stand and watch the arrows fall around him. He cannot be touched."

The Overlord nodded, muttering, "Always they plague us, those who whisper from the stars. Yet I do not see how their forces are maintained—we renew ours from many worlds, but I am told that all the Maran forces are here."

"They are, Overlord, but all of David's warriors now use some new healing tablet, and the Immortals heal them as well. I no longer trust any of them to be dead unless I've seen the sword piece their heart, for they return from all else. I ordered the tablets stolen, but our warriors died the moment they swallowed them."

"Whispers," the Overlord growled. "We face not only this force, but their ancient protectors." His attention turned toward another sudden clash far to the left.

Sword rang upon sword as the Shanda attacked a medic unit. Outnumbered and vulnerable as they sought to protect the wounded in their midst, the Marans floundered with little room to maneuver. The Shanda fell upon them with a fury and brought several Marans to the ground.

With a bellowing roar and the blinding flash of sun off a vast expanse of iridescent metal, a giant leapt upon the Shanda. Warriors literally flew in every direction, strewn across the sand by blows from massive arms. Leaving a blinding arc of light where it passed, the huge axe danced amidst the Shanda until not one remained standing. Assured of that fact, the giant shouldered his weapon and stood guard while the medics resumed their work.

"Scott," the Overlord breathed shakily.

"Our second enemy, sir," Barac confirmed. "At first no one knew this weapon—"

"I know that weapon," the Overlord hissed. "I have faced that weapon, a hundred years ago. Why has it been brought forth now?"

"Rumors have spread, sir, that he took up the axe the night their king Anders was killed."

"Again, their king Anders." The Overlord returned to his chair, rubbing his eyes. "I would not spread this around, General Barac, but our empire fell the day the Seers wrested control from the Warlords. On some whim of the Seer, to rid us of one simple man, we now face two much stronger foes."

"We still face Anders, as well," Barac said sourly. "The Marans refuse to let him die, they carry his name like an accursed banner. I have seen their half-dead warriors drag themselves back to their feet to defend that name."

"You are a warrior, Barac, and you understand." The Overlord studied him intently. "Had we remained as we were, and plundered one world at a time, our empire would have continued to thrive and expand. Now we are mired in a war where we have no leverage."

"If I may suppose, sir, I would guess our other forces are not doing well?"

"They hold their own, but are not progressing. And it is because the Immortals hold these Maran forces up as a rallying point. Therefore I have been sent to crush these forces. How do I do that?"

Barac glanced blackly toward the Maran camp. "Kill the queen who calls the winds. Until she is dead, we will not win."

Bronwyn hugged David tightly. "I'm so glad you came. And the warriors will be so happy to see you. Have you any news?"

"A bit, perhaps, but not for everyone, lest Shandal hear." David hugged her, then looked at the others in the tent. "My researchers have broken the first secrets of the book. 'Tis still a long road, but there is a bit of hope."

"Hope is all we need," Aric said stoutly. "If I tell my warriors you have hope, they will have hope, and not ask where yours arises."

"They have hope already," Bryce added, massaging his aching neck. "They heard you had arrived, and rallied enough to push the enemy back for the day."

"Gray wast right, as always." David smiled briefly at his

friend. “I shalt remain here for a time, where I mayst be of more use than in my council chambers. Mayhap I mayst dishearten our enemy, as well as heartening our warriors.”

“I fear we need that help, Father.” Scott entered the tent, pausing only to leave his stained axe beyond the door. “The Seer hath sent a veteran Overlord from their borderlands to command these units. ’Tis time we force our way to a new base and gather for a major defensive action.”

David eyed him. “Who is this Overlord, then?”

“Halath, Father, from the quadrant of Tilmanah.”

“Halath.” David scowled, clenching one fist. “He who stole the Lhassa and took their world. And hath held it for over a century.” He turned to Nicholas, who had accompanied him from Leahcim Tierrah. “Summon the Davan Immortals from their preparations to assist Asher in freeing the slaves. I want that sector back, I want Tilmanah freed, and I shalt have it whilst Halath faces us here.”

“I shalt find great satisfaction in that.” Nicholas turned to go, then paused. “David, hath Asher found the Lhassa?”

“He believes so, in one of the slave camps.”

“We shalt have their world back for them, then.”

Watching as Nicholas strode away, David rubbed his chin thoughtfully. “Mayhap the Seer hath blundered again. If we canst gain that quadrant and rid ourselves of Halath, we wilt have moved toward a stalemate.”

“Not victory?” Prudence asked flatly.

Gray shook his head. “Victory over Shandal wilt not come fully now, that is all too clear. But winning this war wilt bring peace to our realm for many years.”

“Well then.” Aric scanned the group. “We’d better start our new plans, find the new base Scott suggests, and dig in.”

The small Paladin craft landed at the edge of the new camp and Caleb hurried toward the main tents. Scanning the camp as he went, he approved of this new location in the far north of the planet. The cooler air would greatly help his forces, as would the news he carried.

Gray met him at the command tent. "Thou must bear excellent news, if I mayst judge from that smile."

"I think it's excellent." Caleb hesitated, seeing that his friends were all occupied with the latest assault. "How long has this battle been going on?"

"It began only this morning." Gray pointed to the field. "The Shanda have dug in to the south, and art spreading their fires again, but Bronwyn's winds art blowing most of the smoke into their faces. Two forces attacked from either side this morning, moments before the main body moved in."

Nodding, Caleb studied the melee. "Well, before long they will find themselves trapped and cut off from their camp."

"How so?"

Caleb grinned broadly. "Four days ago my people crushed all Shanda forces in our quadrant. Rahssa is safe now, with Davan Immortals to hold it and the quadrant. The Raas are on their way here by Michael's order, to augment our forces."

"Excellent, indeed." Gray motioned him inside. "Call their escort and have the Paladins bring them in behind the Shanda, as thou suggested. Bronwyn is preparing a major attack with the winds, but that shalt be several days in the coming."

"More, if I can't work out this phrasing," Bronwyn sighed, standing as they entered. "I'm going outside to test some combinations."

"Stay in this area," Shara called after her, then returned to her own scrutiny of the sketches before her, a layout of the enemy camp.

Grasping her staff, Bronwyn turned in a slow circle, then located a fairly large patch of ground behind the hospital tents. Before approaching it, she took a moment to locate Richard, several paces to her left, and Salar, holding guard on an alley near a large skirmish. Jericho and Garth led their groups to guard other entrances to the camp, their shouts lost in the rising commotion.

Moving to the center of clear space, Bronwyn stopped to gather a handful of soil. It remained mostly sand, sharp and stinging when blown on the wind, deadly when propelled by a vortex. Sighing, she cast aside the sand and stood to gaze pensively toward the Shanda camp.

Two more battalions had arrived yesterday, summoned by the Overlord who had stalemated David's forces for so many decades. He knew too well how the Immortals fought, and how to protect his own forces from them. Halath was by far the most dangerous commander her people had faced, and already Maran warriors littered the land around the camp.

"He knows David's ways, but not mine," she whispered, ignoring strands of hair blown across her face by the light breeze. "If I can find the words, and the strength, he will not live to leave this world."

Assuring herself that the area remained clear of her people, Bronwyn closed her eyes and gathered her thoughts. Raising her staff, she was distracted by soft steps from behind.

"Richard, you must stand clear for now." She turned to send him to a safe distance.

Brawny arms swept her off her feet, arms banded with the gold of Seryl, and her staff fell to the ground as she was slung over the man's shoulder. Screaming a warning, Bronwyn saw more men of Seryl creeping out of an alley from the rear of the camp.

"Put her down!" Richard roared, hurling himself at the warriors around her captor.

Salar's men raced into the area, cutting off any escape, but hesitated over the queen's safety.

Struggling wildly, Bronwyn gasped as more Shanda streamed up two alleys. "Salar, Richard, behind you!" Cupping her hands, she battered her captor's ears, then again, until he loosed his grip on her waist and she tumbled to the ground.

Her staff lay far to one side, far past Richard, who suddenly fell to the ground with one thigh completely severed. Scrambling to her feet, Bronwyn drew her golden sword and slipped to the center of Salar's group. The Dacynites formed a ring around her, but it would soon prove futile against the growing numbers of Shanda.

Rolling to his knees, Richard stabbed his sword into the ground to lever himself up before his leg could fully support him. He was swiftly cut down again by two swords slashing through his other thigh even as he saw Salar's group falter. Bronwyn wielded her sword well, but her hands already bled and her forehead was cut.

Dragging himself up again, Richard remained this time on his knees, closing his eyes as he clung to the sword's hilt to stabilize himself. Breathing deeply to focus his concentration, he threw back his head as he screamed from the depth of his heart. *"Scott!"*

Amidst Bryce's unit, Scott spun at the cry that was felt more than heard, borne on the close bond between the men. Grasping his travel stone, Scott ran toward the Maran camp.

Bronwyn's heart sank as the camp flooded with Shanda. That meant all the entrance guards were overwhelmed, and somewhere her husband and son were likely fallen. Tears burning her eyes, she sliced her sword through a vulnerable Shanda arm in the press before her.

Striding from the silvery mist, Scott scowled at the disarray around him. Shanda poured into the camp from all sides now, straight toward the warriors before him, the men from Seryl who remained intent on reaching Bronwyn.

"Halath," Scott growled under his breath. "Thou wilt not take our queen this day." Raising his voice, he shouted, "Marans stand clear! Those of Seryl, die!"

Catching one man on his pike, Scott leveled two more with a backswing of the scythe and a sidestroke of the axe. Whirling, he disarmed the warrior who had slashed his back, then swung the axe into two men attacking from the other side.

The Shanda began falling back, attempting to sidestep the reach of the spinning axe, yet the scythe and pike ripped through their ranks as they fell over one another.

On his feet at last, Richard fought his way to Salar's side.

"This is a fine damn mess," Salar grunted, parrying a blow from his left.

"Indeed." Richard pressed backward, between Bronwyn and her attackers. "We concentrated too much on the field and too little on the camp."

"It won't happen again." Salar drew a long dagger from his boot to fend off two warriors at once.

"Mother!" Garth burst through the fray, Jericho close on his heels.

"Thank God," Bronwyn sighed, dropping her sword as her son crushed her to him. "I was so afraid you were both gone."

"Rolled over, more aptly," Jericho said sourly, quickly kissing her cheek. "They boiled through in such a rush to reach you they forgot to kill anyone on the way. Garth, stand behind Salar, and I'll close the circle here. They'll not reach my wife this day."

Retrieving her sword Bronwyn stood sheltered by the four men, but glanced up as a massive shadow fell across the camp.

Looking skyward, Salar smiled grimly. "Raas ships. Let the Shanda face the half-Immortals now."

Several paces away, Scott also saw the ships, then growled as a dagger was hurled into his stomach. Tearing it free, he lunged forward to impale its owner on his pike, then kick the man to the ground. The scythe tore open another man's leg on the backswing, while another lost an arm to the huge axe.

Turning, Scott saw the Shanda running from the camp, running toward their own base, but running too late.

Their ships down, the Raas poured forth onto the field, flanked by Paladins, and cut off all retreat for the Shanda. The Marans ran in behind them, and the enemy was crushed between two forces.

"Get her back to her tent!" David shouted from behind his son, his face dark with anger. "What in blazes happened here?"

"Stupidity," Salar answered, disgusted. "They came in from the rear, through the alleys."

"There wilt be no more alleys!" David snapped, scanning the group. "I want all tents set in two rings, one within the other, and a perimeter of guards four paces apart around the entire camp. In the center place a ship with a watch set atop it."

"At once." Salar turned to call orders to his men.

Still scowling, David glared at Richard. "Do not let her more than a pace away from thee, or I shalt find someone more capable of protecting her."

"David, that's cruel!" Bronwyn cried, hugging Richard's arm as the blond man hung his head. "I should have been safe in the center of camp. Richard had both legs cut from under him."

Sighing, David squeezed Richard's shoulder. "I am sorry, my

friend. But it scared me."

"And I wast lax," Richard said quietly. "It wilt not happen again."

"I know that." David turned to his son. "Art thou all right, as well?"

"I am fine." Scott rested the axe on the ground. "I must rejoin Bryce's unit, the wounded must be brought in. I am here only because of Richard's ability to call me."

David smiled faintly. "I stand chastised. Now, back to the tent, we shalt have a talk about tightening this camp's security. And ridding ourselves of Halath."

"I had planned to do that," Bronwyn pointed out, "if I could only work out the phrase. I must have space to test it."

"Tomorrow, then, when Richard hath rested." David smiled down at her. "He and Scott shalt be thy guard in that work."

Standing atop the ship centered in the camp, Bronwyn intently followed the movements of Jeremiah's group. Ten days had passed since the attempt on her life, and many Maran prisoners were now held in the Shanda camp. It was imperative that they be freed before she began the command contrived over the past days.

Holding her staff too tightly, she ignored the cramp in her hand as she glanced toward the ground. Jericho smiled up at her, standing with Richard and Scott, ready to leap to her defense.

The rest of the camp was quiet, the warriors falling back as Jeremiah's group now returned with the freed captives. David and Gray stood at the edge of the field, waiting.

For an instant the Shanda pursued the Marans, then they took notice of Bronwyn and fled toward their own camp.

Raising her staff, Bronwyn said, "*Astonal. Wynn ree trahs.*"

The winds rose with a cloud of dust, forming a ring around the Shanda and herding them closer toward their camp. Several tried to escape, but the wind forced them backward into their own ranks.

Sighing, Bronwyn continued softly. "*Hatha, mistra ephnan, nathor jonlac trahs.*"

Separate from the barrier containing the Shanda, a tremendous gale arose to excavate a trench between the two camps. Digging wide and deep, the wind gathered the sand and soil into one huge mass, then transported it over the dusty barrier ring.

Unable to turn away, Bronwyn gave thanks for the murkiness of the wall of wind trapping the Shanda, as well as the roar of the winds. For beyond the barrier the warriors fought an agonized struggle to escape, and their screams were not entirely drowned out by the gale.

The soil fell swiftly, thickly, heavily, rising in a crushing mound that filled the barrier to overflowing. In only moments the dim shadows of struggle vanished, the muffled cries faded, and only the wind could be heard.

Tears streaming down her cheeks, Bronwyn whispered, "*Stonal*. Stop, please stop."

With an unnerving moan, the wind fell silent.

Jericho met Bronwyn at the base of the ship and hugged her close. "You did well, Bron. We will leave this world before they can send another battalion."

Nodding, Bronwyn mumbled, "I'd just like to go inside."

"Of course." Jericho kissed her cheek. "You rest, my love. We'll be in shortly." He and the two Immortals crossed the space to join David.

Gazing at the vast mound rising from the flat plain, David suppressed a shudder. "'Tis unspeakable, e'en to save our realm."

"We have done the unspeakable before," Scott said flatly.

David looked up at his son, then rubbed one hand over his face. "Richard, please, go see that Bronwyn sleeps now. I canst not give such peace to my son."

"My peace is on Maradane," Scott said softly as Richard strode away. "Her touch doth what thine cannot."

"Once we have a new base, Scott, go home for a day." David turned back toward the camp. "Let us look o'er the maps, see where 'tis best to go."

Entering the large tent, Richard looked around the dim interior. "Bronwyn?"

There was no answer, only a muffled sob from a dark corner.

"What is wrong?" Richard hurried to kneel before her.

Unable to stop crying, Bronwyn only shook her head, then pressed her face against her updrawn knees.

"My lady, art thou hurt?" He looked her up and down, then grasped her hand. "Bronwyn, what is wrong? Tell me!"

"Richard, it's so horrible, so ugly!" she sobbed, raising her tearstreaked face to look at him. "All my time is spent devising death, hideous ways of murder. I don't know how I can kill any more, not like that!"

"Oh, my lady." Richard gathered her into his arms, rocking slightly as he kissed her dark hair. "We shalt find another way, I promise thee."

The others entered the tent then, unshading the central lamps.

"Richard?" Jericho caught his friend's troubled gaze and ran to kneel beside Bronwyn. "What happened? Is she hurt?"

"She canst not do this any longer." Richard looked around the group. "She is no longer strong enough to do this."

"No," Bronwyn protested, quieting. "I'm sorry, I'll be all right. I'm just tired..."

"Thou art beyond tired." Scott knelt before her. "The strain on thee is far too great, Bron, and we wilt not lose thee for it. There art other ways to help without the burden of such killing."

To his dismay, her eyes flooded once more and she cried, "I'm sorry! I begged you to slaughter, the night Anders died, and I had no idea what slaughter was. To have demanded you to take it up again, when you long so desperately to be free of it, was the most vile thing I've done. I'm so sorry, Scott."

Scott drew her close, gently drying her tears. "Lessons remain very hard, Bron, the harder still as we try to avoid them. How free wilt I be when my world is dust and all I love enslaved, because I wouldst not face pain? This is the role freely chosen by my people. But thou art mortal, and this is not thy role. From now on use thy winds to harry and distract, to cause disruption and dismay, but do not kill. The armies carry that duty."

"Scott is right," David said. "We art to move now, Bronwyn. For these days I want thee only to rest. Once we have a new base, thou mayst work in the hospital tents. One or the other of us wilt work with thee if the winds art to be used."

Jericho lifted her in his arms to carry her to her cot. "You sleep now, Bron. We'll all be right here." He glanced at Richard.

Grasping his copper, Richard stroked Bronwyn's forehead lightly. She was asleep before he removed his hand.

David stepped to the entrance, where stood one of his Paladin escort. "Gather up all the most recent reports and bring them here, with all current quadrant maps. We shalt choose our ground most carefully."

Chapter Twenty-Three

"Snow." Bronwyn studied the maps spread out before her. "And water. Yes, I could do a lot on this world. But will they follow us there?"

"No, but they wilt push us there." David leaned over her shoulder to point to the quadrant map. "Treasure houses here, here, and here. Quadrant governing centers here and here. And this world neatly in the middle. Our fleets shalt try to force landings on three other planets, until they force us down where we wish to be."

Michael glanced up from his own reports. "We have secured two other quadrants today, freeing the armies from those areas to join us here. That wilt draw a greater portion of Shandal's forces."

"Which wilt serve well to keep their attention shouldst we garner a tactic from the Stalassi book." David sat down again. "The researchers feel they art close now, perhaps only a few more months."

"That does not sound short any more." Prudence sank down in

her chair. "We will need a tremendous amount of supplies for that length of time, and more tents and cots."

"And more medics," Bryce added wearily. "If we will have that many armies, I think we'd better incorporate all the units and place the tents in the center of a spoked camp."

David nodded. "First we need to pack this camp for travel. I and the others of my people wilt finish healing the wounded whilst the ships art landed and loaded. I believe, Prudence, thou wilt see time pass all too quickly."

"This is never going to end." Bronwyn pushed her damp hair off her neck as she paused for a glass of water.

True to form, the Shanda had forced David's fleets down in the center of the small desert region on David's chosen world. But the heat was lessened when Bronwyn established winds carrying cool air in from one ocean, and repeatedly stifled as she summoned rain and snow from the planet's vast resources. With the Marans, five other Davan armies were arrayed in the desert, rallying each time the storms came, struggling not to flag when they dispersed.

Watched closely by everyone, Bronwyn spaced her work with the winds between her time assisting in the hospital tents. The work revived her far more than any rest, for she saw herself helping to heal people, and knew as well that her winds now helped to save lives. Yet the battles dragged on.

Bronwyn set aside her glass. "Gray, will we never go home? It's been over a year and forty months now."

Gray paused, copper in hand, and sought the real question behind her dark eyes. He smiled gently. "Neither thy husband nor Garth wilt find need to visit this tent, milady."

She was too relieved for words. Since Anders' death, her life with Jericho had seemed too tenuous to even ponder. Kissing Gray's cheek, she returned to her work sorting medications.

Her attention was drawn by a gasp from Shonnie, who grabbed fresh bandages and ran to her husband. The other two queens paused in their work to listen anxiously.

"Aric, not you too! Is it bad?"

"No. I just can't see with all this damn blood in my eyes." Aric sat down so his wife could tend the gash in his forehead. "I can't waste a tablet on every little cut."

"Some little cut," she chided, reaching for a needle.

"Oh no, not stitches," he groaned.

"Just four. Now be still."

Aric endured her gentle touch, then kissed her lightly when she finished. Touching her cheek, he asked, "What's wrong? You've been crying."

Shonnie pointed to a nearby cot. "Aarek."

Aric strode to the cot, then knelt beside his son.

Waking, Aarak rubbed his eyes. "Hello, Papa."

"Aarek, what happened to you?" Aric eyed the stained bandage around his son's chest. "What happened to your tablets?"

"I used them all. I was trying to help Drahcir, but Garth had to save us both." The youth winced, then grinned. "Gray will heal me, after those hurt more badly. And I'll get a new supply of tablets."

"You deserve a rest." Aric ran one hand lovingly over his son's red curls. "I'll come see you later."

"Be careful, Papa. I'm not ready to rule beside Jeremiah." Aarek watched his father leave, then closed his eyes.

Bronwyn looked across the table at Shara. Gray still worked with the small woman, but not as intensely, and she filled her days now by assisting Prudence. "Have you seen Jeremiah lately?"

"He comes every other day or so, for a few moments." Shara set aside a package of bandages. "At least I know he is well."

"I'm glad you have that."

Shara sighed. "I'm afraid to go home. This is all so removed, so far away, I can function here. I don't know what I'll do at home."

Bronwyn reached out to grasp her hand. "You will come to your friends. And somehow we will put our world together again. If only I could imagine how."

Her thoughts were disrupted by the low call of a horn, followed by another that reverberated throughout the camp. As the third sounding rattled the jars on the table, Bronwyn leapt to her feet.

"That's Richard!"

Running to the tent's entrance, she saw the blond Immortal running toward the camp, Scott close on his heels.

"What's wrong?" she called, frightened.

"All is right!" Scott skidded to a halt and smiled broadly at the group clustered in the doorway. "David's men have broken the Stalassi script and we have a tactic."

Before anyone could speak the five kings converged on the tent, and a tall blond man stepped from the teleportal mist. Bronwyn recognized the black-clad figure and wondered what Chuck had to do with the plan.

The Maran rulers and the Immortals gathered in the command tent to discuss tactics for the next months.

Reviewing several reports, David said, "We now hold over half the quadrants that began this war. Armies from those areas art being brought here, to localize the battle within Shandal's realm. I must depart now to work with Chuck, but Scott, Richard, and Gray wilt remain here."

Caleb nodded, making random notes on his tablet. "How are we to keep Shandal from guessing what is happening? The Horn of the Rijo was scarcely overlooked today."

"We shalt use that to our advantage," Scott said. "I intend to make them believe the event wilt be centered on this world, so they wilt not look elsewhere."

"I'm not sure I care for the sound of that," Aric said dryly.

"It must be done, though. And with the other forces to bolster us, we wilt make it work." Scott turned to Bronwyn. "We need many storms now, to confuse them. Anything that wilt distract and discomfit them. Those combined with the fortifications I am bringing in for this camp wilt make Shandal believe new wind lore hath been discovered, and keep their attention on this world."

"I'll start deriving commands at once," Bronwyn said. "There are some elusive phrases I have yet to master. And if Salar will help, I may be able to dampen this desert far past Shandal's taste."

"Excellent, I plan to draw everything they have toward us."

Scott caught a worried look from Jericho. "I wilt not leave this camp until our major assault begins, except to assist Bryce. Salar and his men art to guard thee, Bronwyn, with Richard."

Richard glanced around the small group. The women alternated between their husbands' embraces and hugging their sons. Shara sat quietly, settled in Jeremiah's strong arms. Quiet was all she had now, and it only emphasized Anders' absence.

Shaking his head slightly, Richard said, "The arriving armies wilt be arrayed behind the Shanda camps. This wilt encircle the enemy, and when they attack Scott's new battlements, our other forces wilt fall in from the rear. We art holding three fleets in reserve, to land beyond any secondary forces sent by Shandal."

"It sounds like a bloody mess to me," Caleb sighed, scowling at his notes. "Jericho, you and Garth remain near Bronwyn. The rest of us will prepare for the new defense."

"I am going out to await my workers' arrival." Scott stretched as he stood. "The rest of thee get some sleep."

At dawn the Shanda were faced with a walled camp across the field. A corps of Immortals had set tirrschon walls around the Maran base camp, and used this foundation to carry twelve-foot high battlements surrounding the hospital and command tents. There were no gates, no openings of any sort, and the Maran forces passed the walls by hopping over them on the winds.

Ordering his men back for a day, the Shanda Overlord studied the scene and saw several small vortices moving behind the Maran camp.

Turning to his general, he snapped, "Send to Donthas at once for more battalions. The wind witch has found new power."

"Yes Overlord. Shall we attack today, sir?"

The Overlord shook his head. "I want fires set, to surround their camp. If we choke them with smoke they will not see us climb their walls."

Coughing, Bronwyn summoned another wind to clear the

smoke from the area around the camp. The fires had raged for two days now, and smoke hung thickly in the serpentine hollows amidst the rolling dunes.

Turning, she called down to the men at the base of the wall. "Salar, please, send up one of your men who can summon a tidal wave. If he can form it, my winds can carry it and douse these fires."

"He's out with Jeremiah, Bron. Can you see them at all?" Salar began climbing the interior ladder to join her.

Gesturing absently with her staff, Bronwyn mumbled a short command and peered through the swirling smoke.

Jeremiah had taken advantage of the conditions to enter the Shanda camp and damage outlying supplies as he freed the Maran and Raas captives. He had been gone all morning and should be almost back to the camp by now.

Bronwyn caught brief sight of the unit, then drew a sharp breath as she saw movement behind the dunes to Jeremiah's right. A Shanda corps waited in ambush, totally hidden from the young king's view.

"Salar, quickly, send someone to help them!" Bronwyn took a firmed grip on her staff. "I'll try to concentrate the smoke around the Shanda."

"Too bad there aren't sand tigers out there," Salar said as he turned away. "The Shanda wouldn't hide there if those cats could reach them."

Closing her eyes as he slid down the ladder, Bronwyn sought a phrase to manipulate the smoke. Intent only on protecting her people, she grabbed at the first words she found and shouted the command.

Maran warriors leapt the wall and raced toward Jeremiah's group. Yet they stumbled to an astonished halt less than half way there.

"No!" Bronwyn wailed, staring aghast as all smoke in the area coalesced into a gargantuan tiger shape and settled around Jeremiah's group. She was already fumbling for another command when terrified screams reached her ears.

Casting aside their weapons, the Shanda fled in total panic, abandoning all plan of ambush in their haste to avoid the cat.

The apparition loped onward toward the Maran camp, maintaining its shape around the unit, and lazily leapt over the wall with them. As their feet touched the ground, the tiger faded on the wind.

"Jeremiah!" Bronwyn jumped from the walkway to land by his side, where she dropped her staff to hug him. "Oh Jeremiah, I could have killed you!"

"We're fine, Bronwyn." He hugged her close, then grinned broadly. "That was so bizarre, we could see perfectly well, but apparently no one could see us. Take me up and do it again where I may see it."

Shaken, Bronwyn complied. "I hardly know what I did. Salar mentioned sand tigers just as I was forming the command...Well, our men are all back inside. Let's see what I can do."

Warriors lined the battlements to watch the experiment. Jeremiah looked on intently, offering suggestions as Bronwyn worked.

The huge apparition formed again, but this time merely stood until Bronwyn motioned in various directions with her staff. Smiling slightly, she sent it loping toward the Shanda camp, where it was greeted with shrill screams before it veered back toward the queen.

"Bronwyn, I'm going to take my men back outside, to see if it moves with us again." Jeremiah called to his warriors and jumped over the wall.

Turning slowly, he studied the shape from within. The form of the cat was clearly visible, yet the smoke hung in thin walls and the interior was perfectly clear. He and his men could see out, as well, discerning the terrain as if through a thin fog. He set out at a walk, and the tiger shape moved slowly with them. It lengthened to a lope as they quickened to a run.

Widening the arc, Jeremiah ran past the Shanda camp, smiling as the enemy fell over themselves to get out of the way. Their cries of panic faded as he returned to camp.

Leaping the wall with the warriors, the cat again vanished as they landed.

Jeremiah smiled up at the queen. "It may have been a mistake, but I think we can use it well. Shall we work up some plans?"

Bronwyn quickly memorized the segment of David's book outlining wind apparitions and worked closely with Jeremiah to hone the effects.

While the tiger inflicted no physical harm, it opened the way for a more mental warfare. The smoky creature stalked the Shanda camp in the night, seen only clearly enough to put the guards on edge. They became so unraveled that Jeremiah's band could pass them almost unnoticed as he continued his forays.

Davan prisoners were killed after only a few days, so Jeremiah settled into nightly raids to return them to their camps. During one such raid his smoke tiger enveloped a group of Shanda guards, who gaped at the sight of his men and turned to flee.

"Stop them!" Jeremiah ordered. "The Overlord cannot know this secret."

Beyond the apparition other Shanda heard the scuffle, heard cries of pain, but saw only the cat lope away and leave four bodies in its wake.

This added a new dimension to the specter. Alone, the tiger flitted just on the edge of Shanda vision until they were never certain of what they saw, or suddenly rushed forward so that the warriors fell back in terror. It did no harm at those times, but when it sheltered Jeremiah's group it left dead men behind.

Embolded, Jeremiah's group was able to inflict great damage. Hidden with the tiger, he was able to pass deeper into the camp, destroying stores and wreaking havoc throughout the command tents. Within the tiger the Shanda saw clearly enough whom they fought, but none lived to tell this tale.

Bronwyn also used the apparition to clear the field of Shanda if Bryce's units were struggling to carry in the wounded. The Shanda never knew when the cat would kill or not, so they fled at its every approach.

While this went on, the Overlord threw his men at the walled Maran camp, seeking any way to reach and rid himself of Bronwyn. The walls repelled initial battering attempts, and fire lobbed over the tops failed to ignite the tanschor tenting. The Shanda set out to pick off the guards atop the walls at night, but Scott allowed no light on the walls and only the most sheltered lamps within the tents. In the end the Overlord had to focus on a full, open assault of the walls and hope to scale them. Donthas was scouring its resources for shipments of wood for scaling ladders.

"Wood?" David glanced at the report from Asher, then set it aside atop a mound of other reports and communiques. "I think not. Michael, how many more fleets need yet to land?"

"Only seven, David." Michael glanced at his own sheaf of papers. "We dare not pull any others from the ground we have taken. These seven wilt be landed within three days."

"Fine." David reached for another page from the table before him. "Move in a ring of Paladin ships and cut off Shandal's supplies. Allow none to reach the surface. And gather what is on this list for Bryce and Prudence, see that they have it within two days. They need to bolster the hospital camp before the other fleets land."

Nodding, Michael stood as another man entered the room. "I shalt report this evening, then." He left the room after a slight bow.

Looking up, David found the newcomer smiling slightly. "Yea, I am adrift in a sea of paper once more. Sit, Chuck, and tell me if this tactic wilt work."

Chuck sat opposite David and placed a small crystal slate on the table between them. At a motion of his gloved hand, small opalescent particles formed words within the pane.

Provided that I am able to work freely, with a Paladin guard, and unobserved by Shanda patrols, I canst complete my portion. But thou wilt require extensive physical preparation to lay the ambush.

"That wilt be done, also unobserved." David tapped one stack of bound pages. "All I needed wast thy confirmation."

Chuch nodded emphatically. *Oh, yea, I canst do this thing. This wilt end this war, or nothing wilt do so.*

David held forth one report. "This is the timetable, then. Commit it to memory, and work with Nicholas on an exact detail of what thou wilt be doing, as well."

Tucking the report into his Star Holder, Chuch retrieved his slate and nodded as he left the room.

The Overlord hurled the crumpled paper across his tent. "How am I to complete a mission without supplies?" He scowled at the courier, who had been barely able to crawl to the camp after his ship crashed.

"Every Paladin ship from four quadrants surrounds this world, Overlord. Our ships can't get through."

The Overlord dismissed him with an abrupt gesture, turning to his general. "Pull all men back to camp, regroup and rearm, and prepare for a full assault before sundown. And send your best unit to my command. I intend to rid us first of Jeremiah, and so open the way to reach the others."

"Yes, Overlord." The general backed from the tent, then began shouting orders across the camp.

As the horns sounded in the Shanda camp, Scott climbed atop the wall to scan the area.

"What are they up to now?" Caleb called up to him.

"It looks to be a full frontal assault, from their formations." Scott paused to study the gathering forces, then nodded. "He hath received word of the blockade."

"And he expects to crush us with one assault?" Caleb frowned, perplexed.

"No, he wilt have one certain goal, I am sure. Caleb, contact the Raas units and align them for flanking attacks once the Shanda have fallen in. I am going to join Jeremiah and Aric's units to meet the assault."

Wiping a trickle of blood from his cheek, the Overlord gasped as he struggled with the burly warrior before him. This had obviously not been a good idea, at least from his present viewpoint.

Shandal's assault was met head-on by the entire Maran force, led as always by the young king with the clear sword. But this time he was joined by the red haired king, and the giant Immortal.

The Overlord had maneuvered the initial battle so that his unit faced Jeremiah's, and at first he gained ground. Several Maran warriors fell to his men's swords, and he moved nearer to reaching the honey-haired youth. Yet as he focused on the king, the Raas armies swept in from either side, closing the circle around his forces.

Motioning his general closer, the Overlord called, "Split the forces into three, to push back the new attack. And send me more men. I want this boy dead today."

"So have many previous Overlords," a voice called from behind him.

Whirling, the Overlord found himself facing Jeremiah in the center of a suddenly clear patch of sand.

"I am here," Jeremiah said softly. "Perhaps you are the one who can stop me."

Gripping his sword, the Overlord tried to focus on Jeremiah's weapon and discovered he could not see it.

Jeremiah attacked, and the sword became visible as a bloody reflection of the setting sun. Bane Slayer sliced cleanly down the Overlord's left arm, weakening his ability to deflect further blows.

Stumbling, the Overlord suffered a slash to his other arm before he at last concentrated on Jeremiah's hands upon the golden hilt. From that movement, he could discern the direction of the blows and counter them with his own sword. Doing so, he learned that his army's impression of Jeremiah was drastically askew.

Unable to stand against Bane Slayer, the Shanda attributed its power to some vague magic, the same magic that shielded the young king from their weapons. Now the Overlord saw that, despite whatever strange protection Bane Slayer afforded, it killed only through the prowess of its bearer. It was a prowess that far exceeded his own, a realizaiton that dawned only slightly before Bane Slayer pierced his armor and his heart.

Jeremiah stepped back as the Overlord fell at the feet of the returning general, who at first gaped and then sounded the horn at his belt. The Shanda faltered, then fell back at the call of retreat.

"That wilt slow them, whilst they fight out who wilt now rise to Overlord." Scott offered a small smile. "Gather thy men to help bring in the wounded, then we mayst fortify the camp during this lull."

Chapter Twenty-Four

Bronwyn was roused from a brief nap by Scott's hoarse voice ringing across the walls, clearly angry.

"Do not topple the ladders for reuse! Pull them up o'er the wall. Pull them up!"

Peeking out the tent flap, Bronwyn saw Aric glaring fiercely at the giant Immortal. "Tell me how in the name of David to pull up a ladder weighted down by that scum!"

The Shanda had pressed for two days to scale the walls, driven off by Scott's axe and Jeremiah's tiger only to return with fresh men and retrieved ladders. Scott knew that the attempt could be stopped—there were more than enough warriors atop the wide path of the wall to provide the cover of archers while others made the ladders unreachable. Jeremiah had confirmed that there was little wood left in the enemy camp, brought in before the Davan fleets had set up their ring to destroy incoming enemy supplies.

"Pull!" Scott roared in Aric's face and turned to grab the nearest ladder. The buckles of his armor burst as he hauled the crude framework upward and shook loose the man clinging to the rungs. Throwing the ladder to the ground inside the camp, Scott bellowed, "Like that!"

Aric rolled his eyes heavenward, then called along the wall, "Team up and haul those ladders up where you can. Or douse them with oil and torch them."

"Scott!"

Richard's cry caused Bronwyn to turn, to find the Immortal engaged with several Shanda who had finally swarmed over the wall. The men towered over Richard, who made use of that fact to slip beneath their guard, but by their very number they would overpower him. More Shanda poured over the wall behind them.

Scott jumped from the wall to bar the entrance to Bronwyn's tent. Seeing the armor of Seryl before him, he unstrapped the axe at his back and called up to Aric. "Take men and close that breach! Get a group in behind this one to help Richard!"

As Aric ran along the wall, shouting orders, one of the closest Shanda hurled a heavy dagger at Scott, catching him in the mid-section. His armor cast aside on the wall, the Immortal had no protection against the weapons.

Bronwyn flinched as Scott tore the dagger free and drove it into its owner's shoulder. Grabbing a fallen shield she knelt behind it, peering fearfully at Scott's broad back.

Seeing no allies near, Scott began swinging the axe with a rhythmic motion, clearing an arc around himself to keep the melee away from Bronwyn. The men of Seryl slowed their attack briefly, seeking an avenue of escape, but Richard and Lachlan were approaching from either side and Jericho and Salar closing in from behind. No more attackers were gaining entry to aid their trapped fellows. Aric's red head could be seen behind Jericho, his big form bearing down with a heavy broadsword.

Moving forward a step, Scott was met by a spear hurled through his thigh. Bronwyn cried out and started to his aid.

"Stay back," Scott ordered, using the flat of the axe to drive the spear out of his leg. He faltered only a little, the huge muscles of his leg still able to support his weight, and hurled the spear into the press of men.

Retreating behind her shield, Bronwyn watched in horror as the few remaining men hurled their weapons at Scott. The big man bled from his entire body, but he maintained his position, his feet in a sticky pool. Several men attempted to slip under his arms, driving daggers into his sides, but he caught them with the butt of the axe, crushing their skulls.

Richard and Lachlan dispensed the final attackers and Scott sank to the ground, dislodging a small dagger from his shoulder. Bronwyn ran forward to cradle his head in her lap.

"Scott." She tenderly dabbed his shoulder with the hem of her tunic.

"I shalt be up in a moment," he gasped, using the back of one hand to wipe his forehead where a slight cut had already healed. "Get the wounded to the tents and cared for. I am going outside."

"Not before you get cleaned up," Bronwyn protested, sending Garth for a basin of water and clean rags.

"Bron, I canst do that myself," Scott began, reaching for the basin as he settled on his knees.

"You can rest for a moment!" she scolded, dipping a cloth in the water and wringing it out. "You're ready to fall over from exhaustion and you know it. You need rest like everyone else."

Scott did not argue, taking the few moments' respite in the midst of the turmoil of the morning. The water was wonderfully cool on his face and neck, and Bronwyn's touch gentle. With his wounds now healed but for the deepest ones, he took a fresh basin of water and doused his head, running his fingers through his matted hair.

"Scott!" Bryce wind-hopped to the top of the wall. "I need to get the wounded in, now!"

"He's coming," Bronwyn called, reaching up to kiss the man's cheek. She smiled to herself as Scott grabbed his axe and ran up to vault over the wall. He was greeted by a terrible clamor of shouts and shrieks, and Bronwyn knew the attack was routed for the morning.

"Progress report." The gaunt Overlord leaned back in his chair, gazing over the brazier on the table before him. The tent was uncomfortably cool since the supply lines had been broken, leaving few coals for heat. Reaching down to scratch the head of a lanky wolf, he demanded, "Well?"

"There is no progress to report, Overlord," the general said, controlling the anger in his voice. His gnarled hands were balled into tight fists.

"What do you mean?" The Overlord's thin lips twisted in a frown. "Didn't you send men over the wall today?"

"They're dead," the general said. "I sent a contingent from Seryl and they were cut down by the Immortal with the axe. Then he left the enclosure and took the axe to the field. He cannot be stopped."

"He can be hurt, though. Our agent from Seryl awaits only the opportunity." The Overlord laced his fingers together, leaning his elbows on his ornate chair arms and contemplating the raid on the giant's home on Maradane. "I gather the wind witch is unharmed?"

"Of course. My lord, we cannot continue like this!" The stocky general pounded the table. "We're running out of room for our wounded, and the majority of our men are wounded. The wall is impassable."

"Unless that woman dies this war will be dragged on until we're destroyed. Keep the assault constant." The man paused, his dark eyes thoughtful. "How do the Immortals deal with their own wounded? How do they supply them?"

"They don't. The majority are healed at once by David's men, and any who have lost limbs are taken away by ship. Supplies are brought through the travel zone and we have no way to stop them, while they destroy our supply ships as they land."

The Overlord silently cursed the unnatural abilities of the Immortals. How was one supposed to fight an enemy who traversed time and space through fields mortals could not tread? They could not be starved out, they had an endless source of supplies and a totally impervious method of transporting them. And now they had somehow made their mortal followers almost immune to injuries, sending them back time and again to the worst of the battles. He was losing men, and eating up valuable supplies supporting warriors who were trying to heal themselves, huddling on the vast dunes.

Scratching his scruffy chin, he tried to understand how such twisted people had gained entry to Shandal's realm. They had appeared out of nowhere just as the realm was forming and had plagued them ever since with their blinding light and foul ways, proclaiming beliefs in a way of life that would cut out the very heart of his people. It knotted his stomach to even imagine a society where so-called rulers wielded neither power nor wealth over a slave class. How could a man exist without the means to buy his way into control over others? He shook his head and looked at the man before him.

"Propose a prisoner exchange. That will give us more able men."

The general ran one hand over his haggard face, wondering if this fur-bundled dolt was fighting the same war as he. While adept enough at climbing to the position of the recently deceased Overlord, he knew nothing of battle. "My lord," he began as if speaking to a child, "David ships all prisoners to a penal planet to await the outcome of the war. And in case you haven't noticed, we have no prisoners. The youth with the sword they call Bane Slayer has freed them all."

Narrowing his baleful eyes, the Overlord said, "Loose more snakes."

Swallowing the urge to bellow his frustration, the general clenched both fists once again. "The Immortals have brought in some furry little beast which kills the snakes."

"Continue the assault on the wall," the man ordered with a gesture of dismissal.

"But my lord, the wounded! We cannot support them already!"

"Then kill them!" the man snapped. "Kill any man who won't be up in three days. More units are coming from worlds not yet tapped. And loose the snakes anyway. It will slow our enemies' steps."

The general shrugged resignedly and stalked out of the tent. Obviously this entire quadrant was to be sacrificed to quell the threat of the wind rulers. As the Overlord said, the home worlds were yet untapped. Shandal could afford to throw away fifty thousand men if the Seers commanded it. Who was he to argue? He sent a detachment of men to the wounded camp, and another to prepare the snakes.

"Jeremiah, get thine men and join me." Gray motioned to Anders' son, having just returned from the enemy camp. "They art preparing to loose more snakes. We art going to take our little friends visiting." He rubbed the chin of the large red ferret draped around his neck. Native to David's home planet, these cat-sized animals had an intense hatred of snakes and could be relied upon to efficiently kill the reptiles. "I brought a dozen—that shouldst take care of their stock."

Jeremiah nodded, calling his men together and heading for the wall, each with one of the venom-immune animals on his shoulder.

The group crept through the blanket of smoke Bronwyn had settled over the area, moving unerringly toward the abominable stench of the enemy camp. They slipped the ferrets under the tent flap, and Gray entered to do away with the giant snake enthroned within.

In the midst of sorting bandages, Bronwyn was startled by a wave of angry shouting from the enemy camp. They had obviously discovered the snakes.

Smiling to herself, she continued her work. Scott, Richard, and Gray were gone now, joining David to enact the ancient tactic.

It had taken David's men ten months to complete the preparations: organizing and briefing special fleets, honing a timetable, and working deep within Shanda territory.

The first step had been to set up a hidden chain of Davan Transports. These intricate mechanisms provided transportation from one location to another within David's Empire, cutting the time required for travel. They were needed in the new locations to enable David's fleets a safe departure from the area. While this work was being done, David organized orders for the rest of the armies to complete a final cleanup after the plan was carried out.

In William's time, Shandal's home planet was ringed with newly opened portals and was highly vulnerable to their energies. All of that foundling realm's forces could have been caught on that world when Chuck imploded the portals and Shandal would have been no more. It would have taken only a few months to implement the end of the conflict.

Six portals remained around the planet Shandal, five of them expendable. But the planet was now home to few people. It had become a place of worship, a center for pilgrimage to ancient shrines, and the hallowed birthplace of the great snakes. The bulk of Shandal's people inhabited other worlds along with David's enslaved citizens. But David knew now he could hurt Shandal e-nough to halt the current war.

The fleets departed their various fields, making no secret of their destination. The plan would not work unless the Seers knew where David's ships were headed. Shanda fleets were ordered to the planet Shandal at once to protect that world from the flood of David's ships. The Overlords depleted armies on every battle-torn planet to raze the invaders of their central world, the heart of their empire.

Chuck monitored the progress grimly, slipping easily in and out of the access zone encompassing the portals. Each of the five lesser doors was set to explode, a charge of energy on the outside ready to blow the door inward toward the planet. As the door to the sorcerers' realm could not safely be destroyed, it was guarded by three smaller charges that would blow toward the planet and drive the other explosions away from that door.

These detonations would cause a vortex of energies centering on the planet, and would trigger capsules Chuck had set all around it. The second series of explosions would dissipate the energies into the access zone, where they would be absorbed without further damage.

Gray communicated to Chuck that enough of the enemy forces were now on the world. As David's fleets faded unobtrusively into the waiting transports, Chuck positioned himself above the first door and activated the charge. Teleporting to each door, he activated the charges in proper succession, then slipped quietly to a position above the sorcerers' door. From this safe vantage he could monitor the explosions and avert any difficulties.

Bronwyn's scalp prickled as an ululating cry of agony began sweeping the battlefield, and everyone in the tent who was able rushed outside. The Shanda were falling back to their camps, with David's men in full pursuit. The kings and princes were running toward the tent to meet the incoming Immortals.

Richard arrived from David's headquarters to spread the news. Reaching the tent, he hugged Bronwyn joyfully, then turned to face everyone.

"Fully one third of the Shanda armies have been destroyed, disintegrated along with the planet. The remaining two thirds art spread thinly and art now receiving the news. I believe they wilt soon be recalled to their home worlds."

"But why?" Bronwyn was doubtful, her words echoing everyone's mood. "They won't give up so easily."

A slow smile spread over Richard's lips, the first in a very long time. "My lady, 'tis not that they art giving up. But it seems that whilst all the armies have been at war, and their religious center hath been destroyed, someone hath armed the slaves on many planets and they art in open rebellion. Cities art falling to the flames so loved by these vile people. The men left to guard the clan families have been slaughtered. And if these armies do not go home soon their entire hierarchy wilt crumble. Asher long ago conceived this plan and hath been enacting it with his units of men. They art moving the slaves from as many of the worlds as possible."

Prudence stared numbly across the field for a moment, then asked, "It's over, then?"

"Soon, milady," Richard reassured her. "We have cut out the heart of the Shanda Empire; with the loss of that planet they lose the focal point of their religion and the sacred home of their gods. A tremendous portion of their army is gone, and their other worlds besieged. There wilt be a surrender soon, very soon, and it wilt be centuries before they pull themselves together. And to prolong those centuries the winds of Maradane wilt harry them."

Shonnie asked hopefully, "Can David not destroy those worlds and avoid further war?"

The Immortal shook his head. "True, we have freed many slaves, and those worlds art destroyed from within. Yet there art some we canst not reach, neither to free the slaves nor destroy the enemy."

Sensing something grave behind his words, Shara pushed forward. "But your people can pass through the guarding shields."

"Yea, but the shields art not the problem this time." The smile left Richard's face. "When Chuck imploded the five portals around Shandal the sixth hadst to be unguarded, lest the guards be caught in the explosions. Something passed through to many Shanda planets. It remains there as a guard—not anything that wilt attack us itself, but we mayst not pass. Five of David's guards wert lost in the first attempt."

A chill swept down Shara's back even in the steamy air. "But his guards are Immortal!" She stepped back to lean against her son.

"They encountered this black mist and faded, just faded to nothing," Richard said, his voice tinged with horror. "Only men of Shandal canst enter those worlds. So this battle is finished, but the war wilt reawaken in the future."

Scott approached slowly but in time to hear the last words. He stared mutely down at the huge axe that he trailed behind him.

Bronwyn saw the horror in his eyes. "You were there."

He nodded, looking up. "I wast with the second group appointed to enter...I heard the screams of the first five. Always have I met enemies to be dealt with by my sword and ne'er feared for myself. My people knew no fear for our own safety. But I heard their screams..."

Bronwyn backed away slowly, retreating to a dark corner of the tent. Suddenly there was no joy to the ending of the this war, for nothing was truly over. There would only be more waiting, perhaps centuries of waiting, while the enemy grew strong again beyond their reach. And even if they destroyed the Shanda empire, something now lingered beyond it, waiting only for what it considered the proper time to destroy David's people.

Bronwyn shuddered and hugged herself with cold arms. Nothing was safe if the Immortals were vulnerable to this new threat. And the threat could not be closed off without beginning the ruin of their universe. How well she recalled David's explanation of the tenuous balance held by the portals. For the first time she really understood how Gray lived. One simple action led to so many others, and each of those to still countless more. The death of one threat could prove to be the birth of hundreds more.

Her thoughts were broken as a figure knelt before her.

Richard took her hand in his and smiled weakly. "Bronwyn, do not let this haunt thy days. Truly, we have need to fear, but the Gabrellans wilt provide for us. They always do."

"But how can those men have died? Your people can't die!" She grasped for some bit of the certainty she had had before.

"We thought not." Richard tried to forget his own horror in order to comfort her. "For us to regenerate there must be something left besides the spirit. There must be a piece of solid form to build upon. And with those men there wast no solid form. The mist surrounding those planets disintegrated them even as they fought to regenerate. They have returned to the Gabrellans."

"It seems so hopeless," Bronwyn said miserably. "Shandal is only a precursor to something we can never hope to deal with."

"We do not know that," Richard said emphatically. "The Gabrellans always guide us. Perhaps they have already begun. We wilt know only as time progresses.

"Do not lose heart, my lady. At least some measure of peace lies ahead."

"I'll be all right once I've sorted this out." Bronwyn glanced around the tent. "I must get back to work now." Her work was far from over. Many, many warriors needed attention in the hospital tents.

Altan stood on the palace roof, half listening to the reports brought from across the crumbling Shanda empire. People were screaming and rioting below him, angered to the verge of madness by the incoming news. Finally he motioned the couriers to leave him and turned to the general at his side.

"Get your units into the streets and stop that slaughter." His tone was low, level, intense. A Seer of his stature never raised his voice. "My predecessors dallied with little games and led us to this. Stop this depletion of our numbers, and don't maim while you do it."

The general saluted and hurried away as Altan limped down to his dark rooms. Becca was waiting with the steaming bloodfire tea and a concerned expression.

"Is it terrible, lord?"

"Terrible enough. But though we fall, it will not be all the way." Altan eased himself onto the bed and threw a cover over his legs.

"Lord?"

"My Master's plan worked well, and the black mist has taught David fear. The Zha-Dhak have also found a lesser universe to plunder, while we grow strong again. With the guardian mist they have expended all the power they dare in this realm. We are on our own, so to speak, while I establish a line of ruling Seers."

Becca looked hesitantly around the room, as if expecting to see the Master. "What are we to do, lord?"

"Establish a more solid line of tactics," Altan mumbled as he drank. "The Warlords will soon learn that I rule, not they, and the worlds I rule will come in line and not kill one another in feuds. I need to begin breeding warriors, filling every world to capacity while we test the strengths of David. A long road lies ahead of us, and I will not see the end of it. But to compensate that fact I will wield more power now."

Becca stepped warily backward.

Altan smiled, satisfied. "Find me a girl, Becca, one of beauty and not too filthy. I will learn how best to bend wills to mine without betraying the true plan."

Tarmynan stepped from the transport ship, onto a rolling plain of lush green grass and cool, clear air. As the breeze tousled his thick black hair, he hugged his baby girl closely on one bandaged arm and grasped his wife's hand.

Asher strode from the Paladin command ship to speak to this group. "For several days thou wilt rest and be tended in the pavillions here. Researchers wilt gather any family histories and assist thee in either returning to thine homeworlds or choosing a new place to make thine homes. If there art specific clans or heritages among thee, and 'tis thine wish, please group together in the pavillions, and the researchers wilt aid thee in returning home." He paused, turning at last to Tarmynan. "Thee, who led thy people so safely during this time—what dost thou wish, Tarmynan?"

"We want our world back, and we're prepared to fight to take it." Tarmynan met and held his gaze. "Tilmanah was a world of holy people, students of the soul, easy targets for our enemy. We remain the students, but now also are warriors. Only death will move us again from our world once we take it back. All the slaves of black hair and blue eyes who are Lhassa will have our world again."

"Come with me." Asher raised his voice so that all could hear. "All who art Lhassa, come with me."

Curious, still wary, three-fourths of the freed slaves clustered together to follow the Immortal up the gentle slope behind him. The relocation pavillions were arrayed to their left, row upon row of spacious, comfortable tents of living quarters and ample supplies. The rows stopped at the base of this slope, which crested with a panoramic view of the vast plain on its opposite face.

The Lhassa drew a collective sharp breath, then sighed as one.

Lush, pale green grass rippled in gentle waves as far as the eye could see. Centered on this plain, there rose a mammoth rock formation, gleaming white in the bright sunlight, entirely natural but with wings furled at its sides and its huge dragon head raised to meet the dawn.

"The Dragon," Tarmynan breathed, hugging his wife to him.

"The Dragon," Asher repeated, then smiled broadly. "I believed I hadst found thee, after we met. This quadrant wast regained by us much later, and Tilmanah is thine once more. My people wilt teach thine how to hold it."

"My people will learn," Tarmynan assured him. "Once your

worlds are restored, and the battles finished, we will meet our teachers."

Chapter Twenty-Five

Bronwyn's restless sleep was shattered by a deathly stillness. She was heading for the tent door when Jericho ran in and swept her into his arms.

Savoring the closeness, Bronwyn kissed his forehead before asking, "What's going on?"

"The Shanda have gone." Jericho held her tightly for another moment, then glanced outside.

"They've surrendered?"

"No, they've been recalled to their homes. They abandoned everything, boarded their ships, and left.

"At any rate, the war is over for now and we also are going home. It will be many years before Shandal is strong enough for any kind of attack, and when they do they will be met by our winds."

Looking around the tent Bronwyn saw others spreading the news to the wounded men. Yet there was no joy.

"I'm so tired, Jericho; we all are. And nothing is ended, there will always be an unfought war between us and Seryl. It's all ruined."

Looking down at her, Jericho was deeply disturbed by the dark change in her. Caressing her face, he said softly, "We need your faith more now than ever, Bron."

"I don't mean to be like this, Jericho. Everything good seems so distant... What of Seryl's king?"

"The black mist does not guard that world, so the murderer will be found."

"What now?" she asked wearily.

"It will take three or four months to treat the wounded and disperse the armies. Then we'll go home and begin again."

The dispersion and cleanup were interrupted by intermittent raids by suicide units from Shandal's untouched worlds, disturbing the work but causing little actual harm. Those units who dared intrude near Maradane's armies met Scott and his men, who maintained a vigilant circuit around the camps. In the final days before returning home they turned back the last large assault, and Scott returned to the hospital tent to heal the few men wounded in the fray.

Reaching into his belt, he hesitated, then searched the pockets of his vest.

"Scott?" Bryce looked curiously at the giant.

"My silver is gone," Scott said in exasperation.

"Well, you did fall when those three men jumped you," Bryce reminded him. "Shall we go search the field?"

Scott shook his head absently. "No, it wilt return to the storage zone of its own accord. Any of our psychic keys always revert there after thirty days away from us. I have my copper still."

Bryce returned to his work as Scott knelt beside a youth with a head wound. They were going home within three days and there was still endless packing to finish.

Bronwyn stared at the rubble that had been her home. Maradane was now a planet of blackened lands and leveled villages, with makeshift shelters dotting the area surrounding the palace grounds.

"Oh Jericho, it's all ruined! We'll need forever to fix it."

"Bron, we'll do it." Jericho gently brushed the tears from her face. "We'll live in the temple while our people's homes are rebuilt. We built this world once and we will do it again." The throbbing ache in his heart renewed itself as he thought of Anders' work. "And somewhere along the way we'll see Seryl pay for their private little war."

His words were barely done when a young servant ran to him. "Milord, where is my lord Scott? I have looked everywhere, and my lady Jana surely can't last much longer!"

His face ashen, Jericho gripped the girl's shoulders. "Krista, what are you saying?"

Krista wrung her hands. "Just before your arrival a courier announced your coming. My lady Jana sent her children to the temple to organize a clean-up crew of the older children and she returned to her home for something for Scott, from what little home remained standing. If only I'd stayed near to her..." Krista fought to control her trembling voice. "There was a tremendous explosion, the house is a heap of rubble, and I haven't been able to find her!"

"Did you see anyone? What sort of explosion?" Jericho was already running toward the remains of the house.

Krista sobbed, "It was a bomb; it could only have been a bomb. I did see a tall man, dark and wearing heavy furs. He ran quickly away, and had gold bands on his right forearm."

"Cursed be Seryl!" Jericho stumbled to a halt beside the ruined house. "Never in all eternity will they pay for this...Bron, get the others, and find Scott!" He began toppling small blocks from the top of the pile. "Jana? Can you hear me?"

Bronwyn was barely gone when Scott raced through the trampled gardens, terror-stricken. "Jana! Where art thou? Jana!"

"I've found no sign of her, Scott." Jericho never stopped working. "Perhaps she's not here."

Scott raced to the back of the house. "She came back with Laryssa; they art both in here." His voice cracked as he begged his wife to answer him.

A muffled cry rose from the debris to his left. Throwing loose rock and boards in every direction, he rolled away even the foundation blocks. In his wild efforts to reach her he did not even notice the arrival of the other kings and Richard. Bronwyn and Shara returned with Joachim and Kimmel, who plunged in to work beside their father.

Bronwyn looked on, pale with rage and fear. "Shara, it will tear him apart if she's dead—it will kill him inside. He loves her so."

"Bron, be calm. I don't believe Jana's dead." Shara hugged her close.

"I can't be calm!" Bronwyn wailed. "I care not what anyone says, we've borne a loss far too great and never will it be replaced. I can't bear to have Scott crushed like this!"

Shara did not answer, knowing that while the burning ache inside said the loss was too great, her husband would have called it small.

Scott heaved a massive boulder away, pushed aside the debris beside it, and found his wife where she had fallen trying to shield her daughter. Laryssa was unharmed and Richard lifted her quickly into his arms.

Scott gathered Jana's bruised body into his arms, tears falling on her hair. "Jana? Thou must be well, I need thee." He brushed a streak of dust off her forehead with a trembling hand.

"Scott?" Jana breathed, opening her eyes to look blankly at him. "Why is it so dark? I can't see you."

He kissed her dusty hair. "Sshhh, my little one. Thou wilt be well, Jana." He eased her into Bryce's waiting arms and reached into his belt for his silver. Then his hand stopped and he stared at Bryce. "'Tis gone!"

"We can't get it back now," Bryce said quickly. "We'll take her to the hospital ship at the temple." He settled Jana back in Scott's arms.

Holding Laryssa tightly, Richard said, "My copper is at the temple. Hurry."

Scott paced the temple gardens nervously, holding Laryssa on one brawny arm. Richard, Bryce and Shara were going to him as Gray ran down the tunnel.

Holding out his hand, Gray stopped beside Scott. "We found this on one of the last prisoners from Seryl. He stole it, taking it for something of value." He dropped the object into Scott's hand.

Gazing at the silver gleaming against his palm, Scott closed his fist around it, murmuring, "Something of value."

Seeing that something was amiss, Gray turned to Shara for an explanation. Bryce looked at up Scott, a mixture of relief and sorrow in his expression.

"Scott, Jana will be fine with a little rest. Shara and Richard helped me repair the damage to her legs, and her back is healed. We've moved her to a room here to rest." He hesitated. "But she suffered such a blow to her head, there was damage. She is blind, Scott."

"Blind?" Scott tilted his head back. His eyes tightly closed, he envisioned her deep violet eyes looking up at him, so searching a look. Finally he swallowed the pain and said, "I wast so afraid she wouldst die. Let me see her."

Bryce nodded, taking Laryssa from him.

Scott knelt beside his wife's bed. "Jana, how dost thou feel?"

"Much better, Bryce gave me some medicine. Scott, is Laryssa all right?" Jana stared vacantly ahead.

"She is well." Scott closed his hand over hers.

"Scott, your hand's trembling. You weren't hurt?" Jana reached out shakily, trying to find his face. He took her hand and kissed her palm.

"Wilt thou ne'er remember I am Immortal?...I wast hurt inside. I thought I wouldst lose thee...but thou wilt be well 'ere long."

"But I can't see; I can't take care of the house. How will I ever do anything if I can't see?" Jana sobbed softly, "How will I live with never seeing you again?"

"My Jana, my ugly face is not such a lost sight." He held her close, his head resting on hers as he smoothed her hair. "It wilt be hard at first, but thou wilt learn. Bryce and Prudence wilt teach thee.

"I wilt build a new home, with servants, and thou wilt find it not so bad. There is truly little thou canst not do, and I wilt tell thee how everything looks. Please do not be sad. There is nothing I wouldst not do for thee, my little one."

Jana rested her head on his shoulder, comforted by the feel of his calloused hand against hers and the scent of his windblown hair. "I will try to be happy for you."

"If only I hadst gone back to find my silver," Scott whispered to himself.

"Scott, don't. I can't live with it if you blame yourself. I don't think it could have been changed."

"Perhaps not. But Seryl wilt feel our retribution, planetary shields or no.

"Thou must rest now." He helped her settle back against the pillows, tenderly kissing her. "Sleep now and I wilt return later, little one."

David sat at the head of the temple council table that night, his jaw set stubbornly against the arguments being launched by the kings. He had come in response to Gray's summons and his heart ached as he saw his son's torment. Yet he was adamant in his stand.

"Thou art to forget all thought of attacking Seryl! This hurt canst not be healed by another war. Attacking now wilt bring only thine own destruction. My men wilt find these criminals according to the law, and by the ancient laws these men wilt die." David turned his gaze to Caleb's stubborn face. The High King's white hair trailed over his eyes, disheveled by the force of the argument.

David continued. "Caleb, thou shalt see to the rebuilding of Maradane. When this world's people have adequate shelter we shalt see to the matter of Seryl. Is that clear?"

"It shall be as you decree," Caleb said, his voice taut. "Construction will begin while we await your return."

Though rarely called upon, the ancient laws of Leahcim

Tierrah were still in effect throughout David's empire. In accordance with these laws, if the warlords of Seryl did not surrender themselves to a prison planet they would face in a duel the men they had wronged. Gray's men would track down the criminals and bypass the planetary shields through the teleportal zone, and Chuck would bring the men out through a spun portal.

Caleb ended the discussion, knowing as everyone else did that the warlords of Seryl would never surrender.

Bryce stood in the temple records room. Veiled in shadows, the shelves before him were burdened with materials: folders, binders, catalogs, rolled maps. The documentation of a handful of people who built a world...

No, not quite. The lovingly compiled data of a man who shaped a world.

Sinking onto a bench along one wall, Bryce put his head in his hands. Why had Caleb asked him to do this? Why must he be in charge of organizing the reconstruction? It would never be the same, never be a reenactment of those first exciting days. There was a gnawing, echoing gap that nothing in these dusty papers would close. The vision that had forged this place was lost.

Leaning back against the wall, Bryce closed moist eyes and tried to recapture a moment passed away over two decades ago.

** Seated at a desk surrounded by rolls of maps and sheaves of paper, Anders and Bryce were perusing detailed section maps.

Unrolling the first map and reaching for a transparent overlay, Bryce said, "I ordered the printers in Leahcim Tierrah to use the researchers' reports and make section maps with climate notations. I'll draw our sketches on these overlays."

Anders scratched his chin thoughtfully as he studied the open map and the thirty-nine others scattered around the room. He had not expected such a confusion of paperwork connected with landscaping the planet. Working with single sheets like this would never do—he needed a complete picture before him. But one small map would be too minuscule for Bryce to sketch.

Suddenly the big man grinned and began gathering maps into his arms.

"What are you doing?" Bryce asked with a bemused chuckle. He never knew what to expect when his exuberant friend got a sudden idea.

"The garden wall needs a mural," Anders offered over his shoulder as he strode from the room.

For a moment Bryce simply stared after him, then he grabbed up the rest of the rolls and jogged to the gardens. "A perfect idea, Anders. Let's get these laid out by number and we'll work from the bottom up."

Soon curious temple residents had stopped tasks of gardening or study and gathered behind the two men. Shara brought the adhesive her husband had requested, then stood back to study the operation.

She smiled proudly as she saw her husband's plan. The section maps would fit in four rows of ten across the wall of the high-ceilinged chamber. Anders would be able to see Maradane as one whole surface, and his work would be visible to the people. He could see the landscape develop while he noted comments and suggestions from the temple residents.

Having pasted up the heavy sheets, Anders and Bryce began attaching the glossy overlays. Prudence brought out a small table and Bryce's case of colored markers and measuring devices. Caleb joined them then, dropping a huge notebook of vegetation descriptions onto the table.

"That came this morning, Anders. It lists all the plants available for our climates."

Anders nodded, taking a moment to look away from the map. "Caleb, could you order a relief map to be set up in the corner here? That will give us a better idea of actual terrain. And have it marked to match this map?"

Caleb grinned, already able to see the planet taking shape. "I'll contact the researchers now. With luck it will be here in a few days." He headed for the communications center, whistling softly.

Feeling a tug on his sleeve, Anders looked down at a boy of

about eight.

"Sire, is our world that big?" the boy asked, incredulous.

"Come and see." Hoisting the child onto his shoulders, Anders crossed the gardens to stand opposite the map. "It's that big."

Round-eyed, the boy said, "And you're going to paint on all the trees by yourself?"

Grinning at the phrasing, Anders shook his head. "Oh no, everyone will help. I want to know what everyone thinks, so the world will be what they want." He slipped the boy back down to his own feet. "You can watch while we work, and fetch things for us if you like."

"Really?" The boy nodded enthusiastically, then scampered off to tell his parents of his great honor.

Anders returned to stand a few feet from the wall, studying the glossy sheets. "That's one heck of a lot of bare ground."

"Can't argue there." Bryce began setting out his pens and rulers. Holding up a gold and a dark green marker in either hand, he asked, "Desert flowers or forests first?"

Seeing Jericho coming down the tunnel, Anders said, "Forests," and began flipping through the massive volume for the right species of trees for the area of the western wind tower.

Bryce attached a second overlay sheet on the sections marked for agriculture and village settings. Anders was using a long stick with pincers on the end to position markers at various spots on the relief map. Several onlookers were perched on benches, watching intently.

"What is the pale green on the map, Anders?" Prudence asked, looking up from a checklist of medical supplies to be ordered. Since the map went up four months ago people were always bringing small tasks to the gardens so they could share in the excitement. Now the landscaping phase was complete and the men were moving on to construction plans.

"Rain forest," Anders said absently, pushing a marker a little further inland from a coast. The rains would be better there, not too heavy and not too light, and a farming village would flourish.

Farther south he set a marker for a mountain village, and to the east one for a fishing settlement. "What do you think, Bryce?"

The southern king stepped to the table and studied it. "Looks good. I'll transfer these to the overlays."

"Okay. I'm going to take the final seeding order to Caleb, and get the volume on animals."

Bryce nodded, already at work with his pens.

Caleb looked rather dubiously at the five-inch thick binder Anders placed before him. "You sure you didn't overlook anything?" he teased.

"Not a seed," Anders bantered. "There's something in there to suit everyone who made a suggestion."

"I'll send it with the next courier." Caleb reached to a shelf behind his desk and held an equally heavy volume toward Anders. "This one is the catalog of animals. I trust you're ready?"

"I finished sorting the people's lists last evening." Anders took the book with a grin. "By the time the seedings are complete I'll have the order for animals ready to go. **

"No!" Bryce stood, pounding the wall. "I can't do it!" Turning defiantly, he strode from the room and up the long hall to the gardens.

His steps slowed abruptly and he halted in the shadowed doorway.

The map dominated the far wall, unchanged over the years. In the corner sat the relief map, so carefully filled with its colored markers. Yet one thing was different.

Standing beside the table, head bowed and hands cupping the marker of the eastern palace, Shara cried softly.

Somewhere in the distance Bryce heard a chiding voice say, "Maradane lives as long as we dream, my good friend."

Shaking his head, Bryce went slowly to Shara and drew her close.

"I was mad at Caleb, you know, for asking me to oversee the rebuilding," he sighed. "But it was because I was pushing memories away, not holding them near. The people are what make our world, and for them I guess I can be a substitute planet-shaper. For them, and for him."

By the time David returned two months later Maradane was well into its reconstruction. Workers from Leahcim Tierrah had completed re-forestation and re-seeding projects, consulting their original records, and compiled orders to replace the wildlife lost in the war.

David brought with him two brothers, warlords of northern lands on Seryl. On the evening following their arrival these prisoners were brought before the council.

David studied the men, his eyes cold. "Thou art well aware of the laws governing thine actions. This council hath reached its decision, and I give thee one final chance to surrender. If not, thou shalt face Jeremiah and my son."

"But we stand no chance against them!" the tallest of the men cried out. "You condemn us to certain death at their hands."

"Regardless of what happens here thou art sentenced to death for murder." David slapped the table. "Thou mayst choose a painless death on a prison planet, or suffer an open duel with the man thee wronged. Or art thou adept only at bombing women and children?"

The man shrank beneath David's venomous glare, but his brother spoke fiercely.

"I will never surrender! I did no wrong in killing a man in battle, a man barely able to wield his sword and unfit to be called king. Why do you harass us when you are victorious and claim the glory?"

"Glory?" Jeremiah barked, his voice hoarse. "All we have are pain and suffering, and loss. It's a foul creature who calls this devastation glory.

"And where is this great and courageous swordsman who hid for perhaps the entire first battle behind a throne to backstab my father, and to stab and slash again as he lay defenseless?"

"Enough of this!" David shouted. "Those who show no mercy deserve not to seek it for themselves. Thou art not forced to dwell in my realm, but if ye remain thou art subject to my laws." He motioned to the guards, who stepped nearer the prisoners and marched them outside.

Once away from the temple Jeremiah turned to David. "I would use my own sword, please, that I had before Bane Slayer. Though it helped to bring some peace I feel like a murderer as I use it. I will never use it again...I wish you had given it to Papa."

David gazed sadly at the youth. "Thy sword served its purpose, for thou art truly thy father's son. A lesser man, in his greed for power, wouldst ne'er part with it...I give thee my blade, which serves well in skillful hands." He placed his golden sword in Jeremiah's hand, then ordered his guards to form a circle and free the prisoners.

A tense silence pervaded the area as the four men faced each other. Scott's opponent was close to eight feet tall, yet a crude swordsman. Rather than defend his life he tried to evade the fight, seeking a break in the wall of guards. Finally tired of the charade, Scott threw his sword to the ground and reached into his Star Holder. Both men from Seryl paused to stare as the big man assembled his axe, then the one who had placed the bomb in Jana's house screamed in terror and threw himself against the guards.

"Let me go!"

The guards threw him back into the center of the ring, where he lay staring up at Scott. The Immortal simply stood his ground, the haft of his axe resting lightly on the grass. By the ancient laws, if the condemned duelist refused to fight, his opponent was allowed to change weapons or tactics to end the battle.

The other prisoner kicked his brother in the side. "Get up, you idiot. Get up and fight." He kicked again until his brother rose to trembling feet.

"You deal death so freely, you who cannot ever be touched by it," the dark man whined as he slashed feebly toward Scott.

"I am touched daily by it, and I suffer heavily for carrying this weapon," Scott growled low in his throat. "I who loath killing am the most efficient murderer in the realm." He prodded the man several times in the belly with the spear point, pushing him around the ring. "I beg others to show mercy, to thrust hatred from their hearts and fight from love, then I lop people's heads from their shoulders." The man stumbled backward, and Scott used the spear to pop the buckles off his armor. "All because of scum like thee. My wife is blind because of thee. She wilt live her life in darkness, ne'er seeing our children again, ne'er seeing anything because of thee." He deftly drew the scythe point along the man's neck, trailing a fine line of blood. "I must listen to thee whine and crawl and beg, because thou art not man enough to defend thy actions. Strike back or I shalt make thy death so slow thou wilt beg for an end!"

The man cowered at the edge of the ring, looking vainly for help from his brother.

Jeremiah's foe put up a weak show of swordplay to mask his attempts to trip the youth. Sickened by the spectacle, Jeremiah let himself be tumbled to the ground only to run his sword to the hilt through the man's midsection, then pull it out with a vicious twist.

Rising and throwing his sword to the ground, Jeremiah walked into a remnant of forest to gather his thoughts and quell the sickness within him.

In the ring, the remaining prisoner gave a final cry of despair and threw himself on Scott's pike. Freeing the weapon with a look of disgust, Scott rolled the man aside with his booted foot. He cast one glance toward his father, then strode away, returning to the only one who could offer any comfort to his tormented nights.

"Take them away," David told his men tiredly, staring toward the forest. "I wonder if I do right," he said absently, not really caring whether anyone listened. "We tell thee to trust in a path that leads only down long roads of fighting to some distant future none of thee shalt see, to trust in a way of life fighting to preserve some honor, whilst we art tortured by what we must do. My son, such a fragile heart, and I consign him to an endless lifetime of killing. He must tell others not to do what he must do, to fight with hatred."

Jericho put a hand on David's shoulder. "He loves, David, very deeply, or he would not hurt. No, you do what is best, and we can only follow. What is best is not always what is easiest, we know that well by now."

"Yea, I have taught thee well." David turned bitterly away, his shoulders slumped in exhaustion, and followed his men into the mist of the teleportal zone.

Richard watched him go, his eyes filled with sorrow. "If only that man's words wert true and death didst not touch us...Come, we must return home. This day is ended." He walked tiredly away.

David returned to Leahcim Tierrah, leaving the Marans to the rebuilding of their planet while he pulled his empire out of the ruin.

At the next council after the Immortal king's departure, Bryce, returning from a research trip, presented Caleb with plans for the new palaces.

"They are in the style of Stalasia, our memorial to Anders."

Caleb examined the sheaf of papers silently, then said quietly, "They are glorious, Bryce. Through these the people will see that Maradane will rise better than before. We must begin right away."

The kings' first plan had been to rebuild their homes only after all else was complete and their people were safely housed. Yet as the first months passed they realized the people missed the sight of the palaces. They turned often to look at the foundation of their security and saw only blackened ruins. Therefore Caleb had asked for plans from Bryce, who had spent several days on Stalasia studying the ruined palaces in the most ancient city.

Once the palaces were under construction the people pursued their work more heartily, being able to pause and know their centers of government would soon be strong again.

For the ruling families the ensuing year seemed a reliving of their first years on the planet. They worked closely with people from Leahcim Tierrah and the supply planets and soon their world was again alive.

As the artisans progressed with the palaces and the new style became apparent great curiosity took hold of the citizens. Temporary warehouses, vast in size, were set up to house materials being shipped from distant worlds, and people near enough to see the work often stopped to wonder about the huge halls rising from the foundations.

At the end of one year, when all else was flowing smoothly, the Maran banners were unfurled from lofty spires and the palaces opened to the people. For many days much traffic passed through the main entrances formed of two massive oak doors with bronze fittings. Above and to both sides of the entrances the marble walls were intricately carved or overlaid with lustrous ivory collected from shepherded planets. Wide verandas were flanked by silver railings and grates of gold and bronze. The sun glinted enticingly on the veined marble and jeweled ornaments.

Once inside, the curious crowds gently caressed polished banisters and drank in the richness of chandeliers, tiled floors, satin and velvet draperies, and striking tapestries. The children marvelled most at the curving staircases leading upward from either side of the entrance halls centered with graceful fountains.

It was well over a month before the people tired of roaming the vaulted halls and gardens. Gardeners still worked outside, cultivating trees and coaxing blossoms from shrubs surrounding new fountains and statues.

Caleb surveyed these scenes quietly, joyful that all was on its way to normal. He knew nothing of the problems plaguing Jericho, for the next council was days away.

Jericho sat at his library desk, pondering the figures of the latest census report and trying to plan a new device for the wind towers. His thoughts were interrupted as a servant led five men into the room.

Jericho looked up distractedly. "Yes, what may I do for you?"

"We're sorry to disturb you, my lord; we know you're very busy." The group's spokesman bowed formally. "We live on the land between the Sea of Timon and the Gulf of Stalasia, where the mountains run along the coast. Many of our people have disappeared, and though we've looked everywhere we can't find them."

Jericho reached toward the back of his desk, where planetary maps were housed on long dowels. Pulling one map out flat before him, he said, "I'm not extremely familiar with this area now. When did you first miss the people?"

"A little less than a month ago, my lord. Our village had barely six hundred people to start. We looked everywhere except the mountains, for the weather there is too violent. Two of my sons are lost, sire." The man's voice was taut.

"I'm trying to do something right now about this miserable weather." Jericho bit his lower lip. "You return home and I'll send a squad of guards right away to search the area. I'll come as soon as I can."

"Thank you, my lord." The men left, and Jericho rested his chin in his hand as he stared out the window. Then he glanced once more at the map and re-read the census report.

"I just don't understand this at all."

According to the census the sector population was not increasing as it should. Villages and cities showed the expected rise, but in certain rural areas there was a marked decline in numbers. Since these were farming communities operated by large families, Jericho found it unnatural for the population there to decrease.

In comparing the census to the map Jericho discovered the greatest loss was in the same area where the people were missing. The range of mountains lay near all the small villages, and he began to wonder if there was a connection between the lost people and the mountains.

Running one hand through his thick hair he mumbled, "I wish Scott and Richard were here. They could help with this."

The Immortals had all gone to Leahcim Tierrah, for it was long past the time when Scott's eldest sons should have been presented at David's court. Immortal youths were customarily brought to David at the age of thirteen, but for Scott's sons this had been in the midst of the war.

At sixteen and fifteen Joachim and Kimmel found it difficult to curb their impatience. Joshua, who was just thirteen, had been driving his father crazy. Maradane's ruling families could not attend this ceremony, not yet comfortable about leaving their reviving world unattended, but hoped to travel to Leahcim Tierrah when Tully came of age in three years.

"Well, they'll be back in a month, but this can't wait." Slipping the map off its dowel, Jericho headed for the guard headquarters.

Spreading the map on Salar's desk he pointed to the strip of land in question.

"Salar, take some men and make a thorough search of this area. Several people have been reported missing. They may be trapped in the mountains by the storms."

"I'll ready the winter gear and we'll leave at once." Salar studied the map, then glanced up at Jericho. "Will you be coming, or shall I send couriers here?"

"I'm coming but might not make it until the day after tomorrow. I want to finish the weather system—it will make the search easier." Jericho jogged back to his study.

Not long afterward Bronwyn came in and sat on the arm of his chair. "Jericho, aren't you coming to dinner?"

"I'm not hungry," he answered absently, not looking up from the paper on which he wrote. "I must finish these plans, then join Salar at the village."

"What village?" Bronwyn smoothed his tousled hair. "You haven't spoken to me all afternoon."

"I'm sorry, Bron." He frowned, leaning back in the chair. "Some people are missing in the mountains; I sent Salar to look for them.

"On top of that, these computations aren't coming out right, and the census report is not encouraging. When is the next council?"

"In three days. Can't Garth help you with the blueprints?" Bronwyn leaned forward to study the plans.

"Not at this point. Besides, he has to install the control panel in our council room. It has to be ready when I finish this. You go eat. I'll be here for the rest of the night, most likely." Jericho stared at the pen in his hand, wondering what he was doing wrong.

Chapter Twenty-Six

Salar returned two days later, early in the morning before Jericho could leave for the village. He found the king working in the library.

"Jericho, I must speak with you." Shrugging off his heavy fur cape, Salar stood nervously tapping his wristband. "Instead of finding anyone we lost three of our own men. There's no trace of them...Jericho, you know I don't fear things needlessly, but there's a frightening air about this place."

"What do you mean?" Jericho straightened in his chair, dropping his pen.

"I can't pinpoint it, but I sense it. There's something amiss with the whole area." Salar hesitated, his eyes confused. "How could three of our most experienced men vanish like that?"

Jericho ran both hands through his thick hair. Even though he had no solid details he trusted Salar's senses. Sighing in frustration, he stood up.

"Choose ten guards and meet me at your office." Jericho grabbed his cape and staff before rushing to the council room where his son worked on the control panel.

"I have it ready to hook up, Father." Garth set a soldering gun on the counter as Jericho entered the room.

"Later. Right now we're going to that village. Something is drastically wrong there." Jericho hurried Garth out to meet the guards.

Salar piloted their small shuttle to the village, landing on a hill on the outskirts of the settlement.

"From here you can see the surrounding lands." Salar waved one hand toward the village before pointing to the lower slopes of the mountains. "The people had no reason to go there, nor do I believe they did so."

Nodding distractedly, Jericho surveyed the scene for anything out of place.

It was an ordinary village of small houses encircling main buildings such as the market and blacksmith. Storehouses formed the western boundary between village and sea. Jericho could just discern a faint line of blue water in the distance.

"I don't suppose they went to the coast?" he asked.

"No, they're not fishers." Salar shook his head. "Seafood is run up daily from the coastal villages."

"Father," Garth said, pointing to a distant meadow encircled by low stone fences. "It seems very odd the way those cattle are lying. They look dead."

Frowning, Jericho caught sight of a figure climbing the hill toward them. It was one of the men who first reported the missing people. As he neared the group Jericho said, "Sir, do you know anything about those animals?"

"I came to tell you, sire. They were killed in the night by some beast. The herdsman was also killed."

Jericho strode down the hill, the others following closely. They stopped near the cattle, three steers torn apart by animals that had eaten their fill.

"Have any of the people returned?"

"No, sire. Four more are gone," the man replied haltingly. "We found two of them in the hills, torn open like the herdsman."

Turning his gaze to the hills the king said, "Salar, do you think the storms have driven some cats down in search of food? There are snow tigers in these mountains."

"This is not the way they kill," Salar answered. "They break their prey's neck and open the jugular."

"Sire," the man spoke up. "We do lose a few stock animals to the cats, this is true, but the tigers never harm us. The herdsmen allow five or so steers to the cats in the violent storms and they return to the mountains when the storm passes. The cats know the dogs will kill them at any other time."

Jericho sighted a trio of the massive dogs trained to guard the herds. They were a formidable match for the sleek cats, yet they had obviously been too frightened to attack these unknown marauders. He turned grimly to the villager.

"What is your name, sir?"

"Aram, my lord."

"Aram, this may not be the tigers, but it's the work of some beast. Please keep your people within the village, and be certain they are armed with crossbows. There is a council tomorrow and I'll see if we can come up with a solution.

"For the time being the guards will remain here, to continue the search and hopefully ward off this beast." Jericho turned to his friend. "Salar, report any discovery at once."

Salar nodded, then set about stationing his men.

As the council began the next evening Jericho prepared to bring up his problem, but was interrupted by Jeremiah, whose voice was troubled.

"Caleb, before we get to other things I have a problem in the western portion of my sector. I hoped someone could help me."

"Certainly, go ahead." Caleb opened his notebook preparatory to taking down the discussion.

"It has happened primarily in Section 91 Blue, near the mountains." Jeremiah referred to the colored overlay map used for easy reference to the areas of Maradane. "Our population there is decreasing and now people are disappearing from the villages. Two small children were stolen from their very beds."

Jericho began to speak but was cut off by Aric. "Caleb, I've had similar complaints. People from villages in Sections 4 and 5 Red have been reported missing. There have also been several incidents of some beast killing livestock and people near the mountains."

"I don't believe this!" Jericho slapped the polished tabletop. "Three days ago I discovered the population declining in Sections 42 and 46 Blue. One of the villages in that area has several people missing and at least three attacks by wild beasts. I had no idea it was happening elsewhere."

Caleb looked questioningly at Bryce. "Have you had none of these problems?"

"No attacks or missing people have been reported," Bryce answered slowly. "But the census does show a decline in Sections 124 and 125 Red."

Rubbing the back of his neck, Caleb turned to the map on the wall behind him. "These sections are so widely scattered, it hardly seems there could be a connection. Yet it can't be coincidence that similar beasts begin attacking people at the same time for no reason.

"Bryce, are you certain there are no missing people in your sector?"

"That only means no one has come to me yet, not that nothing is happening."

"Perhaps they are still searching on their own," Jericho said. "Before anyone came to me the villagers had been searching for almost a month."

"Which makes it all the worse," Caleb sighed, pushing his sleeves up. "There must be a connection, far apart though these incidents are. Has anyone been to the villages?"

All but Bryce and Drahcir had visited the sites. Aric confirmed Salar's comment to Jericho. "Although I can't name it, there's something in the air which bothers me."

Caleb was silent for a moment, drumming his fingers on the notebook before him. His pen lay forgotten. Finally he said, "Send exploration teams to each of those sections and relay the information to me. There has to be a link here. Once we find it we should be able to deal with it."

The search parties, on foot and by air, combed each area but found neither the missing people nor any of the marauding animals. Then, five days later, the sector kings received reports of people missing from villages beyond the original areas.

Caleb called another council to gather news from the leaders of the search. Salar acted as spokesman for the group.

"So far we have little information. The incidents have moved away from the first locations and so we believe the animals are moving on." He traced the areas on the map. "Each area lies at some point in a range of mountains. The animals are staying primarily in those mountains, traveling through them, and seem to go near the villages only when hungry, we believe to make an easy catch of livestock."

"What of the missing people?" Caleb asked anxiously.

"We found none. But with the exception of the two children all those missing were either out with a herd or cultivating a field. Therefore I believe they were chanced upon by the animals and that no outright effort was made to seek out and kill the villagers."

Caleb nodded. "It's fairly clear the beasts don't stalk out of hatred. I spoke with the mother of the children. The house is far afield and the children were crying about going to bed. It may be that the beast was attracted by the noise.

"Have you discovered any tracks?"

"Only a handful," Salar answered. "They are none I recognize—fairly long feet with heavy claws, and made by a biped."

Caleb studied the map intently, recalling Salar's tracings.

"Salar, are they moving toward each other?"

"Oddly, no." Salar turned again to the map. "Some move east, some north, but there does not seem a unified destination."

The High King shook his head. "It makes no sense. Do your best to track them, try to capture them, and keep them away from the villages. I'm going to contact David and see if this seems like a beast native to any enemy planet. It may be they were left during the war."

"Wonderful," Aric muttered. "I'd like to leave something of our own for those accursed people."

Scott and Richard returned immediately after Caleb's conversation with David and joined the search.

The morning after the Immortals' return Caleb was in a storeroom gathering new tapers for the chapels when he heard a piercing scream from the gardens. Dropping the candles he raced through the wide halls, stopping only to grab a sword from the council room wall. Several women were fleeing up the long tunnel while Tiea backed into a corner to shelter a toddler behind her. Armed with only a hoe, she faced a snarling animal. The shaggy grey beast, five feet tall on its hind legs, had entered through the open tunnel door through which the women had been carrying seedling wind trees. Now it hesitated uncertainly, enormous front claws at the ready as it looked around the unfamiliar gardens.

The child screamed shrilly as Caleb placed himself in front of his wife and prepared to lunge at the animal.

"Caleb, no!" Tiea grabbed his arm to hold him back. "In the name of David, Caleb, just let it go! It wants to go down the hall."

Wavering, Caleb saw another beast creeping down the tunnel. He now had no choice but to stand his ground, pressing the woman and child farther back into the corner. The first beast remained where it was while the second proceeded down the hall and vanished into the shadows.

"Caleb, we must wait," Tiea begged in a strained voice. "The women will send help. If we leave them alone they may not harm us."

"I hope so," Caleb breathed. "And I hope the women send Scott."

Jericho was staring woefully at the latest reports when Salar burst into the library, his dark skin blanched with fear.

"Salar, what's happened?" Jericho jumped to his feet, yelling out the open door for Scott to come from the guard yard. “Are you all right?”

“It was so quick,” Salar gasped, his words tumbling together. “Four of them attacked and half of us were dragged off before a moment passed. The rest of us barely escaped.”

Jericho stared at Salar as Scott ran into the library. A chill crept up his spine as he saw the way the Dacynite gripped the hilt of his sword as if expecting another attack.

“Salar, tell me what kind of animal it is. We have to capture them. Salar, tell me!”

“We’ll never capture them,” Salar said dazedly. “It’s the beasts from the caverns.”

Jericho’s response was drowned out as two women ran into the room calling for help. Seeing Scott, one of the women begged breathlessly, “Please, my lord, the beasts are in the temple! They’ve cornered our lady Tiea.”

“Jericho, call the Paladins at once.” Scott reached into the Star Holder slung over his brawny shoulder and began assembling his axe. “Send Tully out to find Richard and announce on the speakers that everyone is to lock themselves in their homes. Contact the other kings, put extra guards on the palace doors, and meet me at the temple.”

Clutching his travel stone, Scott ran to the gardens and vanished into the teleportal zone.

Sweat beaded Caleb’s forehead and his arms ached from holding the sword before him. But the beast had not moved; it remained still, eyeing him menacingly, its claws still held ready. Sounds of destruction drifted down the corridor. The second animal was apparently tearing apart one of the far rooms.

The beast threatening Caleb spun at the sound of sandaled feet in the tunnel. Racing around the outer wall, Scott skidded to a halt in front of Caleb. More steps thundered down the passage and Joachim positioned himself behind the animal. Only two inches shorter than his father, the youth was armed with a massive broadsword.

"Art thou untouched, Caleb?" Scott asked without turning.

"Yes, we're fine," Caleb replied shakily, lowering his numb arms. "It doesn't seem to want to hurt us. There's another one in back that seems to be looking for something."

The beast's head tilted upward slightly at Caleb's words and it growled softly, "Scroes, scroes."

A misty light flickered beside Scott and a voice echoed in his mind, "Scrolls, Scott. Scrolls of the Talitha."

Scott's head snapped around, his eyes wide as the beloved voice dredged up the long forgotten planet's name. "'Tis truly thee?" he asked the light.

Caleb shuddered as the light melted into a familiar form and a whispering voice said, "'Tis I, Scott." Tiea pressed her forehead against Caleb's shoulder with a small cry.

"Maradane is Talitha?" Scott breathed.

"All that remains of Talitha," the light whispered.

"And these beasts?" Scott asked. "They art the Talitha?"

"All that remains."

Scott turned to stare at the beast, then heard a whisper of steps in the shadowy tunnel. The rest of Maradane's kings looked out toward the garden, following Shara's gaze as tears streamed down her face.

She crept forward slowly, one slender hand over her mouth, then breathed joyously, "It's true, we are truly bound to Maradane!"

"We are bound, my love," the voice said gently and the form was finally the true image of the blond king as he reached toward Shara. "Always will I be with you and our world. Though a long and terrible battle entangles us, I will never let Maradane fall. As long as the power of Stalasia binds me this world will live."

The figure faded, but not before sharing his knowledge with Shara's searching thoughts. She turned to Scott, the last trace of grief banished forever from her life.

"It has taken him these many days to understand what is happening. He saved all but the few people who acted rashly; they will be set free."

Scott nodded, understanding something that no one else grasped. Before him the beast dropped to its knees and gurgled, "Slasia," while holding out one massive forelimb.

Caleb dropped his sword weakly, saying plaintively, "I don't understand this."

"The Talitha bow to those of Stalasia," Scott said softly, dismantling his axe. "Please, I want everyone but Shara to go home. A question far older than I hath come to light and we wilt soon answer it. There wilt be no more harm from these creatures."

Everyone stared at Shara, confused, but no one protested Scott's order. They filed slowly away as Shara and Scott escorted the beast down the long hall. It howled softly, calling to its companion, and the noises of destruction ceased.

Caleb watched them go, one hand grasping Tiea's arm, thankful for her safety. The child sat in the corner waiting to be taken home to Cita, content now to play with her sandal laces.

"Caleb, how is this possible?" Tiea finally whispered.

His glance turned to the spot where the light had been. "When the Stalassi die they remain bound to their world, to guard it. It's part of the power of their race to take a shadow form and be seen and heard. But we were never sure if Anders would be bound here or to Stalasia."

Tiea nodded, tears stinging her eyes. "We'd better take Cassy home. Scott doesn't want us near them now."

"I suppose," Caleb acceded. "I just wish I knew what was going on." He bent to lift the little girl into his arms, knowing Scott would convene the council when an explanation was ready.

Scott and Shara sat at the head of the long table, two dusty rolls of paper on the surface before them. The beast crouched in the far corner, its keen eyes never leaving the scrolls.

Caleb gaped at the giant Immortal. "Do you mean to say that these creatures attacked only because we inadvertently hid these scrolls?"

"In part," Scott said. "They attacked partly because they wert attacked. Anders' people sealed the scrolls in a wall and so wert attacked. Thou wert later attacked because thee always chased them with a weapon. Thine actions wert only to be expected, for none understood what wast happening."

"Well, what are the scrolls, and who or what was Talitha?"

"That is a long story, one that answers a question long ago forgotten by my people. Only my father e'er set foot on this world as it once existed," Scott began. Those seated around the table listened raptly as the tale recorded upon the scrolls unfolded.

The Talitha were a race small of stature, gifted with an understanding of magic and a range of psychic powers. They had existed for many thousands of years before the Immortals came into being, yet they vanished suddenly less than five hundred years into the new life of the Immortals. They lived peacefully on their planet, Talitha, and ventured forth only once in all their time, more than seventeen centuries before David's people were born.

Seeing a tangled fate enveloping their people, the psychics gathered together all the mystics among the Talitha. These travelled to a small world of silver meadows and rolling hills, there to found a new race. The colonists were left with only enough magic to preserve their books and to safeguard their new world even beyond death. It was a thing the rest of the Talitha were destined to do in a different way on their ancient home.

Remaining on Talitha, the rest of the people waited patiently for an event they knew no one had the power to change. Nor did they wish to change it, for to do so would be to deprive Talitha of its destiny and condemn countless worlds to slavery and death.

In his early years of travel David stumbled upon Talitha and dwelt for a time with the quiet people. He was awed by the planet as they had shaped it with their magic.

Talitha's surface was ordinary, a pleasant world of mountains and plains, oceans and rivers. The Talitha lived within a ring of mountains, their tiny city a glittering collection of spires and turrets. Yet they spent little time there. Their true home lay deep within the mountains, hewn by their magic to suit their whims.

Carved deep within the ranging mountains and the upper crust of the planet, linked by tunnels to the surface, were the series of bright caverns. Here the Talitha dwelt amidst crystal mountains and lavender rivers, in a world illuminated by globes casting light reflected off phosphorescent walls.

Entering the caverns for the first time David was enchanted by the jeweled castles and great pillared halls nestled in gold-green valleys. Gardens brilliant with blossoms carpeted the cavern floors, and the air was filled with a whisper of silver leaves. Lilies floated lazily along the streams and children waded in search of polished pebbles.

Great amphitheaters of bronze-flecked granite were filled nightly as the Talitha shared their gifts of magic and wisdom with one another. David drank in the sights and gentleness of the people before continuing his travels.

In the year 450 of the Immortals men of black powers visited Talitha on a quest for allies in their campaign for supremacy. Discovering the powers of the Talitha they urged the people to join them and subjugate the other worlds around them. The sorcerers, the Zha-Dhak, had lain waste their home realm and sought new realms to drain of energy to feed their grasping powers.

The Talitha refused, for this was the enemy so long ago foreseen. The sorcerers turned to threats of destruction, but this served not to sway the gentle people. Their most learned mage came forward to meet the angry visitors.

"Leave our world, for here you will gain only your own deaths. The Talitha have foreknowledge of you, of time beyond your current thoughts, and from us will rise the power to destroy you. Talitha will one day bring forth a power against which you cannot stand, and toward that day we guard our world."

The leader of the sorcerers retaliated swiftly. "You will guard, but for us and not against. When we leave here you will allow no one who sets foot on this world to live, and Talitha will die. Nothing but death will rise from this world or this people."

The sorcerers entered an amphitheater, encasing themselves in a barrier until their spells were woven. The Talitha left them undisturbed, instead going about their own final preparations. Certain scrolls were hidden in a place of safety to escape the destruction to come and a counter-spell was cast, altering the sorcerers' work just enough to ensure the destiny of the Talitha.

The sorcerers departed to seek a new world for their purposes. Behind them Talitha lay in ruins. The caverns were brown and withered, the amphitheaters crushed, the waters poisoned. The Talitha were transformed into monstrous creatures so vicious they would tear asunder any soul who managed to penetrate the outer threat of the howling winds. The sorcerers left the world crushed, nature out of balance, and forgot what the Talitha had promised.

Yet the counter-spell worked effectively. The Talitha retained a portion of their knowledge and were bound into the caverns where they could harm no one. Only if the scrolls telling their history became imperiled would they attack, and then only with enough force to regain what was theirs. Otherwise they would remain in their prison and never venture to the surface of the world. The last portion of their spells protected the surface from the ravages of the winds so that all would not be eroded but would remain for the future colonists.

Pausing, Scott gazed sorrowfully at the creature in the corner. "It hath taken them all these years to coordinate an effort to retrieve their history. They recalled little of the surface and were unsure of how to reach the temple from the outside."

Caleb rubbed his moist eyes. "What may we do for them?"

"Little," Scott said. "They remember their previous existence and why they suffered this transformation. They manage to live in their world and will no longer come to ours. The Talitha freely gave up all that wast theirs in order that Maradane wouldst be free to rise. They ask only the return of their scrolls."

"They shall have them." Caleb pushed the scrolls toward Shara, who took them and knelt before the creature.

"Bow no more to your children, my poor one, for we are home and will guard you as you so selflessly guarded our future." Shara placed the scrolls in the creature's waiting arms. The Talitha hesitated, then ran from the room.

Caleb turned back to Scott. "We must do something for them. How have they survived down there?"

"Their last spell cleansed the poison from the water, and they hunted the other animals mutated by the sorcerers. Now they capture any animals which stray into the tunnels. The mountain ranges across Maradane provide access to the caverns."

Caleb glanced at Jericho, then stared for a moment at his notebook. "We cannot undo what has been done. But we can see that fresh food is sent to them. And we will search for their city within the mountain ring. Perhaps something of it survived the winds."

"I never could understand how the surface survived erosion with the winds as they were, even though Anders sensed that something had thrown nature out of balance," Jericho said. "How many other things are we going to stumble over that have been set by those sorcerers to thwart us?"

"This served only to thwart those who worked it," Scott said. "The winds wert thrown out of balance to repel people from Talitha. Yet why didst thee all come here?"

Jericho smiled. "I came to tame the winds. Anders and Bryce sought the shelter the winds provided. It worked in reverse."

Scott nodded. "O'ercompensation. To many it seems that David moves too slowly, erratically, and doth not compensate enough for the forces against him. Yet the enemy hath, in the instances of this tale and the episode with Justin, sought to sow seeds of destruction that have grown into powerful aids for us. Without Justin we wouldst not have had Anders. Without the sorcerers Talitha wouldst have remained Talitha, ne'er open to thine coming."

Caleb frowned. "We'll be thankful for small favors. Yet we can't sit by and wait for these...Zha-Dhak?...to blunder themselves into oblivion."

"Blunders wilt be fewer, I fear," Scott agreed. "They wilt learn from these mistakes. Yet 'tis obvious that we follow the right path. Albeit unobtrusively, someone is guiding us. If we heed this guidance we shouldst see the promised peace."

"I hope we can see a little of it now." Caleb looked at his friends. "We're tired and it's late. Council is adjourned until the next scheduled meeting."

Returning home, Bronwyn sat in her alcove outside the library, gazing up at the brilliant stars. Presently Richard sat down beside her, taking her hand in his.

"My lady, thou art troubled."

Bronwyn sighed. "It's just all so much at once, Richard. It's so terribly heartbreaking to think of what happened to Talitha, and frightening because of how close to home the sorcerers have come. Yet I want to be happy because our Anders remains with us. It's a terrible confusion of feeling." She was comforted only by the familiar alcove wall at her back, included in Bryce's new design because he knew of her love for that spot.

"What befell the Talitha is indeed tragic," Richard agreed. "But remember they chose it freely. They fight the same war as we. And things wilt be made easier for them. They now know their sacrifice wast not in vain."

"I suppose so." Bronwyn fingered the bracelet that had saved her life, wondering if the Talitha had created that grotto. "Shara says that Anders will be with them, so I am certain they will be happier now. She also says he now understands the mark on his shoulder, something he cannot explain to us.

"Will we see peace now, Richard?"

"I believe so, my lady. There wilt be forays by Shandal, but it wilt take long years for them to recover. They lost so many worlds, so many of their upper echelon, and their center of worship. Maradane mayst begin to enjoy life once more.

"What wilt thou do with thy time now?"

"I must write down all that I have learned about wind control, put it all down in a book. I must go on and practice more, and teach others how to do what they can. Things must continue to progress until the next queen of the winds comes along. And I must tell Jericho we are expecting another child," she finished with a small smile.

Richard kissed her cheek. "Shandal hath seen the beginning of its end. And I am glad to be here to see it unfold."

Bronwyn turned to look into his green eyes. "Richard, are you happy now? You are not lonely?"

"Lonely?" He laughed softly. "No, my lady, I have all I want in my life. My son is a fine man, I am near to my dearest friends, and I have the love I hold for one very dear." He squeezed her hand tightly. "I want no more."

For a long moment she was silent, then she leaned over to kiss his cheek. "Then I can ask for no more, my friend. Tomorrow we will plan a festival to give thanks for the new peace."

Richard hinted at a smile. "'Tis what we need. Good night, my lady."

Bronwyn watched him walk to his small house, thinking of his gentle heart, then said softly, "Good night, dear Richard."

End Book Two

Epilogue

Maradane grew in importance to David's empire over the ensuing centuries, binding the once rebellious worlds around it into a group that ruled their quadrant with an iron fist. Many times Shandal sent raiding parties that destroyed vast areas of the planet, but the people rebuilt and devised ways to save precious structures from these raids. David persisted in offering the hand of peace to Shandal, asking the enemy realm to relinquish their violent traditions and join his growing empire, but Shandal doggedly refused, vowing to crush him.

Bound by their pledge to peace to maintain a military advantage, the Davan peoples realized that true salvation lay within the promised reawakening of the ancient magical powers, so long gone from their realm. The Marans remembered, as well, that their race was but the continuation of the Talitha, who had given everything to hold their world for the future. In turn, it was the Marans' very vocal pledge to keep their world ready not only to defend against Shandal, but to guard and cherish whatever magic should come to them. Their struggle was not to save only themselves, but to save these powers and to understand them before the evils of the Zha-

Dhak burst forth and slaughtered all.

While his scholars sought out elusive knowledge and lore, David's warriors monitored Shandal to crush every surge toward uprising, keeping them from re-establishing the central core of their realm. The Paladins regularly destroyed the rising ruling centers, keeping the enemy too occupied with rebuilding its own hierarchy to even consider an open war. Thus was a forced peace maintained, allowing the Davan peoples to grow in strength and wisdom toward the time when a war of many patterns would engulf them.

Scott and Richard remained in their homes by the western palace, both now alone but visited often by their children. They kept a silent vigil for the descendants of Anders foreseen by Scott so many thousands of years past, but they were long in coming. Their appearance coincided with a growing upheaval of psychic and elemental powers throughout the realm. The promised return of magic was beginning, but in ways that often wrought havoc before the psychics and the Lhassa holy men could fathom the complex events.

It was in the Maran year 9,750 that David rushed to the temple for an urgent discussion with Caleb. The king looked up from his work, the image of the first High King of Maradane. The name had been preserved through all the reigning generations of the Bajoc family.

Putting aside his papers, he said flatly, "Your news is bad."

"I fear so." David sat wearily in the cushioned chair facing the large desk, running one hand through already disheveled hair. "This is not turning out to be as I thought it might, so long ago when we of this blood agreed to fight the Zha-Dhak. Yet I wouldst not turn toward another path."

"Nor would anyone on this world. Say what you must."

Sighing, David studied his scarred hands. "Gray agonized o'er this, made far worse by my tormented attempts to force an alternative. There is none that any in this realm couldst live with, for it means the death of all that we seek so desperately to understand."

Caleb lay aside his pen, absently rubbing a smudge of ink from his thumb. "Will our world die, at last, in this attack?"

"No!" David straightened, gripping the chair arms. Then, more quietly, "No, but the devastation wilt be almost as great as that of her first war. Yet if we stop this attack, the war wilt burst on us before the year is out, and though we crush Shandal the sorcerers wilt crush us, and the powers the Lhassa seek so desperately to nurture."

"That is not a thing any of my world would accept," Caleb said softly, thinking of the descendants of Tarmynan and their growing struggle to find and save new races bearing mystic and psychic powers. "I will spread the word, prepare the defense, and we will stand our ground. But will our rulers survive? Without them, the people will falter."

David caught Caleb's blue gaze and said softly, "Your line will continue, and we take action to save the other four. Richard and Scott art gathering certain members of the ruling families. They know what to say, and what to keep for the moment to themselves. The children must be sent away at once and not told of their destination. If they stay here they wilt die."

"Then they will go. But where?"

"Into the heart of our struggle," David sighed. "One world is central to the psychic turmoil sweeping our realm, and there lies our only salvation. Before all is done, that world wilt be linked with our blood and the heart of the Lhassa, and all that wilt save us from the Zha-Dhak. Yet we send them on their way without such insight."

*

At the same moment Richard spoke with a princess of the eastern palace. "Aislinn, thou must gather thy brothers and sisters and pack for a journey." He hesitated, then continued, "I am sorry I canst not tell thee more, but stealth is imperative."

Aislinn studied him soberly, reading his eyes, eyes she had known so well from her birth. Her young face was intent, as usual, her wide brown eyes seeking his thoughts. With one slender hand she pushed windblown brown hair back from her face, then smiled affectionately. "You mean to save us pain, Richard. You need only say David commands it and we will not question."

"I know." Richard frowned in the direction of the temple,

where he knew his king's words fell heavily. "Yet David doth not relish acting thus, and this decree comes from far beyond him...Let things come as they must and do not suffer them before the fact."

"The code of our world," Aislinn sighed. "Very well, I'll get the others ready. Please..." She hesitated, almost afraid to voice the request. "Say Wind may come."

"Wind may come." Richard kissed her cheek. "Scott and I wilt come to thee soon. Hurry now."

A short time later fourteen members of the ruling families were waiting at the hangar of the southern palace. Gathered from each of the four sectors, the young people ranged in age from twelve to nineteen and were already practiced in shouldering the burdens of their subjects. Carrying small satchels hurriedly packed, they talked quietly amongst themselves, curious about the sudden journey.

Catching their attention, Caleb forced his words to remain calm. "I know you will soon learn of your destination." He looked directly at Veda Barria, inheritor of the ancestral psychic powers. "I am sorry we can tell you so little. Until I contact you. Jeremiah is to be your guiding hand.

"The route is pre-set in the computers, so you need only sit back and relax. I will recall the ship when you have lodging. Please, take care, and know that the Paladins will not be far from you."

The fourteen entered the ship and Aislinn's oldest brother Jeremiah secured the door behind them, then started the ship on its way.

Caleb looked anxiously at Gray, who had stood by wordlessly. "Are you certain they will be protected? The world of Earth is so strange, I fear for them."

"This is not the choice of safety, that I saw all too well." Gray gazed after the ship, but only half intent on it. His mind sought assurances of the already unfolding paths before them all. "From this moment forward we plunge fully into the paths of the elements, and this is only our first baby step. These days wilt be harsh for many, as we and the Lhassa continue our quest to learn. Unless we canst locate and focus the energies beginning to spiral on that planet, all wilt be lost. No, I fear whilst I send our children to safety from one danger, they step into another. Shouldst Earth not be brought to David, chaos wilt be our lot."

APPENDIX

The Davan Hierarchy

<u>David</u>

|

High Under Kings (4)

|

Under Kings (1 per inhabited solar system)

|

High Immortals (500 per inhabited galaxy)

|

Planetary Rulers (per individual custom)

|

Planetary Armed Forces supplemented by

|

the Paladins, 420 per solar system, supplemented by

|

the Under-Travelers, garrisoned in specific quadrants and supplemented when necessary by all other Immortals.

Davan Lineage

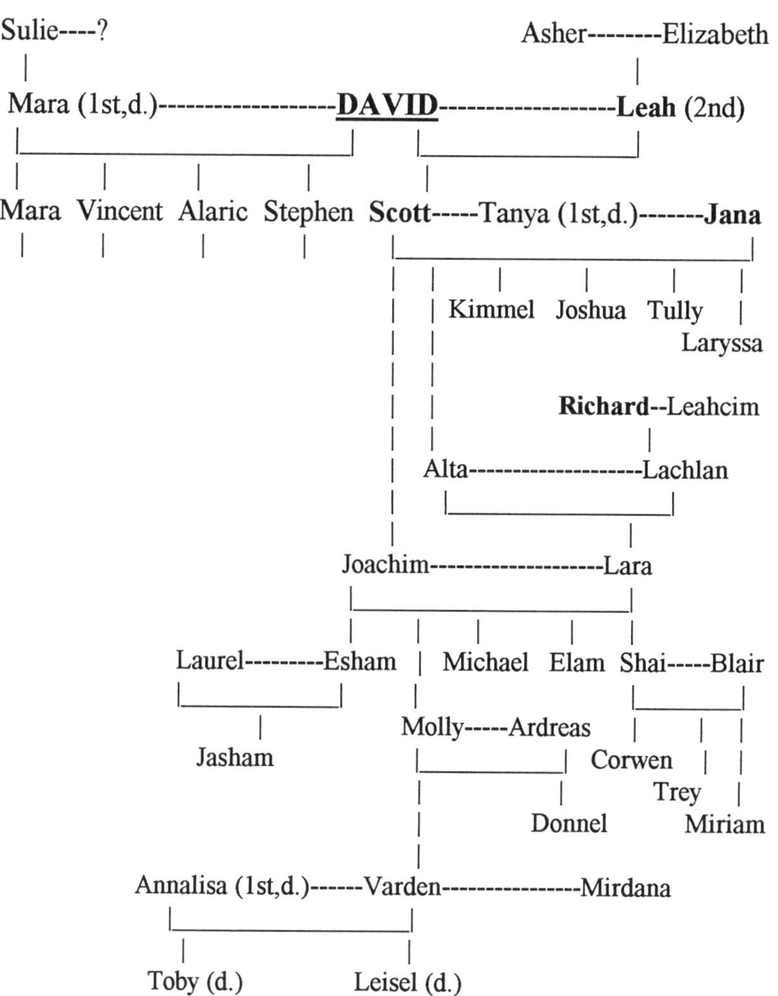

Maran Ruling Families

BAJOC FAMILY

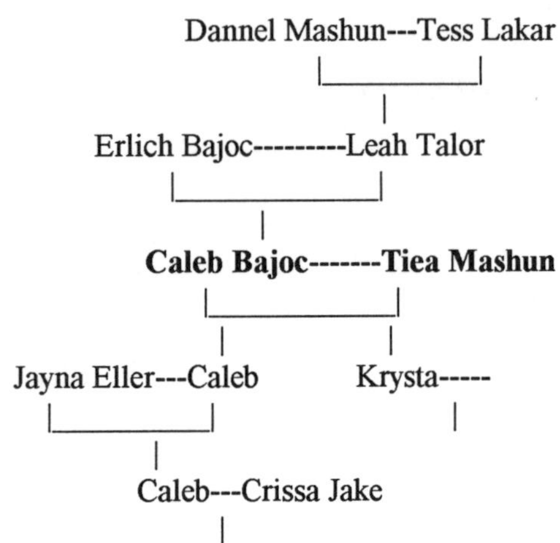

BARRIA FAMILY

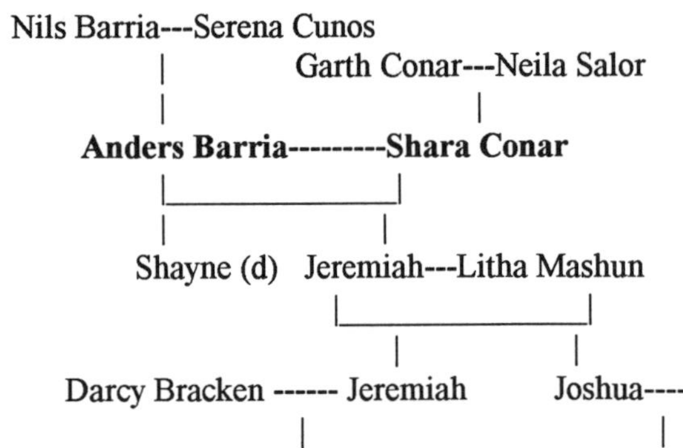

DONNYA FAMILY

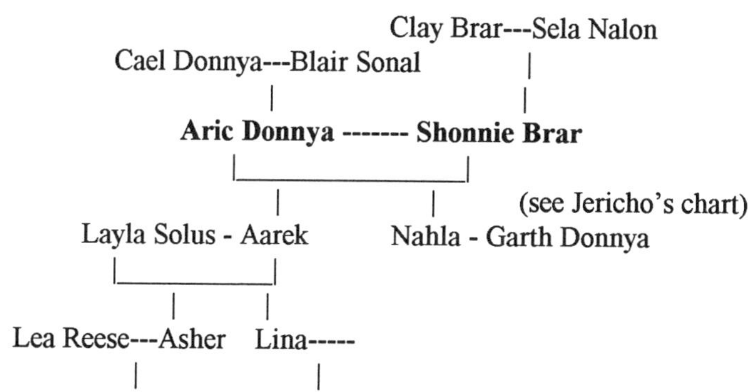

DONNYA FAMILY

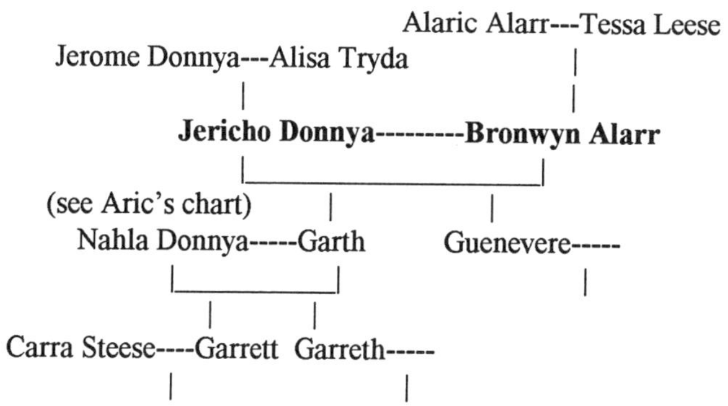

JEREMIAH FAMILY

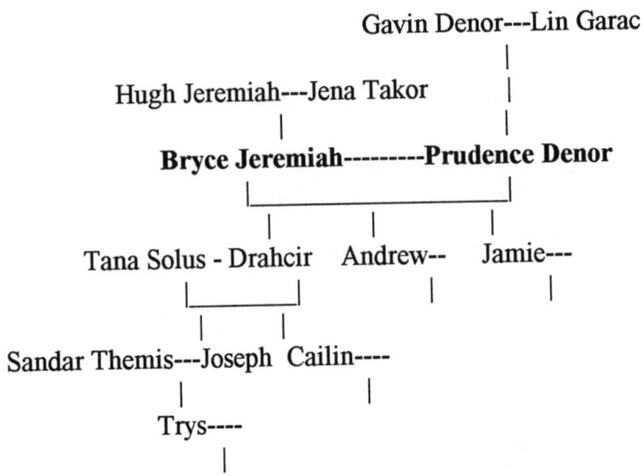

Partial Davan Time Line

17,250 BI	Mystics of Stalasia founded by Talitha
1	Immortals come into being
500	Shandal enters universe
550	Magic begins to flee; Stalassi begin to die
700	David weds Mara
1000	Mara dies; Mara II returns to Adane
1350	Shandal expands to other worlds
1650	Wind Rulers retreat
1750	Mara II dies
1800	David weds Leah; Scott is born; Leahcim Tierrah is founded
1807	David named King
2307	Stalasia seeks help against Shandal
2312	Davan Empire founded
4812	Scott goes into seclusion
4887	Maradane settled

Great
Ice
Stair
Northern Sector
Adani Steppes
Sea of Timon
Palace
Grotto
Gulf
of
Stalasia
Sea
of
Atore
River Mara
Palace
Western Sector
Lake Mara
Palace
Temple
Palace
Raas River Chasm
Winds-haven Bridge
Ocean of Tolar
Southern Sector

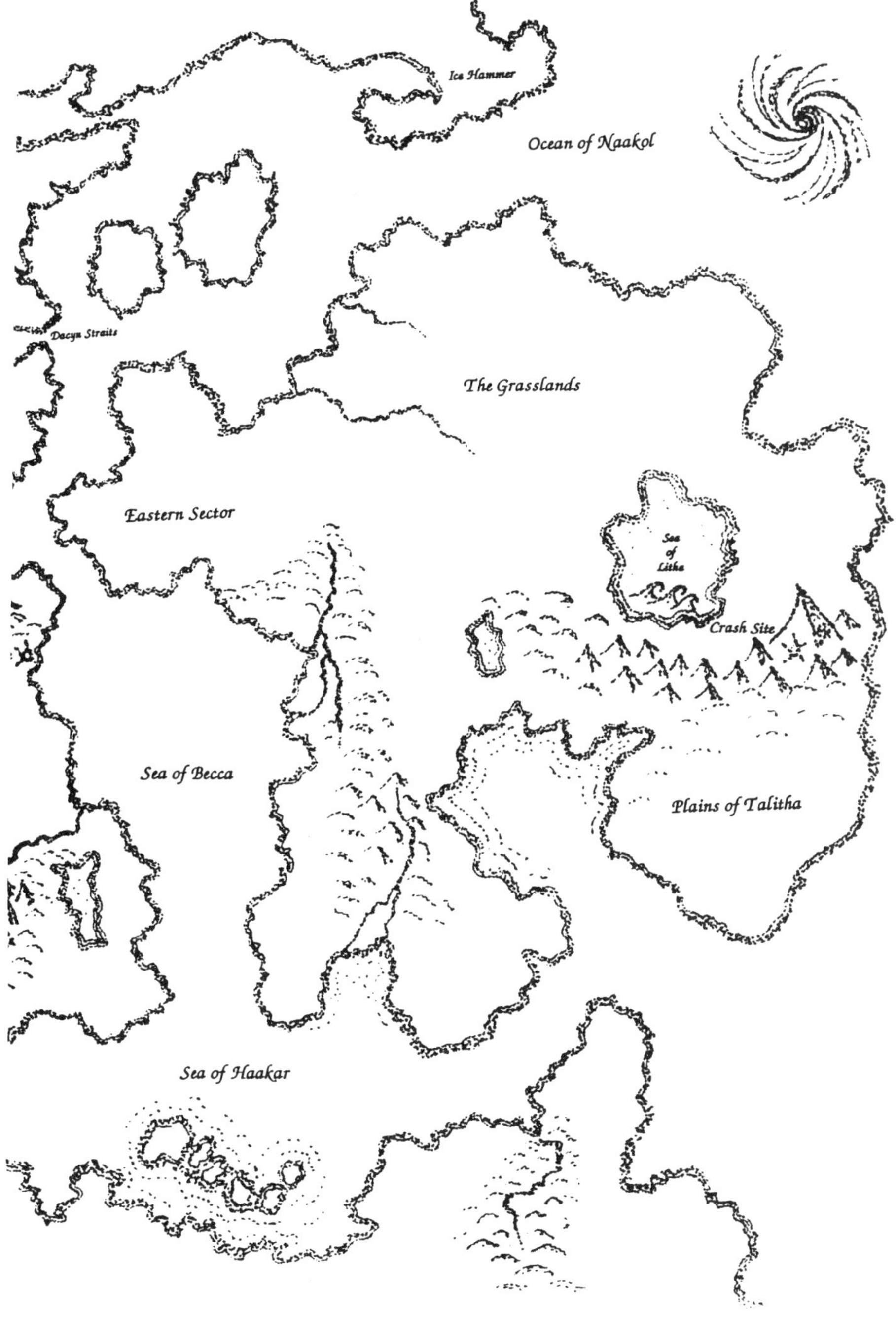
Ice Hammer
Ocean of Naakol
Dacyn Straits
The Grasslands
Eastern Sector
Sea
of
Litha
Crash Site
Sea of Becca
Plains of Talitha
Sea of Haakar

Also Available from Mythspinner Press:

Tales of the Davan Empire...
...three novellas spanning the reach of the Davan Empire...

Passage Through Mourning...

A newly colonized gem mining world is threatened by Shanda marauders barely six hundred years after the close of *Winds of Dawn*. Helpless against a beast imported from the realms of the Zha-Dhak, colonist and Immortal alike struggle to save a group of trapped children. These young lives depend on the desperate search for Scott, who is lost in grief over the death of his wife. His way through his life-long struggle against death is the only hope for the dying colony. 32 pages

The Wind Spinners...

Chasing their fleeing subjects, a new enemy has stumbled through a portal into the Davan realm. Chuck must close the portal before their full armada gains entry and introduces deadly new weapons to Shandal. Yet a strange young woman of Earth hinders his work, rupturing the teleportal zone and creating a vortex that threatens to swallow an entire region of her country. She must accept her own elemental powers and endanger her life to help Chuck stop the enemy invasion. 32 pages

Windfall...

Zed, last of the True-Bloods of Adane, is sent to Earth to thwart slave raiders on the outskirts of a major city. His mission is simple, until he meets a young man with a past too much like his own. Amidst a host of long-suppressed memories, Zed sets this youth on a new road, one destined to carry him to the heart of Adane itself. But Zed's own path takes a heart-rending turn, leaving the regaining of the True-Bloods' ancient wind control in doubt for Anders' descendants. 38 pages

These three titles are now available in a limited handbound softcover edition for $6.95 each. Ordering information appears on the following page.